W9-ABY-982

OTHER EYES

Also by Barbara D'Amato

Death of a Thousand Cuts

White Male Infant

Authorized Personnel Only

Help Me Please

Good Cop, Bad Cop

Killer.app

Hard Road

Hard Evidence

Hard Bargain

Hard Christmas

Hard Case

Hard Women

Hard Luck

Hard Tack

Hardball

Of Course You Know That Chocolate Is a Vegetable and Other Stories

On My Honor

The Doctor, the Murder, the Mystery

BARBARA D'AMATO

OTHER EYES

A TOM DOHERTY ASSOCIATES BOOK NEW YORK

This is a work of fiction. All of the characters, organizations, and events portrayed in this novel are either products of the author's imagination or are used fictitiously.

OTHER EYES

A Forge Book
Published by Tom Doherty Associates, LLC
175 Fifth Avenue
New York, NY 10010

www.tor-forge.com

Forge® is a registered trademark of Tom Doherty Associates, LLC.

ISBN 978-0-7653-2606-5

CIP DATA—TK

First Edition: January 2011

Printed in the United States of America

0 9 8 7 6 5 4 3 2 1

For Adam, Brian, Emily, Paul, Sheryl, and Tony,

ALWAYS

OTHER EYES

1

NOON

MAY 29

CHICAGO, ILLINOIS

Interstate 90 rises in Seattle, less than ten blocks from Puget Sound, skirts the Seahawks Stadium, and heads east. It ends in Boston, throwing a tail across Boston Harbor to Logan International Airport. Between Seattle and Boston, it snakes across three thousand and eighty-eight miles, the width of the continent. When it passes through Chicago, it makes a shallow sidestep around the base of Lake Michigan.

In Chicago, Interstate 90 fattens to eight lanes, ten in some places, and frequent heavy-traffic entrances and exits are needed. The speed limit is fifty-five, which few people heed. Three hundred and twenty thousand cars go through The Loop on I-90 every day.

Just north of The Loop, the road is eight lanes wide with a median of metal posts supporting wide metal guardrails. The right-of-way is fenced with chain-link wire.

The baby had found one of the many breaks in the chain-link fence. Attracted by the activity of the cars going past, he pushed through the gap. He was a vigorous little boy who had loved model cars even before he was able to sit up and play with them, and now, at the age of eleven months, had his own fleet of plastic cars and trucks. These real ones were even more exciting.

He wore a small pair of waist-hung jeans, which didn't stay up very well, since he had no waist. The top of his diaper bulged out on the left side. In the back, the jeans had slipped halfway down his rump. Now he sat up on chubby haunches to watch the cars.

It was just past noon, late May, and quite warm. The grass near the fence had been mowed recently and was comfortable to settle down on. A duo of early white butterflies danced over the baby. However, he thought the cars ahead of him were more interesting than the butterflies. He got back up on hands and knees and trundled toward the highway. His chubby starfish hands made soft plops on the concrete as he crossed the shoulder into the traffic lane.

An eighteen-wheeler roared by, trailing a slipstream of dust and detritus.

The baby sat back, alarmed, then decided that the big truck, as big as a house from his vantage point, was thrilling, not scary. He giggled and chortled as the dust and papers from the roadside danced in the diminishing slipstream.

The baby patted his hands together. Two or three other cars passed. There was a gap, and then a yellow bus went by. The baby laughed again.

The high sun struck a new section of the metal median divider in the middle of the highway, four lanes away from the baby. He cocked his head at the sudden brightness. Then he smiled toothlessly. The bright strip beckoned.

With great decisiveness, the baby started crawling across the highway to the median, right hand–left knee, left hand–right knee, his little jeans riding farther down as he turtled forward.

Brad Oliver had slipped out of New Trier High School after lunch period, even though he was supposed to finish out the day. He thought hanging around just for gym and then study hall was a stupid idea. Brad had wanted his friend Jay to cut with him, but Jay was such a goody-goody he was staying to the end of the school day. Being fair to Jay, Brad admitted that since Jay had European History last hour, his absence would be noted more than Brad's would.

These last two days were stupid, anyway, in his opinion, with exams Monday, Tuesday, and Wednesday. Why not have a whole week of reading period?

However, Brad's absence *would* be noticed. He didn't fool himself about that.

Brad figured if he could get to Wrigley Field before 1:00 P.M. he could get in line for bleacher seat tickets to the Cubs. Otherwise, there wasn't a chance. Used to be easy, but not since the Cubs went so far last year.

Some things were more important than school.

Jay was going to take the El down to Wrigleyville, but he'd better not get there too late to meet Brad outside. Plus, Jay was bringing Aaron, a senior who was eighteen and could buy beer. Brad would be eighteen next week, but that wasn't good enough if they got carded. They had it all worked out. Aaron buys a large beer. Jay and Brad buy small Cokes, and they spread the wealth.

His parents were way too strict. A little beer never hurt anybody.

Brad got onto Interstate 94 at the Willow Road interchange. It was about twenty miles from New Trier in Winnetka, north of Chicago, to Wrigley Field. I-94 merged into Interstate 90 a few miles north of downtown. His old Chevy wasn't running as well as he'd like. He pictured the oil as being the consistency and color of hot fudge by now; he really needed to change it this weekend. The brakes had gotten funny lately, too. The pedal went yay far down before hitting pay dirt. The air conditioner hadn't worked in a year. Brad had all the windows open. He complained about the air conditioner to his friends, but the truth was he loved driving fast with the air rushing in.

But the old tub, which had belonged to his mother, still had a fair amount of go, Brad was pleased to see. He kicked it up to sixty-five in the fifty-five zone. The cop father of a friend of his often said, "We'll give you five and you can take five," which meant they didn't get pissy about ten miles over.

And he'd better push it, he thought, passing a Volvo determined to drive fifty in the middle lane. Arrive at Wrigley after people started lining up and no more cheap seats.

The baby padded determinedly across the rightmost lane of Interstate 90. A Toyota with a Wisconsin license plate sped past in the second lane. The driver briefly had a sense of something pinkish in the road, but it wasn't in his lane, and by the time he was aware of its existence he was past it, without knowing what it was.

As the baby started into the second lane, his jeans worked their way fully off his hips. As he achieved the middle of lane two, the pants slid the rest of the way down and he crawled out of them, padding along now on dusty hands and clean knees.

Unaware of leaving the jeans behind, the baby crossed the second lane to the third.

A carpenter in an S10 pickup, with two hundred one-by-sixes in the back intended for a hardwood floor, was doing seventy in the farthest left lane. He saw the baby one lane over and was so shocked that he swerved when he didn't need to.

A woman driving a Jeep Cherokee in the third lane saw the pickup swerve, saw the baby in her lane, grabbed for her cell phone to call 911 at the same time as she swerved sharply right to avoid him and braked. The driver of a semi, following her, noticed both cars swerve and, without seeing the baby, stood on his brakes.

Farther back, in the second lane, a taxi coming in from O'Hare with a passenger noticed there was trouble ahead and started evasive action, slowing and pulling right from lane two. A terrified driver of a panel truck behind him braked frantically.

The shriek of brakes startled the baby. He was not quite frightened yet, but his single-minded advance toward the shiny median divider had been interrupted, his train of thought broken. He paused and sat down on the white line dividing the third and fourth lanes. His face contracted into furrows of worry.

Brad was behind the panel truck and following too closely. He braked hard, but seeing the cars ahead of him swerving right, stayed in lane. He saw the pickup hit the Cherokee on its right rear. The Cherokee spun out of control sideways, rolling across the two lanes on the right as the pickup sideswiped the metal median dividers and crashed into a guardrail around a median light stanchion, coming to an abrupt halt, while the lumber in its back kept going, shooting across the roadway ahead.

Brad saw the panel truck crank to the right, where it was hit by the taxi. The truck tumbled end over end into the lumber.

At that instant, Brad saw the baby.

The infant was sitting up on the white line, puzzled.

There was just a glimpse of the baby before Brad slammed on his brakes. The pedal went way down, then grabbed. Brad swung the wheel of his car, slewing the old Chevy onto the right shoulder. It hit the ditch and rolled onto its side. Brad shoved himself through the open driver's side window, which was now a sun roof.

He popped out like a cork and sprinted fifty yards back up the roadway, sure he would see a mangled child.

The baby still sat on the white line. A small yellow school bus had just missed him. Its driver had his mouth open as if screaming and the bus fishtailed as it tried to stop before hitting the Jeep Cherokee. A semi and two other cars were bearing down on the baby.

Brad scooped up the baby like a football player snagging a fumble, vaulted to the median and tumbled onto it, cracking his shoulder hard. Crawling over the metal barrier, holding the baby under his arm, he crouched on the far side, just out of the lanes where the northbound traffic was speeding past.

He huddled there as several more vehicles plunged into the back of the wrecks, as one ran into the ditch and struck his car, as northbound traffic began to slow down and gape at the pileup.

A quarter of a mile back in the southbound lanes was a gondola truck carrying tons of ledge stone from a quarry in Montana to a site in Oak Park where a Frank Lloyd Wright look-alike house was being built. The driver was doing seventy.

As Brad held him, the baby screamed, the first time he had showed fear. Brad cuddled the infant into his shoulder.

At seventy, the truck full of stone covered the quarter-mile in just over ten seconds. The driver saw the pileup and hit his brakes, putting his full body weight onto his foot, but it was too late. Laying rubber, the screeching juggernaut plowed into the mass of cars and trucks, corrugating metal and pancaking flesh.

Brad leaned against the median divider, holding the baby close. They were both crying.

2

"What. A. Mess." Detective Horace T. Pollard of the Chicago Police Department repeated the words a second time, trying to utter them like Tommy Lee Jones in *The Fugitive*. Great movie. Magnificent actor. Horace came pretty close, but Hollywood wasn't going to be knocking on his door any time soon.

The "T" in his name stood for Thomas, and he liked to be called Tommy.

There were seven ambulances on the scene. An eighth one had just departed with a body. Living or dead, Pollard wasn't sure. That wasn't his job, thank God. Tommy Pollard approached the accident scene, pausing only for the breath he usually took in situations like these to distance himself enough from the carnage to get the job done.

The Illinois State Police, not the Chicago PD, patrolled the interstates. This was their I-90 patrol route N-3, if he wasn't mistaken, from here to Addison or some such thing.

He glanced around for the honcho and picked a rangy trooper who was giving orders to three men. One of the younger men looked green. The other two were clearly shocked and trying not to show it. The trooper in charge showed no such queasiness. He seemed to Tommy Pollard like the kind of guy who wished he could wear mirrored sunglasses and above-the-calf leather boots.

The tangle of cars and trucks steamed and hissed. One young woman in uniform was foaming down the sizzling metal, and a hazmat guy sprinkled fire-retardant, an absorbent sawdust material, over the gasoline spills. A pair of firefighters in turnout coats stood near a fire engine, watching the progress of the cleanup, alert for explosions.

The fastest-moving people were the paramedics. But just beyond the second ambulance Tommy saw a body stretched out on a gurney with no one in attendance. He knew what that meant.

"Lassiter," Tommy said, reading the rangy trooper's nametag. "I'm Pollard."

"Yes?" His radio squawked "One-oh-five" but he ignored it. "You're the CPD detective?"

"Yup. What do you have here?"

"Four dead. One about-to-be-dead. Eleven injured. And I think maybe three-four buried in there." He gestured with his chin to the fuming pileup. His whole manner said he was too busy to spend much time with Pollard. "But that's not your problem."

"For which I'm grateful."

"*That's* your problem."

Tommy looked where Lassiter pointed, this time a pistol-gesture with his hand.

"That kid?"

"That kid. And that baby."

3

Detective Horace "Tommy" Pollard said, "All right, son. Where did you get the baby?"

Brad raised his head, which had been bent over, his cheek resting on the wispy hair of the baby, and Pollard could see the teenager had been crying. The baby, on the other hand, gurgled delightedly, pulling on the kid's left ear.

"What's your name, son?"

"Brad Oliver."

"So where did you get the baby?"

"Right over there, sir," Brad said, pointing to the center of the south-bound traffic lanes.

Pollard realized he should have extracted more details of the accident from Trooper Lassiter. He had let his distress for the dead, dying, and injured throw him off his usual methodical course. Even as he thought it, over in the tangle of cars somebody screamed.

"Help me out here, Brad. What exactly happened?"

Brad told Pollard what he knew. He had seen the panel truck brake and the Cherokee swerve. "I think then the panel truck hit the taxi. But that's when—I think that was when I saw the little guy right in the road. Then—um. There was this truck heading right for him! So I kind of drove into the ditch and jumped out."

He'd heard the other cars caroming into each other. But he'd been so focused on the baby and then his broken-field run to grab the child that he had missed most of the actual pileup.

"But the truck missed him," Pollard said.

"Yeah, well, but a whole lot of traffic was screaming down at us—"

"So you never saw this kid before today?"

"No. He was just in the road. Sitting right on the white line in the middle of the road."

"Why aren't you in school?"

"Well, see I was going to the Cubs game—"

"Maybe I don't need to know that. Yet. That your car?" Pollard pointed to the old Chevy in the ditch.

"Yeah. Jeez! My dad's gonna kill me."

When Brad spoke in a worried tone, the baby snuffled and started to pucker up his face.

"Aw, come on, little guy. It's okay," Brad said, jiggling the child up and down. The baby quieted.

Pollard was puzzled and worried. Babies didn't just wander onto roads alone. And if Brad's story was true, the baby hadn't come out of one of the wrecked cars. Pollard studied the lanes of the expressway, his eyes finally noticing a tiny pair of jeans over in the middle of lane two. If the jeans belonged to the baby, that tended to corroborate Brad's story.

"Let's put you and junior here in my car for a minute," he said. Brad looked at him in some concern. "It'll be safer. You can't sit here in the median all day."

"Okay."

Two more ambulances, driving on the grass shoulder, slid into place near the upended pickup. An ambulance that had arrived earlier pulled slowly away from the scene, lights and siren going, edging around Brad's vehicle. As Brad and Pollard reached the unmarked squad car, the baby said, "Bo, bo," reaching out for the pretty ambulance lights.

Brad said, "Bo, bo."

Pollard put the two in his car, walked far enough away that Brad wouldn't hear, and called Henry Corden at Area Three.

Pollard told Corden where he was and asked, "We got a missing baby?"

Pollard's partner, Corden, had broken his foot last week. He had not been chasing an evildoer, but stepping off the curb in front of a pizza shop with the pizza obscuring his view of the ground, and he was now relegated to office work. Corden said, "Yo, Tommy. Gonna be cooler tomorrow."

"Yeah, that's nice, but do we?"

"Have a missing baby? No. It's been a real quiet day. Grass fire near where you are. Started by a fire in a trash can, but they've struck it now. That's about all the excitement."

"Well, I've got a baby."

"Where?"

"Picked him up on I-90. At the pileup."

"Yeah?"

"The baby may have caused it. He was jaywalking. Jaycrawling. Sorry. I shouldn't go in for dark humor. But seriously, babies don't just go missing. Check, will ya?"

"Sure. But how'd he get there?"

"Crawled. On hands and knees. Must have, because they're dirty little hands and knees. There's no indication of where he came from. But after all, how far can a baby crawl?"

"Beats me. You'd think somebody would have seen him crawling along. Let alone somebody should've missed him. But I think there woulda been an all-call if there's word out."

"Also, send me somebody from Department of Children and Family Services. Or a Youth officer. I don't care which. Somebody with a child seat in their car. I'm at the accident scene."

"DCFS? You thinking neglect?"

"No. He looks well cared for. But who knows? What kind of person wouldn't know they'd lost a baby? Plus, until we find the mom, somebody's got to take care of him."

. . .

By now helicopters from Channel Two and Channel Five were snarling and whomping around overhead. Beyond the fence, the access road was lined with media and gawkers. The outbound lanes of the expressway, which had been physically unaffected by the catastrophe on the inbound lanes, had come to a near standstill from a gargantuan gapers' block. One Illinois State Police guy stood in the median, just south of the pileup, waving a light-truncheon at the cars to tell them to keep moving. He was having no effect whatsoever.

Pollard walked back over to Lassiter. He said, "You have anything on the baby?"

"Nothing new."

"Well, give me the old, then. Where'd he come from?"

Lassiter was only minimally courteous. Pollard couldn't quite blame the guy. The trooper was dealing with a lot of unpleasant things at once. Lassiter said, in a rather clipped manner, "The pickup driver—the guy with the load of lumber—is alive. Very lucky guy. Lucky plus he was smart enough to be wearing his seat belt. He said he saw the baby coming across the road. That was why he swerved."

"The baby was coming from where?"

"From the west. Crawling across the right lane, going to the middle lanes. That's all he saw. He thought he was going to hit him. Swerved. Lost control. And so we've got *that*." He gestured at the horrific pile of wreckage.

"Has anybody else said anything about the baby?"

"Only two of them even saw the baby. Of our conscious survivors, that is, of course. Most of the drivers were just trying not to get killed."

"Jeez."

Pollard thought he could ask more questions, but Lassiter was truly busy, and he wouldn't get any answers that told him where the baby lived.

A great distant multicar honking came from behind them, where all the inbound lanes were stopped dead. Two patrol cars blocked off traffic into the accident scene. The closest exit ramp where anybody could get off was several blocks farther back, and the cars trapped between the accident and the exit could not back up. At that exit, other cops were funneling four lanes of traffic off through a single-lane off-ramp. But cars accumulated from the north faster than the ramp could get rid of them.

Pollard walked along the edge of the grass, next to the roadway. He started fifty feet south of Brad's jalopy and walked slowly toward it, then past it, in the direction of his own unmarked car. But he wasn't looking toward his car, except for two seconds to see whether Brad and the baby were all right. It looked like Brad was singing to the child. Pollard studied the grass. Assuming that Brad had screeched to a halt as soon as possible after he saw the baby, the child would have entered the roadway about here. But there was a chain-link fence the whole way along to keep people out of the highway. A baby certainly wasn't going to be able to climb a six-foot chain-link fence.

Okay. Here was the little pair of jeans. Pollard took a paper evidence bag out of his all-kinds-of-stuff pocket, unfolded it, and reached for the jeans. Then he thought better of it and rummaged out a disposable camera and photographed the garment first, both a long shot and a close-up. Having done that, he picked up the jeans and put them in the bag.

Ordinarily he would try to preserve the place where an abandoned baby was found as the scene of a possible crime. Accident Reconstruction would go over the site for the causes of the smashup, particularly the sequence of which cars hit which cars first and their trajectories. They'd measure and photograph and then tow the wrecks to the investigation site. Not his job, thank goodness. Then later everybody would try to sue everybody else. But the baby was, so to speak, his baby. If there was any evidence here of where the child had come from, it would vanish quickly. Already the emergency vehicles had driven over the jeans, across the baby's path, and even across the grass margin of the road where he might have found traces of the child's passage. You couldn't fault them. There were people dying in that mess of twisted steel, and getting to them was a priority. For that matter, in an hour, two at most, Lassiter would reopen the highway.

Pollard visualized a line from the spot where Brad and the baby had been sitting in the median, through the place where he had found the jeans, over to the fence. Not that a baby would likely crawl in a straight path. Still—

He walked to the fence. "Lo and behold," he mumbled to himself. About five feet north of where he stood, a part of the fence was not attached to its support post and a narrow triangular opening ran from the midpoint to the ground.

There were broken weeds there, too, Pollard saw, feeling like the Deerstalker. He crouched and studied the terrain. He was a city cop. Tracing critters through the underbrush was not his forte.

Pollard took a handkerchief out of his pocket and tied it around the post. He wanted to be able to find this spot from the other side of the fence later when the emergency vehicles were gone and everything looked alike out here. Pollard rarely used cloth handkerchiefs. In fact he thought the idea of blowing your nose in one was faintly disgusting. But his wife insisted that carrying one was the proper thing to do. He briefly wondered whether he should tell her it had come in handy—and in what way—but decided he'd better not.

He made a phone call on his cell while he was still outside the car, to Corden again to get him to arrange a couple of teams to canvass the surrounding area for the child's parents. Nothing especially secret in that, but there was no reason to let Brad hear everything, either. Then he walked to his unmarked and opened the driver's door.

Brad was singing. He sang, "Eighty-one bottles of beer on the wall, eighty-one bottles of beer. If one of those bottles should happen to fall—"

The baby giggled and made hooting sounds that were probably meant to be singing. The baby caroled "Beeee, waaaalll! Beeeer!" Brad had a dreadful singing voice and the baby adored it.

Brad said, "I think this thing here is leaking."

"This thing? Oh, you mean the diaper?"

"Guess so."

"Don't you ever babysit?"

"Nope. Never."

A blue Chevy, passed along the margin by the patrol cops, drew up behind Pollard's unmarked. As it came to a quick stop, it rocked on the uneven ground. A woman of about thirty-five, plump and bouncy, got out.

"Well, kid, it looks like the little fellow's ride is here."

"What?"

"Come on, kid," Pollard said. "Get out of the car and bring junior."

"What? What are you going to do?" Brad got out of the car, but he held the baby tight to his chest.

"DCFS is here."

"What? You mean that woman is going *take him away?*"

"We can't keep him, Brad. He's not ours. We can't even drive anywhere with him. I don't have a child car seat."

"But—no. You don't understand—"

Brad glanced back at the highway. The flattened jeans were no longer there in the road, but not far away was a squirrel. At least Pollard was pretty sure it had once been a squirrel. Its leftovers were mashed flat into the roadway, a kind of broadened silhouette of a squirrel with flattened dirty gray fur like soiled felt. No part of the little body was thicker than a quarter inch. Pollard exchanged a flicker of a glance with Brad. In a flash of understanding, Pollard realized that Brad had pictured the baby just that way. The kid had been terrified that the baby would die and in that single instant of terror he had bonded tight to the child.

The woman said, "You're Detective Pollard."

"DCFS?" he said.

"Youth Services. Ms. Goodbody. My real name. No dumb jokes, please." She presented ID.

"You've got a child seat for your car?"

"Yes, I have."

"Got a diaper?"

"As a matter of fact, yes." She smiled.

Pollard told her briefly what had happened. He let her take several minutes with her paperwork—you didn't just hand a baby over—intentionally not rushing her, so that Brad could spend that time with the child.

"We're going to need pictures of him right away," Pollard said. "For our 'Have you seen this child?' handouts."

"Will do. You'll have a .jpg of him by the time you get back to the station."

Finally, the woman approached Brad and held out her arms. Brad began to cry and the minute the woman took the baby, the little guy howled, too.

"Can I come visit him?" Brad said.

"Is he related to you?"

"No. But I just wish—"

The woman studied Brad for a few seconds. "I'll see if we can arrange something."

"I love him."

"Okay, kid," Pollard said. "I'll drive you home now."

Brad was still sniffling. He tried to distract himself, saying again, "Jeez! My dad's gonna kill me."

"Because your car got wrecked?"

"No. It was already a wreck. And it was mine, anyhow. Because I cut school."

"Hmm. I think I have a cure for that."

Pollard performed a complex maneuver around a newly arrived truck spraying more decontaminant and fire-retardant foam on the gasoline and brake fluid leaking from the tangle of cars. He waited while two EMTs trundled a gurney with an accident victim past the upended pickup truck. The victim's face was covered. Pollard then drove on the grass verge to the off-ramp up ahead, turned back along the access road, and stopped at the crowd of news people. "Get out for a minute, kid. I won't leave you."

"What are you going to do?"

"Trust me on this. Just get out."

Pollard exited the car, too. Every reporter's eye and several cameras swung toward him.

Pollard said, "This is the young man who jumped from his car and at the risk of his own life saved a baby from a horrible death. He is a true hero."

Half a dozen video cameras swung from Pollard to Brad. The reporters mobbed him.

4

Professor Blue Eriksen had spent the noon hour at Channel 12, being interviewed by Forrest Sabin for his program *Paging Chicago*. Live and actually pretty popular, it had a viewership as high as any of the noon news programs. The reason was Sabin himself. Unlike a lot of TV interviewers, he didn't rely on good looks. He actually read books.

But Blue was aware you had to watch yourself with him. He was smart. He did his homework. And he was a shark. A triple-threat guy. He was perfectly willing to play get-the-guest. Blue once saw him destroy a colleague of hers from the English department who claimed that Shakespeare's works were written by Queen Elizabeth I. Blue doubted they were, but many respectable scholars thought so. Sabin reduced the man almost to tears.

He had large mobile features that somehow looked good on the small screen. And a chummy manner that let him ask the most intrusive question as if it was a fascinating notion that had just occurred to him.

The four or five times she'd been on his show, he had tried to trap her into saying something inconsistent, or something controversial. Blue didn't mind the controversial. In her opinion, people ought to think. In fact, they should be challenged, surprised, irked, even enraged to the point of thinking. Which is why she didn't mind coming on his show. But you had to watch out, just the same. His goal was an entertaining half hour, no matter whom he attacked. Her goal was to boost archaeology and not look like an idiot while doing it.

The Dean at school liked his teachers to do public-appearance events, and while she didn't do everything he wanted, he was right about this. It was good for people to realize that the stuff professors taught in universities was pretty much understandable to everybody. Blue liked to demystify her job.

While Forrest finished with his first guest, a man who wrote inspirational literature—which Blue mentally called "desperational literature"— she ran through the TV don't-dos in her head: Don't look at the camera. Don't fiddle with your hair. Don't adjust your clothing.

The idea was to pretend you were having a nice chat with a friend in his living room. Oh, sure.

Sabin said, "My second guest today is Professor Blue Eriksen, an archaeologist from Northwestern University. She was last on our show to talk about her very popular and very controversial book, *Goddess*. Welcome aboard, Blue."

"Thank you, Forrest." *Do they really need lights this bright?*

"I asked you to come on and describe the book you're working on now. It sounds quite controversial."

As a matter of fact, when he had Blue on the show six months earlier, she described the project. He knew she knew that, and he knew she knew that he knew. But he was too canny to count on every viewer having seen the show back then. Or if they did, remembering it.

Blue said, "We're studying the fact that virtually all the world's religions developed in partnership with naturally occurring hallucinogens. Mostly plants and fungi."

"Oh, surely not, Blue."

"It's really not debatable that they began that way, Forrest. Think of the visions of shamans and the peyote of Native Americans. For that matter, think of religions today that use fasting to inspire visions. The idea isn't original with me, either. You've probably read that Professor Benny Shanon at The Hebrew University in Jerusalem believes that Moses was using an hallucinogen when he saw the burning bush and heard the voice of God."

"Well, but—" Forrest said, possibly trying to change the topic.

Blue said firmly, "The Bible mentions the use of acacia bark, which is similar to the hallucinogen ayahuasca."

"That may be—"

"But what we're doing that's new is quantifying it. We're testing the tissues of ancient humans, mummies and skeletons at their actual burial sites, to describe exactly what and how much they used."

"Mmm. I seem to remember you mentioning this when you were on the show a while back."

"Yes, I did."

"You enjoy a good debate."

"Why else would I come on your show?" Blue smiled at him. And she didn't look at the camera.

"But how would you know these drugs were used in religious ceremonies, not just for fun?"

"We don't call them drugs."

"All right. But how do you know?"

"You know by context whether they were involved in rites. Sometimes they are found in bowls used in ceremonies. They're found in residue of organs like the liver, along with ceremonial substances—special foods, for instance, or spices. They're found in human sacrifice remains. Also, quite often the ancient cultures have left paintings or sculptures of the substances actually being used in ceremonies."

"But still, maybe the drugs were just to keep the people quiet, or some such thing."

"It depends on the substance. They're all still around, so we know what their effects are. Hallucinogens are not sedatives."

"I don't see—"

"We're not just studying whether they were used during ceremonies. We're asking whether they were involved in the actual development of religions."

"That sounds a bit far-fetched to me."

"Have you heard of the Good Friday experiment?"

"No. And right after we go to break, I'll have you tell me about it."

They went to break. Forget having a nice conversation with Forrest while on break. He dropped his head in his hands and wouldn't talk. Blue thought, maybe he's gathering energy. She spent the time checking her clothing for wrinkles and touching an itchy forehead, fidgets you didn't do while on the air. *Make one fussy move and you look like you're dissembling. It's times like these that make me feel sorry for politicians.*

"Now tell me about this Friday experiment," he said, looking fresh as a daisy when the break was over and he raised his head.

"It was on Good Friday in 1962. Dr. Walter Pahnke, who was both a minister and an M.D., designed an experiment that's become famous. In the basement of Marsh Chapel at Boston University, he assembled twenty young men. They were all theology students. He gave half of them thirty milligrams of psilocybin, the active ingredient from hallucinogenic mushrooms, and half of them a placebo. While they were there, all the men participated in a worship service. During the next few hours, the ten who had been given the psilocybin experienced hallucinations. Some of them had some frightening moments, but they all said later that they felt deeply positive overall. They felt a sense of sacredness and a sense of unity with each other and with the world."

"Oh, Professor Eriksen. That was probably just the fuzzy warm effect of comradeship."

"No. All twenty were friends, or at least people who knew each other. But that feeling of deep oneness was only felt by the ten men who had been given the psilocybin."

"That happened because they knew they'd been given it. It was all suggestion." While his voice was serious, there was a tiny smile on Forrest's face when the monitor showed Blue was onscreen.

"No, it can't be that, either. Pahnke first randomized the meds. Even he didn't know until later who had been given the psilocybin."

"Well, they'd know by how they felt."

"No, that objection doesn't work. He had given the ten men who didn't get the psilocybin the B vitamin niacin, a substance that made them think they were getting the active hallucinogen. It made them feel warm and somewhat relaxed, at about the same time that the other men were beginning to feel the effects of the psilocybin. But the men who got the niacin didn't have the feelings of sacredness or unity and so on."

"And just how did he judge that? Wishful thinking on his part?"

"He had all twenty fill out a questionnaire at the end of the day, before they or he knew who had been given what. Then the questionnaires were graded by assistants who didn't know which man had received which substance. The results were as I've told you. Feelings of sacredness, of oneness, and besides that, several of them reported that the fear of death had left them."

"So, okay. They got a little lift. But it's like a parlor trick. Can't last."

"They were given follow-up interviews a month later and then six months later."

"Well. They were impressionable young men."

"And then, twenty-five years later, a man named Doblin decided to find out whether there were any lasting results. Pahnke had died in a scuba-diving accident. It took Doblin quite a while, but he found eighteen, all but two. Sixteen were willing to be interviewed. Everybody he talked to who had had the psilocybin believed *twenty-five years later* that it had been a genuine, positive, religious, mystical experience."

"And I suppose they all went on to cocaine or meth?"

"Now *there*, Forrest, is the most amazing thing of all. They didn't take to hard drugs. The psilocybin group seems mostly to have gone on to become ministers."

"Do you realize, Professor Erikson, that this notion of yours could lead people to think that drugs are harmless?"

"Personally, I don't think anything is harmless in excess, including food. I'm not pushing a point of view, Forrest," Blue said, sweetly. "I'm stating facts. Like alcohol, I suppose, it's a question of how you use it. I'm giving you facts. You can decide for yourself how to interpret them. But the idea we're beginning to test is even more revolutionary."

"What would that be?" He had perked up. This must have sounded good for his ratings.

"I'm looking into whether the psilocybin experience tends to prevent the use of hard drugs."

"What!"

"I began to notice that civilizations that used psilocybin or psilocybin-like substances seemed not to make much use of other, more dangerous substances."

"But it *is* a dangerous substance."

"Actually, it isn't. The LD50, which you know is lethal-dose-fifty, the amount of something that is lethal in half of a group of experimental subjects, is lower for caffeine than for psilocybin. It takes less caffeine to kill a person than psilocybin."

"But—that can't be."

"I was surprised myself."

"Wait—the Netherlands is thinking of outlawing psilocybin because they had a couple of deaths where people got nuts and got into danger." Forrest almost stuttered in his surprise. "And. And. And the Netherlands is the drug capital of the world."

"They supervised it incorrectly. In fact, not at all. Completely unprepared tourists went to Holland to do drugs. Just willy-nilly. Out on the street. Psilocybin should be taken in supervised settings. And the Good Friday experiment makes me think maybe once or twice in a lifetime would be enough. Like a vaccination. If this works, we might prevent drug addiction."

"Ah—uh." Forrest was uncharacteristically out of words.

"It's already being used in the U.S. for end-of-life therapy. But my idea is new, as far as I know."

Forrest sat straighter. His eyes opened wide. "Cure drug addiction! Are you joking?"

"No. It's a valid research area," Blue said calmly, but underneath she was fascinated at Forrest's heightening reaction.

"Pushers would be after your blood!"

"Oh, I don't think so—"

"Drugs are very big business!"

Blue was not sure whether Forrest was really unnerved or just trying for added audience reaction. She said, "Well, maybe a lot of people would have to go into some other business."

Forrest regained his footing. Smoothly, he said, "And you're putting it out here for the first time on my show?"

"Close. I wrote about it in a professional archaeology journal that came out a couple of months ago. Well, sort of. This would have been too speculative for a professional journal. So I did what academics do with speculative stuff. I put it in a footnote."

5

Blue went directly from the TV studios to the Northwestern campus. This was the last day of her Anthropology 101 class, Introduction to Archaeology. At Northwestern the archaeology and anthro departments were one, which is fairly common in colleges today. Blue was an archaeologist and paleopathologist, not that she had anything against anthropologists. It's just that the further back in prehistory she looked, the more fascinating she thought it was.

Anthro 101 was the big chance to hook the kids on prehistory. She loved it.

The kids were a bit end-of-term silly. Not like grade-schoolers exactly, but people all have a little bit of elementary-schooler left in them. The kids would now have a week's reading period, followed by the quite difficult final exam, for which toughness Blue was either praised or blamed. Since archaeology as taught by Blue was not a course they could take for an easy A, these were the better students, some of them very good, and Blue had enjoyed teaching them. It was a big class, for archaeology, close to eighty kids. Blue's classes had increased in size since her book, *Goddess*, had broken out into bestsellerdom, with nobody more amazed than she. It was scholarly; it had footnotes! Who would have thought?

"Okay," she said. "With five minutes left of the term, I'm going to show you something. This will *not* be on the exam."

There were a few dramatized sighs of gratitude in the audience.

She pulled a Styrofoam box from the shelf inside the lectern. Lifting off its top, she took out a slab of stone about fourteen inches tall, ten inches wide, and not more than an inch thick at the thickest. She held it up for all to see.

It was hard, gray stone into which had been incised two arrows and several dots. The shaft of one arrow, outlined by two parallel lines, rose up the left side of the slab, made a right turn and ended in a perfectly modern-looking arrow point on the right side of the top. Just below it a second arrow shaft began, running vertically down the right side, making a right-angle turn and running to the left along the bottom, ending in an arrow point. In other words, there were two bent arrows indicating a clockwise direction. Small dots, about an eighth of an inch in diameter, were scattered around the slab in no apparent order.

"The dots," she said, "are so perfectly round that they were probably made by rotating a burr point, maybe set into a stick and rotated with the help of a rope or leather thong." She illustrated rotating a stick by placing a pencil between her palms and moving them back and forth. "The lines of the arrows were probably incised with a sharpened stone."

"How old is it?" Stan Metz asked. Stan's father was a soybean farmer in central Illinois. Stan was an avid student, who had showed an interest in ancient agriculture.

"It's from about two thousand years B.C.E., and was found near Valdivia, in Ecuador."

Rosie Barranaco, a bouncy child with freckles, who looked too young to be a college student, said, "What is it?"

"Well, that's what I'd like you all to tell me. It's been called a 'star stone' or 'star chart,' but the community it came from didn't go to sea except to fish near shore, so navigation can't have been a big issue. And they weren't nomadic, either; they didn't travel long distances overland. So why would they need star guidance? Besides, the dots don't conform to the sky as it was back then. And even so, what are the arrows all about? Why would somebody living in a fishing village four thousand years ago the Valdivia mystery stone

spend hundreds of hours incising two clockwise arrows on a rock? Nobody knows why. In other words, your guess is as good as anybody's."

Maria Laird, a little older than the others, and the kind of kid who always gets an A, said, "It's calendrical." Maria had told Blue to pronounce her name like "Mariah." *There's a lot of that going on these days. Some day a kid is going to tell me her name is Ellen, spelled J-A-N-E.*

"A calendar. Yeah," said Stan. "When to plant and when to harvest."

Blue said, "Could be."

Rosie said, "But it doesn't look like a representation of the seasons or the position of the sun or anything like that."

"The site where it was found was active between 2500 and 1500 B.C.E. It's one of the first sites in the Americas with any real body of artistic work. But it was a simple fishing village, with no large ceremonial architecture and no big sculptures."

They puzzled over this in silence for half a minute. Then Rosie said, "Do those figures, the arrows, turn up in later things, artifacts, in that area? I mean, like, things that we *do* know what they mean?"

Blue was pleased. That was a very, very good question. Rosie was a bright student. "Sorry to say, no. Practically nothing survives from this culture, and the later Valdivia cultures are quite different."

"These guys were wiped out?" Stan said.

"Either wiped out or flooded by another culture. Or literally flooded. El Nino could have caused torrential rains. Or for that matter, there could have been a tsunami."

"But those arrows are so *modern* looking!" Rosie said.

"Yes, they surely are."

"Maybe it's like a traffic sign," she said.

"What do you mean?"

"If they had a, um, like place of worship, and you had to approach it from the left and circle around to the right. Clockwise."

"That's a good idea."

"Or maybe," Stan said, "men were to go to the right and women around to the left. There may have been another guide stone for the women. Those dots may have been decoration."

"And without a written language," Rosie said, excited, "it could have been that three dots meant women and two dots meant men, because—" Some of the class started to laugh. "Or whatever," she finished up, shyly.

They became silent, thinking. Picturing people who lived long, long ago. Picturing themselves living long ago. A lot of misguided individuals think archaeology discovers the differences between people, Blue thought. It doesn't. It discovers the sameness.

She added, "Think of these as being people almost exactly like you genetically. Clive Trotman says that if one gene in thirty mutated enough to change one amino acid in the past one hundred thousand years, which is probably average, that's only a thousand genes changed. A hundred in the past ten thousand years. Out of maybe twenty-five thousand protein-coding genes in the human genome. Since most survivable mutations are probably inconsequential, he says we are in no significant way different from a person born ten thousand years ago."

Rosie was round-eyed.

"He says that a baby born in the early Stone Age, adopted into a present-day family, could grow up to pilot a 747."

You can tell just by looking which students get it, Blue thought. They developed a far-off, thousand-yard stare that, paradoxically, caused their eyes to focus just beyond the ends of their noses. They were looking back into the mind and life of someone who lived two thousand or ten thousand or a hundred thousand years ago. They were trying to see into the essential nature of humanity, to people without any knowledge of the internal combustion engine, the composition of water, the events leading to World War II, how blood circulates, or the fact that the earth is not flat.

"I have photocopies of a sketch I made of the stone for anyone who wants to take one home and puzzle over it. As I said, no one knows what it is, so your guess is worthwhile. And let me repeat, it's not on the final exam. In conclusion, I hope you will remember something Winston Churchill said: 'The further backward you look, the further forward you can see.' Thank you all for taking Anthro 101. It's been fun meeting you."

They applauded. The kids often did at the end of a term. Blue thought it was nice gesture, and nice that it hadn't yet gone out of favor.

6

The two out-of-town agents had caught the plane in D.C. at quarter of six this morning, arrived at O'Hare at six-fifteen local time, having gained an hour. They stopped by their hotel only long enough to dump their bags in two separate rooms, then headed for the Agency's Chicago office.

Marcus clapped his hands. "Okay. Let's get started. We don't have much time." Marcus, Diana, and the seven others filed into the Agency conference room. He and Diana had race-walked from the hotel, ten blocks, and he was still fighting not to appear out of breath. Diana had been able to chat the whole way while walking.

Marcus and Diana knew they were in the position of people from the main office—resented.

The room was tastefully decorated in gray, taupe, and mauve, and Marcus hated it instantly, but recognized it for what it was: the your-friendly-government we're-just-here-to-help-you statement.

Marcus took the head of the table. The Chicago Admin, Keller, immediately seated himself to Marcus's right. Diana slid into a seat halfway down the table, with the windows at her back, and Marcus noticed that she began studying the six men and one woman, as Marcus was doing himself.

The Navy SEAL type, Conrad Brader, folded his arms and sat still as a statue. Strong silent type, Marcus thought. Very short hair. Half of one eyebrow missing. A notch out of one ear. Marcus had a friend who owned a bull mastiff with similar characteristics. Clay Dunne, the only agent here Marcus had met before, had a half-smile on his face. Maybe he always had, as Marcus thought about it now. Poor Clay spent his days liaising between the Agency and the CPD, or the Agency and the Illinois State Police, or the FBI, or Treasury. It probably wasn't the role Clay hoped to play when he joined up.

"All right," Marcus said. "As you know, I was originally from Chicago PD before I moved to the Big Onion."

Clay laughed, understanding, but the others just stared.

Marcus said, "Sorry. If New York is the Big Apple—"

Then the rest of them chuckled sycophantically, except Brader. Too tough to laugh at anything. Marcus had run enough cop meetings in his Chicago days to know the type. There's one in every crowd.

"You all have copies of the photos I e-mailed?"

There was a general mumbling of agreement.

"Now—the reason Diana and I are here, as you know, is Felix Hacker. Hacker is a very bad guy. I've got copies of the original video grabs here that are better quality than the e-mails. For all the good it does." He handed a stack of glossies to one of the younger men, who got up and passed them around.

"We have five different pictures of him, and when I say different—" Somebody shuffled the photos and groaned. "Yup. That's the problem. He relies on never looking like himself."

"Whatever himself looks like," said Keller, the admin.

"He looks like Robert Duvall," the Chicago woman said.

"And Robert Duvall looks like a different guy in every movie," said Keller.

Marcus studied the group. By now they all had the photos spread out in front of them. They were looking at Felix Hacker in different clothes and five different places, four of them airports.

Marcus said, "Right. It's not that he's heavily disguised. And our analysts tell us he's never had cosmetic surgery. He has a very 'everyman' face. He doesn't stand out. Beyond that, it's acting and clothes. In the two full-length shots you have, you'll see he looks half a foot shorter in one than the other. We know that's an illusion, from measuring the background he was standing against in each place. He wasn't even slouching much. But his attitude in one is dumpy and tired, in the other he's brisk, alert, in your face. In fact, he's exactly five feet eleven inches."

Clay said, "Looks fifteen pounds thinner here, too."

"That's mostly clothes, and partly stance. Now notice that in four out of these five shots he wears his hair over his ears. In one it's a low ponytail; in another it's a mullet. In this one," he held it up, "the hair is just long and sort of professor-floppy. He'd know that ears are often used to i.d. people and has decided that if they can be covered up without looking fake, then they should be covered up. You'll also notice that in only two photos does he have facial hair. Well, three if you include the three-day stubble in the one where he's looking like a homeless man. Other than that, one trim mustache, one short beard. I assume that he has decided that to have a lot of facial hair would look fake. That's our Felix. And this tells us another thing. He's very careful. Nobody's ever going to catch him by noticing him wearing makeup or cheek fillers or eye lifts."

Clay said, "Smart."

"He's been here a full day now. He may have killed his target yesterday, but I doubt it. He likes to get set up first. He will probably kill today. So it's urgent. Hacker never stays around after he kills."

"How does this help, knowing more or less what he looks like? It's a needle in a haystack, sir." One of the younger Chicago office agents, the guy with pink ears and a pink chin who had passed the photos around, was brave enough to argue with the Washington honcho. Marcus was pleased. Not about the negativity, but glad the kid had spoken up. The young man went on, "According to this data, we have no known associates, no idea where he's going. Really nothing more than a few pictures."

Keller said, "We certainly can't run around the city looking for somebody who looks like Hacker. Do you want them to just go out and stand on street corners and watch?"

"No. That's not our role. From D.C. last night I talked with the Chicago PD and seventeen contiguous suburban departments and I've given them his pictures. A BOLO has gone out at every roll call since eleven last night." He noticed Keller's eyebrows rise.

"They'll keep an eye out. That's the kind of thing they can do well," Marcus said. "But of course it isn't enough."

"We don't usually involve them," Keller said.

"Well, we do this time. He's going to hurt somebody. Fatally. That's why he's here."

"We steer clear of the locals—"

Marcus overrode him. "And as I said, more than likely he'll do it to-day. I called cab companies last night, too, from D.C.," Marcus said. "And the CPD has got pictures out to them and El engineers and bus drivers."

Keller said, "Hey, you've got the CPD into it. Why don't we let them try to find him?"

Keller was going to need straightening out, Marcus thought. But not now. There wasn't time. Judging from the faces of the other agents in the room, they were impatient with Keller, too. Brader averted his face about one-sixteenth of an inch.

"What I need you to do is this. Get a list together of possible targets. Fast. Like in ten minutes."

"What kind of targets?" the woman asked.

Good. They were listening. He wanted to convey the urgency he felt, without letting them see his fear that they might be too late.

"These are two types of people Hacker targets: Example: 1998. Hackensack, New Jersey. A man named Aldo Moffo is found dead, shot twice in the back of the head. Aldo turns out to be the son of a man who had run mobs in the area for decades. A big man in Hackensack. Dad had died recently, passing the business on to a lieutenant, being well aware that Aldo wasn't up to the job. Unknown to the lieutenant, Aldo had taken over about a third of the staff and income while Dad was dying. This was not smart. While the lieutenant was still trying to convince Aldo to retire, somebody sent Hacker to retire him permanently."

Clay said, "How do we know?"

Marcus liked the "we."

"That it was Hacker? Look at the third picture. The one with the three-day growth of beard. It's from a security camera. Our witnesses, both of them, said a bum had been hanging around the convenience store where Aldo picked up his hazelnut latte every morning."

"So Hacker didn't try to avoid the security camera?"

"He avoided the one in the store—just didn't go inside—and the one at the gas pump. This one was under the soffit at the Dumpster and he may not have seen it in time. He shot Aldo and dragged him to a spot between his—Aldo's—car and a row of bushes at the side of the parking area. Aldo wasn't found for two hours. Hacker had plenty of time to leave. You bring up a good point, though. Hacker's cautious but he doesn't work scared. He gets the job done and then gets out of Dodge."

Clay was fingering a second photo. "He looks like a lawyer in this picture."

"That was on his way to a killing in Massachusetts four years ago. Douglas Cleary, a member of the Massachusetts legislature, had proposed legalizing marijuana. There were extended hearings, some running late into the evening. Cleary had his throat sliced when he entered the underground parking lot at midnight. The scene was seriously messy, but the victim was hidden between a parked van and the victim's own car. It was late at night. The body wasn't found until the next morning. Again, plenty of time to leave. The knife was left at the scene."

"I remember that case," Keller the Admin said. "Wasn't there a rumor the guy was killed by some anti-drug group? I mean, after all—"

"Right. But neither the Mass cops nor the Fibbies nor anybody else ever found out who did it. Except us, and indirectly. The Agency got word that Hacker had been in town. We had people go through the surveillance tapes from the usual places, and found surveillance pictures of him at Logan Airport in the wee small hours of the morning after the killing. Of course, by the time they viewed the tapes, he was long gone. To Lisbon, in fact, but I don't think he lives there."

"But why would he kill a man who couldn't have been in competition with the large distributors?" the kid with the pink ears asked.

"Well, how do we know he wasn't? Just because the cops never found that Cleary was selling or distributing doesn't mean he wasn't. Working for decriminalization would be pretty decent cover for a dealer." In fact, though it would only confuse them if he admitted it, Marcus wondered, too. At least two other Hacker kills were people who might be called pro-decriminalization. One of the murders was in the U.K. and one in the U.S. But these people didn't need to know about that, certainly not right now.

"None of the local agencies picked up anything?"

"No. Anyhow—one more. Six years ago there was a gentleman operating in South Chicago. Henry Guest was his name. Gunned down in his bathtub. The body wasn't found for twenty-four hours. Plenty of time to get far, far away. Henry Guest was buried in his gold Cadillac, with hundred-dollar bills between his fingers. Guest was a Robin Hood kind of hood. Made serious money running dealers but never touched the stuff directly himself. He didn't actually rob from the rich, because his money came from drugs, but he surely gave to the poor. He had three soup kitchens on the South Side. He had a whole staff that took appeals from people in need of money and gave money out when they thought the cause was a good one."

"You don't *admire* this asshole do you?" the admin asked.

"Admire? Not really. But I had a sort of grudging affection for him."

"The guy was a drug dealer."

"Yes, but he was a Chicago original, you might say. Anyhow, there were so many possible killers, we didn't even imagine that the job was Hacker's until about six months later, when we got word."

"From?"

"Oh, Good Citizen. Anonymous Good Citizen. It must have been somebody who knew the hit had been ordered up. Pretended not to know Hacker's name, but he gave us a good description. Then we checked airline records. There was one man in the right age range who couldn't be traced. His plane went to Uruguay—don't you love it?"

Keller said, "So you want us to do what?"

"This is an unusual opportunity. If he has his victim in his crosshairs, let's get him when he's ready to pounce. Pull the names and whereabouts of your major drug figures. You already know them. Hacker doesn't run around the world doing piddly ass hits. Identify the heavies. Your mafia guy in Northbrook, your westside Hispanic honchos, Russian mob, South Chicago black mob, anybody who might be skimming big or trying to take over from the really big people. That's what Hacker does. He keeps people in line. He cleans up."

Keller said, "So we assemble names. Then what?"

Ticked off at the admin's constant carping, Marcus said, "Listen. I don't want to hear that 'it's hopeless' shit."

"Like we've got nothing else to do! We had two tons of cocaine a month coming into Chicago just from two brothers, the Flores twins. Twenty-eight years old, outta Mexico."

"Yeah, I know about that."

"Resulted in the biggest narcotics trafficking indictment ever in the states. Forty people—"

"And they only got jammed up when the cartels on the Mexican border went to war and told the Flores boys, pick sides or die. So they ran to the Feds. Would you ever have caught them otherwise?"

"We were *that far* behind," Keller snarled, holding his finger and thumb half an inch apart.

"Sure you were. In just ten years Chicago has become the principal U.S. center for drug distribution. You've been doing just great!"

Diana winced as Keller stood up, tipping his chair over behind him. But Marcus said very, very quietly, "I suppose it's our central location, huh? Location, location, location. The reason why Chicago was a railroad hub. Well, maybe it is. But the Flores and their friends aren't our problem now. Hacker is."

Keller righted his chair and sat down, as Marcus went on almost in a whisper.

"Hacker is an enforcer. And for the first time in several years, we have a chance to get him. Of course, we're not good at standing on street corners watching randomly. I've already got people doing that. But individual surveillance stuff is exactly what we *are* good at. You've got most of these guys under observation already. Broaden the scope of who you look at. That's why I brought up these examples. And change the direction of your gaze, people. Instead of looking in, watching what these gentlemen are doing, look outward and watch for somebody who may be trying to do something to them."

"Protect them?"

"Yup. To catch Hacker, sure. Well worth it. Who can get me a list?"

"I can do that," Brader said.

. . .

"No prob," Brader said, ten minutes later. "Forty-four good possibles. Eighteen are already under light surveil. Five close surveil. I doubled the guys on the eighteen, warned the five, sent teams to the rest."

"Magnificent," Marcus said, meaning it.

Marcus was thinking, what else can I do? Is there anything I've overlooked? He felt like pacing back and forth, but that was a bad idea. You shouldn't look fidgety in front of the troops.

"You know this pretty well strips our personnel," Keller said.

"You haven't seen any sign that he has already completed his kill, have you? How many murders do you have a day in Chicago?"

"Little less than two. One point eight. Average."

"Any in the last twenty-four hours look like Hacker targets?"

"Nope."

"Let me see them, anyhow."

Marcus tamped down his anxiety. His shoulders were so tense they wanted to climb up around his neck, but he forced them down. There was no point in his going out and standing on some street corner watching for Hacker, but he wanted to.

The long tech room was next to the communications room, and he watched live feed from an agent at O'Hare, knowing even that was useless. Hacker would not be leaving yet. He would be killing.

Besides, it would take fifty agents to keep just door-watch at O'Hare. They had eleven.

Hacker would soon be killing.

He could be killing somebody right about now.

Marcus made his way to the coffeemaker, which turned out to be spectacular. It was one of those ungodly expensive things; you put beans in the hopper and it ground and brewed an individual cup for you. What part of "budget" didn't this office understand? Marcus was used to the big urns in police district offices where you threw any coins in your pocket, plus pocket lint, into the Styrofoam money cup as your contribution and got ghastly coffee.

He must have been staring at the machine, because Brader growled, "No payoffs. We each kicked in a hundred bucks at New Year's."

The young guy came over to the coffee alcove and said to Marcus, "Sir, why hasn't airport security ever caught him?"

There were chuckles. Marcus said, "Airports are sieves. You know the U.S. has three different agencies involved in flight security and three different and only partly overlapping lists of people to watch and stop. If a passenger uses a name that's not on any watch or hold list and he looks average, his chance of being picked up is pretty close to zero. It's sheer luck somebody recognized Hacker coming into the country this time."

"Why didn't they grab him, then?"

"He bamboozled them."

"How the hell did he do that?"

"He came in from Canada. They're no better at screening than we are. Drove from Winnipeg to International Falls with a car full of fishing gear and trout."

Keller said, "And our border guards—"

"Didn't catch on. Our borders are as porous as anybody's. His i.d. looked perfect. He came in as Henry Lone Wolf, believe it or not, with his hair long and tied back with a rawhide thong, and asked them to call him Hank. Whole car apparently smelled of fish."

"Who tumbled to him?"

"The Canadian border guy got to thinking a few hours later and scanned the BOLO. But by then Hacker had a six-hour head start."

A rumbling sound heralded the fact that Conrad Brader was about to speak again. "So how many hits do you think this Hacker has made?"

"In the U.S., we think about seventeen. Abroad, who knows? There's rumor of fifty or more. About twenty of them are well-documented cases. Two in Germany—"

"They document well in Germany," Brader said.

"Yes. Three in the U.K., one in Italy. Probably a lot more nobody ever tied to him. And most of the time there's no evidence and no trail."

"So if," Keller said, "Hacker makes most of his hits look like accidents, we'd never know."

Marcus made a mental note to tell Reed when he got back to D.C. that Keller's negative attitude couldn't be helping the Agency. Personnel was no part of Marcus's job description, but he'd do it anyway.

"That's a fair point, Keller. Somebody with smarts," he said slowly, "should go over accidents in Chicago. See if any of them send up a flag."

Conrad Brader held up his index finger and pointed at his chest.

"Thanks, Brader." Marcus was pleased. He had more confidence in Brader, not knowing him at all, than in most of the others.

"What about biometrics?" the kid asked, coming up behind Marcus as he stared tensely over the shoulder of a communications officer. This kid is stalking me, Marcus thought, but in a good way.

Everybody laughed, except Brader and Marcus. The Feds, in the person of the Transportation Security Administration, had published a paper called "Guidance Package Biometrics for Airport Security," and everybody who worked where the rubber met the road in security had had a good laugh at it.

Marcus said, "Well, if anybody *really* could scan ears reliably, that stuff might work."

"Fingerprints are biometrics," the kid said.

Keller said, "Yeah, like we're gonna fingerprint everybody who gets on a plane?"

Marcus said, "No, no, he's right. Maybe some day. If it gets fast enough."

"But sir," the kid said, "ICESat can measure a half inch change in the elevation of polar ice from three hundred miles above the earth. Why can't we identify a man passing through O'Hare ten feet away from us?"

"Stop trying to suck up to the D.C. honcho, Fetterman," Keller snapped.

Marcus said, "No. He's right again. There's no reason simple surveillance should be so difficult." Marcus was thinking, keep my mind occupied, Fetterman. I hate waiting for something to happen.

Brader, having set accident queries in motion, reentered the room, rumbled again, and uttered. "I get that Hacker's toxic and not here on vacation. But—"

"Yes?"

"Who does he work for? One employer or whoever bids highest?"

"One. I'm pretty sure."

"You had some different categories of victims there."

"Well, rumor on the street—if you can call Washington a street—is that it's one group."

"Who?"

"We don't know yet." And it's pretty much killing me, Marcus thought. "Somebody big, that's all. Somebody big."

"Internationally big?"

"Of course."

Diana put a hand on Marcus's arm as he paced the conference room. They had just finished sandwiches brought in from a deli, and were alone for the first time since morning.

"Marcus, I understand why you'd call on your CPD contacts—"

"Baker got the Hacker photo in the roll call rooms in all the districts and mentioned at all roll calls. There's no other way we could get that kind of coverage."

"But the Boss isn't going to like it."

"The Boss doesn't have to love it, Diana. One of the reasons I came to Chicago myself is that I still have connections here. We may actually grab Hacker this time."

"Haseltine's policy is not to get tangled up with the locals."

"Frequently a good policy. Wrong this time."

"He's going to be really pissed off."

"Look, Diana, it's okay to keep our Agency research to ourselves. I agree that you don't broadcast confidential information on drug dealers that we're trying to watch. I admit there can be cops in the dealers' pockets. In fact, I've known a few. But that isn't what we're talking about here—giving anything away."

She shook her head doubtfully. "If somebody let the word slip, Hacker would know we were looking for him."

"It wouldn't matter. He knows we're always looking for him. We're not giving anything away. We're talking about getting something. Help. Come on. Don't act like Keller. Do we really want to catch Hacker or not, Diana?"

7

Blue crossed Sheridan Avenue to the Anthro/Archaeology office building. At Northwestern, generally speaking, the lecture halls are not in the same buildings as the faculty offices and labs. And large lectures, like her 101, were held in whatever campus space fit the size of it that semester.

Blue thought about phoning Edward and asking how he and Adam were doing, but she had already called at noon and all was well. To a certain extent, she believed it was important to show trust in him. Growing up, Adam would need a father, even though he and Blue were divorced.

One of the students, Evelyn Grantly, had trailed her from the lecture hall, begging Blue to put her exam off a week because she had to go to Delaware, to the funeral of her grandmother, which was tomorrow, and wanted to help her mother over "the next few days. She's going to be, like, devastated, Professor Eriksen."

"I can't do it, Ms. Grantly. It's just not fair to the other students. Take your materials with you. You'll have plenty of downtime to study."

"Oh, all right!" she said not quite huffily.

What sweet Ms. Grantly didn't know that Blue knew, was that she was known as "dead-granny Grantly." She'd run this scam on a math professor, and a good friend of Blue's in the history department, who had already heard about her from a friend who taught freshman English. Blue supposed that Grantly's boyfriend, who surfed, had discovered a place in the world where the waves were just right during the very last week of May. Or maybe she was trying to cheat.

What puzzled Blue more was the girl's lack of imagination. The combination of slyness and naïveté—she apparently believed that professors in one department never spoke to those in other departments—was one of the mysteries of human nature.

As Blue passed through the department office, she pulled the mail from her mail slot and found that another student, a good student named Parker Cotts, had called the office. Cotts had not been in class today. Blue didn't take roll—hardly anybody did these days—but she did notice things.

The note, written by the department secretary, simply said he called to tell the department that his brother had died.

"Lenora," Blue said, "you took the message from Parker?"

"Took it. Checked. It's true."

"That's horrible. What happened?" Parker and Peter Cotts were twins, both of them students at NU. Blue had never met Peter, but they were said to be identical. Except in academics. Peter was a math/computing guy and Parker was history/anthropology/archaeology.

"Motorcycle accident. In Skokie someplace."

"Oh, no! I'll write to Parker. But if he calls about the exam, tell him he can take it however late he wants." Blue thought a few seconds. "He had an A-minus on the midterm. Tell him, if he wants, I'll give him that for the semester and he can forget about the final."

She went on down the hall, sorting the mail as she walked, still appalled at the thought of losing an identical twin. There was a note from the Chair that all professors had better get their grades in on time this semester or else. He didn't exactly say "Or else" but he came close.

At the door of the dry lab, she caught the voices of her colleague and one of the grad students going over the list of what to take on the trip to Peru.

Blue was having a really great day, what with the upbeat end of class and holding Forrest Sabin to a draw. And the excitement of her new project.

Yes, she yearned to be going to Peru with the gang. End of term, just the time of year to start out on a dig. Summer vacation was the time to go—classes over, students gone. Every year since sophomore undergrad she had been packing up to leave about now, figuring what the climate was going to be, what to pack, what to leave behind, the excitement of not knowing what they would unearth—every summer except last summer, and now this. She would stay here with her child while two graduate students, a chemist, a photographer named Drake Rakowski, and her colleague Jasper Martello, flew off to collect samples. Samples for their book. Their planned opus. Her work and she wasn't going.

But that project was drawing to a close. She had begun writing the book months ago, because they had plenty of data already on hallucinogens in the development of religion.

Her new big project was the one she had told Forrest about. The results from the end-of-life therapies other people were conducting had set her off on the new track. Dying patients needed far less medication if they had been given psilocybin. When she found the Good Friday results she knew she had something big.

The use of psilocybin to overcome drug addiction now had a firm financial grant. It was going forward at a private detox facility near Chicago. Blue had an M-2, a stint in medical school when she got her paleopathology degree, but she wasn't an MD, so she had needed to enlist two solid doctors and a full staff to oversee the administration of the hallucinogen.

This was geared toward treating patients with existing drug addiction.

Now she had floated a re-do of the Good Friday experiment with a larger test group. This meant not trying to treat people already using drugs but finding a group of young non-drug-users, giving them psilocybin, and following them for several years to see whether they turned to other drugs. The United States was grudgingly beginning to relax its prohibition on testing of this sort, but she already had a definite bite from Canada.

Blue almost bounced with enthusiasm.

As she rounded the bench table in the lab, the sleeve of her blouse caught the edge of a box of glass slides and sent them tumbling off.

"Jeez! Watch it, Blue!" Jasper Martello sidestepped as the slides crashed onto the floor spraying glass shards everywhere.

Blue said, "Oh, man!" Jasper and she both reached for them, bumped heads, sidestepped, tried again, a real Abbott and Costello routine.

"I was hurrying," she said. "Didn't see them."

"You look upset."

"No, not at all. I'll clean this up." She had already started, grabbing a dustpan and broom from the closet.

"I'll sweep. You hold the dustpan," Jasper said. He tended to be a perfectionist, and Blue knew he would want every shard of glass removed. Tabitha Lincoln, one of the grad students, who was in the supplies room helping them pack, looked over but apparently decided there were enough people involved in the cleanup.

Blue said, "I can do it." But Jasper was already holding the broom and it went a lot faster with two people, anyway.

Jasper Martello and Blue were both full professors in the anthropology/archaeology department at Northwestern. Jasper was five years older. They were coleaders of the upcoming research trip, even though Blue wasn't physically going along, and they had been working for three years toward the publication of a major book, the one Forrest asked about. The hallucinogen project was the first time Jasper and Blue had collaborated. There was an odd power imbalance between them. Because *Goddess* had been a runaway bestseller, the grad students tended to treat Blue as a celebrity, even though she was younger than Jasper. Blue worried whether Jasper found that uncomfortable.

"Wish you were coming with us?" Jasper was being kind, if a little clumsy. He'd been careful for months not to pry. Blue hadn't been out of the country since before her baby, Adam, was born nearly a year ago. To Blue, the most exciting thing about archaeology was being out in the field. On a dig, she had a sense of getting close to people who lived hundreds or thousands of years ago. She loved being out in the field, but she'd been stuck here and Jasper knew she missed what she considered her real work. She had breast-fed Adam for six months, coming in to school three hours a day three days a week, teaching, and then doing the paperwork for their project at home, while Jasper and the team had gone to the Bulnayn

Mountains in Mongolia, a pre-Stonehenge area in Wales, an ice cave in Finland—so much good stuff. When Adam was six months old, Blue found a good nanny, Paula Desnoyers, and came to work five days a week for six hours. Her ex-husband also took care of Adam a few hours a week. *But it isn't what I love most,* she thought, *field work. Scratch that. What I love most is Adam. What I love second-most is field work.*

So I should be happy.

Blue said, "Yes, I wish I were going with you."

"Could you leave Adam with Edward?"

"For a month? I don't think so. Oddly enough," she said, "he's a really good father, even though he's a rotten husband. He's taking care of Adam today because Paula's sick."

Jasper nodded.

She said, "But Edward works long hours. What would he do for a whole month on his own?"

Jasper said, "Could he have Paula in more?"

"I just don't think I should, Jasper. It's not right while Adam's so young."

"I suppose."

Tabitha Lincoln said, "Did you see the news? That thing about the kid who saved the baby?" They had a small television in the break room, with the sound turned low. But right now, rushing to pack for the trip, nobody spent much time taking breaks. Tabitha was a beautiful, tall African American, so lovely she made you think of Cleopatra. *I mean our image of Cleopatra. The real Cleopatra wasn't so gorgeous.* Tabitha, thank goodness, pronounced it "Tabitha," not "Tawbitha" or anything weirder yet.

Tabitha was well aware of her beauty, too. Today she wore a turquoise nubby knit shirt and white boot-cut jeans, with a glittering belt of linked Navajo silver and turquoise discs.

She was also smart.

"No, what?" Blue said.

"Some baby crawled onto the Kennedy, right into traffic, and this teenaged kid"—Tabitha was twenty-three and a teenager was a mere child to her—"drove his car into the ditch and jumped out and ran across traffic and grabbed him and saved him. There was this *huge* pileup."

Blue said, "Where were the baby's parents?"

"Nobody knows. They have a picture up on the news asking for them to come forward."

"Jeez! How could somebody not keep track of a baby?"

Jasper said, "Well, I hope the teenager gets some reward."

"Didn't hear anything about that," Tabitha said.

Andy Becker, looking like Yosemite Sam, with handlebar mustaches, came loping into the room. Andy was twenty-four, their other grad student. His hair was red, thin on his scalp and lush on his upper lip. He had a great admiration for Jasper and constantly tried to do exactly the correct thing to please him.

He said, "American flies out of Midway. You gotta go to Dallas-Fort Worth and then change for Lima."

"Gaaawd, this is so last-minute," Tabitha drawled. Tabitha was inclined to drawl as if she were world-weary.

Andy, apparently feeling that Jasper was being criticized, said, "It's not like *you're* paying for it."

Jasper said, "We had a flight canceled. Be glad we didn't get halfway there and *then* have it canceled. That's happened more than once." He turned to Andy. "What times?"

"Ten-oh-three a.m., twelve-thirty p.m., one-thirty p.m., or you can go to Miami and change there for Lima."

"Which one is fastest?"

"I can't see it makes much difference. Hour and a half to DFW. Eight hours from there to Lima. Gotta allow two hours for changing planes."

"Yeah, at least. There's too much chance of missing connections otherwise. Well, go ahead and make the reservations."

"No way to avoid getting into Lima at the crack of dawn, either."

"Well, when you get done with the reservations," Jasper said, "come back and start bubble-wrapping the fixatives."

"Sure thing."

Tabitha said, "What I don't understand is how, every time we go, we plan six months in advance, start packing up well ahead, and still there's a lot to be done at the last minute."

Blue said, "This isn't *quite* the last minute, thank goodness. You guys still have five days."

"Right."

Blue called home to check on Edward and Adam, but there was no answer. Oh, right. Edward had talked about taking Adam to the park if the weather was good, and it was.

Back at his desk at Area Three, Pollard grinned at the memory of Brad on the *FiveAlive* news. As the reporters fired questions at him, he'd been such a teenager, so Brad-like. When told by a reporter that he was a hero, he had actually said, "Whatever." When they asked him to describe the horrific pileup, Brad said, "It was—was—was uh, bad." The kid would never be a politician.

One of the survivors was a woman who had come on the accident scene late in the chain reaction. She had skidded into the back of the semi, but had not been seriously injured. She said to Channel 5, "That young man ran right across in front of all those cars and he could have been killed and he grabbed up that baby, just when I thought the baby would—" At that point she gulped and burst into tears.

In the break room, Pollard had made a point of watching the streaming news on CLTV. He imagined Brad's parents, caught between telling their son he shouldn't have cut school and admitting that if he hadn't, that baby would surely be dead.

None of which solved Pollard's problem.

He had a baby and no parents. Or, at any rate, the system had the baby and he had a mystery. Usually it was the other way around: frantic parents and a missing child. He smiled about Brad, then the smile faded as he wondered what the baby was doing now—with strangers in a strange place. Sad.

The baby must have gone missing from his home or car by noon. Little Fella was no abandoned newborn. It happened far too often that a woman abandoned a newborn infant in hopes that nobody would have to know she'd been pregnant, but this wasn't one of those cases. This was very unusual. Somebody had cared for this child for nearly a year, and from the look of him had loved him. His hair was trimmed; his face was clean. Pollard had smelled shampoo. Even the baby's good cheer showed that he had been loved.

After he had dropped Brad at home, Pollard returned to the accident scene with an evidence tech. Locating his handkerchief on the stanchion of the chain-link fence, he pointed the tech, Frederick W. Blankenship III, toward the child's probable path and told him to do his bloodhound thing. Pollard himself walked up and down the access road the baby would have had to cross, but found only squashed pop cans, candy wrappers, popsicle sticks, discolored pennies, a condom, lots of gum, gum wrappers, lots of cigarette butts, a very old knit cap, all items impossible to connect to a wandering baby. He had hoped for a tiny baby sock in the access road and another matching baby sock in front of one of the houses that stood just beyond the road. Sure. Dream on.

After crawling on his hands and knees in the grass, the way the baby must have done, Blankenship came up with a few evidence bags and no encouragement. Pollard sent him back to Area Three Headquarters. Pollard had gathered three assistants by then and divided them into two teams, himself pairing with one of them. They visited the houses that backed up most closely to I-90 across the access road from the hole in the fence. They began with six houses along the U-shaped street. The developers who had built this subdivision were coping with the fact that all small streets had to end at the expressway. They could have simply created two dead-end streets, but apparently thought the U-shape would be more attractive. It was certainly easier to drive through. The rounded part of the U abutted the access road and the open end faced west, with both of the ends entering into Milwaukee Avenue. They had placed two houses inside the body of the U and four around its outside. At five of the houses, nobody answered Pollard's ring. This was hardly surprising, since most people would still be at work. A very cautious teenage girl answered at one of the inner houses. She was coughing and red-nosed.

Pollard showed her his ID and made sure his colleague did so as well. "Have you seen anything unusual in the street today?"

"I've been watching television all day," she said, sneezing. "I'm sick. I stayed home from school."

He ducked away from her sneeze. "Did you see a baby crawling by outside?" She goggled at them as if they might be dangerous lunatics.

"Nun-uh."

From that street they fanned out to the next closest, twelve houses on two adjacent blocks. They had no luck there, either. Pollard realized that the number would go up quickly as they worked their way farther out. And become more time-wasting; the farther away they went, the less likely it was that the baby had crawled that distance. After the two teams had rung bells at forty houses, nine where people were actually home, he gave up, left the three to carry on, and went back to Area Three.

Could the baby have been dumped from a car? Could he have been left behind at a park playground by mistake? Pollard envisioned a harried mother of, say, five children, loading the kids into the car after a day at the playground, getting home and finding the baby missing. No, the first thing she would do is call the police.

Horace "Tommy" Pollard did another round of checks through the records for missing children, taking the query into wider parameters this time. There was a missing teenager who lived on Loomis and had run away three times before. There was a woman whose nine-month-old baby had been missing since she came home from work at noon. However, Pollard's baby was white and this baby was black and his mother was involved in a custody battle. She believed the baby had been taken by her ex-husband, who had been at home with the child.

Every day, soon after going-home-from-school time, there were children who didn't arrive home when they should. The info on today's batch was just beginning to enter the system. Almost all of the kids would turn up later, having gone to a friend's house and lost track of the time. None of these was Pollard's baby.

Pollard was deeply worried.

Suppose the baby had been left with a negligent babysitter? Suppose the sitter simply walked away, maybe leaving the baby in the yard? Suppose there was another child abandoned? Or suppose the baby had been at home with his mother, playing out in the yard maybe, and the mother fell into a diabetic coma? If so, she needed help, and no one knew where she was. That was quite possible.

Every minute that went by made Pollard more uneasy.

Something very bad must have happened to the mother. Or father.

The baby had dirty little knees and dirty little hands. But his hair had smelled of shampoo. The jeans were soiled from being run over but were clean inside. Impulsively, Pollard picked up the phone, and checking his notes, phoned the youth services officer, Maura Goodbody. He reminded her who he was, and said, "How is the little guy?"

"Well, not happy. Actually, he was crying at the top of his lungs when I last saw him."

"Where is he?"

"He's in the hospital overnight. We have to have him checked out, you know. There could be almost anything—"

"And what happens tomorrow?"

"He'll go to a temporary foster home."

"When you changed the little guy's diaper, did he have any diaper rash?"

"No," she said.

"Were there any signs of abuse?"

"Not that I could see. And the hospital says not."

She was being very cautious, but Pollard kept quiet and after a few seconds she said, "He's not a neglected child, Detective. I've seen a lot of neglected children and he's not one of them. He responds to smiles. He chatters at us. Somebody loved that baby."

Pollard noted, but did not comment on the fact that she said "loved" instead of "loves."

Pollard was supposed to be working seven to three today, but he called his wife and told her he needed to work a couple of hours more. He was worried about the child's parents. Still, as his wife pointed out, there were other people at the Area Three headquarters fully capable of taking messages and even beeping him if something important came up.

. . .

CHICAGO LOOP, THE AGENCY BUILDING

Diana came into the tech room where Marcus, Keller, Brader, and several field agents were watching videotapes of endless streams of people entering the doors of Union Station, Northwestern Station, the LaSalle Street station, Midway and O'Hare airports, and several major downtown El stops. It was mind-deadening work, and they had to change off every half hour or so for a coffee and walking-around-blinking break. Even at double speed, it would take many hours to cover today and yesterday. And of course more tapes were coming as the day went on.

"We've got a possible," she said.

"What?" Marcus paused his tape.

"Your CPD friends phoned a minute ago. One of their guys saw somebody who looked a lot like Hacker."

"Where?"

"Going into a building at 1177 North Sheridan."

"Let's move!"

8

"Let's go, let's go."

Marcus's blood fizzed with adrenaline as they got out of the Agency cars.

He would get Hacker this time.

The apartment building was a three-high, a building with two apartments on each of three floors. Many buildings in the city had been built this height so that they were not required to install elevators.

Diana had as much field experience as Marcus, and between them they had set up a perimeter around the building in less than ten minutes. Marcus had talked with District Commander James Moffat and the man was willing to let them do their thing as long as he had a few cars around in case Hacker broke out of the perimeter. He extracted Marcus's promise to call in instantly if the bust went bad.

The building manager, Simon Atwood, was a wiry man with a goatee. He wore a leather vest over a red sweatsuit. "Tenants, all of 'em, been here a while," he said. "Can't imagine anybody your guy'd be visiting."

The information that he might have a desperado in his building had energized him so much that he bounced up and down on his toes and made boxing moves with his arms. When they told him the man they were searching for was dangerous, he said, "Well, let's go look!" This despite the fact that he had seen nobody come in. Obviously, the guy didn't get enough excitement in his life. Of course, the fact that Diana was standing there looking gorgeous might have been a factor, too, Marcus thought.

Two agents had secured the hallway. Two others were inside the back exit. All four sides of the building were under observation, including the two sides without doors, in case Hacker tried to climb out a window. Hacker had no history of violence against police officers, but they were ready.

Asked to be more specific about his tenants, the manager explained, without any apparent concern for their privacy, "Three-A is a guy, maybe fifty. Works at a printing shop. Guess he's divorced. Has his ten-year-old kid over once a month and they go to like the Lincoln Park Zoo or like that. Movies. Three-B is two lesbian ladies. Quiet. Clean. Live and let live, I say.

"Two-A is a single mom. She has guys over, though. It's a two-bedroom apartment, so hey. They're all two-bedrooms. Did I say that?"

"No, Mr. Atwood. Go on."

"Well, Two-B is a couple with a new baby. Actually Two-A has been complaining about Two-B's baby crying at night. Wouldn't you think she'd be more sympathetic, kid herself at home? Her kid's seven, but how hard is it to remember?"

"And the ground floor?"

"Couples. One-A is an older couple. Gotta be in their sixties. One-B is, like, yuppies. Making a bit of money, I think. In which case they'll be moving out soon."

"Basement?"

"Basement is all me."

They walked through the basement first, just to be on the safe side. Marcus moved fast, checking every closet. The manager kept quite a tidy apartment, except for one room in which he did woodcarving.

Several people were out at work, he said. Nobody had come in except the mailman.

Reluctantly, Marcus said, "We can't go into an apartment without a warrant. We can knock on doors and ask, though."

"Well, I can go in," Atwood said. "I have keys to all the units. Have to. Suppose there was a water leak? Or a fire?"

"It's not the same thing. We can't do it."

"How would they know?"

"Wait. Wait. Let's see who's home first."

Three-A, the fifty-year-old man, was home. He said, "You can't come in without a warrant."

"I know that," Marcus said. Diana and three agents were backed up down the hall, just in case somebody came out shooting. They would have needed only two agents, except one was there to keep Atwood at the far end, out of trouble. He seemed determined to be James Bond.

Marcus, saying a prayer in his mind, asked, "Sir, if you just let us look around—? The man may be dangerous, and he's got to be somewhere."

"Oh, hell, why not?" the man said.

Nobody was lying in wait. Nobody in the closets. Three-A had not wanted them to see the number of empty beer cans in the kitchen sink, a giant plastic can full and two black plastic bags with telltale bulges. Marcus and Diana averted their eyes politely.

Three-B was not home. Two-B was home and the place smelled of diapers, baby poop, milk, and sweat, the kind of sweat you get from not having time to wash clothes. The kind of thing you get when everybody is too tired to wash clothes.

"Go ahead and look," a red-eyed, rumpled woman said, as she bounced a shrieking baby. "You already woke him up."

"Sorry."

Two-A was not home.

The elderly couple in One-A was home. The wife, a tiny woman with silky white hair, asked them in and offered coffee. "I have some delicious little croissants, fresh this morning."

Marcus was just looking into the couple's fragrant kitchen when Commander Moffat charged in. Commander James Swearingen Moffat was a cop Marcus had known when Marcus was a uniform and Moffat was a sergeant about to be promoted to lieutenant. Marcus was astonished to see him at the scene. Not only did commanders not go out on cases, even lieutenants didn't. Marcus had exclaimed "Sir!" when Moffat said,

"What are you doing here?"

"We cleared it with you and the loo. The dispatcher knows about—"

"No, what are you doing *here*? The sighting was at 1777 North Sheridan."

The building at 1777 was a large motel, only two stories high, but a full block long. There were forty units, twenty on the ground floor facing the parking lot, twenty above, with a stair up and a walkway overlooking the parking lot. It was no-frills, but clean, to Marcus's eye more a businessmen's lodging than a hooker hangout.

Marcus was muttering, "Oh, hell!"

Diana agonized all the short seven blocks to the motel. "Oh, God! Did he say it wrong, or did I write it down wrong?"

"It doesn't matter right now. Let's move!"

Marcus went in with District Commander Moffat, leaving the perimeter buttoned up. He thought Moffat, like a lot of good street cops promoted to administration, wanted an excuse to get back on the street.

Marcus showed the desk manager a picture of Hacker, the most generic and therefore probably the most like the real man.

"Uh, no. I don't think we've had anybody here like that." The manager shoved a few papers around on the countertop.

Marcus was stumped for a few seconds. But the manager seemed a little off. "What's your name, sir?" he asked.

"Gabalson. Mort Gabalson."

"Look here, Mr. Gabalson," Marcus said, pulling a file card from his pocket and writing "Mort Gabalson" on it in letters big enough for Gabalson to read upside down, "we have a police officer reporting that this man entered your building today. He's a dangerous man, Mr. Gabalson. You don't want to get in trouble."

"Uh."

"Uh, what?"

"Well, he may have come in while I was on break."

Marcus noticed sweat beginning to gleam along the manager's hairline. "Mr. Gabalson! Let's stop this. He stayed here at least one night. Last night. You weren't on break all that time. You knew he was here."

"Uh—"

"Let me guess. He came in yesterday and wanted to pay cash. So you thought you could take the cash and let him stay. Off the books. The owner didn't need to know."

Silence. Marcus added, "And we don't need to tell the owner, either."

Marcus waited, and balled his hands, not to hit Gabalson, but to keep from hitting him.

"His name?" Marcus said.

"Well, yes. I think he said his name was Parsons? Ah, no, maybe Partisan."

Thinking *cute name, Hacker*, Marcus asked, "What room is he in?" Uneasy about the phrase "his name was—"

"He checked out."

Marcus's heart sank. "When?"

"He checked out at one-thirty."

"Checked out? He hadn't checked in."

"Yeah. Whatever. Well, he went out of here with a bag at one-thirty. Nope. That's wrong. About quarter of two. Or maybe even two. I'm pretty sure, anyways."

The district cop had noticed the man going into the motel at one-thirty. He'd informed the district at four twenty-five. Hacker had probably picked up his stuff and left.

The district commander got the patrol officer on the line for Marcus. The man admitted he'd waited to put the word in until he got back to the district for his break.

"Why?" Marcus asked, trying not to snap at the cop. They all carried cells. Why not call in?

"To look at the photo. It didn't look like him. He was shorter, fatter, and older. I would've said the guy was sixty, sixty-five. And yours is forty, right?"

"Roughly."

"And this guy looked kind of—well, not all there. You know. His lower lip was slack. His eyes were half closed. And he dragged his left leg just a little bit." The man was talking more rapidly.

"Go on."

"So I headed in to the district to look at the pictures again. It still didn't look a lot like my guy, but I figured I'd better report it anyhow."

Turning away from the phone, Marcus gritted his teeth, rather than scream at anybody. He told Brader, "Double the surveillance at the airports."

"My fault. My fault," Diana said, back at the Agency.

"The officer who called may have misspoken."

Her face had gone stony. "No. I'm upset enough as it is. I *won't* have it blamed on somebody else if it's my fault."

Diana ran the tapes of the incoming phone messages back. The voice of a patrol cop from the district said, "I don't know whether this was your guy. It doesn't really look like him."

"Where did you see him?" Diana's voice.

"Going up the walk to one-seven-seven-seven North Sheridan."

"I've got it. Thanks. We'll check it out."

The call was logged in at four-twenty-four.

"Every agent should either be in an airport, train station, or bus station, or should be here making calls! Call and remind the taxi companies!"

Marcus got on to Chief of Patrol Hollis Baker again and really believed Baker was doing everything he could. He had patrol officers on every outgoing El train, walking the length of the train, scanning every face. Every bus driver had been visited at least once, told again what Hacker looked like and given a photo, whether he had kept the earlier one or not. Billy Mitchell Field in Milwaukee, considered Chicago's third airport, had responded and salted the terminal with its own security and Milwaukee police. Marcus had re-warned all the other Chicago area airports—Palwaukee, Chicago-DuPage, Waukegan Regional, Aurora, Gary/Chicago, Lewis University, Joliet Regional, Lansing Municipal, Schaumburg, Lake in the Hills, and thirteen others. He'd sent follow-up e-mails to all forty-two heliports, which had already been faxed photos, and had agents making confirming phone calls. Most of the heliports were at trauma centers, hospitals, or police barracks, so they were unlikely escape routes for Hacker, but better safe than sorry. He also called and faxed the three seaplane bases.

There had been no phone calls made from Hacker's motel room. Like he should be so careless. Cell phone calls? They'd be a bear to trace, maybe impossible, but Marcus would find somebody who knew how to try.

By now both Moffat and Diana were beating up on themselves. Moffat left the Agency grumbling—probably, Marcus thought, to go back to the District and ream out the hapless patrol officer.

When Marcus had finally exhausted his ideas on where to look next, he said to Diana, "Hacker was out of that motel before we even heard about the place, Diana. It's really not your fault."

"It was unprofessional of me not to double-check. Totally unprofessional."

Marcus understood how she felt. He was angry and frustrated, but he didn't want to take it out on her. "I've made mistakes myself once or twice. Once, anyway," he said. She smiled, but only for a second.

"Once, huh?"

"We couldn't have stopped him, Diana. He was long gone from the motel."

"We would have alerted the airports."

That was true. Of course Hacker wouldn't hang around. He probably wouldn't take public transportation to the airport. Marcus's best guess was that Hacker had previously rented a car using another name and a clean charge card, and they would eventually find the car abandoned in the return lot of some rental company at Midway or O'Hare, where returning a car was so common that nobody noticed, or parked and abandoned in one of the public garages. They'd find it, but probably several days too late.

They checked the smaller airports, too, but generally they were more apt to notice people than big airports, and were not likely choices for Hacker. There were parts of the world where small airports were the best place to fly out of if you didn't want to leave a trail. Easy to bribe people, easy to get yourself "missed" on a passenger list. But here it was not so.

By six o'clock, with no results, Marcus said, "Goddammit to hell! We've lost him."

"Bet he went first class," Brader said.

Marcus said, "Why?"

"Hadn't you heard? First class buys you reduced screening and shorter wait time. Frequent flyer does, too. But he's not going to be on a frequent flyer list."

"Makes you want to spit nails," Keller said.

"All right," Marcus said loudly. "He's killed his target and he's left. We lost him. So who's dead?"

9

The sun was lower in the west, somewhere over O'Hare, moving into a haze of thin, smoky overcast. The air was the color of maple syrup. While it was plenty light enough for Pollard to see his way around, lamps had been lit in a few of the houses. He was back at the U-shaped street again. The mystery bothered him. He just couldn't let it alone.

Pollard took a look at the highway, cleared now of wrecked vehicles and bleeding people. Despite the fires in two cars and the black smoke that had engulfed the accident scene, and the fire-retardant foam laid down, there was virtually no sign on the pavement now of the carnage. A bend in the metal divider, paint scrapes on the divider, and some burned grass showed where the horrific scene had happened. But on the pavement there was no sign at all. The thousands of tires that had passed over it since the road was reopened had erased all the marks. Like a river, he thought, then thought something about: can you step into the same highway twice? Well, that was surely silly. He studied the houses.

The baby must have come from west of the highway. He had been heading east, and anyway, he couldn't have climbed over the median divider.

How far could a baby crawl, really? His knees and hands were dirty, true, but they weren't abraded. He had been wearing jeans, which would have protected his knees until the jeans fell off when he was halfway across the highway, but the streets here were like streets everywhere. There was dust and sand and grime. The child could not possibly have crawled more than three or four blocks without scuffing the palms of his hands.

Pollard stood in the middle of Pebble Lane, the U-shaped street, looking between the two eastern-most houses, the ones closest to the freeway. He could see the cars zipping past on the freeway, their windows catching the orange of the lowering sun. He squatted down to baby level, as much as he could without cracking his knees and risking being unable to stand up again. It would be way too undignified to have to crawl to a tree and pull himself up.

There was still a good view of the highway between clumps of yews. If the baby had been right here, he would have seen the cars and possibly been attracted to their motion. The sun would have been high in the sky when the baby started his journey, but surely it must have glinted off some of the car windows. Just the thing to catch the eye of a child almost a year old and make him want to investigate.

Pollard would check out the houses nearest this spot. He didn't bother with the house where the girl had been home nursing a cold. Next door to the girl's place was a red brick colonial. He looked in the glass pane set into the door. There was a light on in the back, possibly in the kitchen, shining onto the wall in the hall. Pollard rang the doorbell. It played the first fourteen notes of "Home on the Range." The door swung open, letting out a gust of chili con carne fragrance.

A man holding a wine glass said, "Who are you?"

"Detective H. T. Pollard, sir. I'd like to ask you a couple of questions." He added, "About the neighborhood." Pollard said this hoping it would be disarming. Many, many, many people, in his experience, had either done something wrong or were afraid they might have. So they clammed up unless you let them know the inquiry wasn't about them.

But the man snarled, "What about the goddamn neighborhood?"

"It's a lovely neighborhood," said a voice behind the man. An extremely beautiful woman appeared, wearing blue lounging pajamas and a defiant expression directed at the man, not Pollard. She carried an empty wine glass.

"Yeah, it's just swell. High taxes, crummy city services—"

"Sir. Could I have your name, sir?"

"No."

Well, he could get it from the computer easily enough. In fact, he probably had it in his car on the first canvass reports.

"Mine's Brenda Sorenson," said the woman.

"Look, I'm sure you've heard about the accident out here—" Pollard pointed to the expressway.

The man said, "No."

Brenda said, "Yes."

"Seven dead as of now," Pollard said. "There was a baby involved—"

"Ohhhhh," the woman said.

"But he wasn't hurt. We think he crawled out from somewhere along the road. Not from one of the cars, if you see what I mean. Were you home this afternoon?"

This time they said "No" together and the woman added, "We just got home." Too late to have seen anything useful.

"Can you tell me," Pollard said, "which of your neighbors have babies?"

"I have *no* idea!" the man said. "Like I'd care." He poured the rest of his wine down his throat and stalked off.

"The Metzgars," Brenda said. "At 2101." She pointed.

"How old a baby?"

"Oh, I don't know. I'm not good on babies. Under a year, I guess. But I'm not sure whether they're home right now. I think they were going to Banff. Or Maine."

"That's all the babies in the neighborhood? One?"

"No. There's the Eriksens. At 2119. But he hasn't been around much. I think there's been a divorce. She used to travel a lot. And I don't know them well enough to tell you—"

"How old is their baby?"

"Oh, six months, maybe." Pollard was just about to write off the

Eriksen's baby when she said, "Or a year." She smiled sheepishly. "I'm not good on babies."

Both houses, 2101 and 2119, were dark, and the canvassers earlier had found no one at home. The sun had sunk lower and passed into deeper overcast while he talked with Brenda and The Grouch.

Most people at this hour would start to put lights on. In fact, there were lights at many of the other houses now.

At neither the Eriksen nor the Metzgar house was there a car in the driveway. But both garages were closed, so he couldn't be sure there was no one inside the house. Pollard approached 2101. Metzgar. First he rang the doorbell. Then he knocked. Then he pounded. Not a peep from inside. His sense of urgency was growing. Somewhere must be the baby's parent— sick or dead?

The shadows were long and although the late-May evening was golden and warm, for no particular reason Pollard felt creepy. Except for a distant hiss from I-90–I-94, it was a very quiet neighborhood. He longed to see inside those two houses. Of course, he couldn't enter a house without either an invitation from the householder or a warrant. Unless there were exigent circumstances of some kind. Like a person inside appeared to be injured or ill. Or a bad guy had run inside with a gun. That kind of thing. Once in a while you could go in if you'd had a "check on the well-being" call from a relative, but even then, if the outside of the home looked intact, you usually shouldn't break in.

Large and sided with fieldstone, 2101 Pebble Lane was in good shape, its trim freshly painted, the lawn mowed. There was no sign of intrusion in the front. The front door was shut, the windows unbroken. Pollard started around the house, taking the shady east side first, and feeling the coolness as he got into the blue shadows.

He found that the rear of the house was surrounded by a solid, chest-high redwood fence. There was a gate with no handle or latch on the outside, set flush in the fence. He reached over the gate and down to the latch on the inside. There was a padlock hooked over the drop-bar, but it had not been locked. The gate opened and he went in. He was trespassing and could get into trouble, but he excused his behavior by thinking that it was not nearly as illegal as entering the house itself.

The fence surrounded a large patio, which swept out from the house and wrapped itself around an oval swimming pool. This was probably why the gate could not be opened from the outside—liability. On the patio were a baby walker and several plastic toys. The water in the pool was unmoving, dark purple. Pollard stared at the pool, feeling suddenly queasy. Then he realized he was unnerved by the idea of the baby, left alone, crawling across the patio, over the edge, and plunging into that water.

Maybe the baby's mother had fainted, fallen into the pool and drowned, leaving the baby unattended to crawl away.

Very uneasy, he crossed the cement to the pool's edge and stared into the shadowed water. There was still enough light to see that no one floated there and just barely light enough to see that no bodies lay on the bottom. A red and white ball nodded indolently on the surface.

Returning to the patio, he checked the windows of the back of the house. None were broken or forced. The back sliding door was intact and closed tight. He pushed it; it was locked or at least latched.

He exited the backyard and checked the west side of the house. That, too, was intact.

But wait. Dummy. The baby hadn't closed the gate after crawling out, surely. So the baby had not come from this house.

He gave up on 2101.

The people who had designed the small subdivision and put in this U-shaped street had had to make a decision about street numbers. In Chicago, the street numbers on east-west streets run up as they go west, but two legs of this street went west. The house numbered 2119 was on the same side of the street, in a topological sense, as 2101, but faced it, looking north across an intervening pair of even-numbered houses in the center of the U. If 2119 hadn't been clearly numbered, and if Brenda in the pajamas hadn't pointed it out, Pollard could not have deduced which one it was.

2119 Pebble Lane appealed to Pollard more than 2101. He was no judge of styles, but it looked New Englandish to him, with pale gray wood siding and apple trees in the front lawn.

All the windows were dark. The sun was very low now, and the blood red that soaked the tops of the trees reflected little light onto the ground. If there had been a lamp on in the house, he would have seen it.

He circled the house. The yard was more modest than 2101, but pleasant. There was a small flagstone patio with a hammock and two chairs. A couple of cat toys and a small pet dish rested on the lawn. There was a cat flap in the back door. Farther along was baby bouncy seat. A playpen stood under the protective overhang of an awning. Pollard looked into what he assumed was the kitchen window. All he could see was a breakfast table, frog-shaped salt and pepper shakers on the table, four small chairs, and beyond that the end of a kitchen counter.

He circled past the trash cans on the west side, to the front of the house again. This time he peered in the tiny garage window. There was one car parked in the two-car garage. Did that mean somebody was home? Not necessarily.

He stood on tiptoe in the flower bed to look in the living room window. The room was dark, but as far as he could see there was nothing wrong.

A window well for the basement was just below the living room window. He could see nothing at all through it. The basement was pitch dark.

"Hey you!"

A man came out of the house next door, holding his cell phone. *Oh, great.*

"I've called 911. You stay right there, mister."

Holding his hands wide in the air, Pollard said. "I'm a police officer. If you let me get my hand to my pocket, I can show you my ID."

The man shifted from foot to foot, probably trying to remember what they did on television in a case like this.

Pollard said, "I'm not reaching for a gun. Let me do it with two fingers."

The man backed up into his doorway. "Okay. Go ahead."

With thumb and forefinger, Pollard pulled out his CPD star.

. . .

That little bump in the road out of the way, Pollard scanned the neighborhood. The man with the cell phone had not actually called 911. He thought the threat would be good enough to scare an explanation out of a trespasser. As in a way, it had.

"You did exactly the right thing, being a neighborhood watchdog," Pollard said.

"Well, we all gotta look out for each other."

"But the next time you're worried you really should call 911. That's what we're for," Pollard said. "You can always phone us back if everything is okay."

Pollard stood in front of the watchdog's house, hands on his hips. He was extremely frustrated. A call to the Area had told him that there was still no word that anybody had lost a baby.

10

On this shift he had to be at the district by 7:00 A.M., so Pollard forced himself to go home, worried though he was, and get ready for bed.

He had keyboarded a query to the Illinois State Police. He had notified the National Center for Missing and Exploited Children. Then he gave NCIC, the National Crime Information Center, the baby's specs. If there was a missing baby of that description, they'd let him know. He put it out on the Canadian version, too, CPIC. What the hell; it was only a few keystrokes. And Canada was—what? Only three hundred, three hundred fifty miles away.

But he still believed the baby was local.

Usually, there was a missing child and a distraught parent. This time he had the child, but the parent was missing.

"All right," Pollard said to his wife as they turned off the bedside light, "let's forget for a minute where specifically that baby came from."

"Gladly, dear," she said, with exaggerated patience.

"No, I mean, let's not think about the specific place. What *kind* of thing would he have come from? A car or a house, right? What else?"

"What else indeed?"

"There aren't any nearby day care centers—so—"

"Um-mm."

"Now, there were no abandoned cars in the neighborhood. And nobody saw any car stop and put a baby out. Although you're going to say they didn't see anything else, either."

"Zzzz-mmm," his wife said.

"Most likely he came out of a house. Don't you think? But we didn't find any open doors or broken windows or sliders. It's not so easy to get out of a house if you're less than two feet tall."

He wife said nothing.

"Well, that's pretty much what I thought, too," said Pollard.

Horace "Tommy" Pollard had just begun to fall asleep when he sat bolt upright in bed and shouted, *"Cat flap!"*

11

The body lay with its chest down flat on the kitchen tiles, the lower half turned so that the legs were bent at the knees. To Pollard, the man appeared to be youngish, possibly in his late thirties. His right hand was pressed to his blood-covered cheek, fingers spread in a pathetic gesture of denial or horror. A knife lay near his feet.

Pollard did not turn on any lights in the kitchen. He would wait until the evidence techs arrived and began processing the scene before altering anything, including light switches. He would be very careful about moving around the house. Nevertheless, he had a duty to check it thoroughly. There could be other victims, and if so, they might still be alive.

He slipped paper booties over his feet, and with his flashlight moved to the kitchen door. There were no lights on in the hall.

The hall had a wood floor. Pollard crouched down and ran the flashlight beam across it at a sharply raking angle, almost parallel to the floor. There were normal-looking scuff marks but no smears or drops of blood and no foreign particles as far as he could see, other than a little ordinary house dust. Still, he stepped carefully and stayed near the wall.

Without leaving the hall, he shone his light into the dining room. He saw no disruption and no bodies. In the living room, a small armless upholstered chair lay on its back, one leg cracked. A glass coffee table was smeared and several knickknacks had been pushed onto the floor. Then they'd either been stomped on or bashed with something heavy. There were pieces of little ceramic or glass feet, and after a moment he realized that many of the knickknacks must have been frogs—glass frogs, ceramic frogs. When he found a brass frog that was only dented, he knew he was right.

Pollard could see into all parts of the room and there was no one in it. He crouched again, and with the beam of light highlighting the tips of the rug fibers, he saw depressions in the carpet, as well as several long scuff marks. With any luck, some of the depressions might give him an idea of the shoe size of the killer.

The hall ended at the front door. He turned, shone his light into a downstairs bathroom that appeared clean and undamaged, then started up the stairs, staying to the outside of the treads.

Ten minutes later, he believed he could make an educated guess about what had happened here. A killer or killers had entered the house, probably by slipping the absurdly simple lock on the rear door. The dead man had been upstairs, napping, to judge by the wrinkles in the bedspread in the master bedroom. The man had heard sounds, come downstairs, and either he had attacked the killer or the killer had attacked him, most likely in the hall. The fight had moved into the living room. Then the victim had run into the kitchen, possibly intending to get out of the house, or possibly to find a knife. The killer had pursued him and stabbed him to death. The killer might have taken a knife from the kitchen knife rack when he first entered the house. But if so that was more the act of a pro who wanted no connection to himself than a bone-headed burglar surprised by the homeowner.

All subject to what the techs found, of course, but he'd bet on something like that.

The crime scene van with the tech driving arrived fifteen minutes after Pollard's call, which was extremely good response time, made possible because the tech was coming from another case nearby. Fifteen minutes after that, the tech having fingerprinted the light switches, Pollard had lights on throughout the house.

Pollard stood in the baby's room. A blue flannel blanket was wadded into one corner of the crib. Pollard's tentative reconstruction: The baby may have been asleep, and the father taking a nap while he had the chance. Then the killer arrived and maybe made a sound. The father woke and went downstairs to see what the noise was. The fight may have waked the baby, or maybe he woke naturally at the end of his nap. Probably he gurgled, then he cried, then most likely he screamed in great indignation that nobody had come to get him up. Then maybe he climbed out of the crib. He was at the age when they sometimes did that.

Pollard went out into the upstairs hall. There was a small blood smear on the wall.

How did the baby get down the stairs? Pollard remembered one of his own children who could creep backward down stairs before he could walk.

Pollard went to the kitchen and leaned against the sink to see what might have happened when the little guy padded his way in here. The tech was videotaping the scene.

Pollard's mind shied away from visualizing the child crawling on hands and knees into the kitchen and finding his father bloody and dead. But that must have been what happened. Pollard hoped the child didn't understand. Forcing himself, he looked closer at the bloodied floor. There were three little starfish prints, baby handprints in the blood. *But was there any blood on the baby's hands when we found him?* He tried to remember. Odds were the long crawl to the highway had worn it off. And the jeans? They'd been run over by at least a couple of cars and were dredged in dirt, but he would have them checked for blood.

Okay. The child looks at his father in bewilderment. He touches him. Daddy always responded to me before. *Get up, Daddy.* There would be frustration and maybe fear. And then—Pollard could almost see it. That attractive cat flap. The little door that was always "No-no. Don't go out. Mustn't touch the cat's door."

He understood how the baby got out of the house.

The baby's part in this was reasonable enough. But the whole crime didn't make sense. Pollard was uneasy at the picture painted by the evidence here. The drawers he had seen in the dining room sideboard were neatly closed. Maybe there was silver missing, but he doubted it. There had been no sign of anyone rifling drawers or closets upstairs. One of the upstairs bedrooms was an office, full of computer equipment. In the living room was a television, untouched, while the frogs had been smashed. This didn't look like theft.

Unless the killer was interrupted in his robbery by the man waking and coming downstairs? The robber killed the man, panicked, and fled.

But he hadn't panicked. There had been a thin blood smear on the wall of the hall outside the baby's room. The killer had gone upstairs and looked in there for something or someone and turned away, letting the baby live.

Or did he go there first, and that woke the father in the bedroom across the hall? Possible. But then wouldn't the struggle with the father have taken place upstairs, or on the stairs? Plus, the blood smear had to come after the killing.

Could the killer have been looking for something? Something other than money, silver, televisions, electronics, or sound equipment, the most usual targets for theft.

But then he should have riffled through drawers and closets, shouldn't he? Could it have been teenagers, invading houses just for thrills? Not likely. Teenagers almost always trashed the place. They poured cereal on the floor and dumped milk over it, threw bread around, spilled out sugar, soap powder, toothpaste, whatever they found. Except for the smashed frogs, this place was almost pristine.

Pollard really didn't like overdramatizing crime. Ninety-nine percent of the violent crime he saw was dumb, routine, and pathetically ineffective. It was always either large risks for small money, or alcohol or drug-fueled anger stupidly acted out.

This, though, was different. The scene was generally clean, except for the blood. It really looked as if the killer had entered for one reason only, to kill.

12

Since he had not been stopped at O'Hare, Felix Hacker was virtually certain that a time-consuming review of airport tapes from all over the region would have to be done before anybody would even know which airport he had flown out of, much less what flight he was on and where he was going. There was a good chance they wouldn't pick him out even then.

An hour and a half after his plane was wheels up in Chicago, it landed in New York. In five minutes he was in the international terminal. There he went directly to the men's room farthest from boarding. In one of the stalls, he removed all his outer clothing, including shoes he had worn in Chicago, and changed into a new set of clothes.

He spilled a small amount of ink on the uppers of the shoes, just in case anybody wondered why they were being discarded, and put the shoes in the trash can. He packed the clothes in his suitcase.

His plane was leaving shortly. He went to pick up his boarding pass.

He was seething with rage.

13

By quarter of ten that night Blue had had a long day, what with the TV program, and her last class, plus she and the team had been packing—the team all day and Blue since two—everything they could possibly need, including toilet paper.

"Toilet paper?" Andy said.

"The hotels in Peru don't supply it. And the rolls are nice, soft packing material."

It wasn't so much the quantity of equipment that ate up all the time. It was the fragility. And the insurance on each piece had to be checked against the serial number on the camera or lens itself. The problem of extra batteries alone was an hour's checking job, because it seemed like every piece of equipment needed a different size or type of battery, and of course multi backups.

Then there was all the stuff the team needed for bringing material back in good condition. Most of the samples they would take could be brought home fixed onto slides or even dry-packed in pharmacist's folds or sterile baggies. On this particular trip the team would collect ancient pollen from burial sites, coprolites, which were petrified feces, organ samples, hair, and small fragments of textiles. Pollen, for instance, was light-resistant, and most pollen was very drought-resistant, but could be damaged by moisture. Almost everything damaged textiles.

One of the reasons Peru was such a rich site was that the weather in the long plain between the Pacific coast and the Andes was extremely dry. Vegetal material thousands of years old could be found largely unchanged.

Blue had hired Drake Rakowski, a photographer who would photograph most of the large textiles on site, because the Peruvian government had forbidden their removal. The same was true for the old mummies. Drake would photograph the mummies in situ, photograph the team removing the tiny samples, photograph the labeling and sealing of the specimen bags—a kind of chain-of-evidence like police officers use. So Drake would be performing three types of photography: micro, one-to-ones, and macro.

"Coffee!" Jasper said.

"And not decaf," Blue said. "Although I plan to go to sleep some time tonight."

She dropped into a chair in the break room and passed the list of supplies around the table. "I think we're pretty well caught up. Take a look. Anybody see any problems?"

They had a standard printed checklist they used on every expedition, with a supplemental list of items for the specific geographical area and specific goals of the current project. And of course they crossed stuff off the standard checklist that didn't apply to this case. Jasper and Tabitha flopped down at the table to study the lists while Andy made like a waiter and went to the supplies shelf to pour coffee.

"Why take five mountaineering packs?" Tabitha asked. "We've only got two mountaineers in the group."

"Just in case," Jasper said. "The Ice Maiden mummies were found at twenty thousand feet on Mount Ampato."

"I know that, but we're not going there."

Blue said, "If we get permission at the last minute to take a sample, you may climb up to the Old Woman mummy."

Jasper said, "If I got permission, I'd jump there in one bound."

Andy brought over the coffee, four mugs clutched in his two hands, spilling only a fraction of it, mostly on his jeans. "Yipe!" he said.

Blue said, "The Ampato mummies have been moved to Arequipa, anyhow."

"Not the Old Woman, though," Jasper said.

"Look. There's that baby story," Tabitha said, as the Channel 5 *News at Ten* came on.

"—a hero for risking your life to save a baby," reporter Jeannie Sun Hong said, as Andy turned up the sound.

A teenaged boy said, "Mm, sure. Whatever."

"Witnesses say you ran across four lanes of traffic, grabbing up the infant, and sprinted to safety in the median strip."

"Well, yeah." The kid ducked his head. The shot was of just his head and shoulders, but Blue could imagine him shuffling his feet.

The camera panned to the pileup. Somberly, Sun Hong said, "Six people perished at the scene of this nine-vehicle accident. Another has subsequently died in the hospital. Three more are listed in critical condition."

Back to the face of Sun Hong. "The possible cause of it all, a wandering infant. Police are seeking the child's parents and asking anyone who knows the baby to come forward. If you recognize this child, you are urged to call any local police department or dial 311, the police non-emergency number, immediately."

A picture of a baby flashed on the screen.

Blue jumped to her feet and screamed. *"Oh, my God. Adam!"* The table rocked and all four coffee cups toppled and spilled.

14

Blue jammed on her brakes behind one of six police cars and an ambulance in front of her house. Thank God it was only twenty minutes from the archaeology building to here. Jasper had urged her to let him drive her, but she wanted to have her car for whatever happened next. Blue had made more use of the car phone in those twenty minutes than in all the rest of the time she'd owned it. Her whole body was trembling. But the TV had said Adam was alive—

She had called her house on the way, but there was no answer. Edward *must* know what was going on. She called Edward's cell, Edward's office, and Edward's nurse. He was nowhere to be found. Damn Edward! Had he *lost* Adam? Had he fallen asleep and just let Adam crawl away onto the highway? Couldn't she trust him for even one day? Why hadn't he called her immediately to explain?

She tried the house again. A man answered, who was not Edward.

"What's happened to my baby?" she whispered into the phone. She tried to shout, but her voice wouldn't cooperate. Blue had heard that expression, "my heart was in my mouth," but she had always thought it was just a cliché.

"Who is this?"

"Who is *this*?"

"Ma'am, please give me your name."

"My name is Blue Eriksen. You're in my house." He had a cop voice, not a burglar voice. Her own voice was getting stronger, even though her throat was dry. "Where is my baby?"

"Ma'am, are you coming home?"

"I'm ten minutes away. What happened?"

"I can't give out that information over the phone, ma'am. I have no way of knowing who you are."

Suddenly she got her breath back. *"I live there. I saw my baby on the news!"*

"Well, ma'am, if you just come here we can work everything out."

She wanted to slam the phone down, but you couldn't slam the stupid thing. It had a button. She punched it hard and while driving faster called information for Channel 5, which had run the image she saw of Adam. They didn't know anything more than the facts they had broadcast on the ten o'clock news, and the fact that the baby was all right. That wasn't good enough.

She called 911.

She asked, "Is there a problem at 2119 Pebble Lane?"

"Who is this calling, please?"

"Blue Eriksen. It's *my house!* There are police there. What's happened?"

"Are you at the residence now?" the woman asked.

"No! If I were *at the residence* I wouldn't be calling to find out what's happening, would I?"

"I don't know, ma'am, but I can't give out that information over the phone. I suggest you go to the residence."

"I *am* going to the damn residence!"

"If you're in a car, ma'am, please drive carefully. We don't want to add to the statistics."

Statistics? What in heaven did she mean? She called 311, the non-emergency police number. By the time they got through the who-are-you who-am-I stuff, Blue was within two blocks of her house and could see flashing lights in the distance.

Jamming the car in park, she ran across the sidewalk. A uniformed cop stopped her.

"You can't go in there, ma'am."

"I *live* here!"

"Ma'am, this is a crime scene." The officer made a strong-but-patient face. His name tag said YOUNG.

Yellow barrier tape blocked access, but Blue pushed through it. A streamer trailed from her shoulder while she ran forward. "This is my house! Get out of my way!"

"Here's Detective Pollard." Young spoke with relief.

"Where's my baby!" she screamed at Pollard. "Where's my baby!" She pulled the barrier tape off her chest, brushed past Pollard and headed around to the back of the house where lights were set up in the backyard and most of the action was taking place.

"Ma'am, wait! Let's go in the front."

"This is my house, you idiot! I'll go in any door I damn well please."

"I want to explain to you where the baby is. He's fine. Just show me your identification, and I'll take you in there myself."

That stopped her. "All right."

She pulled out her driver's license, and about a dozen ID cards, credit cards, library cards, and so on fell on the ground. He picked them up for her, glancing at them as he did, no doubt confirming that she hadn't stolen the driver's license of a look-alike. Blue followed him in the front door. "Let's sit down for a minute," Pollard said, gesturing at the living room, but Blue had caught a glimpse of people crowded around something on the kitchen floor. Pollard followed her fast as she ran to the kitchen. She saw a hand, outstretched on the floor, just glimpsed it between two men bending over what she now realized was a man lying prone. She skidded to a halt behind the outstretched arm of a uniformed cop.

One of the tech people who had been bending over the body looked up and barked, "Stop right there!"

But Blue had already frozen in place, closing her eyes. She opened them and what lay on the floor had not vanished. *Edward!*

"Edward?" she asked the body, not believing what she saw.

"The baby's safe. He's not hurt at all," Pollard said quickly. He must have realized what Blue feared, with all the blood. "Do you know this man? Is he your husband? Does he live here?"

"No. Yes, but he's my ex-husband. He doesn't live here."

Just then the cat came in, stepping fastidiously around the blood.

"What happened to him?" Blue asked. "And where's my baby? Where's Adam?" She scooped the cat into his traveling crate and latched it. When Pollard walked to the living room, she followed, a little wobbly, her knees feeling numb. She wanted to feel sadness for Edward, but the emotion just didn't come right now.

The living room showed evidence of a struggle, one chair over-turned, Blue's frog sculpture collection swept off the display shelves and stamped to bits. She automatically reached out to sift the wreckage for her favorite green glass frog, but snatched her hand back. She leaned down to right the chair, and again drew her hand back. Pollard said, "It's all right. It's been photographed and the evidence tech has been here." But she left the chair as it was. The sofa seemed untouched, and she sank down on it. Pollard picked an overstuffed side chair that showed no signs of vi-olence.

"Please," Pollard said. "Help me out a little. You are Mrs. Eriksen—"

"I told you that. My name is Blue Eriksen. This is my house. Where's my baby?"

"He's safe and well. Tell me about the dead man."

"He's my ex-husband. Edward Eriksen. Dr. Edward Eriksen. We've been divorced nearly a year. Where is my baby? And I won't answer any-thing else until you tell me where Adam is."

"What was your ex-husband doing here?"

"He was babysitting. He's a very good father." She repeated some-thing she had told Jasper earlier today, "He may have been a horrible hus-band, but he's a very good father." Why was she explaining that? She was talking too much. Her failed marriage was no business of Pollard's. She pressed her lips together for a few seconds and that gesture held back the tears. "I meant it, though. I won't answer anything else—"

"Your baby is well and being cared for. Please, Ms. Eriksen, tell me this man's address and what he does for a living."

"He's an orthopedic surgeon. He lives downtown at 840 North Lakeshore. And you're going to ask, but no, I don't have any idea why anybody would want to kill him. And no, I don't have anything in this house that's valuable enough to steal, and no, I didn't kill him, and I've been at work with other people all day long who can tell you I wasn't here, and now *where's my baby?*"

"He's in the hospital—"

"What?" Blue jumped to her feet. "You should have told me that *first*, Pollard! What happened to him? You said he wasn't hurt! Where is he? Let's go!"

"He's not hurt. He's fine. It's standard practice. Whenever we find an abandoned baby he has to be checked out."

"Well, he's *not* abandoned. I'm here. Let's go."

"They won't sign him out to you tonight, ma'am."

"Why the hell not?"

"Frankly, they can't be sure he's yours."

Blue was so speechless at this she could only make little puffing, inhaling noises.

"Mrs. Eriksen, think of it this way. We found a baby. We don't know for sure who he is. He has no ID, of course, being an infant, and unlike an adult, he can't tell us anything."

"Wait a minute! I saw that picture on television. That's Adam!"

"I believe you."

"What is the matter with you people? He's my son. I want him right now!"

"We don't know what happened here. You could be a confederate of the killer, for all I know."

"But I have identification."

"Ma'am, we just need to be sure the baby is actually your Adam."

"Well, I'm sure! Here. In my wallet. There's a picture. Look on the table. Look at these pictures!"

"Um—the problem is, ma'am—the problem is—"

"Would you just spit it out? Let's get over this idiocy and go get Adam."

"Well, the problem is, ma'am, that one baby looks a helluva lot like another."

15

Adam was in his very own baby seat—thank God he was, Blue thought—in the backseat of her car, as they headed to an extremely important meeting. He'd been three days in foster care, which made Blue scream at everybody she could find, but the third day was Edward's funeral, and she left her anger behind long enough to go. Much as she'd had crushing disappointments with Edward and his incessant affairs, she'd loved him once. His sister came to the service, although she had rarely seen Edward in recent years.

Blue was not proud of how she had behaved those three days. One thing she valued in people was rationality. She prided herself on being calm in the face of crisis. Over the years, archaeology had taken her to parts of the world with real dangers. Sometimes it was danger from weather, or geological factors like volcanoes or mud slides. She had been caught once in the very tail end of a pyroclastic flow—hot gas and rock that was called tefra and flowed more than forty miles an hour—from a volcano. She still had burn scars on her ankle, but if she had been a quarter mile closer she would have been roasted to death.

Sometimes it was danger from people. She took pride in being calm and facing down problems, thinking rationally about what was best to do.

Well, pride goeth before a fall.

She lost her cool. The picture in her mind of Adam creeping happily across the highway, narrowly missed by semis and SUVs, plus the carnage his being there had caused, plus him being kept away from her just when she needed to hold him—she lost it. Shaking and angry enough to fight, she went to the hospital where he was being held—*okay*, she thought, *cared for*—and screamed at the administrators. They were surprisingly patient but wouldn't let him go. So she located the pediatric unit where he was being kept, sat down in the waiting room, and refused to leave. One of the nurses was sympathetic enough to tell her the actual part of the waiting room that was closest to the room where he was. In fact, she told Blue that Adam was just ten feet on the other side of that wall. It may not even have been true, Blue knew, but it was kind. She slept there, fitfully, that night.

When they moved him to foster care the next day, they slipped him out somehow and refused to tell Blue where he'd been taken. She went to the district police station that held the Area Three Detectives and sat all day on a bench, making Pollard feel guilty. He wasn't DCFS, but was her best contact and he might be able to speed things along.

She haunted Detective Pollard. One of the many ironies of police work, as Pollard explained it, was that the faster the processing of DNA material became, the longer it took. In the old days weeks and weeks were required to analyze blood or other tissue for a match. Now with a good sample it took just a couple of days. Therefore many more samples were processed, therefore the system was all backed up and it still took weeks and weeks to get results.

True to his word, Detective Pollard expedited the testing. He felt genuinely sorry for Blue, she finally came to think, even though at the time it seemed to her he was just getting tired of her incessant hanging around. She suspected he went up the hierarchy to get it done, maybe making some departmental problems for himself. And he did one other brilliant thing: he had Adam's handprints from the wall near his crib taken by an evidence tech and compared to prints taken directly from Adam. Which proved he was Blue's boy. And finally the mysterious powers decided he had been neither abused nor abandoned.

Blue had her boy back, and that was what mattered.

Now for the most important meeting. She pulled her little red Chevy up to the curb at the house on Winnetka Avenue. She went around to the back door on the right side where Adam was belted into his rear-facing child seat. He was a happy boy, generally, but was starting to wriggle at the confinement.

Blue had barely lifted him out, when he said, "Down! Down!" and made fussing, impatient kicks with his feet. She let him down on the grass next to the walk. At that instant, the door of the house burst open and a gangly teenager ran out. "You came!" he shouted.

Blue started toward the kid, her hand outstretched. "As I said on the phone, I want to thank you—"

But the teenager ran past her to Adam. "Little guy!" he shouted.

Adam put up his arms and shrieked with delight. Brad scooped up the child and hugged him.

Adam stared to sing, "Beer! Wall! Beeeeer! Wall! Waaaallll!"

16

Marcus Holton had not lived in Chicago in four years, not since he had taken the job at the Agency in D.C., but he came back for certain holidays. His mother insisted that Christmas, his sister's birthday, and Grandmother Swartz's birthday were sacrosanct and had to be spent in Chicago with the extended family. His dad's birthday they now all celebrated in Washington, although it had taken his mother a while to accept that. His mother was not really comfortable in Washington. She considered it a one-industry town, more of a stage set than a real place.

At thirty-eight, Marcus was young for the responsibilities he carried, but his career had progressed in a quite natural fashion. Born in Back-of-the-Yards in Chicago, he'd been a school-hating street-scrapper as a child. By the time he graduated from high school, he realized he'd better start taking academics more seriously. He did well at the University of Illinois in Champaign and immediately applied to the Chicago Police Department.

Marcus was accepted, went through the academy with top grades in everything, and became a patrol officer—a beat cop—as all recruits did.

Three years later he took the sergeant's exam, passed it with high marks, and made sergeant at the age of twenty-seven. Partly he was smart and partly he was hard-working. Partly he got along with people whenever he could without compromising his demanding standards. But also, he had clout.

Clout in Chicago is as ubiquitous as the air. It can come from high position: The Mayor, the Superintendent of Police, and the Cardinal all have clout, even if they originally came from somewhere outside Chicago. But most garden-variety clout is local and inherited. Marcus's father, Jack called Jacko, started out to become an alderman, getting out the vote at elections, driving the ill, the aged, and the uninterested to the polls. Some might say he also took the nonexistent and the dead to the voting booth. But Jacko didn't like the idea of spending his life on the City Council. He was more active than that, more of a street brawler, and while the City Council gave what many would believe to be ample opportunity for fighting, he decided to join the police department. He had risen to the rank of District Commander by the time Marcus joined the force. Very shortly after, a high-rise fire, and Jacko's vigorous response when the fire department communications system broke down and the towering inferno threatened to torch half The Loop, pushed the senior Holton into the national limelight. The ability of big cities to react quickly to potential disaster had become, as Jacko Holton said, "a hot topic if you'll pardon the play on words." Marcus knew it was more his father's natural bossiness than real organizing ability that had saved the day. But there was no doubt that he had done well, and his parade-ground bearing, parade-ground voice, and staccato delivery quickly made him a media darling. Anchorpersons loved the way he barked answers at them. His natural conversational style was the fifteen-second sound bite. Or, as Marcus called it, the fifteen-second sound bark. So when the current congressman was caught in a nasty affair with a prostitute and resigned "to spend more time with his family," Jacko Holton was tapped to fill the void.

Now Marcus had more clout than ever.

He figured clout was like being born handsome, which he hadn't been, or being born rich, which he hadn't been, either. It gave you a leg up, but just one leg; you couldn't run on it alone. In the long run, you had to develop real skills to go anywhere. His father considered clout to be something like friendship. You did something for a friend, he did something for you. What Jacko didn't do was graft. As a result, while Marcus had clout, he didn't have money.

This was fine with him. He was okay with the fact that his father could get him promotions. Ill-gotten gains would not have been acceptable.

In Congress, his father quickly made his police expertise felt. He became a member of the U.S. House of Representatives Committee on Homeland Security and then moved into the Subcommittee on Intelligence, Information Sharing, and Terrorism Risk Assessment.

Marcus, meanwhile, had been tapped to tune up the Chicago Police Department's TAC teams. More or less the equivalent of SWAT teams, in Chicago TAC teams were not citywide, but embedded in each district, and the members ordinarily were chosen by the District Commander. One of their most common jobs was busting into drug houses. They received good, but standard, training. Marcus spent six months studying high-tech products to upgrade their tools of the trade and another six months wrangling with the commanders and other old boys, who thought basic equipment had worked for fifty years and could work just as well for another fifty. The young guys, the actual TAC team members, who were mostly under thirty, thought the new gear was hot stuff. At the end of twelve months, Marcus had incorporated about half of what he had hoped to, and was pretty happy that he had achieved that much. He had become a de facto expert in drug interdiction.

His father thought that a move to Washington would help Marcus's career. Whatever Marcus wanted to do in the future, a stint in a Federal agency would give him credibility. Marcus himself was not so worried about his future career. He disliked the politics of advancement. However, he did think getting out of Chicago for a while would be a good change for his brain. He'd spent all his life in one place. Also, he was eager to find out how big government agencies worked. Plus, with the Agency, there was the chance of travel. Not having a wife or child to worry about, he jumped at the idea. From being a scrappy kid, he had become a man who wanted to accomplish good things.

Being a lateral hire at the Agency placed him in a position that threatened his new boss. He couldn't easily be fired, since his father in Congress was too important. He didn't have the same background as most federal agents, although there was no arguing the fact that policing the streets of Chicago was just as "real" as anything their agents ever did. In fact, he had been through more close calls as a patrol cop in Chicago than most federal agents ever had to cope with. Marcus Holton appeared in Washington with a halo of credibility around him.

That didn't mean there was no resentment, and when he got back to the Agency after his failure to nab Hacker in Chicago, he felt from the Director, at least, a kind of satisfaction that Marcus had failed.

The 11:00 A.M. weekly status meeting today was tense with crosscurrents. Unlike the FBI, which had offices in D.C. itself, the Agency occupied a building in Arlington, Virginia, similar in its stylish blandness to that of the CIA in Langley. The conference room looked out onto an intensely green lawn where a large sheet of fire-engine red peonies bloomed in a central bed. As the others entered, the Director, Coleman Haseltine, stood with his hands locked behind his back, staring at the outdoors. Marcus believed Haseltine saw nothing of the flowers. He wasn't the type to stop and smell the roses.

Marcus had not told Haseltine that Diana's error could have lost Hacker for them.

Aaron Malkovitch, Personnel, seated himself, groaning grumpily. He had the appearance of Santa Claus without the ho-ho-ho, Marcus thought. Malkovitch was the Old Man of the group, and rumor had it that several years earlier he had been short-listed to become the Agency's next director. What had happened to switch him onto a side track, Marcus did not know.

The other people at the meeting were Logan Reed, Intel Admin; and Diana. Diana McCullough was Assistant Administrator for Field Operations. Marcus was Assistant Intel Admin.

Diana was a woman Marcus would like to know a whole lot better and he'd been thrilled when Haseltine has told him to take her Chicago with him, saying she'd never seen the Chicago office. Of course, the whole thing had ended badly and Marcus still had no idea what she thought of him.

Diana had silky honey-colored hair and green eyes. Unfortunately, she also had a no-nonsense manner and had been an agent for thirteen years, longer than Marcus had been here, which led her to behave condescendingly to him. She frequently called Marcus "our Chicagoan."

Diana was famous, in the way members of a closed circle became famous for this or that, for being rigorous about exercise. She arrived at work an hour and a half early every day to run the track in the exercise basement, then swim a couple of laps in the narrow lap pool. Then she showered and rode up in the Agency elevator to be at work at 8:00 A.M. The Agency was proud of providing a complete health spa for its employees. What was less frequently said was that very few of them ever used it. Diana used it. She kept three changes of clothes in her office closet, including a business suit and two track suits, one warm-up flannel and one Lycra or Spandex, in addition, rumor had it, to a full drawer of fresh underwear and socks. Diana frequently arrived at early meetings with her hair just a little bit damp.

Marcus thought she looked even sexier with tendrils of damp hair lying on the back of her neck.

He thought Diana was fascinating.

Get-Together-with-the-Boss Day was the day Marcus liked least in the week. It usually involved Haseltine sneering at them for whatever hadn't been accomplished, and it was very light in the attaboy department.

When they were all seated, Haseltine spun around from the window, his hands still behind his back like the admiral on the bridge of a ship in combat, and said, "We are without a couple of people. Frank Nordmeyer is in Cairo on assignment and Carter is at the Philadelphia Field Division."

Philadelphia was currently involved in a complex case involving locally manufactured methamphetamine. The product came from the University of Pennsylvania area and it now looked like the investigation would sweep into its maw a number of students from the chemistry department and possibly a professor.

"No good came out of your little jaunt to Chicago, Holton," Hasel-tine said.

Marcus said, "Sir, it was important to try."

"Not our ticket, Holton. I told you then."

"Hacker kills people."

"We don't do killers. We do drug interdictions."

"Hacker is a soldier for some very big drug cartel, or—"

"Or what? We don't know, do we?"

"Sir—"

"Plane tickets, Holton. Two nights in a hotel. And you let him slip through your fingers."

"I'll get him next time," Marcus mumbled.

"Enough. Diana, you had a report."

Diana cast Marcus a glance, which he interpreted as gratitude. Then she swung into her Field Operations persona.

"Over and over again we've had to explain field disasters when I know the cause is lack of equipment. We all know that infrared sensing equipment can see through walls. A team that's about to break into a house or apartment can know ahead of time that there's, say, just one adult in the place, or more adults, or children. We could have avoided that mess at Wrangler's Creek if we'd known there were children in the house."

Haseltine said, "Nobody intended to shoot the little boy."

"Of *course* nobody intended to shoot the little boy—whose name, by the way, was Jamie—but he's still just as dead. My point is, with adequate imaging they would have known there were several small people in there. New York City has them for their *cops*, for God's sake!"

"We have them," Malkovitch said.

"We have *three*! They were all—God knows why—in Seattle at the time. We're the *Agency*. We should have one in every field office, at least."

Haseltine said, "We could buy every gadget on earth if we had an un-limited budget."

Reed, putting in a word for the first time said, "We have a *huge* bud-get. We have a budget the size of France."

Marcus said, "I agree with Diana. I'm not so sure budget is even a consideration. If we had better visualization, we'd need fewer agents on the scene. We'd probably save money in the long run."

Malkovitch gave him a Santa Claus smile. Diana definitely looked pleased.

Haseltine made a check mark on a notepad.

17

Walking out the front door of the anthro building was something Blue
Eriksen did several hundred times a year. She was not expecting trouble
and hardly even looking where she was going.

"There she is!"

Twenty or thirty people, both men and women but more of them
women, came screaming up the sidewalk.

"It just serves you right!" said a fortyish woman wearing a beautiful
pink linen suit and viper's face.

"You're a negligent parent!" somebody screamed.

"That child should be taken away from you!"

Blue stopped on the last step of the building. She'd seen these people,
or people like them, a lot when the book *Goddess* came out. One of them,
who was not here today, was the Rev. Hommiller, who had told the world
that her book blasphemously intended to show that God was a woman.
Blue tried to explain that wasn't the meaning of the book at all. She and
Hommiller had even done a *Chicago Tonight* program together. No matter

how many times she tried to tell him that the book was about people many millennia ago who believed that God was a woman, or believed that nature at least was a woman, he screamed her down. She was blaspheming. She asked him where he thought the term "Mother Nature" came from. He never answered.

He wasn't here today, but in the crowd were a few of his minions.

"You are *just* the kind of person who would let a baby crawl into the highway," said a woman Blue recognized as Peggy Darwin. Blue thought a more inappropriate last name had never been attached to anybody. To Peggy, the Bible said that woman had literally been made from the rib of man. She happily called this "the first surgery."

Peggy was the opposite of the pink linen suit woman. She must dress the way she did intentionally, Blue thought. It had to be very hard to find flowered beige limp cotton housedresses anyplace today. And surely she owned other shoes than bedroom slippers. Maybe Peggy was very, very poor, but her new Chevy pickup, which Blue had seen her get into after the last "protest," argued that she wasn't. Even if she were, there were a lot of charities that would have supplied her with shoes.

The only youngish man in the group—the other six or so males were in their sixties—was also a person Blue had run up against before. He believed firmly, and announced it stridently, in the calculation of Archbishop James Ussher, in 1650, that the earth had been created on Sunday, October 23, in 4004 B.C.

Naturally, that didn't leave a whole lot of room for archaeology.

"You shouldn't be teaching children," he yelled.

"Snotty bitch!" Darwin yelled.

"A professor! You think you're better than anybody else!"

"I'm not surprised—"

"People like you—"

"And you're divorced—"

"Go home and take care of your *child*!"

"Man is not descended from apes!"

A year ago Blue had learned that there was no point in arguing with them. They didn't listen to her. They didn't want to agree to disagree. They wanted to beat her into the ground.

She was not sure that she really listened to them anymore, either.

Blue had decided that quiet courtesy, the soft answer that turneth away wrath, was the best way to confront them. Although it rarely turned away wrath. But today it didn't even occur to her to be polite. After Edward's death, and the vision of Adam on that freeway, this was just too much.

"Get out!" she shouted. "You don't belong on a college campus! You pigheaded, pig-*faced* bigots! You—"

She was trembling with anger. "How dare you say that all those brave strong people never existed! These are your ancestors! Your great-great-multigreat grandmothers and grandfathers! They walked across the ice bridge between Asia and Alaska, carrying their children. Spearing fish. Hoping for food. Starving. Your own ancestors walked out of North Africa and trekked across the plains of Turkey to Europe, and gave birth on the trail and survived or died."

"That is not true!"

"We have their bones, and their pottery, and the mementos they put in the graves of their family members. Little necklaces of shells they laid in the graves of their mothers. A stone knife or a favorite hammer stone in the graves of their fathers and brothers. Tiny dolls made of wood tucked into the arms of children. How *dare* you ignorant, foolish, self-centered people say they never existed! How dare—"

Blue felt an arm go over her shoulders from behind. She whirled, ready to hit somebody, but it was Jasper.

In his classroom voice, which reached to the back of the largest lecture hall, he said to the crowd, "A man has died. He died as the result of a despicable, criminal attack inside this woman's home. If you have any respect for life, and death, you'll leave now."

With this, he literally scooped her back inside the building.

Jasper knew that Dr. Neal Swanson, one of the department's more colorful archaeologists, was a Brit who kept a stash of good Scotch in his drawer. Swanson was usually loath to part with it, but Jasper placed Blue firmly in her office chair and came back with a half-full bottle and a paper cup. Without asking, he poured her a couple of ounces, shoved it into her hand, folded his arms, and watched. Jasper was tall and cadaverous and he loomed when he stood over her. She drank the whole thing.

"They just don't get it!" Blue said. "I haven't done anything to hurt them."

"You call their beliefs into question."

"No, *I* don't. Fossils call their beliefs into question. Twenty-thousand-year-old graves call their beliefs into question."

"Blue, you want to carry the lamp of enlightenment—"

"I wish!"

"Have another spot of Scotch."

"And none of these things even call their basic beliefs into question. Most Christians accept evolution."

"Blue." He took away the paper cup of Scotch, and, facing her, took both her hands. "Blue. There's one thing you don't understand."

"Lots of things." She laughed a little, high on adrenaline from the confrontation.

"No, seriously. There's something you need to be more aware of, or you'll keep getting yourself into danger. Reason *does not* conquer all."

Blue finally said, "I'm okay now. I'm so excited about the way the psilocybin research is falling into line I can't really be upset about those—people."

"What's new?"

"My trial is going in the drug rehab center in Skokie. My medical researcher is a great guy."

"If you start getting results, maybe you could duplicate the trials at several universities."

"Actually we are getting early results. It's a small sample, just twenty-four people in the first sample, but we've kept twenty-two in the program."

"This could really be big, Blue."

Several minutes of peace and quiet passed. Finally, Jasper smiled, unusual for him. "Where's the little guy?"

"We're staying at the Orrington Hotel in Evanston. With some of our clothes and Adam's toys and more toys and more toys. Paula's with him right now."

Jasper was a mystery to Blue. Not in a bad way. He was extremely smart and hardworking. And also reliable, a characteristic she really valued. If he said he would be at a meeting at 10:00 A.M., he was there. If he said he'd get the import papers to the import duties people, the papers went out and on time.

But she knew almost nothing about him. She'd known him for nine years and she didn't know what part of the country he spent his childhood in, for instance. He had one of those all-purpose U.S. accents, pretty much like a TV anchorperson but without the portentousness.

He never spoke about his early life, his parents—alive or dead. No cousins in New Jersey, no grandmother in Rhinelander. Never announced that he was going home for Christmas. No day off for a family wedding. He had once mentioned that he had a brother who was some sort of high-powered art sleuth, but then he closed up as if the reference had been too revealing. Like all of the professors, his curriculum vitae was on file at the school and, the times being what they are, also appeared on the school's Web site. Blue knew he had been an undergraduate at Stanford, done graduate work at the University of Michigan—where his thesis advisor was an old friend of Blue's—and had taught at the University of Illinois in Champaign before coming to Northwestern. In that long and peripatetic but perfectly typical academic career, he had taken two breaks for additional study of chemistry and microscopy. He was an archaeological chemist. Blue knew what he'd been doing for the last fifteen years.

It was just his family background she knew nothing about, and she found that peculiar. He seemed lonely. He was a very introverted person. *But hey. We're all alone in some sense.* Blue thought most of the extroverts she knew were people who just didn't realize how alone they were.

Really, she felt she made too much of this. She knew Jasper was reliable, hardworking, smart, and preferred roast beef sandwiches at lunch to tuna fish or ham. He drank coffee rather than tea. And most important, when he analyzed a substance found in a tomb, it stayed analyzed. He knew what he was doing. There was nobody better at the high-tech molecular work.

She had told him yesterday she had decided that Adam and she were going to Peru with him and the rest of the troops. Detective Pollard had okayed her to leave the country, since it was provable she had been teaching a class when Edward was killed.

They were leaving day after tomorrow and would arrive in Lima the next morning. Jasper, Andy, Tabitha Lincoln, Drake Rakowski, Dr. Bengt Jungstedt. And Blue. And Adam. Blue was going to get Adam out of Chicago. Thank goodness.

Blue said, "I rechecked everybody's passports yesterday." Edward and Blue had applied for a passport for Adam not long after he was born, on the theory that Blue traveled a lot in her work and might want to take him.

She had made sure that the equipment was packed and the permits had all come in. Jasper, ever particular, had checked and rechecked their own lists of equipment against the packed stuff before it was sealed, which the grad students had also done, of course, as part of their training, but— news flash!—grad students were not always accurate. Suppose they arrived in Peru and found that a vital reagent or preservative wasn't in their boxes? And would take eight weeks to come in from some supplier in, say, Germany? And they were only going to be in Peru for two weeks, anyway? It didn't bear thinking of.

Jasper held his head up, chin too high, a pose she'd seen him use when he had to tell a grad student to go back and re-do a paper. "Frankly, Blue, I'm worried about Adam. A research site, even if we aren't actually digging, is no place for an infant."

"He's not an infant. He's nearly a year old."

"That's immaterial. There are risks."

"Babies live in Peru very healthily, Jasper. He's had the shots his pediatrician thinks he needs. We can boil water and cook his food. They sell baby food in jars in Peru, just like here. We're staying at the Enca Hotel when we get to Trujillo, and everybody says it's clean and comfortable."

"There are gangs in Peru."

"Few, and not where we're going. The Shining Path and Tupac Amaru are political. We wouldn't even be on their interest list."

"A foreign country is always unpredictable."

"Unpredictable? May I point out, when you talk about danger—that it was right *here*," she pointed generally westward, the direction of her house, "where my ex-husband was killed. Right here in a safe, North American house!"

The word "unpredictable" broke some sort of dam in her emotions. "Unpredictable? I've torn my head up thinking whether Edward or I could have known what was coming. A couple of times I felt watched during the day or two before Edward was murdered. But I thought that was just stupid. Which, no doubt, it was. The attempted burglary was random. Somebody was looking for a house that appeared unoccupied. Edward's car was in the garage and couldn't be seen—"

Jasper was silent. There were issues going into this that Blue had thought about quite a bit. For some time now, she had wondered whether he was jealous of her. She was by far better known. Of course, in the in-bred world of archaeology, *Goddess* was not quite respectable. It was considered *popularized* archaeology, and so it was. In *Goddess* she was trying to take the reader back to a time at the dawn of civilization, before metal-working, before writing, even before farming. It was not so much a book of original research in the go-out-and-dig sense as a consolidation of what we knew about societies that worshiped a female goddess.

Early humans didn't know what triggered the gestation of a baby, any more than gorillas or horses understand conception. Even today, there were societies that didn't tie sexual intercourse very closely to conception. They thought there were other factors involved. But for early humans, it was no wonder they didn't get the connection. With nine months between conception and delivery, the specific event would hardly be remembered. And most of the time intercourse did not lead to pregnancy.

To them it must have seemed that women produced babies in incomprehensible ways, magical ways, and those ways were vital to the tribe. No group of people could survive without the contribution of its women. Blue explained that in many ancient cultures women were revered. They were truly Mother Nature. Some "Venus" figures dated back thirty thousand years. There were massive stone temple ruins on the island of Malta that were outlines of women's torsos.

Her book told the story of some of those cultures.

That book, *Goddess*, provided part of the money for the research for the new book Jasper and Blue were writing together. Many people believed that universities give their professors money to do research. Not so. There were some college grants, true. But most researchers in all fields had to scrounge their own funds. Physicists and chemists got grants from companies hoping to use their findings commercially. Or from the federal government. There were very few commercial uses for archaeological discoveries. They got money from sources like religious groups that wanted to know more about the history of their religion. Or ethnic groups. Or sometimes wealthy enthusiasts—who often wanted to go along on the dig and who got seriously in the way.

Raising money for archaeology was usually hard. After the success of *Goddess*, offers poured in for Blue's next project. It was gratifying. *Gratifying? Actually,* she thought, *it's about time!*

The effect of all this, though, was to put Jasper in a somewhat secondary place, power-wise. Blue didn't think that offended him. The project was close to his heart, too. He'd seemed happy to do the research abroad. The last three months of her pregnancy, she hadn't wanted to travel. And after Adam was born, she thought it was best to stay home for a while. Jasper had seemed happy to go on the research trips with the students while Blue stayed in Chicago doing the paperwork. *Maybe Jasper had been too happy about going without me. Did he want me to stay home this time as well?* She was wondering whether she should ask him straight out—

"Peru is only fourteen days. Could you leave Adam with somebody?"

Aha! *So much for foolish suspicion.* It was just Jasper the nitpicky perfectionist at work again.

Leave Adam! My God! How could he even think—The idea of leaving Adam with anybody now made her heart race. She tried to control her breathing as something like a panic attack washed over her.

Speaking as calmly as she could, Blue said, "There's nobody here who's able to take care of him. My mother has the first symptoms of

Alzheimer's. Not bad, and she's completely self-reliant, but I would be afraid to leave a child in her care. And Edward's parents, you know, are—um—too—um—punitive."

Her own mother was showing some signs of Alzheimer's, yes, but it was more than that. She had never been reliable. When a parent who has never been especially good at parenting started to go downhill, Blue thought, it was really painful, because you realized the relationship you hoped to have someday will never be possible. Blue's army colonel father was one of the two hundred forty-one Americans killed in the Beirut barracks bombing in 1983. Blue was seven years old. Even at that age, she realized that nothing really *worked* around their house except when Daddy was home, and after that nothing much worked except when her grandmother, Dad's mother, came for a couple of weeks. Blue learned to be independent, and to be grateful, unlike so many kids, for school. In school things were planned sensibly.

Jasper said, "I know how much you've wanted to get back in the field."

"I haven't said that."

"I could see it." He took a deep breath. "I worry that we'll get there and Adam will monopolize all your time."

Blue's eyes started to swim with moisture. Jasper would probably be embarrassed beyond belief if confronted by a weeping woman, so she quickly said, "You need to understand. I've been seeing—over and over during the last three days, I keep seeing Adam padding his way across the expressway. All happy, and maybe fascinated at the big shiny cars and trucks. The trucks! It's just killing me! Trucks carrying lumber and steel and God knows what. Somebody, being nice, they thought, told me to be glad that the truck carrying tons and tons of stone had just missed him. She was being nice! Cheering me up! The truck that ran into the back of everybody else and killed four of them." Blue's voice was rising and the tears flowing. She was embarrassed, but she couldn't stop.

"As if he couldn't have been killed by a Volvo," she sobbed. "Or even a motorcycle. He's so little."

Jasper put his arm around her shoulders.

"Oh, I'm so sorry, Jasper. I never do this."

"Of course, Blue."

"I see it in front of my eyes all the time. I don't even have to close them. I can't live in that house any more. The Realtor—I called a Realtor, and he's putting it on the market. Everything is going into storage. I can't look at that house and I can't stay in Chicago right now. I hate this place. And Jasper, I know how irrational I'm being. Wasn't I always the rational one? Sensible. Calm. If we were on a dangerous dig, I was always calm."

"Yes, you were."

"But I just can't stand this. He's so little and so happy."

"I know how you feel."

"You do?"

"Exactly how you feel. Well, not about Adam, of course, but I know how it is to want to turn back time. A few days or a month. Or a year."

"You do? Jasper, what happened to you?"

Then he just closed up and took his arm away from her shoulders.

"Nothing, really," he said.

To cover the uncomfortable moment, Blue said, "I wish I could take Paula with us to help with Adam. But she has her whole family here. Actually, I hinted."

"And she won't go?"

"Nope. Didn't rise to the bait. She's keeping my cat, Tiglath Pilaser, though."

He sighed. "You can find a nanny there, in Peru, maybe?"

A stranger? No, no. Blue wasn't going to let him out of her sight. Would the grad student, Tabitha, help? Tabitha do child care? Dream on.

"What if I can't find anybody to help? It worries me, too. But I have to go. I'll just do my best with Adam. You'll get a full day's work out of me."

Jasper looked no less worried.

Suddenly, a notion hit her. "You know, I have an idea."

18

"Here. It's not that hard, Brad."

"Um."

It was pitch dark outside the aircraft's windows. Blue and her team were somewhere over the Pacific Ocean near the Gulf of Tehuantepec.

Brad, Adam, and Blue were at the fold-out baby-changing table near the rear of the plane. Adam had just woken up.

"See, here's how you can tell that he's wet." Blue slid her finger into the back of the diaper.

"Gross!"

"Well, if you can't stand that, you can probably just tell by patting his rear. If he's wet, it'll feel warm and soggy."

Brad still didn't look happy.

"Okay, Adam. Lie down for me, sweetie," Blue said. Adam squirmed. "We'll be done faster if you help me, kiddo." Adam made a face but lay reasonably still.

"Brad, watch me, please. See these tabs. You just pull and they come off." The diaper came open. "Now you take hold of his feet with one hand, pull his bottom up, and slide the new diaper underneath. You try it."

Brad couldn't get hold of both feet at once. He tried again and briefly got them. Then he lost his grip and Adam plopped back down. Adam made a scowly face at Brad. Finally, Brad got over feeling he might hurt Adam, took a firm grip on Adam's feet with his left hand, lifted him, and with his right hand slipped the new diaper underneath.

"Now you can use one of these wipes to wipe him off."

Brad tried it. "Geez."

"That was pretty good. If we run out of wipes, you can use a cloth and water."

"Yeah, but—"

"Now open the tab and stick the sticky part on that patch there."

"Yeah, but—"

"That was fine. Other side. There. You did that very well." Adam turned over. Brad set him on the floor, where Adam rose to his feet, took two steps and went back to hands-and-knees locomotion.

"Yeah, but—"

"But what?"

"What do I do when it's—you know—when it's—um—worse."

"Which should happen pretty soon now."

"Ahh—gee—"

"You do the same thing, Brad. Only more carefully."

Brad was being paid to be Adam's pal on the trip. He'd been enthusiastic about the job and the travel. But it looked like he wondered whether this part of the job made it all not worth it.

Adam had woken up at his usual time, 6:00 A.M. Local time, assuming they were close to the coast of Peru, was seven, same time as New York. Blue had found in several years of teaching that while her students knew that South America lay entirely south of North America—duh—they thought it was south and *west*. It was an odd perceptual thing she couldn't explain. In fact, Peru, which was the westernmost bump of South America, was east of most of the United States. Lima, where they were headed, was at about the same longitude as Detroit, but three thousand seven hundred miles south. So Adam was waking up on Chicago time. No jet lag here.

Jasper, Tabitha Lincoln, Andy Becker, the photographer Drake Rakowski, the chemist Bengt Jungstedt, and Brad, Adam, and Blue had seats together toward the rear of the plane. This was nice because it was a long flight and Adam had grown restless. When the seat belt light was off, he could lurch and crawl around in the aisle, paying visits to all of his friends. Being Adam, they were all his friends.

Drake Rakowski lounged in his seat, looking like an old-time foreign correspondent, darkly handsome, but a bit raffish, with hooded eyes that he kept at half-mast most of the time. He wore crisp safari clothes, like an illustration out of a vintage Abercrombie & Fitch catalog, and he must have had the khaki shirt tailored.

Dr. Bengt Jungstedt, at fifty-six the oldest of them, courtly and a bit formal but gentle-natured, was a tall, bony man, an Ichabod Crane or Jack Pumpkinhead in neutral colors, the sort of grayish man who would look just the same in a black-and-white photo and a color photo. He had a sterling reputation in archaeological chemistry. Jungstedt was a Dane who taught frequently in London and the Netherlands.

Bengt and Blue had been in e-mail consultation for weeks. Bengt was interested in the chemical basis for Blue's theory that psilocybin might decrease or prevent the desire for hard drugs. Bengt had located an experimenter in the Netherlands, Dr. Adrian Oudendyk, who would be perfect. Blue had a good background in social anthropology, as most archaeologists did, and she had two years of M-2, medical school, but she was not an experimenter. Oudendyk had said he would seriously consider their proposal.

The aircraft was only half full. This wasn't the peak time of year for tourists in Peru. Also, two unusual accidents had happened recently at Machu Picchu, Peru's biggest tourist destination. A mudslide had cut off all access to Machu Picchu Pueblo, the small mountain town that acted as the staging area for people climbing to the citadel. Half a dozen people had died in the slide, and fifteen hundred people were cut off from the outside world for several days. Sometime later a Russian tourist, climbing on Huayna Picchu, Machu Picchu's famous mountain peak, was killed by a double bolt of lightning on an apparently pleasant day.

Blue stood in the aisle, Adam playing swing-around on her legs, and looked at her little band. Jasper had his head bent over a notebook, rechecking everything he had already checked at the airport, in the lab, and at the office. Andy Becker, one of the two grad students, turned the page of a book Jasper had recommended he read.

It had not escaped Blue's notice that the photographer, Rakowski, had chosen a seat next to Tabitha, both on the hop to Houston and the flight they were on now. This despite the fact that seats were assigned to each person by name. Blue hadn't really loved it when he said to Jungstedt, "You don't mind if I change seats with you, do you, old man? I promise if we crash and I survive I won't take over your identity."

Jokes like that weren't very funny. *In fact not funny at all. Nor is that faux-British accent.*

Tabitha didn't object, though. She had been doing quite a lot of giggling, when she forgot to smile in a distressingly adult manner. Rakowski had a reputation as a womanizer. Fortunately, a professor supervising the work of grad students who are well over twenty-one was not *in loco parentis*. Tabitha was going to have to paddle her own canoe.

"How long before we get there?" Brad asked.

"Are we there yet? Are we there yet?" Rakowski teased. All right, Blue thought, maybe she'd have to take a firm stand with Rakowski at some point.

"Thirty minutes," she said. "Watch as we come in. The sun should be up. We'll come in over the coast and you should see three of Peru's four worlds."

"What does that mean?" Brad asked.

"There's no place on earth with such contrast. It's the most amazing country in the world. There are four absolutely distinct climate zones. And they go from one to the next as if somebody drew a line in the sand.

"The Pacific coast of Peru curves out into one of the richest fishing seas on earth. There's sea bass, flounder, shrimp, crabs, and scallops and lots more. We think humans have lived and fished along that coast for as long as twenty thousand years.

"But go just a mile or two inland and you're on a tableland as flat as a griddle. It's an almost endless plain that runs all the way down the coast through Peru and into Chile, where it becomes the Atacama Desert, the driest desert in the world. The plain is where the Nazca lines were drawn on the earth. You've seen pictures of them, haven't you? The spider and the monkey and whale and geometric designs that are so huge that who-ever made them can't possibly have been able to get far enough above them to see what they looked like."

"Oh, yeah!" Brad said. "They were made by space aliens."

"Some people think so. Space aliens who could get above them in the sky in spaceships and give instructions. Personally, I think you could also produce them with good basic surveying techniques, because the land is so flat.

"Anyhow— Moist air comes across the Pacific and slips on over the desert without slowing down or cooling, so it doesn't rain. Then it hits the Andes. The Andes chain runs the entire length of South America. In Peru the moist air rises directly out of the plain and flows eighteen thou-sand feet up the mountains. There are no foothills to the Andes. So the warm air carrying the Pacific water vapor rises against the Andes and as it rises and cools it lets go of its moisture. The rain sheets down the moun-tains and forms rivers that cross the desert plains and run straight for the sea. Early people who lived in these deserts channeled the rivers into huge, complex, irrigated terraces and grew vegetables. For variety in their diet, they traded vegetables for fish with the coastal people.

"If you go farther east, past the mountain people, up and over the Andes, you come to the fourth climate zone of Peru. You come down into the Amazon rain forest, and if you go far enough east, you are in Brazil.

"The fishing people didn't know about El Niño and La Niña. All they knew was that some years suddenly the fish would not be there for the fishing. And the plains people, like the Moche and the Incas, with their huge complex terraced gardens, would one year notice that the rains in the mountains were going on too long. Then suddenly, a great wall of water would rush down out of the Andes and flood across the plains, washing away the terraces that had taken them years to build. The floods would wash away whole villages and lay the fields in ruin.

"So it's not surprising that the nations of the plains were superstitious. They did what they could to hold off the anger of the gods of the sky who sent floods."

"You mean human sacrifice?" Brad asked.

"Sometimes."

He thought a minute, then said, "I'm really gonna learn something here. Right?"

"I imagine so."

"Cool. Isn't it lucky my French class went to France for spring break last year? I mean, I wouldn't have been able to get a passport in time."

"Very lucky," Blue said, thinking that for her it surely was.

"And it's lucky I turned eighteen on Monday, because my parents couldn't have stopped me from coming."

"But you said they were pleased about it."

"Yeah. But *if*."

He was eager and cheerful, but his tendency to behave like a six-month-old Labrador retriever was going to try Blue's patience.

What am I thinking? This young man saved my son's life. I am going to have patience coming out of my ears.

Blue worked her shoulders a few seconds to take the kinks out, then turned around toward the front of the plane. The four or five nearest passengers were looking at her. They'd been listening. Two of them applauded.

Adam climbed into an empty seat.

Outside the window, the sun was rising. They could see it from the plane, which was two miles high in the sky, well before the light would fall on the land. What they saw was the jagged-tooth profile of the Andes, backlit, the tops gilded with light, and sunbeams distinct as rods shooting through a few declivities. Below, the plains of Peru were obsidian-black.

19

Marcus's own office seemed smaller and darker when he got back from Chicago. He worked on genuine Agency business a while, including drafting several e-mails to manufacturers of listening devices. He'd revise the e-mails tomorrow to make sure they said just what he wanted and no more. A few bad experiences with hasty e-mail messages had trained him to be cautious. No more trigger-happy send-finger. His secretary would have been willing to type the drafts into his files if he wanted her to, but he didn't want. The writing, even the groping for words, clarified his thinking.

But what he really wanted to do was review again the murders in Chicago during the time Hacker had been there. He had read and reread the accounts and none of them seemed like a Hacker hit.

He had gotten up to check the view out his window when there was a knock at the door. Before Marcus could reach the door, it swung open.

"Diana!" Marcus was surprised. He thought she had been avoiding him. If she felt guilty about messing up the addresses in Chicago—and he had little doubt that she did, because he certainly would have—then she'd probably see him as a reminder of her error.

"I just had an idea," she said.

"I'm glad to hear that. I sure haven't."

"We were talking about Chicago deep-dish pizza."

"We were indeed. On the plane coming back." Marcus thought this sounded promising. "On the plane where they fed us each one miniature bag of peanuts."

"Well, there's supposed to be a Chicago-style pizza place in Bethesda. I don't suppose it's anywhere nearly as good as Chicago, but we could—"

"Test it?" Marcus asked. Yes, this did sound promising.

The pizza date started out a bit rocky. Romano's Bella Bella looked good and smelled good. And there was indeed, deep-dish pizza.

"Pepperoni and sausage?" Marcus suggested.

"I don't eat pepperoni," Diana said.

"How about sausage and ham?"

"I don't eat cured meat. Too much nitrate."

"Oh." He was flummoxed. Did this mean she didn't want sausage? She'd suggested the pizza. What was pizza without pepperoni?

"Don't look so staggered," Diana said.

"Well, I—of course, I understand your body is a temple."

She burst out laughing. "Yes, I exercise. I eat a lot of vegetables. But I'm reasonably human."

"By which you mean?"

"Flawed."

"Oh. That's good. I'm reassured. Here I was going on the assumption you were perfect."

She smiled. Marcus guessed he'd said the right thing. Diana said, "If only. Humans aren't perfect. But you have to believe you are perfectible."

"Like how?"

"I was a chubby child, Marcus. The fat kid in grade school. And that was nearly twenty-five years ago, when 'childhood obesity' wasn't a sort of respectable disease entity. It was more of a character failing. No, it was *really* a character failing. Plus chubby kids weren't as common then."

"But you're so—"

"Nobody was going to help me. My mother firmly believed that fat equaled healthy. She was about a generation behind, but hey. That was her belief."

"So you did it yourself."

"I slimmed myself down, to her horror. She still thinks I look like I'm wasting away. I have to be careful about food, even now. It's like being an alcoholic. Except that my addiction is to something I have to have some of to stay alive."

Diana leaned back and shut her eyes.

Marcus studied her for a few seconds. "You're still feeling bad about Chicago."

"Yes, and beside that, I *should* feel bad."

"Listen. We got a lot of information in Chicago. This was the first time any law enforcement agency anywhere has found a place where Hacker actually slept overnight."

"Oh. Fingerprints?"

"Well, they found fingerprints, but they're probably not from the most recent tenant. They're all in places the maids don't usually clean."

"I suppose we shouldn't have expected him to be that careless." She looked unhappy.

"Things like the doorknobs, faucets, air conditioner controls, and the tub surround were all wiped."

"I'm sorry."

He wanted to reassure her. He wanted to take her home to his bed, but he wanted her happier, too. "Diana, we'll get DNA! Nobody can stay in a place overnight without shedding skin flakes and hairs."

Diana said, "But unless we have his DNA in the system, that isn't going to help. The AFIS fingerprint base is huge. DNA filing is just getting under way."

"The point is now we have his DNA. We'll put it into CODIS."

"Maybe he's in there, maybe he isn't." The Combined DNA Identification System linked nationally. "And it's just getting started."

"I agree he may not be in the system. But we never had his DNA before. If he's left DNA at other crime scenes—"

"But you already know he's been at other crime scenes. What I'm saying is that we need his real name, and this doesn't give us that."

"I've put in a request to rotate his DNA against any probables. But it won't be quick."

"Well, we can hope."

"The point is, when we catch him, we can link him to that room."

"But Marcus, that room isn't even the crime scene."

"I asked the techs to get trace evidence from the motel carpet and I bet it will connect to the crime scene, wherever it is."

Diana said, "Yes. Good. Otherwise, he could just say he stayed in Chicago a couple days and then went home."

"This is all going to be useful when we catch him. My point is this is evidence we never had before. With some skin cells, serologists can even work up a genetic fingerprint. Our computer forensics guy can produce a genetic portrait."

Marcus was trying hard to make Diana feel better. He had been attracted to Diana the moment he met her in an Agency meeting. It puzzled him a bit why this was. She wasn't his type. His former girlfriends were all soft-looking women. His mother and sister were soft, pillowy, consoling women, not plump exactly, but generous. Well, his mother was plumpish. None of the girls he had dated in high school, even though they were slender, had Diana's sinewy, strong crispness. But then, none of them had lasted very long in his affections, either.

Maybe it was just as simple as the old saying—you either were attracted to women just like your mother or just the opposite. He suspected that, under the businesslike clothes she always wore, Diana would have strong, cut muscles, overlaid with soft skin.

He asked, "If you're so cautious about food, why are we here?"

"Because I love pizza. I do a portion control thing."

"So you're not going to make me eat a whole wheat pizza?"

"Whole wheat pizzas are pretty darn good. But no. Let's get mushrooms, barbecued beef, and green pepper."

"And beer?"

"Of course beer. A bock."

"Why bock?"

She laughed. "Well, you know the rule. Dark beer with meat pizza. Lighter beer with veggie pizza."

"Oh. Of course."

When the waiter came, Marcus ordered. Diana added, "And double garlic on the pizza."

"Double garlic?" Marcus said when the waiter had left.

"Well, yes, Marcus, dear. I don't kiss on the first date."

After half the pizza and one beer, Diana said, "We're doing this backward."

"Doing what backward?"

"Well, ordinarily we have a crime and a crime scene. The techs collect evidence at the scene to analyze. The motel isn't a crime scene."

"We have a crime someplace."

"Well, I hope you're right. I mean, I don't exactly hope that somebody's dead—"

"I understand."

He focused on the warmth his left hand felt lying near her right hand. The chance to begin a relationship with her was a happy thing to have come out of this. Not enough to repay him for having missed Hacker. But he could still be consoled.

She said, "What are you looking so bemused about?"

"Oh, nothing."

"I have another question."

"Shoot."

"If we don't know who he is, how do we know his name is Hacker?"

"Several years ago London had a message from a good citizen after a man running for office there was killed. He said the killer was called Hacker."

"And they believed this good citizen? Could it have been disinformation?"

"Could have been, sure. The name could have been. But it was our guy. He'd been in London at the time of the killing and he was seen on a surveillance tape in a cross street near the murder."

"Which doesn't mean Hacker was his birth name."

"No. It doesn't mean that. But it's what everybody in law enforcement uses. We could call him Mr. X or Dr. No. The point is, when we say Hacker we know who we're talking about."

Diana leaned back and sighed. "Maybe this is wishful thinking, but what about the possibility that his Chicago kill didn't come off?"

"Huh?"

"It must happen sometimes, don't you think? He does all his research and then he goes to the kill and the mark isn't there. Or somebody else is there. Or the mark has died, whatever. You say he's cautious. He's not going to jump into it if something in the target area is really wrong."

"Well, no. You've got a point."

"So he just leaves in a hurry."

"It's possible. Maybe there never was a killing."

It would be quite a while before they discovered they were wrong.

When he dropped her off at her apartment, walking her to the door as his mother had made him promise always to do, she said, "But I do kiss on the second date. Would you like to come here for dinner tomorrow?"

20

In Fribourg, Switzerland, a narrow-fronted house of pink brick stood on a street devoted primarily to offices. To most Americans, the buildings would look like pleasant individual residences, but in fact they were the homes of multinational corporations or large charitable organizations. The pink brick house had white-painted window frames and a door painted in thick dark blue enamel with shiny brass hinges and a brass doorknob. Next to the door was a small brass plate reading

LEEUWARDEN ASSOCIATES.

There was a town called Leeuwarden in the northern part of the Netherlands, but Leeuwarden Associates had no connection with it. Neither were any people named Leeuwarden involved in the company.

At 11:00 A.M. WEST, Western European Summer Time, limos began to arrive in front of the house. The street resembled a fashion parade of top men's clothiers as cars disgorged one splendidly suited gentleman after another. It was hardly surprising that Leeuwarden hosted men in Armani, Gucci, Hermes, Miyaki, and Sulka suits, and John Lobb custom-made boots. The gross sales of Leeuwarden for the year were approximately eight hundred billion dollars, close to the gross national product of France.

The reception room was understated and overfull. Madame Liane Versluis spoke soft words of welcome to the gentlemen, as Helmut Sands took the topcoats of the few who had worn any.

From earlier meetings all the men knew that they were to pass through the reception room and go directly to the boardroom at the back of the house. The boardroom was shaped like a half moon, the curving outer wall entirely filled with mullioned windows that looked out onto a tiny, very Swiss garden, manicured, trimmed, and combed. Helmut would soon bring in coffee, tea, and pastries.

"Dobro jutro," said the Serbian.

"Günaydin," said the Turk.

"Buon giorno," said the Italian.

"Guten morgen."

"God morgen."

"Good morning."

"Goedemorgen."

The American said, "Hi, all." The German frowned.

Madame Versluis spoke ten languages fluently. Not only English, Italian, French, German, and Spanish, which she called "all the ordinary ones," and Hindi, which she called a "cobbled-together" language, Kiswahili, and Dutch, but also Farsi and Urdu, which were especially important to the business. She spoke several others quite well, but not as a native would. Madame Versluis was very highly paid and rightly so.

She nodded at two of the men, who immediately followed her to one side of the entry hall. They were Leeuwarden Director Roberto Pavia of Argentina and Associate Director Brian-Michael Ratigan from the U.K. The two had slightly different ideas about how Leeuwarden should be run, and very different personalities. But so far the teaming of the two had been successful.

"Mr. Hacker is here to see you," she said.

Pavia said, "Put him in the library." The so-called library was used for very private conversations because the floor-to-ceiling books were an attractive cover for extremely thick soundproofing.

"I already have," said Madame Versluis.

Ratigan chuckled. "I'll tell the boys we'll be with them in ten minutes."

The men in the conference room represented all the surface of the planet. They represented not geographical areas, nor common language areas, but areas of differing types of legal systems, and many of them were lawyers.

There are several more or less distinct types of financial law on earth. About a third of the world's population lives under a common law system that grew initially out of the English practice of basing administrative and judicial decisions on the decisions that had gone before. Thus "common," or an outgrowth of human practice.

Twenty percent live under the so-called "civil law" system, a rather formal Franco-Latin legal system that grew out of the Napoleonic Code.

Another twenty percent live under other systems, especially Germanic, which has elements of both English common law and the Napoleonic Code.

But there are further subdivisions; the most important in terms of the population affected is the difference between traditional English common law, used in the United Kingdom, Canada, Australia, parts of Africa, and India, and American common law. The difference was vital to Leeuwarden's interests, which was why having sub-directors familiar with the law in each area was important. American law, for instance, was quite strict about preventing creditors from "piercing the veil" of a corporation. That is, if a corporation owed money, creditors in most cases could not get money from the individual shareholders of the corporation. English traditional law gave shareholders somewhat less protection; in egregious cases it let creditors pierce the veil of ownership and go after shareholders for debt. Civil law was even worse; it protected debtors and had little sympathy for corporations. If Leeuwarden needed that veil, and it often did, an American jurisdiction was the better place to establish a subsidiary company.

Traditional English financial law is lenient on usury, allowing loans to be made with high interest rates. American law forbids what it considers exorbitant rates of interest, and charging high interest, over a certain amount, may be criminal. Islamic jurisdictions, influenced by Sharia moral laws, are even stricter. In some Islamic jurisdictions no interest whatever is allowed on a loan. In some, simple interest is permitted, but compound interest is illegal. These differences, which can be extremely complicated to calculate, were of great importance to Leeuwarden because loans frequently had to be made for fertilizer or farm equipment well before profit came in from the sale of product.

In addition to the American common law jurisdictions and English common law jurisdictions, there were jurisdictions of mixed Roman and common law, as in Quebec, South Africa, Japan, and South Korea. There were Franco-Latin systems in South America, Mexico, and parts of Africa, and mixed Franco-Latin-Germanic in Italy and the Philippines. The U.S. state of Louisiana, which had been settled by the French, had its own mixed Franco-Latin set of laws. There were also emerging jurisdictions like China and the former Soviet Union. Leeuwarden insisted on the use of cash for most transactions at what they called ground level. While the opportunities for thievery by personnel was increased, they could deal with that. The policy was worth it because the chances of countries gathering data about their business was much decreased. Knowledge of local legal systems was all the more important, however, as at some point the cash had to be transformed into real property and even bank accounts.

Leeuwarden had divided the world into twelve jurisdictions, putting the type of legal system first, but trying to give a sub-director geographical areas near each other wherever possible. For each jurisdiction there was one sub-director and one assistant sub-director. The assistant sub-director went to every meeting with his higher-up, was involved in every decision, and usually had an office in the same building. In the event of the disabling or death of any sub-director, Leeuwarden Associates did not intend to waste time bringing a new one up to speed.

Ratigan began to speak, without raising his voice, and in an instant everyone quieted.

"Señor Pavia and I will be back in just a few minutes. Please take full advantage of the beverages and pastries."

"Shall I come, too?" asked Henry Wong, third in line for leadership at Leeuwarden.

Pavia said, "No, have your coffee. We'll be right back."

Morton, the chef, came from the galley, as the directors called it, carrying a large tray with Turkish coffee, American coffee, Viennese coffee mit schlagobers, and milky Indian chai with cardamom seeds, all of which he placed on the sideboard. Then he went back into the galley for other beverages. Morton was reputed to know how to prepare coffee sixty different ways.

Ratigan made certain that the directors had food and beverages, then he and Pavia strode to the library. Ratigan pulled the library door closed behind him with such an ominously soft, slow click that Hacker jumped to his feet.

Ratigan said, "Mr. Hacker—"

"Yes. It was a total fuckup," Hacker said. It never hurt to be forthright. Felix Hacker was a slender man, but very strong. He had grown up on a farm in Nebraska before entering the Marines, and had the muscles of a man who had done heavy farm work during all his teen years—long, lean muscles, with no health-club designer bulges. He was one of the few recruits who had found the Marines training easily within his abilities right from the beginning. Now he watched Pavia closely.

Pavia said, "This shouldn't have happened."

Ratigan said, "Wait a minute, Roberto. We both agreed to go ahead with this."

Hacker said, "Damn right it shouldn't have happened."

Hacker was head of special operations for Leeuwarden, and highly qualified for the job, which made him much more valuable to the organization than any of the area directors. He was well aware of his worth. He said, "It was totally my responsibility to get the facts right. We needed to know that the husband sometimes babysat."

"Who researched it for you?"

"Hammat. It was his second assignment. He was supposed to check her schedule, thoroughly, not just verify where she lived. He seems to have spent the whole time with a hooker."

"And he's doing what now?" Ratigan asked.

"Whatever you do at the bottom of the Mississippi. Look at mud?"

"Good."

"Things have deteriorated with her," Pavia said. "She was on some talking heads television program making noises about research. She is a more serious problem than we had believed."

"I suppose you want me to get it right this time."

"Yes, and soon," Ratigan said.

"Yes. But make it entirely different," Pavia said. "Our motto is subtlety. We are the epitome of under the radar. Two home invasions in the same place will draw police attention."

"That's no problem. There are a hundred other ways to go."

Ratigan chuckled. "Keep a low profile."

Pavia said, "Oh, Ratigan, you and your Americanisms. True, though."

Hacker said, "She's just made it easier for us."

Ratigan said, "In what way? This is not twenty questions. Don't keep me waiting."

"She's on her way to Peru."

"Well, then," Pavia said, "you'd better be spooling up the Gulfstream G-IV, hadn't you?"

Roberto Pavia, even though he made fun of Ratigan's Americanisms, was the one who had actually spent time in the United States. The only son of a wealthy Argentinean shipping and mining family—they had four daughters who would not be encouraged to go into the business—he had been tutored at home and then sent to Harvard, either for the education or for the validation of his importance. The girls were sent to convent schools.

Pavia had seen very early that really, really serious money was not to be made in shipping, but in illicit drugs, and he had the seed money to follow his dream.

Brian-Michael Ratigan, on the other hand, had been born in Belfast and had a graduate degree in gang warfare. His father was a drunk who worked two weeks a year, just long enough for his new employer to realize he wasn't coming to work. His mother cleaned floors at St. Anne's Cathedral. Kneeling and scrubbing were penance enough for her. When she was at home, she took her frustrations out on Brian-Michael. At the age of fourteen, he ran away to London. His passions were American films and the organization of criminal enterprise.

Each had prospered, and in becoming a team they had prospered enormously.

Ratigan said, "Why bother with the girl? She's no threat."

"She's not an *immediate* threat," Pavia said.

"We've got bigger problems."

"Professor Eriksen is a cloud no bigger than a man's hand. I concur. But she's coming closer. Now she's got a larger trial group lined up."

"She's probably just trying to make a name for herself."

"Well, that's another part of the problem. She's already made a name for herself. Imagine what would happen if people realize she's actually curing addicts."

"People won't believe it."

"Oh, please. You want to bet your whole future on that?"

"We can deal with it later. We've got serious problems. Mexico is about to melt down, and it's right on the U.S. border. It's falling apart into civil war. We've got seven major cartels fighting each other there, two of them huge, and they're also holding back our profits."

"Which is why we'll be popping over there to kick them into shape. It doesn't affect dealing with Blue Eriksen."

"Oh, shit, maybe not. It's not like we don't have the staff."

"Absolutely. Right now she's as the serpent's egg, which, hatch'd, would, as his kind, grow mischievous. We'll kill her in the shell."

"I suppose that's Shakespeare."

"I suppose it is." Pavia knew Ratigan resented what he called "an expensive education."

"We'll take the long view," Pavia said. "It's the wise thing to do."

"Yeah, maybe."

"Plus, she'll be easy to kill."

21

The *garua*, the sea fog, saturated Lima.

Thank God we're not staying here long, Tabitha Lincoln thought. After three digs, Tabitha prided herself on being hardy in the wilderness. In fact, her first dig, in northern Illinois when she was an undergraduate, was the most miserable experience of her life. No later privations abroad compared to it. Her entire class camped out on the Rock River, investigating a shell midden supposed to be from the Late Woodland period, about fifteen hundred years ago. The mosquitoes nearly ended her career. She had thought she would have anemia by day two. Covered with bites, she actually lay in her tent the first night trying to estimate: If each mosquito withdrew one milliliter of blood—surely they sucked out at least that much! When you whacked one it made a huge splotch—and if she had been bitten by a thousand mosquitoes—although it felt like ten thousand—then she had lost a liter of blood, which was approximately a quart. Then maybe she would die and be out of this horror.

The next day at Rock River, scrabbling through the little bits of freshwater clamshell, inedible leavings of the food the Late Woodland people had subsisted on, she complained to the professor. He said, "You're seven miles, tops, from the nearest McDonald's. You're going home to Seattle on your summer break. Imagine living your entire life right here. There's nowhere to go to get away from the mosquitoes. And any variety you get in your diet only happens when the blackberries ripen or some of the hickories have nuts in the fall. Or maybe the hunters catch a rabbit. Or a woodchuck. Woodchucks are nice and fat but gamy. Then there's the whole winter to get through, mostly on clams and roots."

And suddenly she could see it. One of the shells in her hand was almost unbroken. It was only an inch long, silvery inside. She could see the person who had found it in the river. In her mind it was a young woman and she was pregnant. Hungrily, she had sucked all the meat out of the clamshell and now she was licking the remains, running her tongue around inside the shell, getting every last bit of the juice.

Tabitha put her tongue into the shell. This same gesture might have been made a thousand years ago.

Tabitha was hooked.

She liked people a thousand or ten thousand years ago better than people today, though. Tabitha disliked the demands of live people. They were unruly, smelly, loud, unpredictable, irrational—all behaviors that Tabitha didn't care for.

And she didn't really like Lima, what she saw of it so far on the way in from Jorge Chávez Airport. The research she had done before leaving Chicago had not prepared her for the smell of the shantytowns they were now driving through. It was sad, no doubt about it, that people had to live in these conditions. By and large they were country people who couldn't survive on farming and had come to the city. But there was nothing for them here, either. The shantytowns had no medical services, no water supplies, and no electricity. Worst of all, there were no sewers.

"What is this *garua*, anyway?" she asked Rakowski. "Smells like more than fog."

"Haven't the foggiest," he said, and he laughed heartily. Tabitha thought maybe he wasn't as attractive as he seemed at first.

"It's a mix of fog and factory pollution and emissions from cars," Professor Martello said. "Basically it's smog."

"When does it blow away?"

Professor Eriksen said, "It doesn't, much. It's here ten months a year."

Oh, great, Tabitha thought.

But Andy said, "We aren't staying in Lima anyhow, except two nights."

There were armed guards everywhere, Tabitha saw as they came into the center of town. Guards followed school buses taking children to morning classes. Armed guards stood in front of large buildings and industrial plants. Private houses were less in evidence than stone, brick, or stucco walls, and she deduced that there were houses hiding behind them. They passed through an area of particularly long walls topped with broken glass. There were guards at the entry gates. "Homes of the rich?" she said, and Blue Eriksen nodded.

22

Blue had booked them into the Hospedaje Plaza Mayor in Lima for two nights. It cost a bit more than most archaeological digs would spend, but she had sponsors and could spend some of the income from *Goddess*, too. She thought if some of them were going to develop turista, tourist tummy, they might as well do it in a degree of comfort. The hotel had private bathrooms and twenty-four-hour hot water. And the Hospedaje was quiet, despite being in the city center. She wanted the group to visit the Museo Arqueológico Rafael Larco Herrera here in Lima. It was a walkable distance from the hotel, about six blocks. It would give them an idea of the history of the area in a nutshell—a gigantic, varied, beautiful museum nutshell.

She gathered the group and they trekked to the museum—even Adam, who was walking quite a bit, now that he was almost a year old. He made it half a block before Blue had to pick him up. Then Brad, remembering his job, put Adam on his shoulders and Adam sang "Beer! Beer! Bottlllll!" startling the passersby.

The Hospedaje Plaza Mayor was located, hardly surprisingly, on the

Plaza Mayor. This big square, where once an Inca palace stood, was now very Spanish. Victims of the Inquisition were hanged here in the 1500s and Francisco de Ávila burned Inca sacred objects here in 1609. There even used to be bullfights in the square.

They spent four hours in the Museo Larco Herrera. Or rather the group did. A person could easily spend four weeks. There were rooms and rooms of the wonderful Moche portrait pots, pots in the shapes of faces of important people, so lifelike that you could tell which person was being pictured on each pot. The peasantry, mostly artisans, were pictured more humorously, and there were animals and fish pots, too. There was a frog pot Blue would have loved, except that it was owned by the museum and, besides, the smashing of her collection had damaged her liking for them.

Blue headed back to the hotel with Adam after two hours. He needed his nap, and actually, Blue needed one also. The others had just discovered the Sala Erotica, the hall of erotica, in the Herrera, and Blue could see Brad, Andy, and Drake Rakowski were eager to study the archaeological evidence.

At eight, fairly early for dinner in this part of the world, they headed off to a highly recommended restaurant. Without Adam. He was eating baby food from jars, just to be on the safe side. Blue had many friends who had taken their children on digs in all parts of the world, and most of them claimed that when infants got *turista* it was milder and lasted less time than in adults. But she was starting out extra careful. Like any small child, Adam had had a couple of stomach upsets and they were no fun for anybody, Adam or anyone in the vicinity. Blue could not begin to imagine how Brad would cope with taking care of a sick Adam by himself if he had to.

There was an order of nuns that had been highly recommended to her by the people on the Huaca de la Luna dig and by a woman professor in the States. In South America various orders of nuns had things they did famously well. The Convent of the Congregation of the Daughters of the Immaculate Mary here in Lima made such a good income from their

moche
stirrup
pot

elaborate wedding cakes, as well as bonbons, chocolates, and candy fruits, that they had no need for support from contributions. The nuns that had been recommended to Blue, Little Sisters of Santa Teresa, specialized in raising extra money for their order by babysitting visiting English-speaking children. Adam was spending the evening with one whose name was Sister Tinkerbell. Actually, Blue realized it was something a little different and more sedate, but Adam seemed to think it was Tinkerbell because he pronounced it that way. He was at the stage where he pronounced what he liked and couldn't pronounce what he didn't like.

In any case, when Tinkerbell arrived, instead of doing the falling-on-the-floor oh-oh-oh-oh-no-no-I'm-going-to-be-babysat crying routine, he laughed so hard at her nun's habit, especially the winged headpiece, that he nearly choked. She thought this was delightful, which confirmed for Blue that she was okay.

She brought with her *Pat the Bunny* in both Spanish and English and a collapsible game that involved rolling different-colored rubber balls down inclined slopes.

Blue thought, *When your child doesn't care that you're leaving for the evening, you're pleased and also not so pleased.*

La Cabana was in walking distance, just three blocks, from the Hospedaje Plaza Mayor, whose concierge had told Blue's group that the food there was very good. He was right. Jasper, Andy, Drake Rakowski, Bengt Jungstedt, Tabitha, Brad, and Blue sat around a long table made from two square tables pushed together.

"Don't drink local water," Blue had told them, ordering bottled water. "And no ice. It's almost always made from water that isn't bottled. Order only cooked food." That having been said, the dinner was wonderful.

The waiter brought them *anticuchos* as soon as they had ordered their drinks. These hors d'oeuvres Blue had discovered on an earlier trip to Peru. They were made of beef heart, marinated overnight, then brushed with oil and spices, skewered and grilled. They also offered ceviche, which is local raw fish "cooked" by lime and lemon juice and salt. It looked cooked and had the texture of cooked fish, but Blue wasn't sure whether bacteria were killed by the process, so she asked her group not to order any. It was not that the kitchen was unclean. People all get used to the populations of bacteria in their home environments. Probably a Peruvian coming to the United States would have traveler's tummy for a while, too, Blue said. But she wanted her group to acclimate with the least possible difficulty.

Andy looked at the menu and asked, "What's this *cuy*? It says it's broiled and served with potatoes, onion, and garlic. Looks good."

"It's guinea pig," Blue said. Correcting him, she added, "Pronounced 'kwee.'"

Brad said, "Guinea pig? Yuck! I had two pet guinea pigs for years. George and Garibaldi. We thought they were Lucrezia and Garibaldi at first and I wanted to have little guinea pigs, but it turned out, well, you know."

Drake Rakowski, their flirtatious photographer, said, "Great! Broiled guinea pig. That's what I'm getting."

Tabitha looked daggers at him. Since he had probably said this to impress her with his sophistication, as well as to annoy Brad, he seemed to have miscalculated.

Blue ordered the grilled *corvine*, a relative of the sea bass.

Jasper wanted a fish stew called *parihuela*.

When Brad realized the *arroz con pato* was duck cooked in beer, he eagerly ordered it. Blue smiled, having seen again and again this adventuresome, I'll-be-a-devil thing when students got really far away from home for the first time.

The other three had *ají de gallina*, chicken in walnut sauce.

They drank bottled beer and bottled carbonated water, waiting for the entrees.

"Why did they name you Blue?" Brad asked suddenly. "It's a funny name."

"Yes, why?" Tabitha asked.

"They didn't. When I was about five and my sister was three, she went through a stage of putting B on the beginning of a lot of words. Like milk was bilk. OJ was bojay. Uncle Stan was Buncle Stan."

"Yeah. My little sister couldn't do 'R.' She used to call me Bad."
Everybody laughed.

Brad said, "So what is your real name?"

"My mother named me Luella. But they called me Lou."

"So she called you Blue."

There was one rather unpleasant incident that marred the evening. Their waiter was not one of the fastest. The pace of life was different in Latin American countries. The group wasn't in any particular hurry, but Jasper was always work oriented, and he wanted to get back to his room to study some authority or other who had ideas on how one should remove and store the brain and liver samples we would collect at the Temple of the Moon to take back home. He had already consulted a number of experts, had brought Dr. Bengt Jungstedt along, and in addition he was precisely such an authority himself, but that was Jasper for you.

And between excessive care and sloppiness, Blue preferred excessive care.

At any rate, Andy, who was always a Jasper-worshiper, noticed that Jasper was getting impatient. So when the waiter approached them glacially slowly with a tray of drinks, including a Scotch for Jasper, and managed to jar the tray, upending the Scotch into Jasper's lap, Andy said, "You clumsy peasant!"

Jasper leaped up and placed himself between the waiter and the group of local people sitting behind Blue's group. Bengt Jungstedt jumped up and made soothing gestures to the waiter, also shoving crumpled U.S. dollar bills at him. The rest of the group smiled disarmingly at everybody around us, as if nothing was wrong.

The waiter made the dollars vanish and smiled, too. Blue drew a breath of relief. Jasper and Bengt sat back down. But Jasper hissed at Andy, "That was rude. And very foolish!"

Andy was abashed, especially, Blue thought, because it was his hero speaking.

Bengt Jungstedt said, "You could have caused an *incident!*"

.   .   .

Felix Hacker, half a dozen tables away, ate a savory *ají de gallina* and drank Inca Kola with a double shot of pisco, a clear brandy made locally. Kola with pisco was called a Peru Libre. Mr. Hacker always drank the local beverages and ate locally produced food wherever he went, even if it meant lutefisk in Sweden. He believed it made jet lag less severe and put you on a more stable physical footing. You would be quicker, stronger, smarter, than those who did not instantly adjust. In China, at a banquet for several Leeuwarden officials, he had been served skewered bamboo mouse, sautéed cow veins, which he had at first assumed to be pasta, and stewed pig snout. When he saw the snout brought in on its platter, he thought it was a gigantic portobello mushroom. Even when he realized it wasn't, he ate it all in good appetite.

And then there was that restaurant in Omaha where they deep-fried everything, including the parsley.

The party of archaeologists and hangers-on he was watching weren't so smart. They were drinking a variety of things, some local, some imported, including designer water from Europe and vodka from Russia. Smart people could be so stupid.

Mr. Hacker had never been in Peru before, but he had been in Colombia several times. He adjusted quickly to new places and blended in well, even when he did not know the language. In this case, he spoke Spanish fluently, but didn't know the other local dialects. Working from a basic everyman face, he could appear alert, stupid, suave, bumbling, aloof, friendly, rich, or poor with mainly a change of manner and clothes. Only in very rare cases did he use anything like a disguise. Today he looked like a South American banker, with white shirt, silk tie, and a vanilla-colored suit.

He studied his target. Finding them had been no trouble at all. Calling the hotels in Lima, working from the most centrally located outward, he had them by hotel number six. He simply phoned each hotel and asked for the party of archaeologists from Northwestern University.

Blue Eriksen was attractive, he had to admit. He had studied pictures of her before his abortive attempt on her life, and he decided she was more attractive in person. Her appearance must have helped the sale of her first book. She probably looked good in TV interviews. Her colleague, that Professor Martello, was what Mr. Hacker's father would have called a "long drink of water." He looked prissy, fussy. The storklike guy next to him had to be Dr. Bengt Jungstedt. You could knock a guy like that on his ass with one push and he'd sit on the ground and whine.

Now, the younger people were another story. The tan man with the camera bag and designer safari clothes looked sturdy enough. Probably thought he was tough. And then there were the three students. The girl moved like a walker, a hiker, but not a fighter. One of the men, the young guy with the mustache who had insulted the waiter, was late-twenties, Hacker guessed, ropy muscles, maybe one of those Ivy League tennis-player types. Hacker hated them. He hated over-educated people. The younger kid was a puzzle. Hacker wondered whether he was losing his ability to assess people, because he just couldn't believe that the kid was old enough to be a grad student. Looked eighteen at most. But why else would he be here? Hacker's research on Eriksen and Martello hadn't turned up any kid brothers.

When the group finished dinner, the younger members still had lots of energy and wanted to go on to a club. Dr. Jungstedt, surprisingly in a man so quiet, wanted to go with them. Jasper and Blue didn't want to go. He had papers to study, and Blue needed to get back to Adam. The nun had been highly recommended, but Blue was still uneasy about being away from her baby for more than a couple of hours.

The restaurant owner made some suggestions to the kids about clubs to visit. They left the restaurant and clumped up together on the sidewalk.

"Negotiate for the taxi price *before* getting in," Blue said. "Official cabs are yellow. Don't take any other kind. When you want to come back, the club will call you a taxi."

Andy said, "All right." He was quite subdued.

"Drink only bottled water where the top is still on the bottle."

"Right."

"Do not drink anything with ice cubes in it."

"Right."

"Drink bottled drinks like beer and Inca Kola. Don't drink anything poured at the bar. Don't even drink what they call 'purified' water. You can have hot coffee or hot tea. Don't eat raw fruit unless you can get it with the peel on and peel it yourself."

Tabitha sighed dramatically. "Yes, Mother," she said.

"Like your mother might say, you'll thank me later."

23

She seemed to be telling the younger people how to be safe, Hacker thought. Wasn't that cute? Especially in view of the fact that she and the other man about her age—Professor Martello, it had to be—put the kids in a cab and then started walking along the main street alone and unprotected. From him.

He followed at the distance of half a block.

Neither Martello nor Eriksen looked behind them. They did scrutinize the other people on the sidewalk, as you would in a strange town where you were not quite sure whether you were in a safe area. But they didn't do a three-sixty check, and certainly didn't notice him particularly. Of course, he was wearing a tropical-weight suit, Panama hat, and nice shoes. No way he looked like a street thug or an assassin.

They proceeded together, the pair, then the single man behind them, along the dark but busy street. Streetlights studded the walk at intervals but were not very bright. Although it was 10:00 P.M., this was not late for a South American town, and Lima was a very cosmopolitan place. The street was filled with people.

This was both good and bad. With people coming and going in both directions, Hacker was able to draw closer and closer to the academics without any likelihood of their noticing him. He could hear snatches of their conversation.

"—ship the first samples home?" Prof. Eriksen said.

He couldn't hear Martello's answer.

"—not complete?" Eriksen said.

Professor Martello shrugged. "You're almost done with the first draft. So I could take a run at the rewrite."

"Great. I want to start spending full time on the psilocybin project."

"You're excited about it."

"We're getting results! Jasper, you know I think all of archaeology helps people understand themselves better. But to actually help people physically in the here and now—"

Mr. Hacker thought, *Oh, oh. Better move soon.*

He knew that if he got close enough, he could slip a knife between Blue Eriksen's ribs and be gone into the crowd of tourists and locals before she even hit the pavement. Martello, too. Generally, people don't die fast from wounds like that, wounds that bled into the lungs. Half an hour or more it might take. In fact, many people stabbed in the back with a very sharp knife walked blocks, sometimes even walked home, before they realized there was a problem and by then they were the walking dead.

He edged closer.

Blue turned to say something to Martello. Hacker thought she caught a glimpse of him. It didn't matter, though. She didn't know him and she was going to be dead soon.

When the two police officers appeared, striding along the street a block ahead, he cursed under his breath. They were the "tourist police," not the city police, he deduced from their regulation white shirts. But it didn't matter which police they were. Now he could not safely strike and leave. All police were armed in Peru, and they shot people who ran from them. It was just too dangerous to make a move against the woman right now. Even as the police passed Eriksen and Martello, the two professors were at the door of the Hospedaje Plaza Mayor. Then they were inside. It was Hacker's hotel, too, but he could certainly not attack her in front of the hotel personnel. And it was better he not go in at all right now. She must not have a chance to notice him twice.

Grimly, he continued to walk straight ahead, knowing he would have to go up the street several blocks before turning around. He tried to tell himself that this was no bad thing. He had acted hastily once before and he was lucky the mistake hadn't done serious damage.

Make haste slowly.

24

"It sure doesn't look like much," Brad said, gazing at the Huaca de la Luna, the Temple of the Moon.

Andy said, "But it's *huge*."

"Yes, but it's all *dirt*."

Blue succeeded in not laughing outright. Brad was so earnest. He was really interested, she thought; not making fun, just puzzled. He must have anticipated an ancient temple à la Hollywood. The Temple of the Moon looked like the world's largest mud pile, constructed by giant children. Speaking of children, Adam climbed happily around her knees as the group sat on a line of raised rock and sun-dried brick at the edge of the path to the Temple of the Moon. Behind it Cerro Blanco, the White Mountain, rose out of a flat plain. The immense bulk of the Temple of the Moon, ninety feet high, was built to the west of Cerro Blanco and up against its lower slopes. The Huaca del Sol, a short distance across the plain, was even bigger, as long as four football fields and the height of a thirteen-story building.

But to an eighteen-year-old who grew up in Chicago in the age of glass and steel towers, it might not look like much.

Finding a particularly round rock, Blue handed it to Adam, who smiled up with indescribable sweetness.

Tabitha drawled, "You just don't get it, Brad. This was the center of an empire!"

Abashed, Brad said, "Well, I don't mean—I mean—the mountain is really awesome. But the temple doesn't look like a temple. I don't see—"

Blue said, "It *is* mud brick, after all. And it's had a millennium and a half of weathering. Now look at these."

There were several partly intact bricks around their feet. The archaeologists had decided they were not interesting enough to protect under an awning. The brick nearest him, as well as all of the others on the wall behind, were marked. Blue said, "See? Clan marks. The clans paid taxes in bricks. This huge mound is their IRS filing cabinet." Mentally, she tried to guess how many thousands of such bricks there were in the temple and lying on the land around it, but thousands didn't begin to do it justice. Millions?

Blue said to their lead guide, "Federico, do you know how many bricks there are in the Huaca de la Luna?"

"Yes, Professor. Fifty million."

Brad said, "Whoa!"

Blue stood up. "Let's go, group. What you see from here is just the size of it, not the, well, the content, you might say."

She picked up Adam, who grabbed on to her hair and shirt as if he were a baby monkey. The team had been admitted to the site without paying the usual tourist fee. But they had made a handsome contribution to the combined Peruvian and foreign investigation into the two temples, Huaca del Sol and Huaca de la Luna. Located only five kilometers south of Trujillo, the temples comprised a prime tourist attraction. Hordes trooped through every day, and the problem was to route them so that they didn't add to the damage done by dust storms, the Spaniards, and the very, very rare but torrential rains. The Huaca de la Luna was open daily, nine to four, although the Huaca del Sol was not entirely excavated and wasn't open to the public right now. But you did have to get into the temple to understand it. Three of the people on the ongoing dig, Federico and two others, accompanied them as guides. Or maybe to make sure they didn't take any souvenirs. Jasper and Blue had good reputations, plus permits from the Peruvian government to get what they had come for, but the rest of their little band were not known to these people. Theft by colleagues of archaeologists—spouses, workers, whatever—had happened before, a lot of times. For that matter, theft by reputable archaeologists had happened far too often as well.

They had arrived in Trujillo today on a 10:24 A.M. LAN Perú flight via Chiclayo, arriving at 2:00. From Lima to Trujillo, the center of Moche country, was three hundred miles as the crow flies. Blue had explained that they were not crows, and it would have been more like three hundred fifty miles by car, but even so she had seriously considered renting a car and driving. The coast highway was winding and slow. Always the teacher, she thought that would give the students a pretty good look at this part of Peru, including fishing villages and the rivers that flowed down from the Andes. But it would eat up valuable time.

They checked into the hotel in Trujillo at three, but Blue had not been willing to give everybody another fun afternoon out. Letting them unwind one night at the Lima clubs had been enough. Blue had a good nest egg to complete the research, but she wasn't the federal government. Not the U.S. Air Force with its $390 wrenches. Her expenses had to make sense. So after checking in, they got two taxis and went immediately out to the site. Andy stayed at the hotel with what he called tourist tummy but might have been a hangover, and Bengt and Drake looked a bit green. Brad confided to Blue that Andy had drunk pisco sours with ice cubes, even though Blue had specifically warned them against ice cubes. Brad added that he thought Andy was depressed about what had happened at the restaurant. Blue was pleased that Brad was keeping track of what was going on around him.

She walked toward the excavation into the Temple of the Moon, trailed by her little party, now eight of them, including the guides. Adam, the ninth member of the party, was trying to cram the hair on the left side of Blue's head into her ear, giggling all the while. "You know that's not where it goes," she said. He shrieked with delight. She nuzzled his neck. He shrieked louder.

Achutallas rolled past them on the bone-dry earth. The achutalla was a plant with no roots. It looked like a dead pineapple top. It was a bromeliad, related to pineapples. It was not dead; it was a fog plant, rootless, living on moisture in the fog in this land where there was almost never any rain. An achutalla as far as Blue knew never looked green. Two more rolled across the road, tumbling over into the endless plain.

"Fifteen hundred years ago," Blue said to her group, "there were twenty thousand people living in this city and another twenty thousand in what you'd have to call its suburbs. In Europe about then, refugees from Attila the Hun were camping in what would later be Florence. This was the center of the Moche civilization, earlier than the Incas and in the arts maybe greater than the Incas."

They had seen the magnificent Moche portrait pots and weavings at the museum in Lima, and nobody gave her any argument on this point.

"If you had been standing on this spot fifteen hundred years ago, you would have seen a market that spread from here to the Huaca del Sol and all round the sides of both temples. You would have heard the tapping of artisans pounding out sheets of copper and gold. There would be chirps of guinea pigs and clucks from the chickens in the meat market. You could smell the scent of fish from the fish market and raw wool from the weavers. There were wool dyers and jewelry makers who polished and cut lapis lazuli imported from the south and spondylus shell imported from Ecuador to the north. And there would be bead makers and toolmakers and the smell of roasting corn. Trains of pack llamas came into the marketplace carrying freeze-dried potatoes and alpaca wool from the Andes."

"And it all died out?" Tabitha said.

Federico almost wrung his hands. He said mournfully, "Yes. It is all gone." He waved his arm. "And then some of the civilizations that followed the Moche used the area as a cemetery and destroyed unnumber—innumerable artifacts. Then the Spanish came and destroyed most of the temple."

"The good part of the story, though," Blue said as they rounded some piles of dirt and approached the temple itself, "was that the chutzpah of the Incas saved a lot of the Moche artifacts. The Spaniards arrived when the Inca civilization was dominant, a thousand years after the Moche.

They looted gold from the Incas—you all know about that—and then just boldly asked the Incas what other civilizations there had been around here earlier that they could go loot. And the Incas said there weren't any. Not to bother looking at old inferior cultures. That theirs was the first and only great civilization that ever lived here."

"Arrogance met arrogance," Federico said.

"Not that the Spaniards didn't find some Moche treasure. But they didn't find all of it."

Even more mournfully, Federico said, "The Spaniards diverted the river to flood the Huaca del Sol. They hoped they would wash away everything but the gold."

They were all looking toward the huge bulk of the Temple of the Sun. It was mud brick and quite dissolvable. "They washed away two-thirds of the temple," Blue said.

Tabitha voiced what the others must have been thinking. "You mean it was three times larger than *that*?"

Federico sighed deeply and added, "And then came the *guaqueros*. Looters. Criminals! They should all be shot!"

Blue thought, *Federico is my kind of guy*.

They found themselves facing a long square-sided trench that went back into the temple area. Because several levels rose above it, toward the top of the Temple of the Moon, which was ninety feet high, the trench appeared to get deeper and deeper as they walked. They saw a side trench, leading quite abruptly to the right. It had been excavated to a deeper level than the one in which they stood. Federico, who was just behind Blue, said, "This is one of the three burials we are working on now."

Two skeletons lay partially revealed in the dirt, one clearly a young woman or a girl, with the entire skeleton visible except the left arm. The right arm was bent upward almost as if saluting. The other skeleton was of an adult, and although Blue could not be sure at this distance, the narrow pelvic girdle suggested a male. Ten *offrendas*, small offering jars, were clustered around the feet of the adult. Lapis beads lay over the rib cage area.

"It is when we open those offrendas that we will give you the samples," Federico said.

Federico then led them up the pyramid by way of a forty-five-degree ladder—almost a wooden stairway—they had constructed to make it possible to climb up a level more easily and to save the bricks of the temple from the wear of feet. Carrying Adam, Blue found it difficult to climb and stumbled after a couple of steps.

"Let me have him," Brad said. He took Adam in one arm and skipped up the ladder as friskily as a mountain goat. Blue mumbled to Bengt, "Don't you hate it when they're fifteen years younger and twice as agile?"

Then she caught Jasper's eye as if to say, "See? I was right." He rolled his eyes and smiled. Blue took that to mean so far so good.

Federico led them to a large, wide-open area protected by a roof put in place by the government and the tourist bureau. The roof, more than two stories over their heads, consisted of flat wooden boards held up by tall wooden poles made rigid by forty-five-degree angled poles at their tops, like the letter Y. Under this protection were two magnificent terraces of gorgeous, bright friezes. The Moche were masters of geometric patterns, and the walls flamed in the late-day light. Drake Rakowski, behind Blue, unholstered his camera. And Brad, who had just a little earlier thought the temple "not much," said, "Wow!"

Blue took out her small camera and a sketch pad. Drake would do the important photos of the trip. Blue just liked to make a record for her own use.

A couple of dozen tourists were lined up at the rail, studying the friezes with the same awe as Brad. Judging from the languages, they were from all over the world. There were several Japanese, a couple speaking Portuguese, a German scholar lecturing three German young people, and several from the U.S., including one in a Hawaiian shirt and straw hat. For some reason the bright Hawaiian parrots on the shirt disturbed Adam. He twisted around on Brad's shoulders and started to whine.

Brad handed him to Blue and he quieted.

Federico led them past the tourists to a barricaded section at the end. The friezes here were an extension of the part the tourists saw—not different, but equally spectacular—and the group was allowed to get closer to them. They included a fierce stylized face inside a diamond shape.

"The *Degollador*. The Decapitator," said Federico.

the Degollador

a Moche frieze

. . .

Huaca de la Luna, like most ancient pyramids, was constructed of a series of terraces. Terracing made it easy to enlarge a pyramid. One generation of workers would start with a single, simple pyramid, made to house the body of a great leader, a king or a high priest, for his trip to the afterlife. When another king died, another generation of workers built a terrace around the pyramid, entombed the king and built a layer over the old pyramid, making it taller and wider. This would go on over and over, until the pyramid was gigantic. The pyramid may become so large that many kings may be entombed under a single terrace, along with their wives, courtiers, servants, and often animals. The flat plazas laid on top of the layers of tombs were used for ceremonies. Because the Moche built with mud brick, not stone, they could not construct interior corridors and rooms. The weight of the structure above would collapse them. So they filled in the spaces above the tombs as they went along with broken brick, mud, and debris. Then they flattened out the top to make a new terrace. Far from damaging the tombs, this process protected them and the paintings on the walls. They never hollowed out the older areas, and probably never revisited the older tombs, underneath, at all.

Each new level had vertical walls with elaborately painted friezes, a pictorial history. At Huaca de la Luna, there was a series of four plazas atop the tombs, and the last plaza built was longer than three football fields. The structure contained an unknown number of tombs and friezes inside, carrying the story of the Moche.

It was now late afternoon.

Blue led the group to an outcropping of stone facing on an excavated area, "Several years ago, all you would have seen here was a plaza laid on top of rubble. Then archaeologists made a grisly discovery.

"You need to realize that what I'm going to tell you about was put together over quite some time, but I'm summarizing. They found the skeletons of about seventy young men. They're pretty sure there were more than seventy, but they can't be positive how many because—"

"Uh-oh," Tabitha said. She was always quick on the uptake.

"Exactly. They were dismembered. Hands, feet, arms, legs. All scattered around. This was a sacrificial platform. We know now that the Moche engaged in human sacrifice, like so many early people. It was part of their religion. But this was different. Many of the skulls were missing. Some limbs were missing. That is unusual. As the archaeologists worked down into the earth, they found layers of hard clay interspersed with looser soil and blown-in detritus like we see around us. Okay, class, why is hard clay unexpected?"

"I don't know," Brad said.

Tabitha said, "Because it hardly ever rains here."

"Right, Tabitha. Clay is sedimentary and stays where it is unless it's washed out or dug. It hardly ever rains here. But in some of the layers, the bones were actually *embedded* in the clay. So it must have washed in around them while it was liquid. There was a pit just over there." Blue pointed to a small dig near a wall. "It was full of bones and pottery and on the pottery were pictures of naked young men tied together with ropes around their necks.

"The clay layers may have been formed when heavy rain washed construction clay into the plaza.

"The investigators analyzed the bones. All of the dead were young males over fifteen and under forty. All were healthy and—Brad, we can tell this from marks on the bones where muscles attach plus the strength of the bones themselves. Athletes have denser bones. All these men and boys were strong and athletic. All had been well fed during childhood. Some of the bones showed that the young men had been injured about a month before they died. The injuries had partly healed. A broken rib, for instance, heals in three and a half weeks.

"Then there were other injuries that never got a chance to heal. Skull fractures for one. And cut marks on the neck vertebrae consistent with a sliced throat. But the joints where the dismemberment occurred didn't show any signs of cutting. Also many of the bones were bleached."

"That's sad," Brad said, looking half sick and half fascinated, which seemed like a perfectly normal reaction to Blue. He was playing some sort of roll-the-stone game with Adam.

"There was one smaller group of bones, though, that did show signs of intentional dismemberment. And not only dismemberment, but defleshing."

"What's defleshing?" Brad said.

"Defleshing is removing the meat from the bones in the way you would a pig or goat for cooking."

"Oh. Yuck."

"I think he's sorry he asked," Drake said, chuckling. Blue gave Drake *A Look*. Blue did not permit *any* making fun of anybody in any of her classes for asking any questions, ever. Drake wasn't a student, but she was in charge of this expedition and Drake had better remember it. He blinked and almost backed away.

Blue said, "So what happened here?" The sun was close to setting now, the light growing more amber and the shadows bluer and longer. The faces of her little group looked bronzed. Their expressions were somber.

"The investigators did what the best of archaeology can do. Bring the past to life. They knew from pictures on pottery and on murals that ceremonial battles and sacrifice of prisoners were part of Moche culture. But why this extreme case and why the scattering of bones and why defleshing? Well, this is the story they developed:

"You might think rain is a good thing. Not for people like the Moche on the Peruvian plain, who depended entirely on irrigation, using the rivers that run down out of the Andes. Rain happens high in the Andes. Not here. Here on the plain, the cities depended on the careful terracing and elaborate networks of canals to distribute the river water properly. Remember, forty thousand people lived in this valley alone, and it's only one of several seats of Moche culture."

Brad listened with his mouth partly opened. Even Adam was listening, but goodness knew what he understood. Brad said, "What happened?"

"What happened was El Niño. Torrential rains fell in the Andes as the climate changed. The canals flooded and burst their banks. The terraced fields washed away and the crops both drowned from the water and dried out when their roots were exposed to the sun. Clay-laden water flooded the temple.

"The first—that is the lowest—level of clay in this terrace—shows that the Moche sacrificed five or six young men, captives who had been held a while so that their battle injuries had started to heal. Their bodies were left lying in the plaza here and the vultures may have pulled apart their bones. But their sacrifice did not appease the gods. When another torrential rain washed away more of the precious fields, even more clay washed into the plaza. So they sacrificed a larger number of young men. Their bones bleached when the sun came out. But the rains came again. This time the Moche dug that pit, engaged in ritual cannibalism, and tumbled the bones of more young men into the pit, and threw clay pots with pictures of the events into it, too."

"Did it work?" Tabitha asked.

"You mean did the rains stop? Not soon enough, apparently. The leaders of the Moche had failed, the gods had failed, and the people were starving. Very little rebuilding happened here after those last sacrifices, judging by the state of the temple, and the Moche civilization in this area flickered and died out."

The sun sank lower, turning the whole valley blood red. Blue had craftily planned to end the story at sunset. Why not be dramatic when you have a chance? But as the shadow of Cerro Blanco washed over the land, she felt a chill.

25

Next morning the party found itself bouncing southward from the hotel to the temples in a rented microbus. It was 9:00 A.M., later than Blue would have liked to start, but the hot water at the Enca Hotel in Trujillo went off between 10:00 P.M. and 7:00 A.M. She had made the decision to conserve funds, since they would be here over a week, and this hotel was definitely cheaper than the Hospedaje.

As they trundled along, Trujillo looked much more livable than Lima. The air was much cleaner, for one thing. The city plan was formal, with streets laid out in a grid pattern. There were many grand old stuccoed houses that reminded Blue of mansions in southern towns in the United States. Wooden balconies on the second floors, with ornately carved wooden shutters, looked out on the street. In the old days, gently bred women would watch the passing crowds from the balcony without the chance of being seen. The stucco was painted in soft, cheerful colors: light lime, terra cotta, pale lemon, and sea blue.

The microbus had no seat belts. In fact, cars here had no seat belts.

Blue held Adam in her lap and worried quietly. *Come to think of it,* Blue reflected sourly, *school buses in most of the U.S. don't have seat belts, either. A crime, but don't get me started.*

Seat belts were a rarity in a lot of the world where archaeologists went. Small wonder more archaeologists were killed or injured in auto accidents than by disease or human attacks.

Brad and Andy were drinking warm Inca Kola, which was yellow and tasted like Little Debbie snack cakes would if they were liquid. It was chock-full of caffeine.

Chatting among themselves about this or that item and whether they would need it and why and how many of them they would need, they unintentionally ignored Brad. He finally said, "Yes, but what are we *doing?*"

Blue said, "Doing?"

"This whole expedition. Why are we here?"

They all laughed, but Blue quickly realized that, even though they had all talked about aspects of the expedition, he couldn't possibly have any coherent idea of what was going on. She said, "We're collecting a variety of samples to check for hallucinogens."

Jasper said, "Vegetal material from the offrendas. Bone specimens, liver residue where we can get it. And hair, of course."

"Hair is great stuff," Blue said. "It's one of the parts of a human that takes a really long time to decay. And it retains trace evidence of what the person ate."

"Or was exposed to. Or even breathed," Jasper said.

"But—but," Brad said, excited and confused in what appeared to be equal parts, "but why?"

"Because hallucinations may have been the inspiration for all the earth's religions."

He looked more worried.

"Think of it this way. Think of early man, maybe just a step up from apes. The tribe is living on the African savannahs, barely subsisting, following migrating herds of animals for food. They know where certain plants are found and what times of year certain plants have fruit. Like baboon tribes do. But they're always just a meal or two from starvation."

"Uh, okay."

"They find a mushroom. Its name is *Stropharia cubensis* and it grows on cow dung."

"Yuck."

"You can say yuck, but they're hungry. Besides, you know human beings. If it's there, somebody is sure to try it."

Brad laughed in a way that suggested maybe he'd tried a few things, too.

"So they try them. And what happens? *Stropharia cubensis* mushrooms contain psilocybin. For one thing, they make you see double if you eat enough of them. What would these humans think that duplicate person was? It's not a big leap to think of it as the soul of the person you are looking at. Also, psilocybin produces hallucinations about absent or dead friends and relatives. How big a leap is it to think that your dead father has appeared from the afterlife? It's his soul."

Brad was silent.

"This isn't some original notion I've come up with. There are quite a few archaeologists who think this was pretty much what happened. Psilocybin has other benefits. In small doses, it helps you see better, which would be a big help to a hunter society. The technical description is that you have better edge-recognition."

Tabitha said, "Then as humans spread out across the world, they carried the ideas of souls with them. Even in the oldest prehistoric burials, you find jewelry or food or weapons buried with the corpse for use in the afterlife."

"As humans spread into other parts of the planet, they found other hallucinogens, and we know from archaeological records that they used them in their religious ceremonies."

Dr. Jungstedt, who rarely spoke, did so now. "Every society on earth has used some sort of consciousness-altering substance."

"But wasn't early man—uh—" Brad said.

"Go ahead. There's no such thing as a foolish question."

"Yeah—okay. Wasn't early man, like, stupid?"

Drake Rakowski gave a slight snort, but must have realized he'd better not say anything negative about Brad's question.

"Have you seen pictures of the female hominid they're calling Lucy?

She lived over three million years ago. She's been on the news a lot because there's going to be a traveling exhibit, the first time she's ever been out of Ethiopia."

"Yeah," Rakowski said. "Ugly gal. She's never gonna replace Paris Hilton."

Without bothering to give Drake a stern look, Blue kept focused on Brad.

"I saw a picture," Brad said. "She was covered with hair."

"That's an artist's reconstruction, you know. But she was standing upright and had pretty much the form of modern-day humans."

"The Moche weren't stupid. I get that. But Lucy probably was."

"Sure. By comparison to modern man. But let me put Lucy in the sequence of things. Go back before Lucy to early chimps. It used to be thought only humans could plan ahead. The idea was that other animals could use tools opportunistically, like birds that use sticks to get insects out of insect nests, or monkeys crack nuts with stones. But it's been shown that bonobo chimps can plan ahead. If they know they're going to a certain place where certain food is available, they'll take the right tools with them. The common ancestor to them and man existed maybe fifteen million years ago. That means it's been a long, long time that humanlike intelligence has been around."

"It's a big step from there to religion," Drake said, smiling at Tabitha. Their microbus hit a pothole, sending all of them up in the air for a half second. Drake used the jolt to slide closer to Tabitha.

Adam went, "Wheeee!"

"Well, sure," Blue said. "But it's not such a big step if you realize that even chimps are conscious of themselves as individuals."

Drake said, "You can't know that."

"Actually, you can—"

"Wait a minute," Andy said. "My Labrador is conscious. He gets happy and sad and disappointed. He even gets embarrassed if he does something stupid, like barking at me before he sees it's me."

"Well, he may. I don't know how to prove that. But I mean *self*-conscious. Tell me this. Have you ever watched your dog when he looks in a mirror?"

"Sure. He thinks there's another dog there. He growls."

"But a chimp knows the reflection is really him."

"You can't *possibly* know what a chimp is thinking!" Drake repeated.

"Yes, we do. They study the reflection for a while, and then they start to see that when they move an arm, the reflection does. So they begin to make gestures, and groom themselves."

"You still can't be sure they know it's them."

"Some researchers put dots of red paint on the foreheads of some of the chimps. When the chimps next looked in the mirror, they made surprised faces, and then they touched their foreheads. *Their* foreheads, not the reflections in the mirrors."

Brad said, "Cool!"

Blue said, "Dogs don't do that. Not even gorillas do that. They appear to think the gorilla in the mirror is another gorilla."

Drake was silent.

"Researchers have even anesthetized the chimps before they dyed the foreheads, so they wouldn't know the painting had happened. Only chimps, dolphins, and elephants can be proved to be self-conscious."

"Elephants look in mirrors?"

"Yes, and study themselves. Then some researchers painted colorless stuff on some elephants and a red color on others. The ones with the red spots touched the spots. The others didn't."

"How did we get on this topic?" Jasper asked.

Blue said, "I was coming to the point."

Jasper smiled. "I thought you were."

"Brad was asking about primitive man. If you realize that even chimpanzees can recognize themselves and reflect on the way they look, and can plan ahead, then it's no stretch to think of the earliest hominids, with bigger brains, as being really very smart and self-aware."

Tabitha said, "We know that they started putting a dead person's belongings into his grave very early."

Blue said, "And painting the dead with ochre—iron oxide, hematite."

Jasper said, "At the dawn of the human race, they may already have been thinking about the survival of the dead person—call it a soul—"

Blue said, "Early humans depended on hallucinogens to give them insight into their world. And hope. And meaning. Their world was full of unpredictable events, earthquakes and volcanoes, and disease."

Jasper said, "The more organized the societies became, the more important the hallucinogen was for religious rites."

"Our culture believes that what people see when they take hallucinogens is imaginary and false," Blue said. "Ancient cultures believed that these visions were true."

"Not so ancient, either," Jungstedt muttered. "Think of the visions of the Christian saints."

Blue said, "Early Christians also produced visions by fasting."

"And scourging themselves," Jasper said.

Brad said, "Well, okay. I've heard about this. But, if everybody already knows that all these early societies depended on hallucinogens, why do we have to come down here and find them?"

Blue had been getting the impression for several days that Brad was smarter than his modest high school record would indicate. There was a good brain working under there, somewhat obscured by his puppylike nature.

"It's not just here that we're looking. Professor Martello and Dr. Jungstedt have gathered samples in Tibet, Scotland, the Aleutian Islands, Mauritania, and Japan. Five sites in the last year and a half."

"But why do it at all if everyone knows it?"

"To test the hypothesis," Jungstedt said.

Blue said, "Part of science is actually *demonstrating* what everybody thinks they know." She thought she sounded pompous.

Jasper said, "People may think they know something but it may turn out to be untrue. You have to pin it down. You have to be able to say 'The X used Y amount of Z on feast days.'"

"Also, while we know some things, we don't know the whole story. We want to be factual. For instance, the Moche used tobacco to produce hallucinations."

"But tobacco isn't an hallucinogen," Drake said.

"Well, actually it is. But that's not what most people use it for today. The tobacco we use isn't very hallucinogenic. But we know from friezes and pottery that the Moche's gave them visions. So, we need to know, was their tobacco different from the tobacco we know today?"

"And of course it was," Jasper said. "They were cultivating descendants of wild tobacco that they clearly selected—"

"To be high-octane," Blue said, earning a nod from Jasper. He went on.

"Tobacco is a member of the nightshade family. It's related to tomatoes, potatoes, eggplants, and peppers, all South American natives. And it's related to some strong hallucinogens. Belladonna, mandrake, henbane, and thornapple. So it comes by its hallucinogenic powers naturally."

Blue said, "Ancient people selected and bred it, almost as soon as they discovered farming."

"*As* soon," Jasper said. "Tobacco was probably the first farmed crop in all the Americas."

"They developed *Nicotiana tabacum* and *Nicotiana rustica* from the wild plants, and we can be sure they were bred for their psychological impact. They aren't food plants. They both have far more nicotine than the wild plants. *Tabacum* can have as much as nine percent nicotine in its leaves. *Rustica* goes as high as eighteen percent. That's a *lot* of one of the most toxic plant substances in the world. Sixty milligrams of nicotine can kill you, if it's just dropped on your *skin*, not even swallowed. If you took the amount of nicotine in one ordinary cigar and extracted it and injected it, you could kill two full-grown men."

Jasper said, "We know that the ancestor of *tabacum* and *rustica* was intentionally cultivated here more than four thousand years before the first Egyptian pyramids."

Blue said, "But for the purposes of our book, it's not enough just to know that in a general way. We have to look at the organs of ancient Moche mummies and see what they actually used back then."

"And how much," Jungstedt said.

"We hope to find some kidney tissue. Nicotine is primarily excreted by the kidneys, not the liver," Jasper said.

"And the way they used it was definitely for its hallucinogenic properties. Spanish explorers from the 1500s talk about shamans in Peru intoxicating themselves with tobacco, and falling into stupors, and waking later, telling about visits to the gods."

"What I wonder," Drake Rakowski drawled, "is why you have to come all the way down here to gather specimens. I mean, it's great for my pictures. But is that why? You want pictures? For your book?" He was implying that Blue and Jasper were doing extra and unnecessary work and spending unnecessary money to make a book that would be popular and sell a lot of copies and presumably make a lot of money.

Smiling his sly, sleepy smile, he said, "Why not just go to a museum in the States and take some samples from an old South American mummy?" Proud of himself, he patted Tabitha on the thigh.

"Contamination," said Dr. Jungstedt.

Drake directed his next question to Jungstedt, but looked sideways at Blue with a grin. This confrontational behavior of his, she thought, could become a problem. He said, "How contaminated could a museum exhibit be?"

"Immensely much!" Jungstedt said.

Drake actually winked at Blue. Maybe he was making fun of Jungstedt's accent. She began to wonder whether she had made a mistake in bringing him. But he made such wonderful pictures.

Bengt Jungstedt sat up straight, pointed a finger at Drake, and spoke softly but firmly. "Mr. Rakowski. Use your mind. Think of what happens to a mummy. First, it's dug out of the ground, maybe by people who aren't very careful about how they work. Suppose wild tobacco is growing nearby. You understand that possibility, sir?"

Drake didn't answer.

"We will look for pollen in the clothing and hair of the dead. Pollen lasts thousands of years. Tobacco pollen looks like little round balls. We can obtain a DNA sequence from it and identify the variety. With tobacco farming a big industry all over the world, there is much information on tobacco DNA types. But there is pollen swirling around us right this minute, pollen in the air in this bus and in your lungs. Take a breath. You are taking in pollen. Unless the samples are taken the instant the grave is opened, modern pollen grains could become mixed and be misidentified as ancient."

"Well, sure——" Drake said.

Jungstedt, usually so courteous, cut him off. "And let us now talk about contamination. Until fairly recently archaeologists sometimes used preservatives on ancient material. A terrible thing."

"So just don't analyze those items."

"Ah-ah! Then there are fumes and moisture that get into the specimens during shipping. And when they arrive at the museum, there is dust in the museum's air. A body may be laid out on an examination table and left there for weeks as it is being studied, with dust falling on it, and flecks of skin from the researchers, products of combustion from the building's heating systems."

"Okay, okay," Drake said.

"Insects, dust mites, moths!" Jungstedt said.

"Let alone the fact that researchers would clean the specimens," Jasper added.

"Other than just brushing off the dirt, you mean?" Tabitha asked, deftly moving her leg away from Drake's hand.

Jungstedt said, "Yes, but even brushes have trace evidence on them. Archaeologists did not routinely sterilize them between uses until recently. Some do not even now."

Jasper said, "Even water contains all sorts of trace chemicals."

Drake said, "Stop! You've convinced me." He cast a sour look at Blue, but he was probably irritated by Tabitha's coolness.

Blue said, "One thing you have to remember about us is that this isn't a typical dig. We're looking for what crime scene technicians would call trace evidence. Past archaeologists—even present-day archaeologists, for that matter—mostly don't do this. Our requirements are so stringent, we need tombs that are opened the first time right before our eyes."

26

The grave lay open before them, shadowy in the early light. The sun touched the very top of the Huaca del Sol, far across the plain, but the shadow of Cerro Blanca covered the Huaca de la Luna.

Their guide from yesterday, Federico, had been joined by Professor Cruz from the National University of Trujillo. She and Blue had met while doing graduate work at the University of New Mexico.

Ana Cruz was a slender woman with dark hair that reached the base of her spine. At the nape of her neck, a jade clip that looked ancient held the hair back out of her face. Blue could almost see her on this spot two thousand years earlier.

Their goal was to take small samples of food, pollen, hair, and bone the instant they were exposed. In cases where they could identify the remains of the liver or kidneys, they would take tiny pieces of them, too.

To do archaeology in Peru required a *credencial*. The INC, the Instituto Nacional de Cultura, checked out all found archaeological objects. What you found became property of the INC. The samples Blue's group planned to take were not precisely artifacts. Tissue samples fell into an un-defined category. They had no intrinsic value, like gold masks or stirrup-spout pottery had, so there was no black market for them, as there was for artifacts. Nevertheless, they had dotted every "I" and crossed every "T" the Peruvian government could think of.

Andy, Tabitha, and Blue hung back a few feet, not wanting to crowd the grave. Andy looked pale and sick after his illness of the day before, but hadn't complained. He hadn't said much of anything today, in fact. Jasper and Dr. Jungstedt knelt with Cruz as she reached into the grave and re-moved three ceramic offrenda jars.

Blue thought it was too bad their photographer, Drake Rakowski, wasn't here to record the moment. He was back at the hotel, the latest victim of turista. Cruz would have made a beautiful picture, leaning into the grave with her slender arms, long hair, and classic profile. She could have been the acolyte who placed the jars here a thousand years ago, re-moving them again. She, Jungstedt, and Jasper were meticulous in brush-ing the last sand off the outside of the jars. Tabitha had set down a satchel of paraphernalia and now laid a large sheet of white paper on the ground to receive the jars, and Andy, a much inferior stand-in for Drake this morning, recorded each move with a digital camera. Drake would have used film and digital both. At least Andy, if no artist, would document everything they did.

The point of all the care, Blue reflected—the point, for that matter, of obtaining fresh, untouched specimens of each cadaver or mummy—was to make it impossible for critics later to claim contamination had produced their results.

What am I saying, impossible? Critics will criticize us anyway. That's what academics do. The point is to have a damn good answer for them.

Slowly, slowly, Jasper and Cruz cracked the seal on the first jar. In it was some light brown vegetal material, which, to echo Brad's words, "didn't look like much."

Jasper and Professor Cruz both uttered a satisfied "Ahhh!" The seal had held—for more than a thousand years. The contents had not been damaged by moisture from the floods.

Tabitha presented containers. Dr. Jungstedt wrote out labels—the date, what time it was, where the material had been found, and who was present. Andy took photographs. Jasper lifted minute samples with a stainless steel spoon. The choreography could have been taking place in an operating room.

What with opening the jars, taking the samples, then taking bone samples from the skeleton still in the ancient grave and soil samples from underneath the rib cage of the skeleton, where the organs had decayed and passed into the earth, and packaging it all, they would be two hours at least.

Blue daydreamed about the chance of finding a full picture here of the ceremonial use of tobacco and ayahuasca. Ayahuasca was similar to the acacia bark used by the Israelites.

Dr. Ana Cruz was helpful, and especially kind in helping Blue because hallucinogens were not her favorite topic. Like many serious archaeologists, she was cautious about feeding into the somewhat woo-woo subculture that found meaning in induced trances and saw spirits everywhere. Some archaeologists virtually ignored psychoactive substances. Blue had read long scholarly books about sites that abounded with peyote or Syrian rue or poppies that said not one word about them. Ana was far more honest than that. She was just cautious.

Blue made sketches of some of what she saw. On a real dig, she would have an archaeological artist along, who would make really good sketches. She just did a few for her own use, to jog her memory, even though she carried a disposable camera as well.

Far down the slope, Adam and Brad played on the sand. Adam's squeals of delight reached up to her. Blue knew he was safe, but she couldn't help looking down every few minutes to make sure.

She set down her satchel next to Tabitha and strode out of the low passage and down the slope to the visitors' entry booth. Adam and Brad were playing just a few feet from the ticket seller.

Has there ever been a child who didn't love sand? Before her dad died, Blue's parents had taken her and her sister to the Lake Michigan beaches as often as they could in the summers when Blue was little. There were long, long stretches of beautiful pale sand just perfect for making into sand castles, or her favorite trick, digging a hole down to water.

No water here in the Peruvian desert, of course, but Brad had come up with a game that involved zooming sticks by hand around an oval-shaped track he had dug. *What a wonderful touch Brad has with Adam!* Brad sat right in the sand, his legs splayed out, making "Mmwwrrr! Zzzzzmmm!" sounds.

"Zuuuuum!" Adam said.

"Wooooz!" said Brad. Adam's car zoomed clockwise around the track. Brad's zoomed counterclockwise. "Oh! Oh!" said Brad.

"Oh! Oh!" said Adam.

"Collision!" Brad said, throwing his stick up in the air after the impact. "*Wipe out!*"

"Ipe out!" said Adam, falling backward, plunging the back of his head into the sand.

Blue sat down in the sand to play with them. Kept her head out of the sand, though.

"You're good with him," she said.

"He's my buddy."

"Bummee, bummee, bummee," Adam said.

Blue said, "He's a happy little chap, isn't he?"

"Aren't all little kids happy?"

"Well, actually no. I wish."

"He sure doesn't like tourists, though."

"What do you mean?"

"Like yesterday. A bunch came by and he sort of whimpered and hid in my lap."

27

The breeze rolled a tumbleweed in a wobbly path across the broad driveway that led uphill. Pavia and Ratigan stared out through tinted windows
onto the plain a few miles out of Santa Magdalena.

The tumbleweed came to rest against the iron fence, where it was
kicked aside by a guard wearing high leather boots.

Two teams of guards seized the halves of the double iron gates, lifting them and walking them open. The other guards, who had searched the
cars and their occupants, stood back in flanking rows and watched. The
weapons taken from the visitors rested in a guard shack off to one side.

Once they had been checked and passed through the line of guards,
the eight Mercedes limos circled up the snaking driveway. They were led
by Osiel Heroles's red Humvee with four guards sitting inside carrying
rifles.

The area around the sprawling casa was utterly bare of vegetation.

"Pleasant spot," Pavia said.

Ratigan nodded grimly. "Homey."

"You were here before."

"No. I saw Heroles last year, but not here. It was about twenty miles east of here. It was a place with plants. Growing plants. Outdoors. Green stuff."

"He moves around a lot, I guess."

The eight black cars stopped when the Humvee did. The driver and front-seat passenger of the lead car jumped out and opened the back doors for Pavia and Ratigan. The driver of the second car got out and opened the door for a tall, elderly priest. From the other cars emerged Leeuwarden's six bodyguards and the Leeuwarden translator.

The Leeuwarden group walked slowly toward the front door of the large central building. The guards watching them muttered, *"Baboso."*

"Hueles a mierda."

"Tonta."

"Burro sabe."

Ratigan asked, "What are they saying?"

"Shh. Just insults. They don't like outsiders."

The priest strolled around back to a small building with smoke coming from its chimney. A kitchen, Pavia thought. There was a sweet smell of wood smoke in the air.

The area around the huge white stucco house and outbuildings was all bare sandy earth. From the rise of land Pavia could see over the surrounding walls across all the countryside for a mile in any direction.

"Could hold off an army from here," Ratigan said.

"All it needs is a moat and a portcullis."

Ratigan, ever annoyed at Pavia's allusions, raised his eyebrows at "portcullis."

One of the jefe's men barked something in Spanish. The Leeuwarden translator said, "They want our bodyguards to wait out here."

Ratigan said, "Shit."

"Tell them okay except for our translator."

Ratigan said, "I always knew we shouldn't both go into iffy situations."

"Think of the upside. Henry Wong is eager to take over."

"Shit."

"Heroles knows we're not the DEA. He knows we're not the *Federales*. He knows we're not competitors."

"Sure thing, Mr. Pavia. He knows we're from Leeuwarden and we're here to help him."

"My friend Señor Ratigan!"

"Osiel! *Buenos días mi amigo!*"

Laughing uproariously, slapping Ratigan on the back, Osiel Heroles shouted out several sentences, which Ratigan, speaking no Spanish beyond half a dozen common phrases, did not understand. Pavia understood, but behaved as if he did not.

The Leeuwarden translator said, "He says you should not try Spanish, as your accent is terrible."

Ratigan laughed.

"He says you sound like a Puerto Rican."

"This is my colleague, Mr. Robert Pavia." Pavia stepped forward into a big hug and backslapping as Ratigan said, "This is Mr. Heroles, our friend."

Pavia smiled, stepped back from the hug and extended his hand, bowing slightly. "An honor to meet you, sir."

Heroles appeared pleased with this and gestured them into a large tile-floored room. Several ornate wooden chairs with thick seat cushions stood around a heavy square table.

"You—there," Heroles said, pointing Pavia and Ratigan to a couple of the armchairs. The translators, his and theirs, he waved to two armless side chairs placed slightly farther back from the table. Three guards lounged next to the only door.

Leeuwarden's translator sat, but shifted uneasily in his seat.

There were drawers in the table, facing Heroles, and he pulled one out, scooping from it a double handful of cigars.

"*Selena! Encendedores!*"

Heroles scratched one armpit gleefully, and then the other one, while a beautiful young woman entered, carrying a wooden tray on which rested long wooden matches and a stone block. Chuckling happily, Heroles clipped three cigars with a cutter, licked all three, gave one each to Pavia and Ratigan. The woman lit a match by rubbing it across the stone and lighted Heroles's cigar. He stared down the front of her lacy blouse.

Then she held a lighted match for Pavia. With a brief glance at Ratigan, he pulled in the flame.

When Ratigan's cigar was also drawing well, Pavia said, "Splendid. Trinidad Extra?"

Heroles said, *"Sí."*

His translator said, "Yes."

The Leeuwarden translator said, "Yes." Pavia suppressed a smile.

At a scratching on the wall, Pavia looked, expecting that one of the guards had lit a match. But it was a lizard. "A gecko, Señor Heroles? It catches insects for you?"

A spate of Spanish emerged from Heroles, which Pavia understood, but did not respond to until the translators had both entered the fray.

Heroles's translator said, "Señor Heroles says that it is a Borneo gecko, not a Sinaloan gecko because Sinaloan geckos are very small and weak and almost transparent. Yes, it catches insects, as do geckos all over the warmer parts of the world."

The Leeuwarden translator added, "Heroles also said the Sinaloan geckos are all—uh—girls and not worthy to catch his bugs."

Heroles's translator looked offended. Heroles belched and muttered.

His translator said, "We import them."

Pavia wondered just how much money this oaf Heroles was worth.

Heroles was the new leader of the Sinaloa cartel, on the job just three years. He had replaced Joaquin Guzman Loera. At the age of fifty-two, Loera appeared on the *Forbes* magazine list of the world's richest people at number 701, just above the heir to the Campbell's soup fortune. Loera was worth a bit over one billion dollars. Maybe a hundred million more.

Which was remarkable, because he had been born in poverty in La Tuna Badiraguato, Mexico. His bullying father kicked him out of the house when he was a child. He had little education and was illiterate as an adult.

He had apprenticed himself to El Padrino "Godfather" Miguel Ángel Félix Gallardo, jefe of the most powerful drug cartel in Mexico at the time. But Loera split off after a few years, founded his own cartel and expanded fast, establishing posts in seventeen Mexican states. When Gallardo was arrested in 1989, Loera took over some of those territories as well.

Loera once went to a restaurant with a small platoon of his bodyguards. His guards confiscated all the other diners' cell phones but instructed the patrons to go on eating. Loera also ate dinner. Then he had his bodyguards return the patrons' cell phones, paid for all the dinners, and left.

There was no word on whether the diners had enjoyed their meal.

In some quarters he was admired—he played a Robin Hood character, making improvements in villages, drilling wells, and putting electric light in cemeteries.

Arrested in Guatemala in 1993, Loera was sent to a maximum security prison in Jalisco, Mexico, and scheduled to be extradited to the U.S. He escaped, hidden in a prison laundry van, adding to his Teflon legend. Puente Grande "Big Bridge" prison has been nicknamed Puerte Grande "Big Door."

Loera bragged that he spent five million a month on bribes.

But Loera's days of power were numbered. His aggressive money hunger inflamed the turf wars and his son Edgar was shot by rivals outside a shopping mall. Then Cardinal Juan Jesus Posada Ocampo was gunned down at an airport by rivals who thought the cardinal was Loera.

Loera went on the run. He was now wanted by the governments of the U.S. and Mexico, and also Interpol, but nobody could find him. Rumor had it that he didn't move around much, less than most big traffickers. In the few cases where the Mexican police had a lead and swooped in, Loera slipped out of the noose minutes before they arrived. The U.S. declared a five-million-dollar reward for information leading to his arrest. No one has claimed it.

However, his ability to run his cartel had been mortally wounded.

Heroles, a cousin of Loera, quickly moved into the vacuum. Either that or it was Heroles who tipped the Federales where Loera was and got him arrested in the first place.

Heroles came into power a more violent man even than Loera. He disappeared his two contiguous rivals from Durango and Sonora. One was kidnapped from his home and was caused to vanish. The other went to church one Sunday and never came out.

Now and then Heroles gave his lieutenants presents tied up in red, white, and green ribbons, the Mexican national colors, containing cigars and one or two fingers. He figured it would keep his men loyal.

In return he was loyal to his lieutenants. A handful of his men were being held at Cieneguillas Prison in Zacatecas. Late one night fifty-three prisoners simply walked out, right past the guards, under the eyes of working surveillance cameras. Accompanied by men wearing fake and outdated police uniforms, they got into fake police cars and screamed away with sirens shrieking. A fake-official helicopter circled overhead. Security cameras showed the guards simply standing around watching the prisoners leave.

The footage was posted later on YouTube.

Heroles had been in power less than three years, but Pavia estimated his worth at around seven hundred million, certainly one of the richest men on the planet.

As a native of Venezuela, Pavia spoke Spanish, but of a Venezuelan type that sounded Italian to most North Americans. In any case, he did not intend to use it here. In British-accented English, he said, "We have come to discuss how we can help you."

A flurry of back and forth translation produced "I need no help."

"Not you personally," Pavia said, smiling and inclining his head in an agreeable manner. He tried not to notice a second gecko scurrying across the wall behind Heroles.

Heroles smiled more broadly than Pavia and said nothing for a moment. Then he spoke and the translator said, "My territory is the largest in Mexico."

"Indeed. Now, the problem as we see it," Pavia went on, "is the perception of lawlessness in Mexico that the North Americans have. *No, no,* no reflection on you! It is an all-Mexico problem."

Heroles spoke. "I do not care," said the translators in unison.

"Let me just make the case, jefe. I do not personally care that the tourist trade in Mexico is depressed. My problem is the effect on the smooth movement of our products. The border wars between cartels are spilling over into Texas and California. This heightens our visibility and heightens resistance."

Heroles cursed and neither translator bothered to try to find an English equivalent.

"It was the ebbing of the Cali cartel, under the onslaught of the American DEA and other forces, that made the trade in Mexico boom. But these things can change. Surely you wouldn't want to attract the lightning here?"

Heroles puffed a stream of smoke toward the Leeuwarden translator, who wisely sucked it up and didn't cough.

"We are proposing," Pavia said, "a sort of high-level parley among the leaders of the seven Mexican cartels. What I would hope to have come out of this is a reduction of inter-cartel violence. And if a real parceling of areas can be worked out, it might be possible to shift product back and forth to cross the U.S. border in different places at different times, depending on where the resistance is least. This could also help confound the U.S. border guards." He waited while Heroles's translator caught up with what he had said.

Heroles pressed the tip of his lighted cigar against the thigh of the guard standing next to him. The cloth of his uniform singed, but the man said nothing.

Pavia said, "Even now, California is seriously considering decriminalizing marijuana. The California action has come about for three reasons, in my opinion. First that the usefulness of medical marijuana has cast question on its criminality. In fact, the U.S. government has announced that people carrying medical marijuana will no longer be arrested at airports. This is a major shift. Second, that marijuana is being perceived as not so very dangerous. But thirdly, and very importantly, the Americans are fed up with border killings. Can you imagine what decriminalization of just this one product would do to our profits?"

"Mierda!" Heroles shouted. He stood up, threw his cigar at the wall and slammed the table with both fists. Then he shoved himself backward into his chair, pulled open a drawer in the table and jerked out a huge pistol.

Ratigan leaped to his feet. A Heroles guard seized Ratigan's elbows and pinned them to his body.

Heroles fired at the wall, splattering one of the geckos.

Heroles shouted "Olé!" and with a big grin dropped the gun back in the drawer.

He said something like "*de serpiente*."

The translator said, "It is snake shot. Like birdshot."

Ratigan subsided into his chair.

Now Pavia, who had sat quietly, languidly, one leg crossed over the other, noticed several stains on the walls. Gecko blood, surely. "But geckoes control the insects, do they not, Señor Heroles?"

Heroles spoke and the Leeuwarden translator said, "We import them by the dozens."

Heroles laughed uproariously, rocking back and forth in his chair. Watching him laugh, Pavia thought, *Ojos de piedros. Eyes of stone.*

As they were leaving, Heroles spoke and looked meaningfully at Pavia. The Leeuwarden translator, who by now was sweating profusely, said, "I would go to such a meeting."

Pavia said, "Excellent."

The translator sighed in relief as they walked through the door—and then uttered a short gasp as Heroles grabbed his forearm. Heroles chuckled and spoke.

The translator said, "Uh. There's always another gecko."

"Well, wasn't that fun?" Ratigan said when they were in the car and feeling far enough away to be safe.

"Very special, Mr. Ratigan."

"Be glad it's not Colombia."

"Right. Paramilitary armies and land mines."

"Shit."

"Indeed. I would like to see him when he's on his good behavior."

"That *was* his good behavior, Mr. Pavia."

28

"Look at that," Obrador said.

Half of Mexico City was spread out before them. Pavia realized that the air pollution, which people constantly complained about, was not showing itself today. The city looked golden. Still, you would probably not be aware of air pollution in this office. The air that sighed softly into the room was cooled and filtered, and had a hint of scent like frangipani. From up here, when the smog came, Obrador would see it as yellow fog filling in the streets below. Up here the sun would still shine.

The Santa Fe section was in the west part of city, in the *delegaciones* Cuajimalpa and Álvaro Obregón. Pavia and Ratigan and their entourage had driven in on Paseo de la Reforma, a broad, straight boulevard planted with trees and flowering shrubs.

"Look at that," Obrador repeated.

"It's beautiful." High-rises, their glass windows glittering in the late morning sun, surrounded small patches of bright jade green.

"It *looks* beautiful. This entire district," Obrador said in perfect, but U.S.-accented, English, "was planned to be accessed by car. There are no street-level perks—cafes, corners where men play music, none of that. Almost no public transportation. No pedestrian walkways to speak of."

"But the buildings are beautiful," Pavia said.

"Oh, no doubt. Beautiful, beautiful high-rise buildings. A shopping mall that is the second largest in Latin America. Three college campuses. Three!"

"It is something to be proud of."

"Oh, yes? Constant traffic jams, because there is no public transportation. A vacancy rate in these beautiful, beautiful buildings of twenty-seven percent and increasing. Santa Fe was built with great optimism after the 1985 earthquakes. Built to be near high income neighborhoods and the new tollway to Toluca. The master plan was laid out during a big boom in the economy. Then, in 1994, comes the economic tumble. Not all the planned buildings were even built and still we have a huge percentage of vacancies. It shows a criminally stupid lack of farsightedness."

Obrador was dressed in a meticulously tailored charcoal gray suit— Kiton, from Naples, Pavia thought. Hand stitched. The bespoke version, twenty thousand at least, and Obrador could no doubt afford a new one for each day of the week every day of the year. Pavia had been told that Obrador employed a man exactly his height, weight, and shape to jet to Naples four times a year and be fitted. If Obrador gained two pounds, his stand-in must gain two pounds before leaving for Italy.

He had the high, thin arched nose of the pure Castillian Spaniard, with dark eyes a little too close together. A harpy eagle, Pavia thought, *arpion*. Obrador's cheeks were freshly barbered and powdered and his nails showed manicuring and subtle clear matte polish. His office was an entire three floors of the glossy business tower, and included the penthouse, where he and Ratigan and Pavia now stood, Pavia admiring and Obrador criticizing the view.

Obrador was their last visit. Pavia and Ratigan had called on five cartels in the five days since they saw Heroles. Both wanted to get home.

"Well, but don't let me dishearten you," Obrador said. "Come and sit down." He led them to an arc-shaped nest of five leather armchairs upholstered in a deep plum color. A humidor of glossy bloodwood stood in the center of a small round table, flanked by a lighter fashioned from an Aztec wind whistle.

"Smoke if you like, please."

He gestured at the cigars in left side of the humidor. "Behike," he said arrogantly. "From Altadis."

"Named for the chief of the Taino tribe," Pavia said. "I collect Taino artifacts."

A slight tightening around Obrador's eyes showed displeasure. He gestured at the other cigars in the box. "And Gurkhas."

Pavia knew enough to resist saying, "Yes, made by His Majesty's Reserve. I buy them myself." Instead he said, "Wonderful. We certainly appreciate your hospitality." Around thirty thousand dollars for a box of forty. He picked out a Gurkha.

Ratigan took one but stared at Obrador sourly.

"You've come to talk about the increasing violence," Obrador said.

"Yes. We are very troubled—"

"If we thought there were economic problems in Mexico before, tourism is off another fifteen percent in the last quarter. The repercussions extend into manufacturing, the service industries, even agriculture!"

"Yes, and the underlying cause is the product with which we are all concerned."

"Which is why you're here. Exactly."

Clearly, Obrador, for all his elaborate courtesy, liked to control the conversation. But now, as if to make up for his brief pique, he said, "I am aware of the advantages of Leeuwarden's existence, and I believe our contributions to the general Leeuwarden fund are well spent. I am entirely alive to the realities of the world of commerce. Supply and demand. The demand changes. Supply perhaps even more so. The best poppy growing regions of the world are becoming warmer and dryer. What if production has to move? Methamphetamine production has become a basement industry in many places. Freebasing was in. Now it's out. We need to have mastery of shipment of ingredients, so we need a global presence."

He hit a touch screen on a small controller near his hand and a large flatscreen on the wall came to life.

"Mexico!" Obrador said, throwing his arms wide, as if presenting them with the entire nation.

"Here you see my territory. I control the largest cartel in the country." He flicked his finger at his touch screen and the area on the map from

Guadalajara in south central Mexico, up past Chihuahua to El Paso, Texas was highlighted in red.

"Now here is the Golfo, the Gulf Cartel." The screen showed the southeast coast of Mexico, facing toward Florida on the Gulf, highlighted in blue.

"Now this is where the Cali Group has a hold," he said, highlighting the tail of Mexico in purple.

"Gulf Cartel Federation here," he said. The area facing the upper Gulf of Mexico up into Monterrey and Brownsville, Texas, appeared in yellow.

Pavia said, "And the Tijuana—"

"Yes, the Tijuana Cartel Federation, as the DEA calls it." The Tijuana group was at the top of Baja and the southern end of California. Obrador chuckled. "Makes the DEA furious. Right up there like a burr under their saddle." He went on.

"Juarez Cartel." From Hermosillo up through Tucson.

"And Sinaloa. The old Loera area. And Loera had Juarez, too. Some of Hermosillo and up to Tucson in Arizona."

Ratigan started to say "Heroles claims to be the largest—" but Pavia stopped him with a minuscule shake of his head, just before Obrador said, "Heroles! Osiel Heroles is a peasant! He is a cultureless, bumbling pig."

Ratigan said, "Uh—"

"It's no wonder he raises hackles. I had hopes he might keep his head down. But he's no better than Guzman Loera."

"Nevertheless," Pavia said, "it's becoming more and more important that you all work together. This constant fighting on cartel borders is wasting your energy, your resources, and even your people's lives."

"Ah, well, I can't allow these donkeys to grab my product or my routes."

"This warfare is doing nothing but attracting the lightning. This is how it was internationally before we organized."

"It would be better if we had just one man in charge in Mexico."

"Possibly. But we don't have to address that yet."

"And I suppose you're just going to say to these tough men, 'Let's all be nice now.'"

"Close. I am going to set up a summit meeting."

"Like the Apalachin Summit? The conference of Mafia chieftains? That didn't work out so well," Obrador said.

"Not because the capos couldn't have worked together. It failed because they were stupid. They drove into a small upstate New York town in dozens of expensive cars and attracted the attention of local law enforcement. Over a hundred crime bosses from as far away as Italy descend on a little town of a thousand people. Please!"

"True."

"Señor Obrador, surely if you undertook this summit you'd plan it better," Pavia said.

"I certainly would."

"And there are only seven of you chieftains. No reason to attract any attention at all."

"Seven plus entourage."

"Of course."

"Well, I suppose it couldn't hurt."

Pavia said, "I will set it up."

"Yes, if I were to set it up, they would think I was taking too much power on myself."

"Exactly. But you and Heroles, as the two largest, will pick the spot. You know the territory."

"Yes."

"And you seven will get together and work out a détente. Draw boundaries and stick to them."

When they reached their guarded car and could talk freely, Ratigan said, "You noticed how his fancy flatscreen maps peeled a whole lot off his competitors' areas?"

"Yes. He thinks we don't know who's who and where's what."

"And you noticed he slipped in the idea that it would be better if one man was in charge."

"Yes. He wants all of Mexico for himself."

"You're dreaming if you think you can get them together and hammer out a détente."

"Maybe. They'd be like two scorpions in a bottle."

"Seven scorpions in a bottle."

Once Ratigan and Pavia were back on the company jet, they fully relaxed.

Ratigan said, "If we had to pick one man, I'd pick Heroles."

"I don't like him."

"I don't like him, either, but the distributors in-country aren't going to be able to get along with a playboy like Obrador."

"He's a smart playboy. He's kept himself Teflon."

"He runs everything by word of mouth. He talks to three trusted lieutenants, they each talk to ten. Each of the thirty instructs another ten. Nothing is in writing or on a computer. The Federales can't get anything on him. But the man on the ground resents that."

"Not when they're paid."

"It can't last. Sooner or later the U.S. will indict him."

Pavia said, "Heroles is a blusterer." He didn't mention the gun incident and Ratigan's reaction. He was somewhat surprised that Ratigan favored him.

"Suppose we wanted to force them into line?" Ratigan said.

"What would you suggest?"

"Sabotage them. Get some inside people who can sabotage the product. Dilute it, so they're running in a cheap product."

"And we could get people who'd take that risk?"

"Pay them."

Pavia said, "True. And then get them out of there."

"Or not. If we cared."

"We might want to be believed in the future."

"Oh, *future! Future!* You're always worrying about the future."

"Well, that's how you make sure you have one."

"So we spirit them away. Second suggestion. Have a couple of saboteurs poison the product. Now *that* would destroy a cartel's trade for a long time."

"And make all product look scary to people."

"It could work once without much blowback. Third possibility. Poison their fertilizer. Kill their plants."

"Not bad. I like how you think, Mr. Ratigan."

Ratigan smiled.

Pavia said, "There is one more way."

"Oh?"

"If we have a hold-out, If somebody's stubborn, give all our info on him to the DEA and Federales."

"God, no, Mr. Pavia. Not law enforcement. That's dirty pool!"

29

At dusk they all headed back to Trujillo.

As they pulled the group together to get in the cars, Jasper came over to me.

"It's so good to have you back," he said, meaning back on a dig, or in this case on a collection trip.

"It's great for me. I love it."

"I was wrong about Adam. He hasn't been any trouble."

"Thanks to Brad."

"Only partly. Adam—well, I don't exactly know how to put this. Adam enriches our lives."

Blue's first order of business at the hotel was to shampoo Adam's hair.

Then, quickly, before the hot water ran out, she took a bath in the strange oval bathtub.

Adam and Blue had played in the dust while the crew took more samples. Blue carried a bottle of water, as they all did. There were a few stones in the dusty earth near the Huaca de la Luna.

They sat, legs outspread the way children love to sit, and Blue would pick up a rock and say, "Gray."

Adam would clap his hands, because now he knew what was coming next.

Blue poured a few drops of water on it. She said, "Red!" The stone, once wet, showed its true colors. Adam grabbed at another stone. She poured water into the bottle cap and handed it to him. He poured it—about a third of it, since most went on his leg and her foot—onto the rock. It turned a dark red. He chortled and shouted, "Stop!" He pronounced it "Pop." But she knew what he meant. Red was the color of stoplights. His father had told him that.

Blue blinked a few seconds, thinking of Edward. He would never see Adam grow up. Nor would Adam have a father to teach him father-things.

Dr. Ana Cruz met them for dinner at El Mochica on Bolivar. It was unpretentious inside, but well known by business visitors, like Blue's group, for its food.

Adam, in a booster seat, was killing his dish of roasted corn and grains, with special attention to mashing corn kernels into small flat coins, when Ana said, "Would you like to help me find the Last Lord of Sipan?"

THE RISING PLAINS, PERU

JUNE 10

They convoyed east in three ancient Jeeps. Dr. Ana Cruz drove the first, with Blue in front next to her, and Tabitha in the back with a lot of gear. Behind them in a second Jeep were Dr. Jungstedt, Andy, and Drake Rakowski with more gear, especially cameras. Jasper, two representatives from the Instituto Nacional de Cultura, and a whole lot more gear were in the last car. The land east of Trujillo sloped upward very gradually, but had a feeling of flatness unless they looked back and saw all the country they had passed through falling away behind them.

Blue had said that there were no foothills to the Andes. That was true but not the whole story. The land rose like a ramp, and on it the terraces near the rivers where the crops grew in irrigated patches stood out green or gold against the brown un-irrigated land around.

Most of the way, the road followed the line of the river. There were small villages with children chasing chickens, rolling balls, and, Tabitha said, wearing some of the most beautiful, colorful clothes she had ever seen. Potatoes, squash, and fruit grew in the fields. The soil looked rocky. Soon they saw llamas and alpaca.

"Do they grow coca?" Tabitha asked Dr. Cruz.

"Most of the coca is grown over the Ceja de la Selva," she said.

Tabitha asked, "What is that?"

"The Brow of the Jungle. See the mountain crest?"

Blue was proud of Tabitha that she didn't say "Duh!" or the equivalent.

No one could miss seeing the mountains. The Andes dominated the whole eastern side of the world. Jagged white peaks loomed ahead and looked just a few hundred feet away, even though Blue knew they were many miles off.

Ana said, "People don't understand how close the jungle is when they see the glaciers on the mountains. But just over that range, you drop quickly down into the Amazon rain forest. As you drop down, it gets hotter and hotter and wetter and wetter. In the upper jungle there is a perfect climate for growing coca."

"Isn't cocaine illegal?" Tabitha asked.

"Not coca leaf. The ENACO, the Empresa Nacional de Coca, licenses growers to grow a certain amount for chewing and drinking in tea. And for their own personal consumption. The government is going to put coca leaf in children's lunch next year." She glanced in the rearview mirror and smiled at Tabitha's surprised face.

"We'll stop for some coca tea in a little while. It's supposed to prevent altitude sickness."

If it got hotter as you went down the other side of the Andes, it was getting cooler as they went up this side.

Blue thought how upset Brad would be to learn he had missed the coca tea. He'd think that was an adventure for sure.

He was in Trujillo with Adam.

Brad and Adam were to spend a day and a half at the Little Sisters of Santa Teresa in Trujillo, the same order of nuns who had sent one of their number to babysit Adam the night they spent in Lima.

Blue had gone with Brad and Adam to check out the facility, which was next to the convent. It was still difficult for Blue to be away from Adam, even though she knew it was foolish to be frightened. Whatever horrible set of circumstances had placed him in danger in Chicago certainly wouldn't happen here, thousands of miles away.

As far as going back to Chicago was concerned, her house was up for sale and she hoped it sold quickly. She never wanted to set foot in it again.

They had entered the visitors' residence next door to the convent, with Blue completely willing to walk away if it wasn't perfect. But it was beautiful—whitewashed stucco walls, spotless terra-cotta floors, bright Peruvian textiles on the walls.

Adam saw none of this. He took one look at the three nuns who had come to show them around and fell on the floor laughing uproariously. His face turned red. His eyes teared and still he giggled. It was the headpieces, those soaring white headpieces.

One of her friends told Blue about a feeling she had frequently had when her children were little. Blue had never experienced it so strongly as she had then. What she wanted to know so badly was, what did they look like to Adam? *What did he think they were?* Did he think they were women with the heads of birds? What? Her friend had told her there would be times when she would very, very much want to know what he was thinking. And she would wish she could ask him when he was older and he could tell her what it was. But by then he would have completely forgotten it.

The three nuns began giggling, too.

Clearly, they weren't grim and punitive. Blue felt okay leaving him there.

He would room with Brad. Brad, being male, could not set foot inside the convent, but the nuns would come to their room in the annex in the morning, fix breakfast, stay and play with Adam if he liked, and so on.

"Brad," Blue said, "you stay right with him."

"Every minute, Ms. E."

"And only bottled water."

"Absolutely, Ms. E."

"Even when—"

"Even when he brushes his teeth."

Adam had been finding it hard to believe that he could only brush his teeth—he had six of them now—in bottled water. And only rinse his toothbrush in bottled water. In fact, Blue suspected Brad found it hard to believe, too, but tap water was just not safe here.

"We should be back tonight. Tomorrow at the latest."

And now they were halfway up the mountain and Adam was left behind. Blue had decided the mountains were no place for an infant.

Why were we here? I, of course, have visions of ceremonial hallucinogens dancing in my head. It would be months, maybe years, before the find could be fully analyzed, but still—

Ana Cruz said, "A woman came into the university looking for an archaeologist. She'd found a pot, she said. Far up the mountain."

"What made you think it was important?"

"It was a very late Moche pot. So beautiful it must have been buried with a very highly placed person. Somebody at the level of a lord."

There was a brief silence in the car.

Blue said, "They were all buried in the temples, though, weren't they? The Huaca de la Luna and others?"

"Exactly. This is very unusual."

30

"Of course, he won't really be the Last Lord of Sipan," Ana said to Tabitha as Blue drove. "Sipan is farther south."

"So who is it?" Tabitha asked.

"Probably a lord of the Huaca del Sol people. It's a very big mystery, if what our pot-finding friend said is true."

"Who exactly is our pot-finder?" Blue asked.

"A hiker, not a guaquero, thank God."

"Guaqueros are tomb robbers?" Tabitha said.

"Tomb robbers, artifact robbers, grave robbers, *thieves*," Ana snapped, nearly losing her usual serenity.

"Tell me about the hiker—"

"She found a stirrup pot in a streambed. In gulley-wash, from the way she described it. It was almost undamaged."

Blue said, "Could it have been planted?"

"I don't think so."

"Why would anybody plant artifacts?" Tabitha asked.

Ana said, "If she found it someplace else, she could claim to have found it here. She could take it to the university to be authenticated. Once she knew it was authentic and valuable, she could give it to the nation, which she would have to do, then go back to the actual site and loot whatever was there, knowing it was good stuff."

"Jeez! That's nasty."

Blue said, "There are lots of nasty crooks in the ancient artifacts business."

Ana said, "I don't think this woman was a crook. The pot's round, so it could have rolled down a gentle slope without breaking. It had lost its spout. The main thing was she didn't try to sell it to us or get us to authenticate it."

"Okay."

"It's a very late Moche portrait of a priest. Beautiful workmanship. Because it's such fine work and such a late type, I think it could have been buried with the last lord of some city. Probably from the Huaca."

"Because after the El Niños and the killings in the plaza, the civilization around Huaca de la Luna died out," Tabitha said.

Ana shot Blue a glance as if to say "you've got a good student there."

Complimenting me, though it was hardly my doing that Tabitha had all her marbles.

Tabitha added, "I thought they buried their dead in the Huaca de la Luna or the Huaca del Sol?"

Ana said, "Exactly!"

"So this is—"

"So this pot is far away from where it should be. So it is a very big mystery."

Ana and Blue and their convoy continued along the rising track until there was no track, just scattered rock and gullies near the river. In two hours they had covered a distance that would have taken the ancient Moche two days. They parked crosswise to the slope, in addition to turning off the ignition and pulling on the hand brake, so that if some bizarre accident dropped the gear out of park, the car was unlikely to roll down the mountain.

"From here we hike," Ana said.

The two other cars pulled into position and everybody got out, opened the back hatches, and unloaded gear. Andy, Jasper, Dr. Jungstedt, and Blue selected sampling equipment. Drake Rakowski packed his North Face pockets with film and lenses, then cradled his two cameras and looked about him. Jorge Blanco and Clodaldo Mamani from the INC had larger backpacks than the rest of them. Clodaldo spoke the local languages and looked exactly like the faces on the Moche pots. Jorge looked to Blue like a blend of Spanish and native.

On the hood of the car, Ana spread an aerial photograph of the upper river and lower slope of the mountains. She and Jorge each carried a GPS. Fortunately, Blue thought. You could get quickly lost among the many mountain valleys.

The Altiplano was a great tableland lifted up—and up and up. It was cut by erosion from the fast-running rivers. Peru was an active volcanic region, and the Andes were still rising. At the top edge of the rising plain there were what looked in high-altitude aerial photographs like broken concrete blocks. These were immense pieces of tectonic plates broken in the volcanic surges where the Nazca crustal plate was forcing itself under the coastal plate. Some fertile valleys lay in the breaks, such as those the Incas inhabited. At the very top of the plain rose the sharp Andean peaks, many of them over 22,000 feet high.

They stood on the high plateau. But calling it a plateau didn't do justice to the ruggedness of the terrain or the fact that they were coping with high altitude and thin, cold air. This was the highest plateau on earth, and was now beginning to be used as a real-life laboratory for modeling what Mars may be like if humans ever land on the planet and want to colonize.

They were fortunate, Blue thought, not to have strong winds today, but the maps flapped in the breeze.

A Jeep came up the trail behind them and angled toward another branch of the stream. Two hikers came down from the east, walking on the other side of the stream. They looked cold and exhausted.

On the map, the river and its tributaries resembled the snaking pattern of veins of blood on the back of a man's hand, thick and contorted as the river ran toward the sea, thinner as the vessels snaked up into the mountains and toward the glaciers that fed them. There were five main tributaries here running westward down out of the mountains, meeting at the palm of the "hand." Blue hoped Ana had a good fix on where they were going.

"Our hiker put it right about here," she said, placing a red fingernail halfway up one of the tributaries, the first of them, the northernmost. The polish on her nail was scuffed from digging.

"Did she have a GPS when she was up here?"

"If only!" Ana said.

"Damn."

"Actually, one of the two other hikers she was with had one but apparently he dropped it in the river along with half their food supply."

"No kidding."

"Gave her extra backpack room to carry the pot downhill, though. Anyway, I sat down with her for an hour and talked her through it. This is our best guess."

That started Ana on a conversation with Jorge Blanco. Blue spoke only adequate Spanish, but it was enough to know that Ana and Jorge were arguing, not unpleasantly, about which one had the best GPS. Apparently Jorge's was accurate to within three meters and with four AA batteries could support eighteen hours of continuous use.

"Mine," Ana said in Spanish, "has a lithium ion battery that will give twenty-four hours of power."

Jorge made a "wow" noise.

Two techies meet in the Altiplano! Jeez!

"And optional battery packs, which are in the glove compartment"—she pointed—"that give power for fifteen days." She probably needed the reserve power, Blue thought. Ana did some fairly risky solo wilderness exploring.

"Mine," said Jorge, "has a function that can tell you how steep the path ahead of you is. And a download for geocache coordinates."

Ana said, "Multilingual menu. Waterproof, rubber armored—"

"Mine has raster support, which lets me check against DOQQs." DOQQs were Digital Ortho Quarter Quads, which were basically aerial photographs.

Blue said, "Sheesh! Get over it. Whatever happened to good old-fashioned testosterone battles?"

31

The line stretched out as Tabitha, Andy, Ana, Bengt Jungstedt, Jasper, Jorge, Clodaldo, Drake, and Blue struggled up the slope next to the rushing stream. Blue had stopped briefly to stick two fingers in the water and it was so cold her whole hand ached.

"What I think happened," Ana said, "is that a chieftain and probably several members of his entourage were interred up here."

Tabitha said, "Why? Why not at the temple like before?"

"Maybe the flooding worried them. Maybe parts of the temple were crumbling from the floodwater and they decided to entomb the lord where he would be safe."

They trudged uphill. Ana said, "Safe until global warming."

"The glaciers are receding," Blue said to Tabitha. "There's more runoff."

"And maybe the Moche placed him up here for protection from theft, if theft was a problem then," Ana said. "It's possible the glacier even crept down to cover the tomb and froze there. Until recently."

They could already feel the chill from the glacier, sighing down the mountain. It was frightening to look up at it, and at the fangs of the mountains above, even though, in fact, the terminus of the glacier was at least two miles uphill from them. Bluish white, it seemed tremblingly poised to slide down and engulf them.

They had to follow the cold freshet now, because, while they could see the glacier and peaks above, they were no longer on the rising plain but the shoulder of the mountain, and the rocks and eroded crags closed in the view. Their route twisted and turned. Seeing far ahead was impossible.

The insects that had followed them from lower altitudes were gone. Blue's thigh muscles were starting to scream in protest at the constant climb, and they were all breathing hard. She didn't want to be the first to wimp out. Drake was carrying two cameras as well as his backpack, and both the INC reps had extra gear, including a tent, firearms, and food, so that they could camp out and guard the site. The rest of the team carried somewhat lighter loads, mostly backpacks and emergency waterproof sleeping bags, although they didn't plan to stay overnight. Jasper and Bengt had collection equipment to use at the site.

If there was any site.

They struggled up and up. Finally Ana stopped, and Blue halted gratefully behind her. Her thigh and calf muscles twitched, ridding themselves of the products of overexertion.

Ana gestured at the rivulet. "This isn't the place."

Blue realized what she meant. They were farther up, nearer to the glacier water source than the hiker had indicated. There was no human debris of any sort in the water or along the bank. No pieces of pottery, no bone fragments except for parts of a recently dead bird and strewn-around tufts of some soft-looking, toast brown fur that might have been from a guanaco or vicuña. Killed by a puma, most likely. *Puma concolor bangsi*, killer of the Andes, and one of the reasons Jorge and Clodaldo were carrying firearms.

"But maybe it came from higher up," Blue said.

Ana had them all sit down. "Great!" Blue said. "Give my leg muscles a complete rest." They flattened out the aerial photograph between them. Above them hunkered the great glacier.

If the watershed were a human right hand palm down, they were two-thirds of the way up the thumb. "She was sure it was here?" Blue asked.

"She was as sure as she could be, but it was her first trip to Peru." Ana pointed at the index finger. "We'd better try over here."

"Just because we haven't seen any signs yet doesn't mean this is wrong," Blue said. "The stream may pond up ahead someplace. And if it does, artifacts could sink there."

"But I don't think it ponds."

Out came the relief maps from her kit. She discarded one and spread out another, of just this area of tributaries. Its scale gave elevations of the land in increments of a foot.

"See? It's almost straight upgrade from here."

"You're right." The land fell away from the glacier sharply at first, then more gradually but continuously, down to well below where they were now. There was no fold in the land or level area where water could pool.

Andy said gloomily. "So as far as the accuracy of your hiker is concerned, maybe we'll have to search all five of the streams."

Ana nodded. They put their heads together over the map.

Tabitha said, "Look. Maybe we don't have to go all the way back down. If we just crossed this mountain ridge, we'd intersect the next stream at about this same elevation."

Blue said, "She's right. The ridge isn't *that* high. And it would save us a mile downhill and a mile back uphill on the other side."

Bengt Jungstedt said, "I think crossing the ridge is more dangerous. More chance of somebody getting hurt." He was the oldest of them, although he seemed in good shape.

The sun was almost at the zenith. They'd spent half the day getting this far. Blue said, "We could go back down and climb up the next valley today, but we won't get all five done before dark."

"Well, let's try the next one," Ana said.

Jasper said, "If we have to come back tomorrow, then we have to come back tomorrow. We really have to keep at it. If this is a major discovery—"

"I think it will be," Ana said.

They climbed back downhill. Hiking downhill was harder than hiking uphill, Blue thought. *For one thing, you're more afraid of tripping and falling. Going up, if you fall, you're already naturally hunched to fall forward self-protectively, plus there's a shorter distance to the ground. Going downhill, you're leaning backward unnaturally and taking the impact of each step on your heels. The body isn't made for this.*

Halfway back to the main river, Bengt Jungstedt fell. Blue had noticed he was moving less flexibly, rocking from foot to foot with his feet rather widely spread, like an older person with hip trouble. *You shouldn't do that on downhill scree because it doesn't give you balance. You need to bend the uphill leg at the knee with enough power to hold your body weight and then place the other leg down almost in front of it.*

He tumbled sideways, his backpack sliding with the momentum, pushing him farther onto his right side. With his right arm wedged underneath his chest against the ground, he couldn't stop his slide for several feet, until a gentler section of the slope brought him to a halt naturally.

They all rushed to him. His face was badly abraded by the rocks. Blood ran down his forehead and neck, and he lay on one side, stunned.

Ana, Jorge, Clodaldo, and Blue all had antibacterial wipes out of their backpacks before you could say staphylococcus. Ana asked him to stay lying down. Blue said, "Bengt. Where does it hurt?"

"Just my face."

Great. Maybe he hadn't broken anything. Visions of carrying him back to the car, his leg splinted, ran through Blue's head.

Jasper sat down next to him and put a hand on his shoulder. "Move your right hand for me." He did. His left arm had never contacted the ground at all. It was probably just as well he hadn't been able to break his fall with his right arm or they might be dealing with a broken wrist.

"How about your legs?" Blue asked.

He wiggled both feet. Very slowly, watching for any sign of sudden pain, they sat him up and Ana gently wiped his face. There were bits of rock and some plant material ground into the skin.

"This might hurt," Ana said, "if I try to get more of the dirt out."

"Go for it," he said. She did.

With Bengt cleaned and disinfected as best they could do it here, they continued the climb down. Jasper walked next to him the whole way.

Bengt wanted to continue the search. When they reached the division point, where this stream met the other streams, Ana turned them to what would be the index finger. It was past midday now. A sigh of warmer air from far down the slopes countered the cold drift from the glacier.

Andy said, "This is discouraging. It took us two hours to do that one stream."

Drake said, "Yeah. It could be any one of these. Or none of them. We don't even know whether there really is a tomb."

"Maybe somebody just left the pot here," Andy said.

"What do you mean?"

"Well, like a hundred years ago some grave robbers found it, but they had too much stuff to carry and they left that one piece behind."

Ana said, "I did ask about how it was lying. If it had been out in the elements for a hundred years, it would have been buried in sand and debris."

"But—"

"If it had been out there even a few months, the stream would have washed it into a drift. But it hadn't been."

"So maybe somebody abandoned it recently. I mean, they got it someplace else and left it here. We might never find where it came from." Andy was quickly becoming the Eeyore of their group, Blue thought.

"It's a valuable pot. You don't just abandon a thing like that," Jasper said firmly, which shut Andy up, but not Drake.

"Well, we still don't know where she got it." Drake turned to Ana. "Like you said, maybe she found a tomb with lots of stuff she thinks is valuable, but she isn't sure so she brought it to you to get confirmation. She wouldn't tell you where the good stuff is."

Ana said, "All I can say, Mr. Rakowski, is that she's not a known dealer."

"And certainly not one of our known guaqueros," Jorge said.

"From what we could find out about her, she really is a college student from Michigan who agreed to come along on a mountain hike because she's something of an exercise freak and one of her two friends is interested in birds."

Everybody was silent for a minute or so.

Blue said, "As coleader of this happy group, I declare lunch time."

. . .

While they were not at a really dangerous altitude, they were high enough up to have to make sure everybody was kept fed and hydrated. Especially hydrated. The cars were a short hike downstream. All of them carried bottled water in their backpacks, but they didn't want to use it up before going farther up the mountain. Same with the packed food.

They hiked down to the cars.

Tabitha and Andy unloaded water bottles and cups. Ana pulled out a bag of bread Blue had bought on the way up on the outskirts of Trujillo. Jasper had bought big sandwiches of Peruvian beef and lamb from the nuns where Adam and Brad were staying. Blue had found some bricks of cooked dried fruit that ought to have been safe from traveler's tummy problems because it had been baked. It was very much like fruitcake, but better. Ana had also ordered about a dozen thermoses of hot coca tea, which should give them all the energy they badly needed. The two INC men, Clodaldo and Jorge, were being treated to lunch by Blue's group. Jorge was effusive in his thanks. Clodaldo not so much so. Blue thought Clodaldo didn't really like North Americans.

Bengt plopped down next to Blue. "I didn't have a chance to tell you the good news before we left this morning," he said.

"Good news? I'm always ready for that."

"Adie is eager to run the experiment."

"That's great. When can you start?"

"Maybe September if we can assemble a team that quickly."

"Wonderful."

"One piece of news that is not so good."

"Oh?"

"Adie seems to have mentioned this to the Netherlands media."

"Mmm. I wish he hadn't. It's far too early. But I suppose if it's just in the Netherlands, if it's not picked up by extremists, maybe nobody much will hear about it."

Blue sat on the ground, munching a roll baked just that morning in

Trujillo. As she gazed up at the mountain, wisps of mist eddied from the glacier where the warmer air from the plains passed over it.

"The breath of the glacier," she said.

Blue said, "We have time to try one more. Then we'll have to go back to Trujillo. Or camp here."

"We could camp here," Jasper said. "But it wouldn't be very comfortable."

They carried small emergency tents, just in case. You don't go into the mountains without them. But they were really skimpy and Blue suddenly wondered whether everybody had sleeping bags. She had told them, but with the cars not far away she had not checked the packs, except for Tabitha and Andy, who were her students and, of age or not, were in her care. She said, "No. Let's do just one more and then go back to Trujillo. It's one o'clock. We have four and a half hours to sunset."

Ana spread out the relief map and the aerial photo. "I think we can get far enough up the next one in an hour and a half to know whether it's right or wrong." She pointed at the index finger.

Blue looked at the tributary on the map. "It's wrong," she said.

"Why? How do you know?"

"I don't know, really, but look at this." She pointed to the five branches. "We've been up the thumb." It jutted out the side of the "hand." Of the four fingers, the longest and straightest was the ring finger, which somewhat upset the comparison to a real hand.

"The Moche were very familiar with the river, even though they lived in the valley, right?"

"I would say so. They traded with the mountain people," Ana said.

Jorge said, "And we think they even went over the crest of the Andes through the pass and down into the Amazon rain forest."

"All right. It makes sense that they'd be familiar with the watershed of the river that was so important to them. Look at it this way. If they buried a lord up here, in defiance of their usual custom, why did they do that? The river is their lifeblood, but when the El Niño rains came, it destroyed their crops and flooded their homes. It was their builder and their destroyer. And nothing they did made the rains stop. They tried human sacrifice and it failed. Cannibalism failed. So what I think they decided was to go to the head of the river and give their dead lord to the source of their troubles."

Jasper said, "They killed him as a sacrifice?"

"I doubt they'd do that," Ana said.

Blue said, "I don't think it matters. Maybe he died naturally."

Jasper said, "So why do you think they'd go up this particular tributary—"

"They'd go as far up as possible, wouldn't they? This branch"—she pointed at the ring finger—"is longer and straighter than the others. It goes higher up. So I think they'd see it as the real headwater. The source."

32

An hour later they were struggling up along the bank of the stream. The glacial meltwater had eroded the rock to some degree, producing a landscape that was more uneven than most of western Peru. Of course, if you got as high as the mountain crests, the landscape was like shark teeth.

Many of the mountains were over twenty thousand feet and topped with perpetual snow. They were at about eight thousand feet, the lower end of what is considered high altitude, which ranges from eight to twelve thousand feet. There was no particular danger of altitude sickness, or *soroche*, as it's called here, Blue thought, although they all watched each other to make sure the others appeared well. Reaction to high altitude was quite variable. People become confused and are unaware that they're not thinking clearly. They had walked up, which Blue knew was always a help. Flying in to a high altitude camp was much riskier because there was no time for acclimatization.

The going was rough, with soft spots that their feet sank into without warning. Much of the trail wasn't really a trail, just a rocky eroded streambank. They were moving in single file, and even that didn't provide a lot of foot room. The creek, which was now too narrow to be called a stream, was about eight feet wide here, but fast-moving. It might have eroded down through the valley and shifted slightly since the Moche lived.

Blue said, "The creek bed looks like softer rock, so it might erode fast."

"I was thinking that," Jasper said. "Ana, did your hiker describe something like this?"

"As a matter of fact, yes."

"But don't all the streams look the same?" Andy grumbled.

Jasper snorted. Andy looked abashed.

Tabitha said, "Andy, you need to take a course in basic geology."

Andy ducked his head farther down between his shoulders.

Tabitha said, "Why would your hiker choose to come this way? There're a lot of easier trails farther down."

"My guess," Ana said, "is that nobody wanted to be the first one to quit."

Tabitha simply nodded. Then she added, "I've been on *that* date."

At one point they thought they heard another hiker on the path. Ana said, "Jorge, drop back and check, please. I don't want anybody else along if we find something really valuable."

Jorge let the rest get ahead of him, and he moved off the trail a distance and waited. After half an hour or so, he caught up with them, saying he hadn't seen anyone.

At the time, Blue was hiking in the lead. Suddenly, she said, "Look!"

"A skull?" Jasper said.

Blue was ahead of him and saw it better. "It's a pot."

Ana said, "You may have been right, girl."

It was just part of a pot, about half, and the rough edges gave it the appearance at a distance of a skull with a few teeth. They pushed farther up along the creek bank, then came to a steep rise in the path. The creek came over a low cliff, maybe fifteen or twenty feet above, making a waterfall.

"No wonder it was broken," Jasper said, "if it washed over *that*."

There were steplike cuts in the rock near the fall that looked man-made. Ana and Jasper thought so, too, and their excitement grew. This enthusiasm was a good thing, because their exhaustion was growing undeniable at the same time. Wearily, they climbed the steps. At the top of the fall, the path, such as it was, ended.

"We have to cross the stream here," Jasper said. "The path continues on the other side."

Blue said, "I guess so." There were enough stones to cross on without getting wet, if they watched their step and kept their balance.

"I'll go first," Jasper said. "Make sure it's safe."

Blue said, "Let's be careful. I don't want to risk the kids."

Both Tabitha and Andy snorted at that. *Too bad.*

Jasper shifted his shoulders, making sure his backpack wouldn't move around and unbalance him. Then he stepped across the stream, maybe seven feet across here, sticking to the rocks, not even wetting his feet.

"Simple. See?"

Ana went next. When Dr. Jungstedt started toward the crossover, Blue realized that his face had swollen on the right side, where he had hit the gravel, and the flesh around his eye was swollen. "Bengt, be extra careful. You may not have good depth perception with that eye half shut."

And then he tripped. He went down on one knee in the stream, teetering over the drop-off.

Jasper bolted across the gap from the far side just as Andy ran over from Blue's side. For an instant it looked like all three would go over the edge. Andy held Bengt under the arms and Jasper took his left hand and pulled him across.

"Good going," Blue said. Andy looked at her and smiled, probably remembering that she had talked about "risking the kids" only minutes before. Bengt had got one shoe and his lower right leg wet. Andy and Jasper had managed to stay dry.

The coffin-shaped valley faced east-west. An hour's rough climbing from the pot had given them another pot and a clutch of beads. At the end of the climb was a stunning find.

Most of the small valley was filled with rubble. An even larger accumulation of rubble, like a little moraine, backed up into the diminishing upper crevice.

Blue held her breath. *My God, this could be what I most hoped for.* Unopened ceremonial graves from one of the most artistically creative societies on earth.

Taking in a gasp of air, Blue said, as casually as possible, "That's not a natural drift. See those timbers? They must have collected rock to pile up behind the timbers and then bring down over the graves."

For graves there were. Ana, who was usually unflappable, stared with eyes big and astonished.

A huge glacier terminus hung over the valley. Melt water coursed down it, the streamlet about thirty inches wide. It flowed over one side of a slab of rock at the top end of the valley, past the rubble drift, then down along the south side of the valley itself, where it had begun to wash away the rubble covering the graves. One and a half millennia had passed over the area since the dead were laid down.

"Oh, my!" Ana said.

Jorge and Clodaldo were equally amazed. So were they all. Several items had washed out of the farthest south grave, the one nearest the streamlet. A second grave, the westernmost, contained a skeleton sitting up.

Into the stream had washed jade beads and a spondylus shell earspool.

Jasper fell to his knees next to the stream, peering at the objects in the water. Andy went next to him and did the same, knowing enough not to touch anything. Drake fired up his camera. Tabitha stood, rapt, drinking in the view of the valley. Bengt Jungstedt took out a notepad and a package of vials. He also knew not to disturb the site, of course, but he uncapped a vial, walked a few steps downstream and filled it with stream water. He did the same with soil from the bank of the stream and then a bit farther away.

Ana and Blue stared at the most eroded tomb. The sun was well past the zenith and was burning down at the grave's contents. Parts of the skeleton, which lay on its back, were visible—the beadlike bones of the feet, the long bones of one leg, brown ligaments like rubber bands. Part of the pelvis was uncovered. The rest of the body was overlain with deteriorated fabric. Wool, no doubt, Blue thought. Wool could stand up to a lot of weathering. They couldn't see the arms, but the way the cloth draped the upper body, they were probably intact and crossed over the abdomen. Over the face was a mask of pure copper. Around the neck were beads of turquoise and bone. Not because of the beads, but because of the shape of the pelvis, Blue said, "A female."

"And a young one," Ana said. "Early teens."

They gazed at the layer of rubble that covered the tombs. It had clearly been flattened by the Moche workmen—assuming this was indeed Moche—after the burials, but had sunk a bit in certain spots. There was a very large rectangular depression in the center, not more than a few inches deeper than the surrounding rubble, but deep enough to tell Blue there was something man-made underneath. It was subdivided, with a rectangular depression about three feet by seven feet in the center, its axis pointing east-west; four narrower ones, two on each side of the big one; and two other narrow ones at the east end, above the big one, but crossways, pointing north-south; and three narrow ones at the bottom, pointing east-west.

"If this is like the Sipan tombs," Blue said to Tabitha and Andy, while hope and eagerness fizzed in her blood, "the Lord will be in the center, with a mask of gold and turquoise over his face. Young women or his wives will be in the tombs on each side, with their bodies pointing the other way from the Lord. Then the tombs at the ends will be soldiers, and maybe a sacrificed dog or llamas. There would be gold rattles and gold and silver scepters, and earspools and jewelry made of turquoise, feathers of jungle birds, pearl, and red spondylus shells. And there will be jars of food and medicines."

"Which is what we came for, right?" Tabitha said.

"It is, but we won't see it. Not now anyway."

Tabitha knew that they would not open the graves. The excavation would take months, possibly a couple of years, and would require governmental permission. But her face fell anyway.

Blue understood. She longed to see what was under that rubble, too.

"Tabitha, you and Andy need to know that as of this moment you may be present at the discovery of one of the biggest pre-Columbian finds ever. Even without looking inside those tombs, we know this is out of the ordinary."

Ana said, "I'll make sure they send you samples of everything."

"I'd a lot rather come back and help," Blue said. "With Tabitha, if she wants to."

"I want to. I really, really want to."

The other eroded grave was more than likely a young man, but they couldn't see enough of the skeleton to be certain. They could see, despite some fabric covering and rubble, that his right arm was crossed over his chest and held a knife, which was pretty good proof that it was not a woman.

It was a deeper grave, permitting the dead man to sit partially upright. The left leg was visible from the knee down, and ended in a stump.

"There's no foot," Tabitha said.

Andy and Jasper came over to look.

"A guardian," Jasper said. "His feet were cut off."

Andy said, "Why?"

"Nobody really knows. The speculation is that then he couldn't run away. He had to stay and guard his lord."

Andy said, "That's so, so primitive!" Andy, Blue reflected for the dozenth time, had way less of a feel for archaeology than Tabitha.

"Look," Tabitha said. "What's that?"

"Don't touch. And don't get too close," Ana said.

"But what is it?"

Under the edge of the fabric was a small figure apparently made of clay. It was about five inches long. One end had eroded, possibly from rain, since it looked like it was raw clay, not fired. "It looks like a cuy."

"A guinea pig? Were guinea pigs sacred to the Moche?" Tabitha asked.

Ana shook her head. Jasper and Blue said nothing. They were stumped. "I suppose," Ana said, after a minute, "it could have some ceremonial meaning."

Drake, who had been taking photos, said, "If this is a royal tomb, with all that gold and whatever, what do you suppose the whole thing is worth?"

Ana looked at him sourly. "To archaeologists, it would be beyond price."

33

They set about labeling the site and making plans to preserve it. It had been exposed to the elements for fifteen hundred years, so throwing a tarp over it or trying to put up a tent didn't make much sense. Protecting it from human depredation did. While Ana took bearings and made notes from her GPS on the map, Jorge and Clodaldo unpacked their gear, including rifles, since they were planning to stay overnight. Jasper and Blue wandered up the slope to look at the scree pile and get an idea of the way the Moche had brought down half a hill onto their tombs. Blue also wanted to get a view of the tombs from a bit above. Drake went with them, to take photos from a higher perspective.

They climbed well outside the tomb area as they went up, not wanting to damage any artifacts. The going was quite rough, even avoiding the scree pile. Rock and gravel had continued to slide down over the centuries. Blue stumbled and went to her knees a couple of times, tearing her khaki pants and pretty well lacerating her right knee. Drake slid at one point on a drift of rounded pebbles, and went down but managed to hold both cameras up and land on his back.

It was worth it. They reached the lower end of the scree pile and couldn't go any farther because of the danger of it sliding, but they were twenty feet higher than the tombs. This was the equivalent of looking down from the third floor of a building, and the tomb pattern was laid out beneath them.

Jasper said, "Wow."

Drake said, "If we could just stay until the sun is low, I could get spectacular shots in raking light. The shadows would bring out the tomb pattern."

Jasper said, "Well, we can't. It's too dangerous to climb back down to the cars in the dark."

"Maybe just until late afternoon—"

"Everybody's safety comes first, Drake."

There was a grating roar. Blue looked up, expecting to see an aircraft flying too low, and just as she did she was pushed forward. Her feet left the ground, but she was tumbling over backward, then rolling and rolling, and then she was losing consciousness, trying to stop the dimming, and she blacked out.

Blue was a ball of pain when she became conscious again. Her eyes were filled with dirt. She saw enough light through the dirt that she knew she wasn't blind. Somebody was yelling "Blue! Say something! Blue! Say something." It was Tabitha.

Blue yelled, "Adam! Where's Adam!"

"What?"

"Where's Adam?"

"He's back in Trujillo, Professor Eriksen," Tabitha said, more quietly, but sounding even more worried. "Please be all right."

"Adam's gone!"

"No. Please—"

"But *where's Adam?*"

"He's with Brad. In Trujillo!"

"Oh. Oh, yes."

A man's voice was screaming, but Blue couldn't get the words. A couple of minutes must have passed, she thought, while Tabitha pulled rocks and brushed stones off of her, whimpering with worry as she did, and Blue finally realized that the screamer was Andy yelling "Professor Martello!"

Blue coughed dirt out of her throat and swiped at her eyes. She said to Tabitha, "I'm okay."

"Thank God!"

Several yards away, Drake sat on a pile of rubble, cradling one of his two cameras and moaning while blood ran into his eyes. Blue tried to strain around and see what had happened. When she did, she saw Ana, Jorge, Bengt, Andy, and Clodaldo frantically tossing rock away from one side of the drift.

"What are they doing?" she asked Tabitha.

"Don't worry yet, Professor Eriksen. They'll find him."

"Find who? Tell me. Find who?" Who was missing? "Oh, *Jasper?*" Blue sat bolt upright and screamed with pain. It felt like all the ribs on my left side were broken.

"Please lie down. *Please!*" Tabitha said.

"Okay. But why are they digging?"

Ana came racing over. When she did, Tabitha left Blue to go help the others dig. Ana said, "Lie back. I'm going to examine you."

"No, I'm okay. Tell me what's happened."

Ana felt her arms and legs, which were only bruised, but when she got to Blue's left side, she could scarcely keep from screaming. It felt like she was pressing glass shards into her chest.

"You have a broken rib," Ana said, "and maybe two."

Ana ran back to dig. Blue got up and stumbled over to the others, now joined by Drake, who apparently was not seriously injured. They were frantically throwing rocks and stones from an area that they hoped was where Jasper had been standing when the slide happened. It was hard to tell because the slide itself had changed the landscape.

Bending down, throwing rocks away from the area, Blue called "Jasper! Jasper!"

Blue scrabbled faster. She felt a sharp pain in her chest and she couldn't help gasping. At which point, Ana realized what Blue was doing.

"No!" Ana yelled at her. "You *idiot*! You want to puncture your lung? You could bleed to death right in front of us!"

Blue backed off.

"Tear a blood vessel in your lung," Ana said, "and we'd have to pack you down the mountain in a rush, over the waterfall—"

"I'll stop." She couldn't be any significant help, anyway. The pain was too sharp. Tears were running down her cheeks. Andy was crying, too.

Jorge, Andy, and Ana had already worn the fabric from the palms and fingertips of their gloves and then the skin off their fingers and were bleeding onto the rocks they grabbed and threw down the slope. Clodaldo and Bengt must have had tougher gloves. They were throwing rocks as if the rocks were light as Styrofoam.

Tabitha kept one eye on Blue as she dug.

This was hideous, Blue mourned. Wrenching, and past understanding. Jasper had simply vanished. The last Blue remembered, he was standing next to her. Now he was gone.

Then Clodaldo shouted, *"¡Mire! ¡Dedos!"*

He pointed at the bottom of the hole they had made in the pile of rocks. Where he had just lifted away a hunk of stone was the back of Jasper's hand, index finger protruding.

Now that they knew exactly where to dig, the rocks flew faster. The hole enlarged, first Jasper's arm coming into view, then guided by that, Andy, Jorge, and Bengt found and uncovered his head.

"Is he breathing?" Blue whispered. They couldn't hear her. Andy had already shouted the same thing, as if anybody knew.

"Get the rocks off his chest first!" Ana said, flinging them fiercely aside herself. Then as others took up that job, she pinched Jasper's nose and blew into his mouth, waited a couple of seconds, then did it again. And again.

Rocks flew; bloody hands scooped away stones. Blue crouched over to the desperate group, staying back just far enough not to be in the way. Jasper's shape emerged, streaked with dirt but pale. So pale.

Ana rolled him carefully onto his side, helped by Andy and Clodaldo, then the three of them plus Jorge and Bengt carried him quickly to higher ground, where they could work on him better, out of the pit they had dug. Ana leaned down and listened to his chest.

She pounded his chest. Andy took up breathing into his mouth, once out of every five chest pumps.

After fifteen minutes, Bengt took over the chest pumps and Tabitha the breathing.

And after half an hour, nothing had changed.

Andy squatted on the screen slope, arms wrapped around his head, sobbing in tortured gulps. Tabitha cried silently.

They laid Jasper near the stream several yards above the tombs on a ground cloth from Clodaldo's tent and covered his face with the extra part of the cloth. He was gray and pale and there was dirt in his hair.

Ana cleaned Drake's cuts, disinfecting them with premoistened wipes from her kit. The two slashes that would not stop bleeding she covered with gauze and tape and told him to put pressure on them. She had ordered Blue to sit down and stay sitting or else. When she was done with Drake, she passed disinfectant wipes to everybody and told them to thoroughly cleanse the cuts on their hands. Finally, she came to Blue.

"Any symptoms of concussion?"

"My eyes are still a little funny."

"In what way? Double vision?"

"No. Just misty."

"That's not your eyes. There's fog coming in."

The fog was so dense now they couldn't see the mountains. Tabitha said, "Ana, you know where we are from your GPS. Can't you get a message to—to some rescue people to ask them to come and get us?"

"I already told them where we were," Ana said, but Blue knew from her voice that she saw the same problem Blue did.

Blue said, "Tabitha, they know exactly where we are, but in these conditions they can't hike in or helicopter in safely."

"Well, maybe not helicopter, but why can't somebody hike in?" Tabitha sounded stressed, which was hardly surprising. She realized that without help they'd be spending the night on the mountain, cold

and damp, and with the dead body of a man she had known and respected.

"Would you really want any rescuer to try to cross that waterfall
without being able to see where they were going?"

"I guess not," she said. "I guess that lets out any of us going for help,
too." Her voice was steadier. She was already getting her fears under control. *Good girl*, Blue thought.

Blue said, "Right. It doesn't make sense. Going for help or for help
getting here. Tabitha, if one of us were seriously hurt or sick, somebody
would have to go. But we all know there's nothing to be done for Jasper
now. He's beyond help."

"You do understand, Blue," Ana said, just to be sure. "You're not seriously enough injured to risk anybody else."

"Of course I do."

Andy started to moan.

"The fog will burn off in the morning," Jorge said.

The three women had three sleeping bags, and all the men did, except
Drake, who hadn't brought one, probably doing his macho thing. So Ana
gave hers to Drake and she and Tabitha zipped two together to make a
large one all three of the women could squeeze into. It was a good idea,
anyway, to share body heat in chilly circumstances, however uncomfortable the arrangement was. Plus, Ana and Tabitha wanted to keep track of
whether Blue started coughing in a way that suggested a lung puncture.

It was no surprise to Blue that she couldn't sleep. With broken ribs
there was no comfortable position. Ana put Blue on the outside, with
Tabitha on the other outside. She took the middle. Blue knew Ana did this
to be able to listen to her breathing.

It was cold. Even with the thin tent over them, the wet fog edged in
everywhere—it invaded their ears, ran down their necks, slicked their eye-
lids, their hair. All the surfaces were slightly damp. Thank goodness for the
waterproof sleeping bag, Blue thought. She was chilled and kept shivering,
and shivering hurt her ribs.

But far worse was thinking about Jasper. He'd been Blue's friend for years. *Fussy, particular, reliable Jasper.* His fussiness might have been part of his nature, but it was also a product of his love for archaeology. He believed you should get it right.

He'd been supportive always, Blue thought. Good with students, generous with his time. They'd had a student once who talked so loudly it was annoying. Jasper said to Blue, "He's not doing it to bother us. I think he's slightly deaf."

Jasper's death was a terrible, unbelievable loss.

It was my fault. I set this whole thing up, and now he's dead.

She could hear Andy sobbing in the other tent.

An hour earlier, Blue had sat and held Andy in her arms and let him cry. She squeezed his shoulders, her ribs shooting pain as she did. "He can't be dead," Andy kept whispering. "He can't be dead."

There was nothing to be said that would console him. All you can ever do, she knew, is show you care. "We'll keep his memory alive," she said, and Andy gulped. It wasn't much, but it gave him something to think about. "We'll finish the project and dedicate it to him."

Andy sobbed.

"Will you help?" Blue asked.

Andy moaned and nodded. Then he said, "He can't be dead."

"He was a good person."

"He was so good to me," Andy said hoarsely. "He got me into the program, when I wasn't sure what I really wanted to do."

"I know."

"If I didn't understand something, like the chemistry of it, he'd talk me through it."

"I know. Jasper thought you had real promise."

"He did?"

"Of course he did. You must realize that."

"I guess." He started hiccupping. Ana came by and gave him two aspirins. He went to a sleeping bag and lay down. Finally, they all had gone to bed except Clodaldo, who stayed up on watch with his rifle, planning to trade places with Jorge in the small hours.

The night was utterly black. The stars were invisible behind the fog. Several times Blue heard a sort of sigh-shriek. Was it the call of a predator or the creak of the glacier? She would have to ask Ana or Jorge in the morning. Maybe it was the air leaving the lungs of a small mammal as a night-bird swept down and seized it in its talons. Then there was a different, hideous shriek, like a child in agony. Ana said quietly, "Puma."

Blue could hear pebbles rattling down the scree slope. Once in a while there was a grunt of settling rock. She was scared. They had pitched their camp far on one side of the valley, where the scree slope would not come down on them even if it did slide. But even so, every sound brought back to Blue that moment of confusion.

Slow tears ran down her cheeks, hot against skin cooled by the air sinking off the Andean glacier. It was her fault, she thought, no matter how you looked at it. *I should have known the scree slope was unstable. After all, I had seen the erosion around the side of the Guardian's tomb.*

But that was near the creek, on the other side, the low side of the valley, away from the scree slope and upper, royal tombs. How could there be erosion under the overhang of the great shield rocks on the upper slope?

Possibly melt water from the glaciers seeped under the scree. Maybe it pulled out sand and support material, making the scree unstable. Freezing and thawing could create voids. In which case, the scree would slide at unexpected times, nothing to do with our presence. *Not my fault.*

It didn't make any difference what the reason was. She was the leader of the expedition. It was her job to protect everybody on her team. And she had not done so.

Automatically, her mind veered off from sadness and into her old pattern. She pictured this area as it might have been nearly two thousand years before.

34

Taka had walked all day, and while he was used to long treks, accustomed to accompanying trading parties to cities to the south, walking thirty miles a day on flat sandy trails, now they were going east, climbing up and up with the constant, gradual rise in the land. A hundred men and four women, they were making twenty miles a day, and hard work to do it. The women were borne on litters, the litter-bearers taking turns because it was so arduous. Taka's breathing was coming faster. He was aware of stress on his knees. Taka was a top player in ceremonial games. His knees were calloused from striking the hard leather ball, and even though he was young, beginning to show strain from running after the ball, running down other players.

They had camped last night in the ruins of three potato terraces. The potato farmers had vanished. Some struggling vines remained and in the mud lay a few blue tubers, which they roasted and ate, in order to pre-serve the store of food the bearers were carrying. The rock borders that had maintained the terraces were now just uneven remnants, swept away by the floods. The fields themselves were brown and scarred with gullies as if a giant animal had clawed them. What was left of the central irrigation canal was a rushing icy stream fed by meltwater from the glaciers in the mountains above.

All day they marched, with breaks only for coca tea and corn cakes.

Taka was fifteen years old. His body was strong and healthy, nourished always with fish from the coast, and the best corn and squash from the terraced farms. He had never been sick, as far as he could remember.

But the last year had been hard. The rains had washed everything away. His people rebuilt quickly, every handworker in the city pressed into service, but before the canals were really finished, the rains came again and all the work was lost. The fish market flooded first, and the fish flowed into the rest of the marketplace, rotting and fouling the vegetables, sending the metalworkers packing and running. Then the whole plain flooded, waves of water washing clay down from the terraced fields higher up. Torrents of brown, thick water swirled down gullies and through the streets. The bodies of the dead were creamy with liquid clay, as if they had been dipped in the slip the potters used. Dead men, women, and children were everywhere; corpses drifted into houses or draped over adobe brick walls. The bricks themselves soon turned to mush. The night-soil collectors had been taken from their usual jobs, setting down their stinking pots and turning to collecting the dead. His father the Lord had decreed the sacrifice of the warriors Taka and his friends had won in battle, but the sacrifice had not appeased the gods and the rains had come yet another time. And when they ate the captives in an unusual, desperate ceremony, giving the respect to the gods and their ancestors, there was still no improvement in the weather. A day or a week might be dry and the rains would come again.

His uncle, the chief priest, had tasked his father with a final test, the killing of five of their own men to appease the gods. It was the ultimate sacrifice, painful and yet hopeful, and the men went to their decapitation with great courage. But it had not helped. The rains came again, and everything was gone. Famine and disease was everywhere.

Then his father the Lord had died, suddenly, vomiting and stumbling, going numb and falling into coma and death. The gods were angry.

The people were in despair. His uncle announced a possible solution—although he did not phrase it that way. He said this ceremony would surely save the people. Taka was not as sure, but he hoped. His uncle said that they would entomb the Lord, not in the city as was the custom, but at the headwaters of the river that gave them life and was now giving them calamity and death. There, he said, the Lord would be their guardian and prevent any more of the catastrophic floods.

A party of four hundred workers had been sent on ahead twenty days ago to dig the tomb. They were to hack a large burial chamber out of rock and glacier.

The distance from their ravaged city to the mountains was only two days' trek, but once they had crossed the flatter part of the plain and begun to climb it was hard walking. In ordinary times, clear trade routes led up into the high land. Trains of pack llamas carrying bales of wool and potatoes and mountain herbs and medicinal bark came into the city daily. And trains went out again with dried fish from the coast, and from the city pottery, fabric, and worked metal. Taka had never been permitted to go with them, but he liked to watch them; they looked like ant armies, he had thought, the single-file line of traders coming in, and the single file going away, getting smaller and smaller to the eye, vanishing up into the mountains.

There were no pack trains now. There was nothing to trade.

He supposed he and the cortège in which he walked would look like a pack train to the people back in the city. If he were standing in the market square, watching himself, would he have become a dot in the distance or vanished now into the mist and haze? It was the city that was hazy and blue as he looked back, bluer the farther away he was. Taka thought a lot about color. If his life had been different, he would have liked to be an artisan—a potter, maybe—instead of being the son of the Lord and having to spend his days studying religion and astronomy. He would have been good at pot-making. Even as it was, he played at making things with his hands. Sitting around after a raid or a march or a ceremonial battle, he would pick up bits of wet clay and work with them. Some of the other young bloods joked when he produced a llama or a cuy and called him handworker, which at his caste level was an insult. But he could produce their faces in clay, too, and they took that seriously. It frightened them, he thought.

Of course, playing with clay when he was resting was as much as he could do with it. He was of the ruling class, not the artisan class. It would be laughable for him to try his hand at real pottery. Laughable and reprehensible. He was to be Lord, and he was already a warrior. The young men of the city waged war with neighboring cities. While this was often ceremonial rather than bitter, a brief battle rather than a protracted siege, if the bloods from his city were taken captive, they could be held indefinitely by the victors. Sometimes they were used as barter between the cities. In many cases they were used as ceremonial sacrifices, beheaded in public as expiation to the gods.

His cadre had never been captured. If it had been, he would have gone willingly. The individual was just a part of the community, he believed, and there was no sadness in dying for your people.

The path wound slowly upward. While the trade roads had been washed out, there was no difficulty following the route their four hundred construction workers had taken. Their feet had beaten a crude trail next to the river. As he came over a small rise that led to a washed-out gully, he smelled dead human. It was a sweet-greasy odor he was familiar with, but much more so in the recent months of cataclysm.

He came around a bend. A rock blocking the left side made the path exceedingly narrow. The man ahead of him slipped sideways and righted himself. This warned Taka to be careful, but he didn't realize how soft the gravel and sand was, having been freshly washed into the path, and he went down, twisting his left ankle.

He had been taught all his life not to show pain. Scrabbling quickly to his feet, he walked on, the ankle shrieking as he stepped. Below on his right was the deepest part of the gully and in it was the body of a man. His neck was broken, judging from the unnatural angle of his head. Flies swarmed on the rotting flesh. From the color and pattern of the loincloth, it was the body of one of their workmen. Maggots spilled from the lower side of the belly.

The workmen the man had climbed with would have left him where he lay. They were loaded down with equipment and food supplies and had no time to carry a body. Besides, a workman was of no particular value if he could not do his job.

With a last glance at tracks down the slope, Taka concluded that one or two workers had scrabbled down to the dead man, more likely to take whatever supplies he had been carrying than to make sure he was beyond help. There was no room for ceremony out here where the mountains rose.

With some trepidation, he looked ahead. The peaks mounted so sharply they seemed to lean over the cortège, a range so knifelike they could have been obsidian blades if obsidian were white. Taka thought they were the most fearful thing he had ever seen.

The footing was worse now. Rain and floodwaters had carried down rock and scree and sand and gravel from the mountain crevices and glacial moraines above, sluiced them down, and left all the debris in soft, irregular, porous deposits. He stepped on sand that looked solid and sank into a hole filled with bubbly voids. At the bottom was a sharp rock that knifed the side of his foot next to the sole of his sandal.

Trying not to limp, he trudged on. He pulled a small dried mushroom from his medicine bag and chewed on it as he struggled upward.

The narrow stream that tumbled along near them made a sudden turn. Above the bend was a waterfall, twice the height of a man. At its base lay two bodies. They had fallen from above, where the path crossed over, close to the higher water.

They, too, had been stripped of their tools and upper body clothing and abandoned.

The column climbed the stairlike rocks to the top of the waterfall and crossed over by stepping in the water at the top. It was so cold Taka's feet were numbed immediately. Up ahead in the column he could see the four young women, whose bearers had put them down to cross the stream. They cringed as they stepped into the water, hobbled drunkenly across, and curled into balls in their chairs when they got to the other side.

The path now crowded the south side of the stream. Rock walls rose on both sides. The rock was darkened up both sides to a point far above Taka's head. There were scrapes and gouges along the rock face, most of them horizontal. No trees or large plants grew here. No plants at all, in fact, except for some gray-green tufts in the crevices and small sprouts in sandy patches. Taka concluded that the stream had recently risen to a torrent huge enough to fill the gorge to the brim, scrape it clean, and wash the trees downstream.

They were high up now. When they came around a turn to an open place and he could see far down the river, he could not see his city or the ocean beyond. The air was colder. The midges that had danced around his face in infuriating clouds from the time they left home were gone and he couldn't remember when they had fallen behind. There were fingers of glaciers reaching down into the ravines, sometimes stretching across the trail. He had never seen ice on the ground like this, only the jars of it that the runners brought to the city from the mountains.

He was fascinated and thrilled to be allowed on this expedition, although as his father's son it was a necessity. Everything was new about this ceremony. Lords were always entombed in the Huaca de la Luna; it had been so as long as anyone could remember.

But nobody could remember such disasters, either. There were occasional floods and earthquakes. In living memory the plains had been shaken by an earthquake that leveled most of the residences, ruptured the canals, and tumbled the terrace walls. The terraces had been quickly if not easily repaired. This was utterly different, and his uncle believed it called for utterly different measures.

Despite the seriousness of the expedition, he was elated. He mourned his father, the Lord, but had never known him well. After he had left the women's house run by his mother and female relatives, other men had trained him in combat and statecraft. Taka would become the next Lord, with his older male relatives to advise him.

Everything around him here was new. The whole world was different here—the air clearer, the rock sharper. He had been to the seashore three times, and remembered the air being meaty, different from home in ways he did not have the knowledge to understand. Sometimes it had smelled fishy, but more of the time it reminded him of tea or beer or buried things. This mountain air was different again, both from home and from the seashore. It was not quite odorless, cold and spicy in the nostrils, and had a very faint tang of iron.

Because he had spent all his life on a wide plain, the farther they climbed into the mountains, the stranger he felt. There was no flat land here at all. Crags and sheer rock faces rose on his left. Boulders lay along the path on his right, with the stream hissing around them as it fell downhill. He felt compressed. Ahead there was nothing but vertical stone, deep, sharp valleys, and in the far distance the tops of mountains. The birds here were unknown to him. He saw a big bird he assumed to be a type of vulture because of the sharp angle at which it held its wings, but it was no vulture he had ever seen before. He was used to black vultures with red heads. This bird had a mostly white body with many colors on its head, blue and green and yellow and orange. Once during the afternoon a truly huge bird passed overhead, a bird that looked big enough to carry off a small llama or a child. It made two perfect circles in the air, its wings scarcely moving, and soared away, dismissing the long line of humans as beneath its interest.

Taka was both exhilarated and terrified by the mountains. The combination bubbled in him, like too much beer. He kept his face impassive and soared in his mind like the giant bird.

His foot and ankle were hideously painful, but he could override the pain with his feeling of soaring and also the thought of the honor that was given him, to come here and inter his father.

He was solemn, a bit afraid about becoming the new Lord, somewhat stunned at the sudden loss of his father. His father had not been involved in Taka's schooling; in fact they rarely saw each other except during ceremonies. The older men, his uncles and the priests, had been closest to his father. Most of Taka's life after leaving the women's house had been spent with boys his age, now in their teens considered young bloods. Two of these friends were with him today, the young man who marched ahead of him and another friend several bloods behind.

There were a hundred people in the cortège. At the front were four drum bearers in single file. Following them were ten armed veteran warriors, even though any attack by the mountain people was very unlikely. Behind them strode his uncle and seven priests, also single file. Following them were the only men who walked in pairs—five pairs carrying slung between them the body of the dead Lord, wrapped in embroidered wool, balanced on slings covered in gold.

Behind them came six more priests, followed by the four women sitting in litters, each litter carried by two bearers, front and rear. The women drowsed, sedated. They might or might not realize that they would be placed in the tomb with the Lord.

Following the women were four more warriors armed with spears. Then twenty of the handsomest bloods, including Taka, carrying obsidian knives.

The rest of the cortège was composed of food-bearers, gift-bearers, water-bearers, wine-bearers, and oddments-carriers who bore baskets of charcoal, live coals, extra clothing, cleansers, tinder, and forty live white, black-headed gulls to be released as the tomb was closed.

At midday they began to pass construction workers heading the other way. Of the original four hundred, one hundred had been left to close up the tomb.

The path became a zigzag, then steps cut roughly into the face of the rock. The men carrying the dead Lord lashed extra ropes in place securely around the body as they climbed, but climbing two abreast carrying the body became more and more difficult.

The freshet of meltwater splashed louder and louder. The sounds almost covered the scream of a pallbearer at the back of the bearers as he lost his footing. The Lord's body slipped sideways a few inches. The bearer plummeted over the rock edge, quickly stifling his shout as all men had been taught from childhood to do. He fell into the icy stream at the top of the cascade, tumbled over and over on the wet rocks, and rolled down the side of the mountain until he was lost from sight in the mist.

Another man moved up immediately to take his place and the climb continued.

At a still steeper incline, the bearers of the women took the women from their seats and urged them to walk. They were too weak and unsteady to climb. After one had fallen and was caught just before she went over the edge, four of the strongest bearers were assigned to carry them on their backs.

It was late afternoon when they reached the burial site. How well it had been chosen, Taka thought. A deep, east-west valley, so sharp that it could have been a slice made by the single blow of a giant stone blade, formed a natural, wedge-shaped room. The workers had enlarged the center and smoothed the walls, carrying the scrap and scree and pebbles and sand away and packing it behind a wall of large rocks and timbers at the top of the declivity. High above loomed a blue-white glacier, but the slab of stone that was the side of the mountain angled away from the valley at its top. Runoff from the glacier slipped sideways along this natural roof and into a gully parallel to the valley floor. Down that gully the water bounced and tumbled, becoming a rivulet that became the vigorous stream they had followed for two days and was, far away, the slower river that nourished their city.

Studying the valley, Taka could see that in a few hours the setting sun would shine directly in. He had been taught as a child about the sun's yearly path through the sky and knew it would shine in here at sundown for several days in the spring and several days in the fall. The rest of the year, the burial site would be in shadow.

The front of the cortège halted in the center of the ravine. Bearers moved forward into groups by category, the pallbearers taking the position at the spearhead of the party.

The rest of the column clumped up behind them. Taka was tired from the climb and the unfamiliarly thin air. He sank gratefully into a respectful crouch, as did the other bloods, though he unobtrusively put most of his weight on his uninjured foot.

35

Orange light from the setting sun filled the sharp valley. Rock that had earlier been dull gray glowed red, redder than the best of the red slip that the potters used to decorate drinking vessels, as red as coals in a fire. Taka loved the changes of light at dawn and twilight. His earliest memories were of the changing shape of the patch of sunlight that fell through the slit window onto the wall of his room. As an infant he would watch the shape and then the color change as night came closer. He was sad, as a child, each night when the light snuffed out.

The room of rock grew darker, the reds more purple, and the torches brighter, as the sun touched the horizon. Taka could see nothing of the valley below where his home city lay under the fog. The fog was a solid, unwrinkled, red-clay-colored shroud over the plain, with the light of the dying sun lying on it. There was no reflection from the fog blanket.

It should be cold, here, with the glacier overhanging and the updraft of the wind that came from the sea and crossed the plain. But a hundred workers and a hundred mourners packed the ravine's mouth tightly, keeping out the wind and mingling their body heat with the warmth from a large altar fire and the torches. The red light added its blessing to the heat.

In addition, almost everyone was smoking, everyone except the women, who drowsed, drugged, in their litters.

The wedge-shaped valley funneled sound. It acted like the megaphone the priest's assistants used at the temple. Every sound was amplified and yet absorbed by the bodies, turning it into a group-sound made of hissing torches, breathing, chanting. Sighs and scraping of feet. Taka thought he could hear his blood flow.

In the past twenty days the stoneworkers had removed boulders from the floor of the ravine, hacked off projecting rock from the walls, and leveled the front part of the ravine floor. Then they had hacked a huge rectangular tomb down into the rock at the center of the ravine for the Lord and those who would go with him, and poised above the tomb the large amount of loose rock and scree, held in place with bigger rocks as well as timbers brought to the site from lower on the mountain. The result was a small amphitheater facing west toward the faraway ocean and overlooking the rivulet that flowed from the glacier.

His uncle stood in the back, above the rectangular grave. "Lord go before us," he boomed.

"Lord go before us," everyone responded.

"Protect us, Lord."

"Protect us, Lord," was the response.

"End this time of catastrophe. Watch over us from the source of the river, the source of life. Protect us from the anger of the gods."

"Protect us, Lord," they repeated.

And again and again, "Protect us, Lord. Protect us, Lord. Protect us, Lord."

Taka stood in the center of the double row of bloods, the place of honor as the son of the Lord. His uncle waved the brazier, and the aroma of burning resin and tobacco filled the air. The man wore a headdress made of thousands of tiny blue and red feathers from jungle birds, iridescent in the torchlight. He wore a solid gold blackflap and across his chest a necklace of lapis lazuli. Now Taka's uncle presented him a ceremonial cigar to smoke, then in turn a cigar to each of the other priests, then smaller cigars to the bloods. The Fire Holder lighted the cigars with a coal, beginning with Taka.

His uncle's regalia was splendid, but not as fine as the clothes on the dead Lord lying in the tomb. A mask of gold covered his face, mold-cast and thick, with emerald eyes. On his chest was a gold plate with a giant spider hammered into it. When Taka was young, one of his teachers had taken him to see the metalworkers and he had been fascinated by the artisan who placed a sheet of copper on a sand base and then with specific hammers tapped the metal into a form that made sense as a human face when it was turned over. Small straight hammers made hair or eyelashes. Round hammers produced eyes and cheeks. Long dents became lips. As Taka grew older, he wasn't taken to the metalworkers anymore and had to spend his days studying subjects more appropriate to his station. But he knew how the beautiful spider plate with the lapis lazuli eyes had been made, and he admired it.

He watched as assistants placed earrings in the grave, then jewelry of turquoise or conch shell. Then a parade of men brought offering jars with sealed tops, hundreds of them, probably full of tobacco, ayahuasca, and cactus skins. There were utensils to use in the afterlife.

The sun set, leaving the little valley lit only by the torches. Their light barely reached the walls of the ravine, and extended into the air above only as far as a high drift of ice-mist smoking from the glacier, which they colored copper.

Taka felt a deep rising of warmth in his body, as he always did with the ceremonial medicine. He felt a love for his people, and a sense of solidarity with them. They were all taught oneness. All were as the separate seeds in an ear of corn, making a whole. Some of his friends made mock of the teachings, although the older they got the more they accepted it. Taka might have wished a different role in life. He had not asked to be the son of the Lord, after all. But he knew none of them would survive without the others and he knew they were people chosen to be great.

When the chanting was finished, a cloth of red and blue and gold embroidery was laid over the Lord by two priests. The priests and eight assistants guided the four young women to the long graves inside the tomb, parallel to the grave of the Lord. The four women, their faces oiled and sweating, were unable to walk, although they placed their feet as if they were walking. While supported by assistants on either side, holding them under their armpits, they allowed themselves to be lowered into the graves, two on each side of the Lord, their feet toward the Lord's head, their heads at his feet. The priests gave offering jars and silver jewelry to the assistants, who then placed the offerings next to the women. One of the women briefly moved her hand, trying to touch the jars. The assistant simply waited until she stopped, then placed her hands over her abdomen in the same position as the other women. Their eyes were half closed, just a bit of white showing, like crescent moons, and the lashes painted dark, looking like millipedes were walking over their eyes.

The ceremony seemed rushed to Taka, compared to the way it was usually done, but there had been ceremonies for many days in the city. And of course nothing was the same now, not since the floods. Even at the temple, they had been skipping parts of the ceremony, sometimes because the products to celebrate it weren't available. With the crops mostly a failure, they had very little to trade to the mountain people for metals or the jungle people for the rare bird feathers. What little they had to trade with the jungle people went for ayahuasca, vital for the religious ceremonies. He felt the warmth of the ayahuasca now, binding him and his brothers in a great united whole.

Four bloods, two on each side of Taka, collapsed, sinking slowly to the ground. He knew immediately that they had been chosen to be sacrificed, stupefied by their cigars, probably with medicine-cactus skins wrapped into the tobacco leaves.

Acolytes picked up the four bloods and reverently carried them to the graves. After they were laid in a straight position, arms initially at their sides, the right arm of each was bent across the chest and an obsidian knife placed in the hand. The young men blinked and one smiled. Like the woman, one straightened the arm holding the knife. A priest went to him and replaced the arm in a flexed position and told him to leave it there. The young man did.

There was still the grave of the guardian to fill. Taka watched his uncle as the man sprinkled ayahuasca over a bowl of heated beer and handed it to Taka. As next in line to be Lord, Taka took the bowl and drank. He was already feeling the light-headedness of the strong cigar. Tobacco could be dizzying or even fatal in large amounts. The workers in their tobacco fields wore protective clothing while the tobacco was green and women washed the clothing for them every few days. Tobacco was a dangerous god.

Now even the spiced beer tasted like tobacco to him. There was so much smoke in the air, he was not surprised. His mouth watered at the strong taste of the liquid. No, he was actually drooling. That was strange. Like his father—

He sank to his knees. His uncle and one of the senior priests took hold of his upper arms and turned him around to face the lancer.

His body was becoming numb. It was good of them to care for him. They placed him in a supine position. The lancer stooped to work on Taka. He cut Taka's left foot off at the ankle. How kind of him, Taka thought, because that foot had been causing trouble for two days. It had made him shift position several times when he should have stood straight and respectful.

But why was he cutting off the right foot, which was perfectly good?

They sat him upright now in the sunken space. There were offering jars being packed around his body and earrings next to his knees. He heard a snarling roar as the gravel and sand and boulders slid down. Someone must have pulled away the retaining wall.

36

A party of rescuers reached Blue and her team shortly after dawn, just as they were making their way past the waterfall. The rescuers took over the dreary task of carrying Jasper's sleeping-bag-wrapped body, a burden Andy, Bengt, Drake, and Ana had been carrying since they left Clodaldo and Jorge at the site.

The procession of cars along the road into Trujillo felt like a cortège. It wouldn't have appeared that way to anyone watching. They would not have seen Jasper's body, which lay in the back of the third Jeep, and would not have wondered why the Jeep had just one rider, the driver, and the other cars were crowded, or even why an official SUV was with them. They stopped in front of the nunnery.

Brad came running from the abode, carrying Adam.

"Listen!" he called. "He's learned all his colors! Well, five colors. Go Adam—"

"Lello," Adam said firmly. "Pur*pooo.*"

He stopped. Brad said, "And—?" Then Brad really noticed them, and took a closer look at their faces.

"What happened?"

37

Felix Hacker had never been so angry in his life. He was a man who always kept his cool. His survival depended on his being always, always on top of things, and primary of those things to control rigidly was himself.

He hated that woman. That she would thwart him this way was beyond belief.

Hacker had made a camp for himself in a hiking lodge just five miles northwest of the valley where he had triggered the scree slide. The lodge itself was bare bones, three wooden sides and a roof, with its back to the prevailing winds.

The car he had rented in Trujillo under the name Sydney Sheldon was parked only another half mile downslope. Too bad. He'd get it in the morning, not because there was fog coming and he was afraid to drive. He'd drive if he wanted to.

No, he was going to sit here, his legs folded under him, and sit and sit and punish himself. It was getting cold. Fine. He had one bottle of water and one fig-nut bar. Enough to stay alive. Fine.

He was going to be miserable in the fog and the cold, with no satisfying food. He wouldn't scourge himself, though, not even now. Years ago, he used a three-strand scourge with a long handle, based on that used by Saint Peter Damian, but now he rarely resorted to it.

Tomorrow morning, when the sun came over the Andes at his back, he would get up and go to the car. Right now he would be miserably uncomfortable. An hour or two from now he would be shivering. This was a good plan. Misery would stoke his anger. This whole clammy, chilly, ghastly night was her fault. It would stay in his mind forever, and feed his hatred of the *professor*. He would hate her more each minute—no, he would hate her more each second. All the long night his loathing of her would grow. His body would be marinated in hatred for her. She had evaded him twice now.

She had called his professionalism into question.

Nothing would come between him and her death.

38

"It is the *River Landscape with Ferry*," the little Dutchman told Joseph Stryker, holding out a glossy photograph. Although the Dutchman was sleek and dressed in a beautiful glen plaid suit, his shaking hands and the sheen of sweat at his receding hairline detracted from the masterful image he wanted to project. The photograph trembled so much Stryker took it out of the man's hand to study it.

"Salomon van Ruysdael," Stryker said, reading the notation on the photograph.

"1649," said the little man.

"133.5 by 99.5 centimeters." Joseph converted this in his head to roughly five feet by three and a half feet. "Biggish piece to get away with from a museum this well guarded."

Although this sounded like praise, the little man took it as a criticism. "The painting was very well protected. A tilt detector in the frame. A tracking sensor on the back of the canvas itself. Much like those you Americans have in your stores that sound a noise when you leave the store."

"Yes?"

"Let alone the security we have here in the building itself."

The little man, whose name was Reinert DeGroot, spoke English with a very slight British accent and a quite pronounced Dutch accent. But then, Stryker thought, the man spoke English better than Stryker spoke Dutch. Stryker had himself been in the Netherlands frequently and for long periods, and nevertheless he spoke Dutch very poorly, but could read it reasonably well.

The painting was on loan from the Rijksmuseum in Amsterdam, a gigantic collection of collections, with five thousand paintings, many of them the most valuable on earth. It housed thirty thousand historical objects. Its numismatic collection was the finest and largest in the world. There were also immense collections of silver and gold objects, rare stamps, and several kings' ransoms of jewelry. This small, well-respected museum in the Hague, fifty kilometers from Amsterdam, was no less careful about its collection.

Naturally, Joseph thought, it was very well guarded. But somebody had got away with an important painting, right under the guards' noses. "What would you say it was worth?" he asked the little Dutchman.

"I—I can hardly guess."

"Guess."

"It's priceless. But if you force me, possibly four to five million dollars. In artistic terms it is worth much more."

Joseph Stryker studied the glossy reproduction in his hand. *River Landscape with Ferry*, SK-A 3983, was in fact a lovely thing. The ferry looked a bit more like a barge to his eye. On the barge along with several people was a cow, apparently being taken across a river. There were other cows on the bank, a church, ducks, and in the center a tree, all very Dutch. "What is that cow doing?" he said to DeGroot in mock horror, pointing to one in the back.

"He is—ah—"

Cows mating. The old Dutch painters had a sly sense of humor. "A wonderful glow the painting has," Joseph said.

"That is partly the varnish. The painter intended the varnish to give it that golden glow. We do not overclean our paintings here, the way you do in the United States."

Well, you still had to come to me, the semi-savage American, to solve your mystery.

A second man, taller than DeGroot, with spiky wheat-colored hair, stood a bit off to one side, staring angrily at the ceiling. He had been introduced as Gerritt Heidema. DeGroot said that Heidema did not speak English. Joseph doubted that. Some people claimed not to speak English for political reasons. People like Heidema, security people, often feigned not to speak a language in hopes of overhearing more than they would otherwise.

The room in which they stood was square. The walls were white, the ceiling ten feet overhead, not very high for a gallery. Standing in the doorway, he faced, on the wall opposite, two paintings in heavy frames, one about two feet wide, the other three feet. The wall to his left showed a much larger painting of a castle on a rocky crag. Very dramatic. "Jacob van Ruysdael," said DeGroot, noting the direction of his gaze. "Salomon's nephew." The three were all on loan for six months.

On the wall to his right hung two frames. The painting in the closest showed a still life of fruit. The second heavy frame was empty. A small copy card, a pasteboard square with a little reproduction of the painting and the words "removed for cleaning," had been pinned in its place.

The picture had disappeared on DeGroot's and Heidema's watch—DeGroot was curator, Heidema chief of security. No wonder they were angry. They were also frightened. Because the theft was mysterious, they were both under serious suspicion.

They were angry, too, that the government had forced them to call Stryker in. Joseph Stryker had a reputation for discovering things. They'd reached him in Hyderabad yesterday where he had been trying unsuccessfully to locate a very old sculpture of Kali, goddess of creation and destruction. He had leads on the stolen Kali, and he hoped the leads would wait until he returned. The van Ruysdael theft was fresh. He felt like saying that he had come here out of the goodness of his heart, but Heidema and DeGroot wouldn't care. Nor would it be true, really. He had come because of the painting. It grieved him when a painting was stolen, since it would so likely be damaged. Or lost. Some stolen art was never found, and while the belief was that the vanished work had disappeared into the hands of miserly collectors who hoarded it in secret, one couldn't be sure. Given current worldwide economic conditions, odds were that the missing van Ruysdael was on its way to the Middle East.

The painting could not possibly get the care it deserved while it was being stolen and transported.

Stryker said, "Tell me what happened."

DeGroot sighed. Then he straightened up and said something to Heidema in Dutch. Heidema replied, handed DeGroot a sheet of printout. Joseph Stryker reflected that, while Dutch sounded a lot like German, the Dutch didn't think so. Many Dutch people claimed not to be able to understand German. That was more political than real. Joseph knew German better than Dutch and picked up a bit of what was being said by Heidema. It seemed to translate as, "If you bloody well have to."

"On Monday at 1400 hours the guard on this corridor made his regular entry into this room. He has only four rooms to circulate through, all on this hall. You may have seen the others as we entered here."

"Two on this side of the hall, two on the other side? Each pair contiguous?" Joseph asked, looking at Heidema, even though DeGroot would translate to Heidema and then translate back. He knew, as did Heidema no doubt, that the most likely person to mastermind a theft in a high-security situation is the chief of security.

Heidema said, "Ja," to DeGroot's translation, which DeGroot wisely did not bother to translate.

"So the guard was never more than, say, fifty feet from the missing painting?" Joseph said.

DeGroot himself answered this. "Yes."

"Go on."

DeGroot continued. "As I say, his regular pass through here is on the stroke of two. The gallery next to this is five minutes later, the one directly across the hall ten after the hour and the last at a quarter past the hour. He surveys the hall for a bit each time he enters it. There was nothing remarkable at any time."

"Is the routine that regular? That predictable?"

DeGroot correctly took this as a criticism. "We have to balance two needs," he said, huffily. "We need to know where the guard is—"

"To be certain that he's doing his job? Not sitting in a corner drinking coffee?"

"The need to know where he is balanced by the need for some unpredictability. He varies the timing by a few minutes, stopping when any visitor catches his eye. He takes very little time when a gallery is empty, for instance, and arrives in the next gallery ahead of the rotation."

"And when he came in here?"

"The painting was simply gone. Gone!"

"Who was in this room?"

"No one."

"Was the guard searched?"

"He was questioned and *thoroughly* searched immediately. As you see, though, the painting was not small. One could not conceal it in one's mouth or—body orifices. And he was stripped and his clothes searched minutely."

"Was the room otherwise the same?"

"Completely. The only change was the single missing van Ruysdael."

"And on the guard's previous pass, the painting had been there?"

He received pitying looks and an impatient nod, but he wasn't in the business of making friends. He added to their annoyance by saying, "And this guard has a long history of trustworthiness?"

DeGroot turned red, but he shoved a folder of papers into Joseph's hand. Clipped inside was a photo of the guard. A sheet detailed his entire childhood, education, and every home address up to the most recent. Another two sheets covered his work history. There was his application to the museum, summaries of interviews before he was hired, and various formal papers from which Joseph gleaned that the man had begun work here in 1991. At the end of the file was a clipped-together stack of job performance evaluations and descriptions of which galleries in the museum he had guarded, covering the fifteen years of his work here.

"He has been utterly admirable," DeGroot said in an offhand voice that implied, "We do not hire anyone who isn't."

"So let me summarize the time sequence," Stryker said. "The guard operates on a twenty-minute cycle. Five minutes are spent in this room, then fifteen altogether in the other three rooms. Therefore the thief had no more than fifteen minutes to grab the painting and make off with it."

"Well, but the people who left this gallery didn't have it—"

"That's my next question. What people who left? Who was in this room?"

"There was a woman in here who left a minute or so after the guard."

"How do you know?"

"Not just the guard's word. We have videotapes."

Joseph pointed to a camera over the door. "From that? What is its coverage?"

"We will show you what it sees," said DeGroot. Then he spoke to Heidema and the two went to stand at opposite sides of the room, DeGroot about two feet in front of the empty frame and Heidema just three feet in front of the painting of Bentheim Castle. "From me to Mr. Heidema."

"So your camera does not see either of the paintings on the side walls?"

"No. But it does not need to. It sees all the center of the room and angles downward to the entry threshold. No one can come in or go out who is not observed."

There was a burst of angry Dutch from Heidema, which DeGroot frowned at and did not translate. Joseph picked up enough of it to know Heidema had asked the administration for better cameras and been turned down for budget reasons. Money of course was the reason that most museums could not afford to have a guard in every gallery.

Stryker said to Heidema, "We'll take a look at the tape in a few minutes. I assume on the tape you don't see anybody making off with the painting."

Heidema mumbled what might have been a curse.

"Are visitors screened when they arrive at the museum?"

DeGroot, after a quick exchange with Heidema, said, "Incoming visitors must leave their packages, large purses, and even books at the entry desk. You need a specific permit to bring in a drawing pad. Actually, the woman who was here just before the theft had been here several times. She was making a small painting of the van Ruysdael."

"Really?"

"Well, of course that is permitted. It is in our charter that we are an educational institution. This is true at most of your museums in the United States as well."

"Did you ask her whether she saw the painting missing?"

"Yes. She said it was still in place."

"So unless she and the hall guard and the guard at the exit are conspirators—" He didn't add, "and you."

"But neither can have taken it. They were searched immediately!"

Stryker pointed at the copy card stating that the painting had been removed for cleaning. "Is the card yours?"

"No. The thief left it."

"The thief took the time to put up the card?" Cards like these were used in galleries routinely.

DeGroot's expression hardened. "Yes. He was making sport of us."

"You fingerprinted it, of course?"

They both nodded. "It was not one of ours," DeGroot said. "Or any other museum as far as we know. It was run up on somebody's laser printer and cut to the right size."

"All right. So—visitors are allowed in as long as they don't carry anything that could contain a painting. Of course, they could slip a small painting under their clothing."

"But when they leave from this wing," DeGroot said, "they are patted down. Discreetly, by a guard of the same gender, of course. The guards are even more painstaking in the numismatic collection."

"I don't doubt it. And in any case this painting was too large to conceal under clothing," Stryker said, again thinking that a dishonest exit guard was all you'd need to get around that part of the problem if the object were small enough.

"Now," he said, "I want floor plans and construction plans of the building. You renovated parts recently—"

Heidema slipped a roll of blueprints from his bag with a grim smile, as if to say, "Way ahead of you."

Stryker smiled back as if to say, "And you understand English quite well."

Aloud, he asked, "Was the tilt detector in the frame set off when the painting was stolen?"

DeGroot said, "No. We think the frame was never moved. The painting was cut out"—DeGroot winced at the thought of the damage, as did Stryker—"obviously. When the guard came in on his regular rotation, the painting was gone. Altogether the thief cannot have used more than ten minutes."

"What other security devices does the painting have?"

"The tracking sensor sets off an alarm if the painting is taken past the exit scanner. It is painted to look like canvas and fixed very unobtrusively to its back."

"It never went off?"

"The alarm never went off and the device must still be on the canvas, since it has not been found in the museum."

"So the painting may never have left the gallery," Heidema said, giving up entirely on the pretense of not understanding English.

Stryker said. "Let's see those building plans."

The room was essentially no more than a commercial "vanilla box." Unlike the Rijksmuseum, the Hobbes had been designed to be as little ornamented as possible so as not to detract from the paintings themselves.

Stryker knew this, but he didn't know what the building was like structurally.

"Let's go from top to bottom," he said. "What is above this ceiling?"

The building plans showed a dropped ceiling hanging twenty-four inches below the true ceiling that carried the ventilation ducts and electrical conduits. Stryker asked for a ladder. When Heidema bellowed for one, it came in so fast that Stryker, suspicious that it might have been used in the theft, asked where it had been kept.

"Ordinarily, in the supplies room under lock and key," Heidema said. "We brought it here after the theft to do exactly what you want to do. We searched all the ducts within ten minutes of the theft. We know there's nothing up there."

Stryker did what he wanted anyway. He climbed up and checked the ceiling, moving the ladder a few feet at a time. He pushed hard on the ceiling and found no loose spots. If nothing else proved helpful, he would have them cut out a piece of ceiling and search above it for the missing painting, but for now he thought they wouldn't find it there.

He removed the grille from the ceiling air duct and shoved his head and one shoulder into the large feeder duct itself. A very slender person could slither inside. The plans, however, showed that the main duct that fed air to this gallery ran directly from a high-powered central fan that boosted the power of the general air system. Anyone crawling into the fan would be cut to ribbons. On this side of the fan, the main duct ran to this room and the three other rooms on this hall, the ones supervised by the same guard. There had been visitors in all three. A branch went up from the main duct here to the second floor, feeding air into the four galleries above these. Stryker looked. "What about the branches upstairs from here?" Stryker said.

"Narrower," said Heidema.

Yes, on the plans they were two-thirds the size of the ducts on this floor. No average adult could even squeeze into them, much less move along. But could a rolled painting be fed through it? He would check from upstairs to be sure the grilles had not recently been removed.

"The grille over this air duct is outside the range of the video cameras, isn't it?"

Unhappily, Heidema said, "Yes."

"And right near the stolen van Ruysdael."

Next Stryker climbed down and checked the wall panels. The new white panels were plasterboard, laid over a concrete wall. The joins were loose in a couple of places, and Stryker, thinking that a painting could be hidden behind them, worked his fingers into one crack and simply pulled. The panel came part way off with a screech, showing underlying concrete.

Heidema said, "That panel is loose because we pried them all away to make sure the van Ruysdael hadn't been hidden behind one of them."

DeGroot said, "The panels were intact and flush to the walls up to then."

Stryker took notice of white paint in the seams between the panels. The Dutchman was probably right; the panels had been painted in place and the paint appeared to have been recently cracked when the searchers pried them off.

Stryker turned his attention to the floor. It sloped just slightly to a drain at the far right-hand side of the room, just in front of the empty frame.

"Why is there a drain?"

"God forbid we should have a flood," DeGroot said.

"The Netherlands is very rainy," Heidema added. "There have been water leaks."

"And there are restrooms upstairs," DeGroot said, pursing his mouth. "The tourists demand them on every floor! And there is the sprinkler system." He said the last words as one might utter "dry rot." "Very dangerous to paintings."

Stryker by now was ignoring them and pulling the grate off the drain. "This, too, is out of camera range," he said cheerily. Neither man responded.

The round grate was rusty iron, but came out of the cement opening fairly easily. The grate itself was five inches in diameter and it was set over a drainpipe four and a half inches in diameter.

"We looked in there immediately," Heidema said. "The painting wasn't there."

"It could fit in here, though, rolled up. Where does the pipe go?"

"It curves down a bit and then goes directly outside. You couldn't push the painting through because of the curve. Probably you couldn't push it through anyway. We ran a fiber-optic probe into the pipe right after the theft. The painting wasn't there."

Stryker paced into the hall. It was absolutely straight for thirty feet in one direction and forty-five feet in another. The floor plans seemed perfectly accurate. At the shorter end, the hall dead-ended just past the door to the second gallery on that side, but there was no exit from that gallery or any of the galleries except through this hall. No way to get outdoors. At the longer end, the hall took a right-angle turn, went past two gallery doors, one on each side of the hall, and then opened into a large rotunda, where guards sat watching everyone who came and went.

"Now I want to talk with the guard," Stryker said.

"We did that." Heidema was annoyed.

DeGroot said, "Of course you may. He's waiting in the rotunda."

"Let's have him in here."

The guard was a mixture of humble and truculent, standing with his hands clasped behind his back, his chin up, but his replies soft. He spoke no English. DeGroot translated.

Stryker, who was closely watching the man's eyes, said, "You were in charge of guarding four rooms?"

DeGroot translated.

The reply was that he indeed had that honor.

"Isn't that quite a bit? One can hardly be in four places at once."

The man looked, with his eyes only, at DeGroot, keeping his head faced forward. When DeGroot nodded, he said, "I am very careful. I take particular note of the people."

"Well, then, tell me about the people that day."

"There was a small family group, an old lady with, I think, her son and daughter-in-law. I am judging this by the similarities of appearance between the old lady and the man."

"They came in, when?"

"About ten minutes before the—before everything happened."

"And stayed how long?"

"Not more than five minutes in the gallery. I checked. They seemed not so interested in the paintings."

"So when they went in, the woman painting was already there and when they left she was still there?"

"Yes."

"Then she left after you did your check of that room?"

"Yes."

"Exactly how soon?"

"Each time I go into the hall, I walk past all three doors and then go into the gallery that is next on my rota. I was in the hall perhaps three minutes. No, two. I saw her come out as I was entering gallery 241."

"Which is contiguous to this, the next one along the hall?"

"Yes."

"She was alone with the painting maybe three minutes?"

"Two." The guard began to sweat a little.

"Then what?"

"I gave the alarm but stayed in the gallery. I carry a phone. The woman who had been painting was in the rotunda and was stopped there. She had only her painting materials, a small canvas on which she had been painting, and some conté crayons in a small cloth bag."

"A palette knife?"

DeGroot translated the question. The guard frowned but answered that she did have one.

"We checked it," Heidema said. "It had traces of her paint on it, from mixing paint on her palette. But there were no traces of her paint on the frame of the van Ruysdael."

The fact that it could be quickly wiped was so obvious Stryker didn't even mention it.

"The woman had been under observation in the rotunda?"

DeGroot said, "You are thinking she could have passed the painting to a confederate. But she was seen chatting with the guard at the desk. He says she had been there since he saw her come out of the hall to the gallery. And all other visitors were held and searched as well."

The guard said, "Please! I did nothing to that painting. It was there and then it was gone. Just gone!"

"What do you think?" DeGroot asked, after he dismissed the guard.

Heidema said, "It's a complete mystery!"

Stryker said, "No, I don't think so. I think somebody has been reading too much Jacques Futrelle. And they say the criminal classes are uneducated."

39

Joseph Stryker had told DeGroot and Heidema that he would return the next day, after he did a bit of research, and tell them what had happened to the van Ruysdael. He was well aware that Heidema, the head of security, didn't believe he knew. But DeGroot accepted with bad grace, even though he must desperately want the crime to be cleared up.

Stryker arrived at the desk at the appointed time, 2:00 P.M., carrying a small box of the sort artists and sketchers use. From the desk attendant, he picked up one of the stools they gave visiting artists. Loaning this equipment was safer for the museum than letting painters bring in their own. Knives and other tools could be hidden in the legs of painting stools.

"You're going to blame it on the woman, I see," Heidema said. His English had improved even more in the last day.

"It's almost always the simplest explanation that's the true one. Who was the last person alone with the painting? The woman. Any other explanation would have required a conspiracy of two or more people, including her."

"Go ahead."

"That's all very well, but she didn't."

"Have you circulated her photo to the police?"

"No, of course not."

"When I show you that she took the van Ruysdael, you can circulate her photo and have a good chance somebody someplace will know her. It's a small world, art theft."

"But she couldn't have taken it."

"I want you to look in this box and be sure there is nothing here she wouldn't have been carrying. Nothing the guards wouldn't have let through."

Heidema reached for the box.

"Ah-ah-ah!" Stryker said. "Search it only as much as an unsuspicious guard would. On her *arrival*. You told me they search more carefully when a person leaves than when he or she arrives."

Heidema shrugged. He opened the box. Inside were some wadded cloths, six tubes of paint, several pencils and brushes in a plastic cover, a small canvas rolled and covered with plastic, and a small jar of linseed oil.

Heidema brandished the roll of canvas. "This is the size she used, and we realize hers was similar to the van Ruysdael in size."

"I know."

"And the woman's canvas was inspected when she was leaving. Because the theft was discovered before she was gone, her canvas was confiscated. We still have it. I can show it to you. It's not a painted-over van Ruysdael."

"I don't need to see it. I believe you."

DeGroot, the little Dutch director, got tired of this talk and said, "Let's proceed." He marched to the gallery. Stryker followed and set up his stool, his painting materials, and his canvas.

"The camera sees from here"—Stryker paced from a spot in front of the large castle painting on the left wall—"to here." He stopped about three feet in front of the absent van Ruysdael. When neither Dutchman answered, he said, "Yes?"

"Yes," Heidema growled.

"The woman could not store the painting in the ceiling, or the air ducts, even though there's space for it. Because it would be found almost as soon as you started searching. Which you did."

"We did," said DeGroot.

"The next thing you would do is pull off any loose paneling."

"We did that, too."

"So she didn't leave the painting here, hidden. She took it away."

"She did *not*," said DeGroot. "She was searched. She did not hide it on the way from here to the rotunda, either, or pass it to anyone to hide elsewhere. We searched everyone in this wing, and soon after that we searched the other three galleries in this wing. And no one else had been allowed in here in the interim."

"She got it out of here through that floor drain."

"Impossible," DeGroot said.

"You can't push anything through it," Heidema said. "We tried."

"Probably not, but you can pull something through it."

"Impossible," DeGroot repeated.

"Sitting here painting, she had all the time in the world. She could wait until there was no one in this gallery. And after just two or three visits, she certainly would know the guard's very regular itinerary."

Heidema made a noise in his throat.

"She could also hear whether there were people coming and going in the hall. The place is very quiet."

"Yes, yes," DeGroot said impatiently.

"Let's say it is now the first day that the hall is quiet. Day One. There is no one in the galleries on either side. The guard has left on his rounds. I am the painting woman. I get up."

Stryker took from his box a tube of paint, a wadded-up rag, and from the roll of brushes a small spool of thread.

He took the top off the paint tube. "This is actually Super Glue," he said. He reached in the rag and pulled out a small, squirming gray creature. A mouse. Holding it by the tail, he dabbed the back of the mouse with the glue and affixed the thread. He did this as if mixing paint. The side of his body was turned away from the video camera.

Tossing the rag into the box, he backed up, cocking his head as if studying the painting of the castle, then comparing it to the copy he was painting. He paced backward until he was in front of the empty space that once held the van Ruysdael. Then he quickly pulled the grille off the top of the drain and placed the mouse in the drain. The animal scampered away.

"A hungry little mouse," Stryker said, as he paid out the thread. After a few seconds, most of the thread had disappeared into the drain, and he Super Glued the end of the thread to the side of the drain wall and replaced the grille. Then, again cocking his head as he studied the castle painting, he walked back to his seat on the painting stool.

"Forty seconds," said Heidema.

"The drain is on your building plan. It bends gently, but just to go down a little. Then it levels off and goes outside. It goes right under that wall"—he gestured at the wall where the van Ruysdael had hung—"and outdoors. The distance is less than fifteen feet. The drainpipe sticks out a few inches above ground in an area on the side of the museum where there are bushes and flowers. My confederate is sitting on a bench near the sidewalk, feeding birds and watching a little trap. Inside the trap is peanut butter, and now a mouse."

"So now you have a thread in the pipe. So what?"

"Day Two," Stryker said. "This is the next time the hall is quiet, there is no one in this room but the woman, and the guard has just left."

He got up and took a small ball of heavy string from the painting box. Holding it next to his body, he again stepped away from his painting. At the drain, he pulled up the grille and quickly tied the string to the thread. He pulled three times on the thread. After a few seconds, the thread disappeared and the string snaked into the drain. When the string ceased to move, he Super Glued one end to the inside of the drain and went back to his seat.

DeGroot said, "Oh, dear."

"Oh, dear indeed," Stryker said. "It is now Day Three."

"But you can't pull a canvas through a pipe. It'll snag," Heidema said.

"We'll see. To continue. You realize she has to bring only one roll of string or thread any particular day," Stryker said. "And fifteen feet is a small roll. If found, it looks like painting supplies. Some painters use string to establish a straight line."

"I still say—"

"Day Three." Stryker took another small roll from his case. "This is four-hundred-pound-test monofilament fish line. You can land a two-hundred-pound thrashing tuna on this and have strength to spare."

He tied it to the heavy string, gave three pulls, and they all watched it disappear into the drain.

"But you can't pull a canvas out with that."

"Watch. Day Four." He picked up the canvas he had been pretending to paint. "Here. Go stand with this near the wall." Frowning, Heidema carried the canvas to the wall where the van Ruysdael had hung.

Stryker took from the box the plastic tube that had held the paintbrushes and pencils. It was a long cylinder. "Umbrella cover," he said.

He rolled it up in one fist, and holding it out of sight of the camera, walked to Heidema. He took the canvas that Heidema had held flat. "Pretend I'm cutting the van Ruysdael out of the frame," he said, gesturing. Then he rolled the canvas into a tube, inserted it in the plastic tube, closed the end, tied the fishing line around it and Super Glued the line to the plastic for greater strength. Then he pulled the line three times and the tube and canvas slithered into the drain and disappeared.

"Less than a minute," he said.

For a few seconds no one spoke. Then Heidema said, as if denying it all, "But the guard said she was really painting. The canvas progressed from visit to visit."

"Of course she really painted. And possibly she worked on it a bit at home, too."

DeGroot said, "You are telling us she brought the mouse every time up until she could use it?"

"That's what I would have done."

"But even in a rag, it would have been found when she was searched on the way out."

"Doubt it," said Stryker. "I imagine each time she brought one, she just let it go before she left."

"*Here?*" DeGroot said. *"In my museum?"*

40

Marcus sat at his desk and tried to see the Washington Monument through the haze of heat mist. On rare clear days, he could see it, a white needle in the far distance. His office was on a low floor and had just one window, unlike Director Haseltine, who had a corner office with four windows, the status equivalent of the E-ring, if they had been in the Pentagon. Marcus's window looked out at the parking lot and the cloverleaf mess where Interstate 395, two state roads, and Washington Boulevard inefficiently came together. He dragged his gaze gratefully back from the view, but his mind had never left the problem of Hacker.

It was not, Marcus thought, that fake drivers' licenses, various IDs, foreign passports, even U.S. passports, credit cards, and so on were so hard to get. Unfortunately, they were easy. But good ones were expensive. The more subtleties nations built into them—holograms, embedded metallics, etching as fine as on paper money—the more expensive they became. He supposed the cost cut out a lot of dangerous amateurs. It hadn't even slowed down the professional crooks and the canniest terrorists.

Building a better class of criminals?

Lately he'd heard that not simply perfect but real, genuine IDs were entering the international market. Apparently, you just paid a worker in a government passport agency in, say, Pakistan, to make one up to your specifications, with whatever the validating elements used by the country it was from. Presto. Instant, blameless Pakistani citizen with no outstanding wants or warrants.

Hacker had access to the very best ID. As far as Marcus could discover, the man had never been stopped or even queried because any of his ID looked hinky. To have such good work whenever he wanted it argued for one of three things, a very good income from freelance assassination, so that he could afford the fakes, or the backing of a foreign government, or the backing of a big and very lucrative criminal organization.

Marcus believed the last. There was a kind of thread that ran through his killings, as if one organization with its own purposes kept him on retainer. The thread was drug involvement.

Against this was the fact that some of his killings were hard to fit into a single organization's purpose. A couple of the killings were of people like the Massachusetts legislator who wanted to decriminalize marijuana. They were all drug-related, but exactly how?

In the two weeks since he had been back from Chicago, Marcus had dealt with a lot of day-to-day work that came across his desk. There seemed to be more of it each morning when he arrived at the office. But the puzzle of why Hacker had gone to Chicago never left his mind. He assigned four agents to scan all the surveillance videos of people entering or leaving O'Hare, Midway, and Milwaukee/Mitchell airports. It was a gargantuan task. Two hundred thousand passengers went through O'Hare every day, and that didn't count the building employees, pilots, attendants, security people, ticket agents, cleaning staff, restroom suppliers, plumbers, electricians, tech support, food suppliers, window washers, paramedics, painters, laundry workers, air systems techs, baggage handlers, cooks, waiters, mechanics, and an endless list of others. Surveillance cameras watched the entry and exit doors on the two arrival and departure levels, and pretty much everything else inside—security checkpoints, food lines, boarding areas, and the tarmac.

Fortunately, the agents didn't have to study all the footage. Even speeded up to double-time, that would take too long. And the higher-ups at the agency weren't going to spend a lot of staff time or money on it. Agency Director Haseltine's attitude was, "He's left the country. Good riddance."

"He can come back."

Haseltine said, "At least as far as we know, he didn't kill anybody we care about."

Marcus's men were now actually watching "picked" scenes. The tapes had been scored for scale and had frozen clips of people between five feet seven and six feet. They couldn't confine their search to men, because the program wasn't good enough at that type of discrimination yet. It was possible that Hacker could disguise himself as a woman, even though Marcus doubted that he would. His pattern had been minimal disguise.

They also had to include people in wheelchairs and medical patients on gurneys.

But after several days, the men had pulled nearly twenty-three hundred possibles, which they carefully winnowed down to forty-nine probables. And from there, it took Marcus only minutes to pick Hacker out of the group.

They had him on video entering the terminal at O'Hare through an Arrivals entrance, not Departures, on the afternoon of May twenty-ninth, the day of Marcus's failed raid on the Chicago apartment building. Hacker may have figured if anybody was looking for him, they'd check the Departures tapes first, as indeed they had. But it was just an escalator ride from Arrivals to Departures, and they had him five minutes later going through a security line on the Departures level, his bag passing blamelessly along on the conveyer belt, Hacker himself striding happily through the metal detector.

Of course he wouldn't carry any weapons.

Having located him, it was a simple matter to chart his path to a flight with a Kennedy/New York destination. Knowing his arrival time, they picked him up on Kennedy, tapes, then lost him again.

Then found the next part of his trail. Under a different name, he had flown out of Kennedy standby, going to Monte Carlo.

What galled Marcus even more was how happy Hacker looked as he passed through O'Hare. He was wearing a purple and white baseball cap and a bright yellow shirt with the words LAS VEGAS—WHAT HAPPENS HERE STAYS HERE in cobalt blue. He carried a blue soft-sided overnight bag with LAS VEGAS—BE ANYBODY YOU WANT TO BE on the side in pink letters. Just a good old boy coming home from a naughty weekend. Adding a slap in the face to law enforcement?

The happiness on Hacker's face looked real. A man satisfied. And not by a Vegas showgirl. Marcus could have sworn it was the look of a man pleased with a job well done. But of course the man was an actor.

Some murder in Chicago on May 29, or much less likely May 28, had to be his. Which one?

Frank Ayala had been sixty-one when he died. He came to the United States in 1964 as a teenager, and within five years converted his father's Maxwell Street pushcart business to a small storefront grocery. He moved the grocery to a larger location on West Grand in 1993, and the big, well-equipped, well-stocked Mexican food store had blossomed as the Mexican population increased. In the late evening of May twenty-eighth, after the two regular employees had gone home, Frank began to close down the store. A last customer, or maybe two, entered. The video on the cash register showed only one man, seen from the back, and wearing a hooded sweatshirt too baggy to permit identification, pointing a revolver at Frank. There was no audio on the tape, but Frank is seen shaking his head. The assailant shoots. Frank grabs a display of candy and gum and hurls it at the attacker, who shoots again. Frank goes down behind the counter. The tape shows nothing interesting after that, except an arm dipping into the cash register. The attacker turns, his face still invisible in the sweatshirt hood, and then he must have run out the front door.

Was Hacker the killer? The man was the right height, but this guy looked too slender, and he moved like a teenager, fluidly but impulsively.

Surely Hacker was a great actor, but he couldn't make himself that much thinner.

Marcus sighed. There were a couple of "natural" but unexpected deaths on those two days. There were a few deaths that were not in the physician-attended category, but which were not believed to be homicide. Marcus spent some time looking at the case of Letty Stein, seventy-nine years old. Ms. Stein had been found dead in her apartment on north Sheridan. A brittle diabetic, she had either skipped her insulin, eaten a lot of forbidden Turkish paste, which she particularly loved—there were seven one-pound boxes in her pantry—or possibly her insulin had been withheld from her. Who could tell? A perfunctory autopsy had suggested she had been eating sweets. And certainly she was in ketoacidosis. She had been found at home, alone, in bed, in a locked and perfectly orderly apartment.

What would Hacker have wanted with Letty Stein?

Letty's son, Benny, came into $700,000 worth of silver mining stock at her death. The stock had been bought, with considerable prescience, by her husband several years earlier. The husband had also purchased the condo on Sheridan and then died, quite suddenly, in the lobby of a Phoenix hotel where he and his wife were spending two weeks in February. Marcus talked with the detective who worked Letty's death. She said there was no evidence that Benny had been in the apartment during the two weeks before Mrs. Stein's death. Her insulin prescription was new. Only one of the vials had been used. Mrs. Stein could have opened her new batch before finishing the old batch. She could have gone back to the old batch later, and if it was plain water substituted by Benny, could have used it, thrown the packaging in the trash, and later died. The detective, a Regina Fetalli, said that she had considered it, but the stock would have passed to Benny eventually anyhow, and any other notion was "way too Agatha Christie."

For Marcus, the point was, there was no connection between Hacker and silver mines, and Mrs. Stein was hardly a drug dealer in competition with anybody.

They were all like that, one way or another. If Mrs. Stein was a possible drug underdose, there were several overdoses of various street drugs. None of them had been recorded as a homicide, and to Marcus's eye, he agreed. They were sad but accidental.

Just west of The Loop, a man named John Smith—and nobody ever found any identification more believable than that for him—had been gunned down late Friday. One courageous or foolish street person and an angry prostitute told the investigating officers that the man was a drug dealer. Marcus phoned one of the detectives. Might as well be thorough.

"Jacko's kid," Detective Solway said. "I heard of you. Eighteenth District a while back? Right?"

"Right."

"What do you need?"

"May twenty-eighth. Shooting at West Adams and Halsted."

"I remember. Greektown. Not a place we get a lot of homicides."

Marcus asked, "This guy John Smith important?"

"More important than he looked, you mean? No. Couldn't be. He had a pocket full of little Baggies with the corners missing."

"Oh. A retailer."

"Yeah."

That pretty much let John Smith out. A man who personally stuffed the product into the corners of Baggies, tied them, cut them off, and sold them, was not a man in charge of anything. Marcus could think of far-fetched explanations for Hacker killing him, but they were way, way too far-fetched.

On May twenty-eighth, there had been a murder in Aurora, Illinois, a western suburb on the Fox River, thirty miles from The Loop. That was pretty far for Hacker to drive, and he probably wouldn't take public transportation to a suburb on the way to a killing. Too many people might remember him.

Still, from the faxes the state sent him, the case sounded promising because the dead man was a pharmacist. The man had been shot while closing up his store in the late evening. Hans Overmet, the dead man, owned four pharmacies in two western suburbs, a set-up that was perfect for distributing illegal drugs and legal medications bled off for illicit purposes. The method of murder was also typically gangland. As the sheet put it:

"Responding to report of shots fired, at 2213 hours R/O examined the premises of 332 Arbor and discovered the rear door of premises ajar. Discovered a W/M approx. fifty years of age proned out on floor with small wound to back rear of skull. Notified C. EMTs responded at 2227 hours."

Working through the turgid prose, Marcus pictured a middle-aged man executed by a shot to the back of the head from what proved, in later reports, to have been a twenty-two. This was typically a mob executioner's weapon and the head shot the preferred location. The twenty-two was popular because it was fairly quiet, even without a silencer, and the low power produced a round that usually bounced around in the skull, causing massive brain damage, unlike higher-powered weapons that could go on through and leave the victim alive.

He Googled the Aurora Police Department, which was located on North River Street. Sounded like a pleasant location. The officer he caught at the desk was pleasant, too. "Susan Capresso. What can I do for you?"

He identified himself and gave call-back numbers so that she could verify he was who he said he was. However, her CLI was no doubt printing out that he was calling from the agency. She said, "Go ahead."

"I'm interested in the Hans Overmet homicide."

"Why?"

"There was a killer in the area. I'd been watching him on and off for some time—"

"You're out of luck. Sorry. Shouldn't interrupt. But we solved it."

There was justifiable satisfaction in her tone. She added, "Not that it was too difficult."

"What was it?"

"We went out to the widow's house yesterday to follow up on a few things. I'm ringing the doorbell—front door—when my partner sees a man climbing out a window on the side of the house. Well, we pursue, of course. Coulda been a burglar. Turned out to be the widow's boyfriend. So the widow's all flustered, and long story short, they actually *kept* the twenty-two they shot the guy with. Can you believe?"

"I can."

"Sorry. I'm not much help on your thing."

"Congratulations, anyhow."

Marcus spent several minutes lingering over the account of a dead prostitute. Her game name was Samantha Dee. Marcus knew right away Hacker hadn't killed the young woman. She was too unimportant. But it was just so sad he couldn't quite shuffle it to the no-go pile. That would be like writing her off. She was seventeen. She was found in an alley off Sixty-third Street. She was wearing a cheap fringed bra and orange plastic shorts. She was strangled. Any money she may have had was missing.

Sighing, he finally set the case aside.

So May twenty-ninth.

He reached Sgt. Horace Pollard in mid-afternoon, and heard Pollard set down a mug near the phone. Visions of his own years of dreadful district coffee swam before his eyes.

"Pollard," came the voice.

"Hey, Pollard. Marcus Holton. We spent a while in the Seventh together, way back."

"Hey-y-y." Pollard chuckled in a way that warned Marcus something was coming. "Marcus. You're the sweet chap who put the dead woodchuck in the air vent above the commander's office."

"I did *not*."

"Mmm-mm?"

"At least that's my story and I'm sticking to it."

"And you told him it had probably crawled in there because woodchucks are attracted to peanut butter."

"Commanders shouldn't eat other people's peanut butter cookies when their backs are turned."

"The commanders' backs? Oh, never mind. What can I do for you?"

"One of your homicides. Dr. Edward Eriksen. Two weeks ago?"

"Oh, I remember it well."

"Why? Didn't seem so gory from the description."

"It wasn't the blood. It was the baby."

"Explain."

Pollard explained.

"So did you find anything odd in Eriksen's life?"

"Oddly boring."

"Drug involvement? Political connections? Mob stuff?"

"He was a doctor. He administered drugs, sure. No sign he used and absolutely no hint he sold."

"How come you looked at whether he sold?" Marcus was aware that an ordinary murder/burglary at a spouse's place probably wouldn't go that far.

"Well, we looked at the wife, too. She traveled a lot before the baby was born, so she might have been bringing in drugs. But no hint that she was. Also, I am proud to say we have some very reliable snitches in the undocumented pharmaceutical world."

"I know."

"You would."

"No word on the street." He paused. "Other reason I looked around. No clear reason to actually kill the guy. Nothing stolen. Why not take the money and run? So, yeah. I looked a little deeper."

"And?"

"Like I said. Nothing."

No apparent connection to Hacker.

Dead end.

Marcus had set NCIC to search for the name Hacker, and it would automatically search for other names that sounded similar. Marcus added some variations of his own—Hagard, Haggard, Hatter, Hecker, Haecker. He knew this was not likely to achieve anything, since Hacker itself was probably an alias. But possibly Hacker had used it because it was like his real name. Or possibly he had used variations of it even if it wasn't his real name.

Marcus studied accidental deaths in the Chicago area his aide had pulled for him for May twenty-eighth and twenty-ninth. It was desperation thinking, though, he knew.

A hit-and-run of a child in Oak Park.

And another of the exit ramp stupidities. When he had still been in the

CPD, the cops would sit around at a bar after their tours and marvel at highway drivers who would take an off-ramp, suddenly realize it was the wrong exit, and *reverse back onto the highway*. It seemed there was one every couple of weeks, with the idiot driver dead and often deaths in the car that hit him.

There was a window washer who had fallen to his death in The Loop. That was unusual, but didn't look like it could be Hacker's work. The man was thirty-eight, had washed windows for thirteen years, and had lived a peaceful, normal life, except for his occupation.

What drove Hacker to kill? Just money? Even if it was psychopathy or rage, there still appeared to be an element of perfectionism to his behavior. Maybe an obsessive need to get it right.

Maybe a little like me, Marcus thought.

Obsessively, over and over, Marcus studied the tape of Hacker leaving Chicago. He ran the O'Hare footage, with Hacker in his "I've been to Vegas and I feel fine" clothes, bouncing through the terminal. He had changed clothes and persona before he boarded the plane in New York. Hacker had become a grim soul in worker's overalls, a bad haircut, and what looked like a two-day growth of beard but couldn't be, since he'd been clean-shaven in the O'Hare pictures two hours earlier. A little dirt dabbed on his face could achieve that, though, and if he included dirt under his fingernails and on his cuffs and shirt collar it wouldn't look like makeup. His seatmate on the plane might be disgusted, but airport security would think it par for the course.

The Transportation Security Administration had recently announced that it was phasing in the use of "behavioral profiling" at airports to pick up suspicious behavior. They started at Logan Airport in Boston and then expanded to Miami. Presumably the technique had been used for years in Israel with great success. The keywords were "stress, fear, deception." Whatever that meant, Marcus thought. Screeners were even now being trained in "behavior pattern recognition," the press releases said, with practice sessions going on in forty airports nationwide.

Did this really separate the terrorist from the nervous flyer? Maybe it picked up the amateur crook, the man trying to take a large amount of cash out of the country. Certainly a religious zealot, willing to kill himself in the process of crashing a plane would look quite different, possibly even happy. He's going to heaven; what's to worry?

And the point Marcus was making to himself was that he certainly would never have picked Hacker out as suspicious, and he didn't think any amount of training would give him new eyes. After many, many hours of studying passengers, Marcus still would have thought Hacker was just coming back from Vegas, if he had not been looking for him specifically.

The man was a great actor. Okay, Marcus already knew that. But which of the two Hackers on this May twenty-ninth, only a couple of hours apart, was the real one? If either. Marcus had been angered and challenged at the gleeful Hacker in O'Hare. But now that he looked at the man, the face didn't look as real as the grim one.

Was it possible that Hacker had failed on his trip to Chicago? As Diana had said, the man must fail occasionally, no matter how careful he was. No matter how skillful, or how ruthless.

41

The Monday meeting was in the round board room. There were nine people, with Nordmeyer, back from Pennsylvania with stories about arrogant chemistry professors, and Carter back from Cairo with no stories at all. Marcus intentionally did not sit near Diana. They'd been seeing each other a couple of times a week. She'd stayed at his place last weekend. He'd much rather look at her than pay attention to Haseltine's bragging.

Haseltine said, "We interdicted half a million dollars worth of meth last night in Raleigh."

Marcus made a calculation, applying the 60 percent fudge factor he used for all reports of drug busts, and decided they might have captured $300,000 worth.

"That's great, boss," he said, with anemic enthusiasm.

Reed said, "Not bad at all."

"Hmmmp," said Malkovitch.

Diana was silent. Marcus caught her eye and gave a small nod, just saying hi without words. He didn't smile. Haseltine tended to view any facial expression other than rapt interest as mockery. A lot of the time he was right. After a full hour of self-congratulatory accomplishments by "his" agents, Haseltine gave Reed five minutes to report.

Then he stood, letting the others know the meeting was over. Marcus was just about to suggest coffee to Diana, when Haseltine gun-pointed his index finger at Marcus's chest.

"Come to my office."

The office was on the top floor. On the way up in the elevator, Haseltine did not say a word. He brushed past his secretary's desk, even though the secretary leaped to her feet holding a sheaf of papers. Marcus hadn't been told not to follow, so he did.

Whirling around to place his back to the north window, Haseltine said, "You've been making calls to the CPD." He stepped forward and sat in his custom-engineered, sculpted desk chair and did not ask Marcus to take a seat. For a moment Marcus considered sitting down anyway, but he decided not to push it.

"I need Chicago information. I'm lucky I have the contacts."

"Don't."

Marcus stared at him. "Don't?"

Haseltine said, "You're still tracking your pet assassin."

"Yes. He's a killer."

"I've told you before. He's not our *mandate!*"

"He's a danger to American citizens."

"Then give him to the FBI."

"I've sent them everything I have. I don't think they've moved a finger."

"Look, Holton, this is a government agency. Government"—Haseltine steepled his fingers and spoke in a singsong voice which he must have thought was kindergarten-teacher style—"government involves a division of labor. Some agencies oversee the introduction of new medicines. Some provide supplies to the Navy. Some provide policing for Native American communities. We have a mandate, too." He smiled. "We watch for drugs coming into the U.S. And we watch for drugs being manufactured or distributed in the U.S. What part of that don't you understand?"

"I understand all of that, Mr. Haseltine."

"This Hacker does not manufacture or transport drugs."

"He's an enforcer."

"He may be. But we don't know who he is an enforcer for. From my study of the man, he seems to be a freelance."

"I'm beginning to be pretty sure he isn't."

"Intuition?" Haseltine sneered. His frown morphed into a chin-up haughtiness that was almost presidential. "I am telling you, Holton, don't waste the Agency's time on this."

Haseltine was Marcus's boss, and Marcus accepted the fact. He'd been a cop. He accepted that hierarchical organizations had hierarchies. Duh. But he didn't like it and couldn't resist saying, "I would never waste Agency time, sir. I work at least sixty hours a week, sir."

"Then make sure all your sixty hours are spent on Agency business."

Finally, after having expressed disdain both verbally and facially, Haseltine suddenly said, "We've got to go into this later. I do not make the President wait. Neither do you." As if the delay was Marcus's fault.

Haseltine hit his intercom switch. "Get Malkovitch and McCullough to the car."

To Marcus he said, "Let's go."

Marcus stared. "What? Sir?"

"You're going with me. The great man asked for you."

Puzzled, Marcus stood still.

"Let's get moving. Limo's waiting in the garage."

The limo swung onto Army Navy Drive and aimed briefly at the Pentagon before slipping onto I-395, out of Arlington, and crossing the Potomac. It cruised smoothly past the Jefferson Memorial and then the Washington Monument and up along the Ellipse to the White House. You could choke on the history around here, Marcus thought, briefly homesick for Chicago. Chicago had its history, of course, but it wasn't a city that stared at its navel all the damn time.

Why take Malkovitch along? Marcus found it plenty odd that he himself would be going. Malkovitch had been sidelined a long time. Unless there was background of which he had no idea.

The President was glossy-looking. Shaven and powdered. Slick, in fact, Marcus thought, with a twinge of regret that a person had to be slick to sustain himself through the months of scrutiny leading up to the election. Say one unguarded thing and it would be played and replayed until you looked like an idiot and you'd be out of contention. Which meant a man of simple honesty couldn't enter the race. Make one ugly face, and photos of it would be repeated around the world.

What a prison the Presidency would be. How horrible to never, ever, be able to let down your guard.

The President had a lot of hair, too, Marcus noticed. He was tall, like most Presidents. Tall and good hair. Both virtually requirements. When had we last had a bald President? Marcus couldn't remember. Wasn't Dwight Eisenhower bald? That was a long time ago, though.

All the same, Marcus also thought, holy shit! I'm right here in the same room with the President of the goddamn United States!

While he'd been studying the guy, the President had taken two strides toward him and seized his hand. "So this is the new kid on the block," he said, at the same time that Haseltine said, "Marcus Holton, Mr. President."

"I know. I know," the President said in a pleased tone. "Your father is a good buddy of mine. I call him Jacko. Did Coleman tell you I asked especially to meet you? I know how important you are to your father. I have two boys of my own, you know." He patted Marcus on the shoulder.

Always the politician, Marcus thought, but against his will he was frankly flattered and briefly speechless. After all, wasn't this man the most powerful person on the planet?

He finally managed, "Thank you, Mr. President. I know my father admires you greatly." Boy did that sound suck-uppy.

"And Aaron," the President said to Malkovitch. "Always good to see you."

"Mr. President," Malkovitch said, shaking hands.

"Glad to have you aboard," the Prez said to Marcus. "Man of your experience. Young. Just what we need."

Marcus thought, *Hmm. A mild slap at Haseltine?*

"So," said the President of the United States, "what good news do you have for me, Haseltine?"

Seven minutes later, Haseltine was winding down.

"And very successful seize and intercepts. Three hundred seventy-one kilograms of heroin in 1998. Five hundred and forty kilograms of heroin in 2000. Seven hundred five in 2002. Close to a thousand this year."

"Well, that sounds very impressive."

Marcus could not tell whether the President was being sarcastic or serious. He felt sorry for Haseltine, a new emotion indeed. Haseltine had put in a request for an increased budget. But of course, there was an unavoidable dilemma for him. He had to say the drug problem is horrible. Worse than ever. He needed more money to fight it. And in the next breath, he had to say, "We're making real progress. Doing wonders at reducing the drug problem."

Not an easy stance and Haseltine wasn't especially adroit anyhow.

"Cocaine. Thirty-four thousand kilograms in 1998. Thirty-six in 1999. Fifty-eight thousand in 2000. Sixty-one in 2002. Seventy-five—"

The President said to Haseltine, "Please. Coleman. I've read the reports."

"Uh—"

The President pulled out a sheaf of papers from underneath a leather folder on the table.

He said, "Methamphetamine hospital admissions are way up. As are oxycodone."

"Yes, sir."

"We seem not to be stemming the tide, mmm? Let's talk about your budget, shall we?"

"Of course, Mr. President."

"Now, Coleman. If my numbers are correct, you received one hundred forty-one million dollars in 1975."

"Yes, Mr. President, I believe we did. Under my predecessor's predecessor."

"Bear with me. Jump ahead five years. In 1980 two hundred six million. Is that right?"

"Yes, Mr. President."

"Jump five more years. 1985 you received three hundred sixty-two million. 1990 six hundred fifty-three million."

"Still my predecessor, Mr. President."

"1995, and here you come in, one billion dollars. The year 2000, one billion, five hundred eighty-six million dollars. 2005, two *billion* one hundred forty-one million dollars. Mmmmmm?"

"Yes, sir."

"And now you want more. Bit of a boondoggle. Right?"

"Certainly not, Mr. President. With all respect."

Marcus thought, *I get it. The reason the President asked me and Malkovitch along—he wanted an audience while he reamed Haseltine out. It certainly made it more painful for Haseltine. Washington politics isn't pretty.*

"Now, son," said the President to Coleman Haseltine, "back in Missouri"—he pronounced it Missourah—"we know what boondoggle means. Boondoggle—fine old word. The old cowboys used to carve little pieces of leather, craft 'em into fancy shapes and used 'em to decorate horses' trappings. When the Depression came along the government hired the unemployed to do bit leatherwork, making things that nobody especially needed. That was a boondoggle. Now, son, you want to tell me why your agency work isn't a boondoggle, mmm?"

42

Frustrated with trying to squeeze in a search for Hacker that nobody wanted him to do, Marcus had an idea. He could call his father. This was not something he really wished. Not because Jacko would be annoyed. If anything, it was worse; he'd probably be delighted to hear that Marcus needed him. Marcus wasn't happy with the idea of running to Dad for help.

However, he was certain that if Hacker weren't stopped, people would die. That was not an outcome he could ignore. If he had to feel uncomfortable, eat a little crow, so be it.

He reached out his hand to call his father at his office in the Rayburn Building.

"No, maybe—" Marcus mumbled to himself, pulling his hand back. Rather than use the landline in his office, he waited until he went home after work, before he headed over to Diana's for dinner. It wasn't that he thought the Agency recorded all outgoing calls, but they might. He certainly did not think they had tapped his home phone line. But out of some sense of unease, he at least didn't use his cell phone, which could easily be scanned. Briefly, he even thought of stopping for some odds and ends like Gatorade or candy bars at a convenience store and using their phone.

But there were fewer pay phones available now that nearly everybody carried cells. And also it seemed just too cloak and dagger. He'd use his landline at home.

All he was doing was calling his father.

"Hi, Dad."

"Who is this?"

"Dad—"

"I used to have a son. Maybe he's returned. Could this be my son who only lives a mile away and never visits?"

"Dad, that's for moms."

"And you know this how?"

"We went out for dinner two weeks ago."

"A quick bite at that taco place doesn't count."

"Actually, it was you who had to get back to your office. Congress had a late session or something—"

"So what do you want?"

"Dad, I don't just call when I want something."

"Do you want something?"

"Uh, yeah."

"What?"

Marcus told him about Hacker, about the problem at the Agency.

"So I thought in your position on that subcommittee—"

"The Subcommittee on Intelligence, Information Sharing, and Terrorism Risk Assessment."

"Exactly. Or SIISTRA for short, which sounds like a sorority—"

"Marcus, enough blathering. Have you tried COMINT?" This was communications intelligence.

"Of course I did. It's not that great for finding Hacker, for the same reason it's not great for finding terrorists. If you don't know the guy's country, you can't winnow down all the crap they have."

"Language, Marcus."

"I've tried all the usual things. NSA. I don't think NSA gives out all they have."

"Have you tried ICE?"

"I don't have a sprain."

"Marcus! Immigration and Customs Enforcement."

"Of *course* I did! I queried them when I first got back from Chicago."

"Nothing, huh?"

"Daaa-ad."

"Now you sound like when you were twelve."

"Dad, if there's one reason our government too damned often doesn't work, it's the stupid separation of agencies. If it isn't something they can get credit for, they don't want to spend the time. If it's something the other agency will get credit for, they *really* don't want to spend the time."

"I called it 'the Balkanization of government' when I was on *Meet the Press* with David Gregory a few days ago."

"I must have missed that. Dad, will you help?"

"Of course. Didn't I say that?"

43

"How could you have let my brother be killed?" Joseph Stryker asked Blue.

Stryker and Blue were walking away from Jasper's interment, a horribly sad event. The cemetery was located in Crystal Lake, thirty miles or so north of Chicago. The funeral itself had been in Winnetka, three suburbs north of Northwestern University.

The ceremony had been made harder to take by the presence of a lot of press. News stories had painted Blue as "an unlucky mummy-hunter." Or "author of controversial versions of human history." A nasty one said, "Professor Eriksen's husband was mysteriously murdered in June. The killer is still undiscovered." There was even a story on Jasper and Blue that asked whether Blue was cursed. As if they had been opening King Tut's tomb.

Even worse was the message the department secretary had taken from Forrest Sabin and passed on to Blue. Forrest wanted her to come on his show and discuss her curse.

Blue, of course, had attended the funeral. She hadn't meant to go to the interment, but there were no relatives except the brother, Joseph Stryker, and he looked so bereft, she went along.

Stryker, who had been mostly silent up to now, said to Blue, again, "How could you have let that accident happen?"

"I didn't *let* it happen, Mr. Stryker. I'm as sad about this as you are." She bristled at the attack, but he was bereaved. She certainly was not going to let herself become annoyed with him.

"You should have checked that scree slope before you went charging in there."

"We didn't go charging in there. If you don't think I would have checked for Jasper's sake, I certainly would have done it for my own, wouldn't I?"

"You mean you hadn't started digging?"

"Of course not. We didn't even have a permit. It will be months before *anybody* can dig there. We couldn't remove anything from the site. The most we could do was make a few photographs."

"You must have moved rocks."

"We moved *nothing*."

"But then why did the rockslide happen?"

At the funeral Andy had cried and cried, and finally Tabitha took pity on him and led him out of the church. They did not come back, so Blue assumed she had driven him home.

Brad had come, too, and Bengt. But even though the university had tried to locate Jasper's parents or other relatives, there was no contact person in his file except Stryker.

There were a lot of students and other faculty at the funeral. It didn't quite make up for the lack of relatives. And none of the students—and only a couple of faculty members—had gone on to the cemetery.

Blue was unnerved by having to be in Chicago, which was still tainted by her memories of Adam on the freeway. But she resisted the fear because it was irrational. She *had* to attend the funeral. It wouldn't have been right to stay away.

Stryker said, "How long had the scree slope been there?"

"A little less than two thousand years."

He frowned.

"But Mr. Stryker, there had probably been slides occasionally during that time."

"If you saw evidence of slides, you shouldn't have been on the slope."

"We were on the slope, but not on the scree."

They had reached Blue's car. She clicked the unlock button on the key. When she pulled open the door, her broken ribs gave a stab of pain and she gasped.

Stryker said, "What's wrong?"

"Broken ribs. They'll heal."

"You were caught in the slide, too?"

"Yes." She started to get into the car.

"I've been insensitive," he said. "I'm sorry."

An hour later, they were in Chicago at Greek Islands on Halsted Street. Joseph had said that he'd been in Amsterdam until two days ago, and couldn't get good Greek food there. So Blue drove downtown to show him the way and he followed in his rental car.

Blue said, "I feel wrong, eating dinner and enjoying it, when Jasper— after a funeral."

Stryker said, "Don't. There's no point. Anyway, I made you come here."

"I guess. I suppose there's no real difference between enjoying dinner tonight and last week or next week."

"Jass liked gyros and the fish roe salad. I'm having memorial gyros and fish roe," Stryker said.

"Even though you can't stand them?"

"No. They're great. For what it's worth, Jasper wasn't a guy who liked sad faces, either. Neither of us ever cared much for those 'It's what he would have wanted' statements. Mostly they're self-serving. Jasper definitely thought life was too short to spend in gloom."

"Jasper was a very good person, Joseph."

"I know."

"The school had only your name on a next-of-kin list for Jasper?" she said on a rising note, hoping he'd explain why.

"I'm the only next of kin."

This gave Blue an opening into a question she had been too polite to ask. "You have two different last names—"

"Jasper Martello and Joseph Stryker." He smiled. "Did Jass ever tell you about his history?"

"No. He never said a word about anything that happened to him before college."

Stryker was as tall as Jasper, had the same dark eyes and intense expression. Stryker was more hawklike, though. With the same general features as cautious Jasper, Stryker had the look of a buccaneer. Whatever the differences, he made Blue miss Jasper more than ever.

Seeing that Joseph was hesitating, she said, "Tell me. I always wondered why we never heard about his family."

"Our father was Arthur Hammer."

"Arthur Hammer? Oh. Arthur *Hammer*!" Oh indeed.

"Yup," Stryker said. "A man in the same infamous league as Ivan Boesky, Michael Milken, Ken Lay, and 'Fast Andy' Fastow. And more like the last two. He didn't just sell junk bonds. He brought a whole company down and pretty much destroyed three thousand families in St. Louis. Wiped out their life savings."

Arthur Hammer had been brought into the company as a hotshot who would save the elderly and somewhat stodgy business. He gave himself shares in the company, stock options, and a whopping salary, all with the agreement of the hopeful board of directors. When he cashed in his options and then started selling his shares, he had to notify the SEC, of course, but there were no red flags to worry them. Unknown to them, he was buying puts. He had manipulated the accounting to hide debts and inflate profits. When it all hit the tipping point, Hammer was caught getting on the company plane with a flight plan to the Philippines. Whatever assets he had left in the States were frozen by the Feds, and two years later he was convicted of fraud, conspiracy, lying to banks, lying to auditors, and insider trading.

"He's still in prison, right?"

"Oh, yeah. He's still there. Missed Jasper's funeral. Poor Father," Joseph added grimly.

"But so what happened to you and Jasper—oh! I get it. Your names are—you changed your names. Stryker for Hammer. Martello, Italian for Hammer." She stopped. They must have been deeply humiliated to do this.

"Jasper was more hurt by it than I was. He was younger. He was twelve at the time. I was seventeen and about to leave home for college, anyway. When he was old enough, he changed his name legally, and I did, too, a couple of years later, because by then I realized how many people still hated us."

"But it wasn't your fault."

"Duh. And people are always fair?" He said this sadly rather than unpleasantly.

He went on. "It wasn't just the humiliation and the media scrutiny and people pointing at us. Jasper and I both were horrified, really horrified at what our father had done."

Blue noticed that he always said "father" not "dad."

"You could argue that insider trading," he said, "like what Michael Milken did, is illegal but not so terribly immoral. It would be pretty hard to prove that any widows and orphans lost their life savings because of it. Not like Ken Lay, who tells his own employees that Enron is a great investment, while getting out himself before it vanishes like a soap bubble."

"And your dad—father?"

"He knew what he was doing. And he left them all holding the bag. It was a company that had been in business for over a hundred years. The family that founded it had run out of grandchildren who wanted to take over—the only grandson had started a pretty successful barbecue sauce business—and they hired my father to bring it back to its former glory. He seemed to be doing it for a while, too. And got the employees all investing what was basically their life savings in it."

"I don't know what to say."

"Some of their stories came out in the local papers. At one point I found Jass reading one of the St. Louis papers and crying. Crying! Twelve-year-old boys hate crying."

"And—was your mother—is she living?"

"She was living."

"Did she know what your father was doing? I probably shouldn't ask this."

"No. It's been asked plenty. She hadn't known exactly what he was doing, so far as I could tell. But as soon as the world knew, her rich friends ostracized her. She became a nonperson to them. And she drank herself to death. Took her nearly three years, even though she was really working at it. I guess she figured that was more respectable than outright suicide."

"Good God!"

He was silent for just a few seconds. Then, satirizing date-talk, he grinned and said, "But hey! Enough about me."

44

Madame Versluis placed a papier-maché tray painted white with green tendrils and ivy leaves on the low table in the sofa-and-chair nook of the office of Leeuwarden Director Brian-Michael Ratigan. Ratigan was seated in a wing chair set at a right angle to the sofa. He said, "Thank you Madame Versluis," and leaned over, slightly adjusting the position of the tray.

The door to codirector Roberto Pavia's adjoining office stood open. As Ratigan straightened up, Pavia entered. Madame Versluis withdrew, quietly closing the soundproofed hall door behind her.

Pavia took a second wing chair, directly facing the first and also at a right angle to the sofa.

It was a three-cushion sofa, and on the center cushion sat Cosmo Tilton, bookended by Pavia and Ratigan. He wore a Brioni suit of the softest wool, Lobb loafers, and a Charvet tie. On his left wrist was a Patek Philippe stainless steel Nautilus, and his right hand closed over it in a fierce grip. He relaxed the grip, probably in an effort to appear nonchalant, but while relaxing the hand, he raised his shoulders into a protective hunch.

Ratigan reached over to pick up the silver coffeepot and poured slowly into the three cups that stood on the table. "Cream?" he asked Tilton. "Sugar? Brown sugar or white?"

"Neither. I mean cream. Yes. No sugar. Neither sugar." After a couple of seconds, he added, "Thank you."

Ratigan said, "Try the little tarts. Raspberry, with what looks like almond underneath."

"Uh—"

"Very sweet, of course," Pavia said.

"Yes."

Ratigan said, "Sugar. Such a ubiquitous but amazing substance. Did you know that until the early nineteenth century sugar was extremely expensive? It was hard to ship, you see. And made from sugar cane, a warm weather crop. So in northern latitudes it was hard to come by."

"The invention of beet sugar changed all that," Pavia said.

"Beets, of course grow in the north countries."

Tilton said, "Yes. Yes."

"Sugar cane is a grass. It's cut down by men wielding sharp machetes." Ratigan gestured a sharp blow with the edge of his hand. Tilton cringed, then smiled, passing his reaction off as a joke.

Ratigan said, "The cane is hauled to the factory in trucks, or in some rural areas on the back of a donkey. At the factory gigantic rollers crush the cane."

Tilton stared as Ratigan spread his hands and crushed them slowly down. "And the sap gushes out."

Tilton backed up slightly on the sofa, but Pavia and Ratigan had him between them. He sat rigid.

"The sap is very dirty," Ratigan said, frowning disapprovingly. "There are all kinds of bits of sand and soil and unfortunate *impurities* in the juice."

Pavia said, "It's strained and cleaned with doses of slaked lime. Then it is poured into a big pan over fires and is boiled and boiled until it turns to crystals."

Tilton coughed.

"Have a pastry," Ratigan said.

"Ah, no, yes, thank you."

Ratigan said, "When the Crusaders were returning home, they came upon caravans carrying purified sugar, and were amazed. They called it sweet salt."

"For a time, pure sugar was worth its weight in gold," Pavia said. "Far more precious than opium."

"It drove the commerce of nations. The chance to grow cane in the West Indies was one of the reasons European nations colonized the warm islands of the New World. You might almost claim that the history of sugar is the history of the modern world."

"Economics, always economics," Pavia said.

"Which is similar to the reason we asked you here."

Tilton put down his pastry and swallowed several times.

"You see," said Ratigan, "marijuana production in the U.S. runs about thirty-five billion dollars annually."

"Yes, indeed, Mr. Tilton," Pavia said. "It's really quite amazing. More than the value of the U.S. corn and wheat crops put together."

Ratigan said, "Corn: twenty-three billion dollars worth. Wheat: seven and a half billion."

"People just don't realize," said Pavia.

Ratigan said, "Did you know, Mr. Tilton, that Tennessee, Kentucky, Washington, Hawaii, and California—each one grows over a billion dollars worth. Hmmmm?"

"Well yes, I did."

Ratigan leaned across the intervening cushion and patted Tilton's shoulder. Tilton flinched.

"I know you keep informed. So do we, of course."

"Ah—of course."

"So we were just a bit puzzled when California—which is the biggest single producer, isn't it?"

"Yes. Mmm-mm."

"Puzzled when it came up a little short this year," said Ratigan.

Pavia said, "We looked into weather-related reasons, but couldn't find any explanation there."

Tilton nodded his head.

"Or state police-related reasons. Confiscation, for instance."

"We looked. But nothing there," said Ratigan.

Tilton nodded.

"So we thought we'd ask you to drop by."

Tilton did not remind them that Fribourg was halfway around the world from the U.S.

There was a long silence. Pavia looked at Tilton. Ratigan looked at Tilton. Tilton looked at his pastry as a drop of sweat ran from the back of his head past his ear and down his neck.

Tilton drew an uneven breath. "Mr. Pavia. Mr. Ratigan. I think I should go back to California and audit production. From the ground up. Uh. Thoroughly."

"A *good* idea, Mr. Tilton."

Pavia and Ratigan saw Tilton to the door. Ratigan shook his hand for a full thirty seconds, not letting go, while Tilton tried to stand on wobbly knees.

They turned back to the office.

"Think he'll straighten up?" Pavia said.

"Oh, yeah. Too scared not to."

They sat, holding fresh cups of coffee.

"How's Mexico?" Ratigan asked.

"Proceeding. I got in contact with all seven men and set a day. Obrador found a meeting place."

"In his cartel area?"

"No, he was smarter than that. In Colima, because it's far from the U.S."

"Good. If partitioning doesn't work, I'm still for building Heroles."

"I'm not, Mr. Ratigan. He's too stupid."

Ratigan shifted uneasily. "Well, what about our Mr. Hacker?"

"He's not happy. He failed again."

"Maybe we should drop it for now."

"She's a danger. Ultimately, she's a bigger danger than territorial squabbles."

"In the distant future."

"The future is tomorrow's now."

"Nice to say—"

"If we had been bossier, Mexico wouldn't be falling apart today."

"Maybe."

"In any case, Hacker is on it. He needs closure."

"I hope he doesn't screw up again. We'd have to neutralize him and get somebody else."

"I doubt that will happen. As I said before, she ought to be easy to kill."

Hacker was, in fact, on his way to Turkey.

45

Tunisair TU682 from Djerba taxied to the jetway in Nice. Arsène Dou stood in front of his seat and prepared to be one of the first off the plane. Ordinarily, he thought it was stupid to jump up and then stand in the aisle, but he had to make sure his target didn't get too far ahead of him.

Around him were Tunisian Jews, Berbers, French colonials, Arabs of all sorts and costumes, people carrying sausages, blood oranges, and loaves of bread in many shapes. Arsène loved the smells on these southern flights.

Arsène was becoming hungry. He was always hungry. Arsène loved food. If only he could smoke right now, it would keep his hunger at bay, but of course these days on planes it was forbidden. This was all the Americans' fault.

He kept his eyes on his man, five people ahead of him. No, six, since a woman in a headscarf had pushed her daughter into the aisle. Now the woman herself had pushed in. Seven people. Look sharp, Arsène, he told himself.

The woman with the child had a brown cardboard box as her allowed carry-on. It was held together by a band of duct tape wrapped around it, and Arsène wondered how airport security had inspected it when she boarded. X-ray? The box gave off a strong odor of cumin.

Arsène loved cumin. He was becoming even hungrier.

As they deplaned, Arsène expected his quarry to go to the carousel to pick up baggage, but he didn't. He had only a small leather briefcase.

Arsène, a functionary of the French Direction Centrale de la Police Judiciare, had flown to Djerba, located on an island off Tunisia, to pick up and follow Jakob Naphe back to Nice. Naphe was assumed to be bringing several pounds of very fine hashish into France. But the briefcase didn't look large enough or heavy enough to make the trip worthwhile.

Arsène moved up closer to the man as his fellow travelers fanned out into the Cote D'Azur airport. It wasn't difficult to follow the man now, as Naphe was just a bit taller than most and had a bald spot the size of a fried egg yolk at the crown of his head. His hair hung black and lank around it.

The whole idea was that Arsène Dou would see Naphe meet someone and pass or be passed a package. Arsène would then leave Naphe and follow the other man, thereby expanding the agency's knowledge of the gang. So he was surprised when his quarry continued to walk briskly, not looking around for a contact, and head to the Turkish Airlines counter. A Turkish Airlines flight to Konya, Turkey, was leaving at 17:05. Naphe collected a ticket, saying "Ekonomi Sinifi?" and was apparently reassured that it was indeed economy class. Arsène was puzzled again at the destination. Djerba was an island off the point of Tunisia that stuck up into the south central part of the Mediterranean. To go to Nice, on the southern coast of France, they had flown northwest. Now to go from Nice to Konya in the middle of Turkey they would fly almost due east. Naphe was making a long very indirect V shape.

There was not much time before the flight, no time and no way to find out whether Naphe had noticed Arsène and was simply trying to lead him astray or whether this was actually Naphe's most efficient available connection to somewhere else. Airline connections were quite irrational, in Arsène's experience. While his quarry proceeded to boarding, Arsène quickly asked for a ticket.

"Passport?"

Arsène had showed his police card, so he was annoyed to be held up by this functionary, but there was no time to argue that he was entitled to quick service. Grinding his teeth, he displayed his passport, got a ticket NCE to KYA, Airbus Industrie A319 equipment, also economy, and hurried to the jetway, coming to a halt behind two men in turbans and a sulky, gangly teenager Arsène guessed was British. They moved forward by fits and starts.

In the old days you used to see live chickens carried on planes, their legs tied together. Once he had even flown with a goat.

Not anymore. All these regulations. All the terrorism precautions. It wasn't like the old days.

He let his mind wander, briefly, imagining exploding chickens. Maybe an exploding goat.

Suddenly, it didn't seem so funny. Explosions in midair in general didn't seem funny at all. He found his seat, an aisle seat toward the front, with an earlier boarder in the window spot. He looked around the cabin at his nearest neighbors. Did anybody here appear to be suicidal? How could you tell? Maybe a suicide bomber would appear happy and carefree, doing what he wanted, and going to heaven for it.

No, nothing seemed so funny anymore.

As soon as they were allowed to remove their seat belts, Arsène got up and headed for the restroom as an excuse to check on his man. He had lost sight of him during boarding, even though the man must have gotten on. The A319 was a smallish jet, the smallest Airbus made, and it could carry only a hundred and twenty-four passengers. It was barely over half full.

A dozen or more passengers had been between him and Naphe, so Arsène had not been able to see where the man was seated. The restrooms on the 319 were in the rear. Moving casually, he spotted his quarry about halfway back in the plane. That was good. Arsène would be able to precede Naphe as they exited and follow him, so to speak, from in front. Targets were less likely to suspect a tail up ahead of them.

He closed the restroom door behind himself and was hit by a tickle of uneasiness. Something had caught his eye. It was as if his body knew there was a problem before his mind caught on. He replayed what he had seen while walking along the aisle.

My God! Hacker!

Felix Hacker!

He closed his eyes and mentally reviewed his trip down the aisle. Several rows in front of Naphe. The man in the business suit—

Hacker always looked different. Today he was clean-shaven, prosperous, a little chubby.

The American BOLO had asked them to look out for Felix Hacker and had sent four very different photographs. Arsène was especially interested because he had actually run into Hacker once. Arsène had been responding to a call of a man who had fallen in front of a train in Nice, the west line to Marseilles and Paris. Hacker had been leaving the scene as Arsène arrived and Arsène, not nearly as suspicious then as he was today, now five years older and wiser, had not realized what was later decided— that Hacker had pushed the victim. The victim had been a distributor of heroin on his way to Marseilles. Arsène should have realized that anybody walking away from an accident was suspicious. The average person crowded forward to see all the gore.

At that time, when he saw photos come through of Hacker from Interpol and realized his naïve mistake, Arsène had had to tell his boss. Had to admit that he had seen Hacker that day and had innocently let him walk right past. Well, it was the honest thing to do, even though his boss had sneered at him for letting the man get away.

Arsène hated Hacker.

Since then, Arsène had made a bit of a hobby of Hacker. He thought Hacker lived in North Africa someplace, with an employer in Switzerland. But his closest colleague thought Hacker lived in Portugal and had an employer in Algeria. They both realized that Hacker had organized his life so that pinning him down would be very difficult.

Now Arsène started having doubts. Was it really Hacker or wishful thinking? Could he be sure on the basis of a one-second glance?

Of course he was sure. And Hacker was a killer. Murder was what he did and as far as anyone knew, all he did. And Arsène was meant to stop him. Immediately he made the decision to follow Hacker to his destination and forget about Naphe—after all, how important was hashish? There had always been hashish; there would always be hashish.

First he must call his office. He had left his cell phone with his bag on his seat. *Merde!*

Arsène left the restroom. As he returned to his seat, he was careful not to obey the impulse to take another look at Hacker and be sure.

Once in his seat, he took out his cell phone and started to dial.

"Non, m'sieu!" the flight attendant hurriedly appeared over Arsène's shoulder.

She said, "*Aucun telephoner de cellules.*" Then, unsure of what language he spoke, added, "No telephoninck." She pointed at the Airfone, hanging on its cradle on the back of the seat in front of him.

Arsène was not eager to talk while the person in the window seat next to him could hear him. He had hoped to get up carrying his own cell phone and pace toward the front of the plane. He glanced at the man, an elderly Turk from the look of him, dark hair and dark circles under his eyes. Well, this was an emergency.

Arsène suspected that cell phones would not interfere with the plane's navigational equipment, even though airlines said they would. Always a skeptic, he figured they wanted the revenue from their seatback phones. After all, most passengers forgot to turn their cell phones off, even if they didn't actually use them to place calls while airborne.

Arsène picked up the seatback phone and worked his way through getting the Airfone to let him call. French was not its first language. Two languages he did not recognize later, he got through to his office at the DCPJ. He described his problem to his subordinate, Henri Nez. Henri said that of course he would send gendarmes to Côte D'Azur/Nice airport immediately.

Arsène explained. Not to Nice. To Konya.

Henri said right away. To Côte D'Azur airport.

"*Non, vous idiot! La Turquie!*"

Henri told Arsène carefully that they did not have jurisdiction in Turkey.

Arsène explained again that he was to send *Turkish* police to the Turkish airport.

Henri explained that he couldn't *send* Turkish police anywhere.

Arsène explained very, very slowly, wondering why, since they both spoke the same language, this was so difficult, that he was asking Henri to *request* Turkish police in Konya to meet him at the airport and arrest Felix Hacker, who was wanted in many nations. Henri would be praised.

Why, Henri asked, was he only being told now?

"Je n'ai en le temps avant d'embarquer."

Maybe it wasn't Hacker, Henri said.

"Oui, je suis absolument certain il est lui."

Henri said "Oho!" and averred that of course he understood.

Arsène made Henri repeat the instructions. Henri did, a bit huffily.

Arsène disengaged from the phone and settled back with a sigh.

Two rows behind Arsène, in an aisle seat, Felix Hacker sighed, too. He had heard nothing of the exchange, of course, but he could imagine. He did not know, did not remember Arsène Dou, but everything about the man screamed "Police!" And that determined eyes-straight-ahead on the man's march back to his seat—ach! Almost anyone these days checks the other people on a plane. Really, if confirmation were even needed—

46

"Are your parents comfortable with this?" Blue asked Brad, not for the first time. She had spent an hour one morning at the Oliver's house, two days after Jasper's funeral, inquiring whether they were worried about their son going on a second archaeological expedition. They said they were happy to have him go, but Blue knew that people often covered up fears.

They were now southbound in a Jeep through central Turkey.

Brad said, "Sure. They're fine."

"I mean, they're not afraid of something happening? After what happened to Jasper—"

"No. They know that was an accident." He looked carefully at Blue, probably checking to see whether she was blaming herself. The whole crew seemed to know that she was. He said, "My folks are really happy I'm here. I hadn't done so well in school. You know? And when I got back from Peru, I started telling them about the Moche, and the ancient religions, and all. You know? And I had those two books you gave me. So my Dad says,

'You're reading.' Like he's surprised. And I say, 'Sure.' And he goes, 'In the summer? When it's not homework?' And I say, 'Yeah, it's interesting.' "

"Good!"

"So they're pumped."

"Good."

"So maybe I'm going to do a year of post-high-school classes and get my ACTs up. Because I'd really like to go to a school where they have a good archaeology department."

You gotta love this kid.

"I withdrew my enrollment at the other place."

His parents probably were relieved, Blue thought. Maybe they had wondered what to do with the kid during the summer between high school and college, too. Jobs were scarce right now. He was right that they were thrilled to discover he had a liking for something academic.

The car bounced. Blue changed position. Her ribs hurt no matter what position she sat in, and more when they went over a bump.

They had just moved into an inexpensive hotel in Konya, which was a city of five hundred thousand, located more or less in the center of Turkey. Blue did not understand why Konya wasn't better known in the world. It lay just north of the edge of the Taurus Mountains, in a beautiful farming area, where beets and fruit and wheat were grown. The most valuable Turkish carpets came from here. There were stunning mosques and public buildings, old buildings and buildings older and even older than that and some older than imaginable—there had been humans here ten thousand years before Christ. The Hittites called it Kuwanna four thousand years ago. The Romans called it Iconium. Saint Paul visited the city. Konya probably reached its high point in the twelfth century, when it was the capital of the Sultanate of Rum. It's also the capital of the Whirling Dervishes.

From their hotel in Konya, they drove southeast about seventy kilometers, then turned sharply left toward Cumra, went another few kilometers north through Cumra, where there was a modern mosque and a huge sugar factory, converting locally grown beets into sugar, twelve thousand tons a day in the season. Another few kilometers along the road they saw an elderly road sign, a custodian's house, and a great mound.

They were at Çatalhöyük, the site of what may have been the first city on the face of the earth.

When Blue looked out across the Anatolian plain, she was stunned by the persistence and bravery of early humans surviving here.

Anthropologists currently believe humankind developed in Africa. Forced out by population pressures, droughts, or the desire to find something better over the next mountain, humans worked north out of Africa into the Middle East, east across Asia and down into the southeast Pacific islands. Some who had settled in what was now Siberia—she thought *what a test of survival that must have been!*—may have made their way across a bridge of ice or land to what was now Alaska and from there, over millennia, down the Pacific coast, farther and farther south along the coast of California, the coast of Mexico, through Central America, the coast of Colombia, Peru, and Chile, a few even to Tiera del Fuego.

Some became the Moche.

Others made their way north across Europe, eventually to colonize what later would be Yugoslavia, France, Germany, Italy, Scandinavia, and the British Isles.

As Neolithic man explored north out of Africa, there were only two ways to go. One was up the west side of Africa and over the Straits of Gibraltar. It was a hard route. Not just because of the difficulty of crossing the eight-mile-wide Straits. They would have trekked up through the Western Sahara desert if they came from the south, and the Atlas Saharan wastes if they came from north central Africa. On the east side of Africa, though, they would have walked north up along the Nile, skirted the Arabian desert, passed through what was now Cairo, crossed the Sinai Peninsula, staying near the Mediterranean, each wave going a little farther like an incoming tide, and headed north along the eastern end of the Mediterranean. They would not have had to enter the great deserts of Arabia, even though many of them must have tried, and died.

They continued north, leaving settlers all along the way, but some would have pushed on, into what was now Israel, Lebanon, and Syria, dropping off groups of humankind as they went. North of Syria, they would be in Turkey.

Some went east, some of those turned north, between the Black Sea and the Caspian Sea, and continued north into what would become Russia, and from there all the lands to the east. They set out into not just unknown territory, but into land where no human being had ever made a footprint.

The hegira consumed tens of thousands of years.

Those who turned west found the Black Sea on their north and the Mediterranean on their south, the two big bodies of water funneling them toward the plains of Anatolia, the center of what is now Turkey.

Turkey itself is a funnel, with glaciated, granite mountains, the Kacker Alps, in the north, blocking the way to the Black Sea, and the limestone Taurus chain to the south. Through this funnel, humans crossed out of Turkey where Istanbul stands now, at the Sea of Marmara, and went on west to populate all of Europe.

If your ancestors came from anywhere in Western Europe, they probably passed across this plain.

The mountains north and south were harsh but the central plain was beautiful—rolling hills or flat farmland. In those days it must have been filled with animals to hunt and blanketed with wild cereal grains. There were lakes and rivers, and in the days of Çatalhöyük an enormous marsh with marsh birds and other game. The climate was equable most of the year, but cold in winter.

Saying that tribes of humans moved out of Africa and across the face of the earth gave an inaccurate impression, Blue thought. A move of a few miles might consume a thousand years. To a family living in a hollowed-out tufa stone cone in Anatolia, they had lived there forever. They would have no memory of ancestors ever living anywhere else. Their parents, grandparents, great-grandparents, from time beyond time, had lived here.

How I wish I could go back just for a day. Back ten thousand years and watch. How I wish I could see how they patterned their day. How did they apportion daily living tasks? Who and how did they worship?

Take away the sugar factory, the cars and the electric light, and we are on the plains of Anatolia as they were ten millennia ago.

Blue was often frustrated that she had to see back through the fog of time. The evidence bleached away. The sun-dried bricks slowly melted with erosion, the murals faded.

If only I could just be there. Just to see.

Puttering out to the group's first sight of Çatalhöyük in two rented Jeeps, they passed the sugar factory, and Blue saw Brad looking around.

"Right in this place?" he said. "People lived here for ten thousand years?"

"Way more than that. But the earliest people didn't leave much of a trace. There are caves north of here in Karain that were occupied twenty-five thousand years ago."

Blue watched him gaze about. Like many students, he thought of history as something that happened someplace else. He was thinking, "Right here, under this ordinary sugar factory?"

Yes, right under your feet, she would tell them. In Chicago one year, the school was bulldozing an area near the tech institute for a new parking lot and turned up a skeleton. There was some charred wood near it and the bones were charred, too, so at first everybody thought it dated to a serious fire that had burned several houses in Evanston in the 1940s. Not so. It was the skeleton of an Early Woodland People woman, and was very, very old. For a week Blue's students couldn't talk about anything else. Pre-history? Right here? Under our feet? Yes, it was. Right here.

"Everything that has happened to humans has happened somewhere on the planet," she said. "Well, not the moon landing, of course."

Places that were clement and hospitable to humans in the remote past, if the climate hasn't changed a lot, went on being lived in by people, generation after generation, century after century, through the millennia. The new people built on top of the leftovers of the old and quickly forgot that anyone earlier had called this home.

Çatalhöyük, seen from a distance, didn't look like much, to echo Brad's comment about the Huaca de la Luna. Blue expected him to say it again, but saw him studying the mound with interest as they drew closer.

From a little distance it looked like a big dry hill. It was a high rounded rise in the landscape, and Blue had been told that until recently it had been a favorite picnic spot for people who lived in the area. It was big, larger than thirty football fields.

There were actually two main mounds, east and west. Professor Ian Hodder from Stanford had been excavating the east mound for several years. A couple of other universities worked here, too. Blue's friend, Percival Southey, called Perce, a Brit currently teaching at the University of Chicago, was excavating another part of the east mound.

They met Perce at the dig house, where he and the students lived, at 6:30 A.M., an hour or so after sunrise, which had required leaving Konya about five. This was Perce's idea, not Blue's, and surely not Drake's. Drake complained bitterly the whole way there in the car. He and Tabitha and Blue and Adam and Brad were in the Jeep. Bengt, Andy, and their piles of gear were following in a smaller, very elderly Volkswagen. Drake had maneuvered to sit next to Tabitha, and she let him. Blue had pretty much figured out what was what with her. She had frequently been annoyed with Drake, but she had seen his photographs of their Peru week. They were spectacular. Just the one of the sun setting over the Huaca del Sol alone was worth a king's ransom. Little joke, Blue said to herself. The huaca had been produced by several kings' ransoms. Tabitha was an unusually sincere person. She truly respected ability and quality. The fact that Drake was a superb technician and an artist as well would weigh heavily with her. The fact that he was an insensitive clod to human beings she would, at least partly, overlook. Sheesh!

Blue wanted her whole party to get along happily, but she was not naïve.

Anyway, here they were at the crack of dawn. Perce had a lifetime habit of putting in sunrise-to-sunset days when he was on a dig—or to be accurate, a little after sunrise to maybe an hour before sunset. "The light gets deceptive when the sun gets low," he said.

Perce was chubby, sort of egg-shaped. His hair was the color they called ginger in the UK, a kind of light yellowish, orangish tan. His eyes were pale blue and very alert. He was, not surprisingly at this time of year, sunburned on his nose, cheeks, and chin, and when he took his slouch hat off, there was a white band around the forehead. He met them with both arms outstretched, shouting "Hullo, hullo, ullo-ullo-ullo!"

Then he wrapped his arms around Blue, swung her in a circle—during which time she gritted her teeth and did not mention her broken ribs—let her down, wrung his hands, saying, "Awful about Jasper. Dreadful!" dropped back to give Tabitha a wide-eyed look of admiration, his hands framing her as a picture before his eyes, while Blue introduced her. To Drake he said, "The Michelangelo of the camera! *Loved* the Banff series in the *National Geographic*," thus earning Drake's affection.

Spotting Bengt, Perce lurched forward shouting, "Hey! You old crypto-Kraut!" and whapped him on the back five or six times so loudly that a couple of Turkish workers fifty yards away looked around to see what the fight was about.

Bengt—ordinarily Bengt the Silent—threw back his head and roared, "My pal the slimy Limey!" Then *sotto voce*, in a dreadful stage whisper, Bengt said, "You got beer?"

Perce said, "Hey. I got beer."

When Blue introduced Brad, Perce gave him a thumbs-up. And when she introduced Adam, he fell to his knees in amazement. "The next generation! The backup disk!" He kneed forward and scooped Adam into his arms. Adam shrieked joyfully.

Just your average, stuffy, reserved Brit.

Perce was sunburned, despite the fact that the site team worked under a huge structure designed to protect the dig from rain and sun. The cover looked like an airplane hangar with translucent panels attached to a Tinkertoy skeleton of white struts.

They stood in the parking lot used by Perce's team, well away from the mound itself.

Perce said, "Picture this wonderful plateau and right here, right where we're standing, a field of native peas and grains, a freshwater river slipping by, fish to catch, aurochs and deer and other game in the distance." He spread his arms, inviting us into his world.

"What is an auroch?" Brad asked.

"It's aurochs singular or aurochs plural, lad," Perce said. "One aurochs or ten aurochs. They were wild cattle, really huge, nearly six feet high at the shoulder and with long lyre-shaped horns pointing forward. The males were black and the females were brick red. I'll show you the skull of one in the tent."

"I'd like to see that."

"They evolved in India two million years ago. Spread to the Middle East, Asia, Europe, Africa. Very dangerous to hunt. Very fast runners. Quick with their horns." Cupping his ear, he said, "Can you hear the thunder of their hooves? There was quite an attaboy to a hunter who bagged them. They're extinct now."

He gestured up the slope. Quite a distance away was another protected area and beyond it the dig house of another expedition.

"Now picture that entire rise covered with squarish houses, packed together and almost touching wall-to-wall. The walls were all made of mud brick, faced with white plaster, so from here they would have looked like a jumble of sugar cubes. In each house were three or four rooms, where several people lived. The houses were quite large; some of the rooms were fifteen or twenty feet square."

"Bigger than my whole place in Evanston," Tabitha muttered.

"Most of the rooms had no windows. Some had tiny slits. The light came through a hole in the roof. Fortunately it was not a rainy climate.

"Think of the places as three-room apartments, all right next to each other. There were no doors. The houses were built practically touching. There were no streets. No parks, no plazas, no open space to speak of. You need to think of it as something like a bee colony."

Drake was poking around, sighting things uphill with his camera, paying no attention to Perce. This didn't bother Perce.

"No big houses, either. No civic buildings. No temples. No rich people. All virtually alike. No records of chiefs or big events. No records at all. They thought of time as cyclical, rather than moving forward.

"The houses had walls over a foot thick. Inside was a large room with a hearth and an oven. There was a smaller storeroom, with containers for grain and obsidian and so on. The people of Çatalhöyük imported obsidian chunks and flaked it to make knives and weapons and mirrors. And there was a third room with living spaces and a platform where the people slept. Under the platform in the big room, they buried their dead."

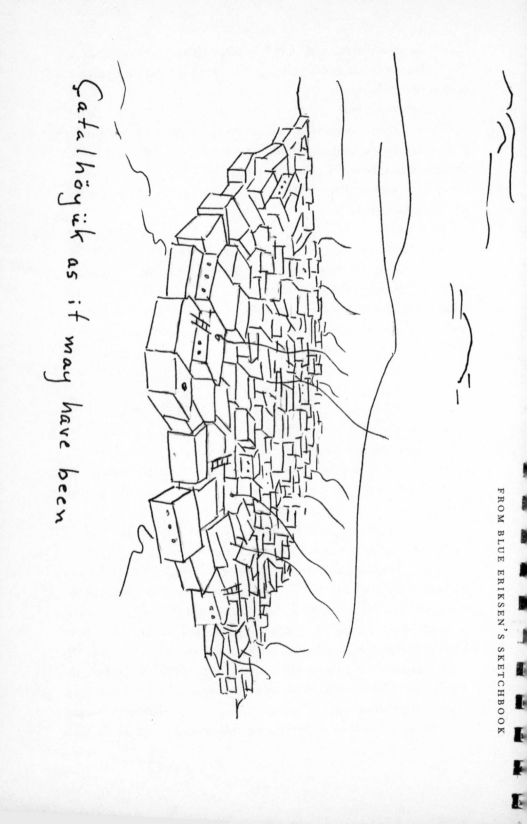

Çatalhöyük as it may have been

FROM BLUE ERIKSEN'S SKETCHBOOK

"Yuk," Andy said.

"Well, I don't know if it was all that yucky. They were extremely respectful of their dead. I'll show you a couple of burials.

"Anyhow, the most remarkable thing about these houses, actually, is that most of them had wonderful wall paintings and sculptures, almost as if every family's home was a shrine. The early discoverers of Çatalhöyük thought there were temples all over the place."

"But with no doors how did they get into their houses?" Tabitha asked.

"Over the roofs!"

"But then—"

"You walked up the outside of the outside houses, up ladders and across the roofs to your house. There was a hole in the roof and you climbed down a ladder—maybe a log with notches cut into it—right into your living room, so to speak." He paused with arms outstretched again, as if to say, "Isn't that wonderful?"

"But what were the roofs made of?" Brad asked. "You can't make roofs of mud, can you?"

"Good question, young man. The roofs were made of tightly woven reeds laid over logs. We think one of the reasons the people settled here in the first place was the big beds of reeds in the marshes."

"But wouldn't they fall through the roofs—walking over them?"

"No. Reeds are tough. You can make a hell of a lot of neat stuff with reeds."

You could indeed make a lot of neat stuff with reeds, as they would see in a few minutes. Perce escorted them to the airplane-hangar-like building that protected his work site and housed the conservation unit. The site itself was under the big white enclosure. Three or four ancient houses were under the protection, two in the process of being excavated.

Perce, like most archaeologists, employed local people to help in the excavation. Many of them here came from the nearby village of Küçükköy. There were students, too, doing conservatorship and excavation. He had local women working on the murals, carefully flaking plaster off the walls to expose the paintings. The women were conservative Muslims, wearing head coverings and long skirts. So he kept his beer well hidden. Blue suspected they all knew perfectly well he had it and where he kept it. They were familiar with beer, since so much was brewed in the area. But it was not sold locally nor drunk by the local people—at least not in any visible way.

The houses in Çatalhöyük were mostly mud brick, so they eroded over time. The practice of the people here was to tear a house down when it was no longer serviceable, and build up another house on top of the rubble of the old. This caused the town to rise up gradually, and produced protected underlayers of information for the archaeologist to dig down through and read.

Adding to this preservation of data was the use of white clay to resurface the floors. In some houses, the floors may have been resurfaced as often as once a month. White plasterlike material was spread thinly on the floor and smoothed down. Fibers, seeds, lead, copper, bone, animal fur—all kinds of trace material was trapped in the flooring and left for people like Perce to read.

And then there were the burials. The practice of burying their dead under clay in a corner also made the level of the house floors rise over time.

Perce was a pro-Çatalhöyük, anti-Jericho archaeologist. You could pick up on this even if you didn't know the background. This happened quite a bit with archaeologists. They adopted their area and became a booster for its importance over everyplace else. In the case of Çatalhöyük, though, there was something to be said for Perce's view.

"This became a town a little later than Jericho," he said, "about nine thousand years ago, but of course Jericho was not a small city, like this. Forget Jericho! Jericho was hardly even a hamlet! Great walls though. Six feet thick and a trench nine feet deep around them. Fewer than two thousand souls, smaller than Ackley, Iowa, while Çatalhöyük was over five thousand. Eight or ten thousand at its height. And the *art*! Good gad, the art here!"

They were now in the conservator's space in the shelter. A mural lay on a table, being cleaned by one of Perce's students.

"Art in virtually every house. This was unquestionably the height of Neolithic civilization. They bred cattle and sheep and goats much better than at Jericho. They made jewelry from copper and lead. They grew grains and peas and made wine from berries. *Can you see it?* Four millennia before the invention of writing, five thousand years before Stonehenge, lolling on their reed mats, with the hearth warm and glowing, venison roasting, sipping berry wine in the middle of the Stone Age! Can you just *see it?*"

The student glanced at Perce and smiled. Probably Perce did this with every fresh audience.

"They made flint weapons. And mirrors from obsidian they chipped right in their houses. Every house was a little cottage industry. They wove and chipped and polished and traded the goods to all of Asia Minor.

"They ate almonds and pistachios. They imported cinnabar and white marble from other parts of Turkey. Lapis lazuli from what we now call Russia."

Brad stared with his tongue caught between his teeth at the deep trench going fifteen feet or more into the earth, going into deep prehistory, every few inches maybe a hundred years. The layers were clearly visible. He said, "All those lives under there. It's like a book with pages. If you could read them."

It's been said before by others, Blue thought. But when you saw a young person really *get* it, there was an electric thrill.

Perce said, "When Çatalhöyük was first discovered and investigated in the late 1950s, it set archaeology on its ear. Çatalhöyük pushed the dawn of civilization back three thousand years."

Perce bounced on his feet. "Pollen in the floor plaster tells us what time of year the resurfacing was done, naturally. Look, you can even see the pattern of the reed mats, pressed into the floor surface."

Perce scarcely stopped to draw breath.

"Domed ovens. Hearths. And take a look at this. These things are mysterious. Or were."

He pointed at a great pile of ceramic balls, most of them about the size of golf balls.

"Some archaeologists think they may have been used as tokens. Like an early form of money."

"Or maybe—" Tabitha started to say.

Brad had also begun to speak, eagerly, and Tabitha stopped to let him. "Or for cooking," Brad said, and Tabitha nodded, unseen by him. "You know. Like, if they didn't have good pots to boil things. You put the balls in the fire and get them hot and then drop them in the water to boil it."

Perce said, "Very good, young Brad. Is it Bradley? May I call you Bradley?"

"Sure. Yeah, sure."

"How did you know that, Bradley?"

"I didn't, sir. I just guessed. We did that in Boy Scouts once. We used heated stones, anyway. Like."

Brad's face glowed. Tabitha glanced at Blue and Blue gave her a smile. It had been generous of her to let Brad get the glory.

Why is Çatalhöyük so important to me? Blue wondered. Mostly because it was so much *before* every religion humans now know about. Here religion, if you can call their attentiveness to their ancestors' bodies a religion, was personal. There was no evidence of priests or municipal shrines. Like their crafts, religion was domestic.

Blue didn't think archaeologists would ever discover much about the psychological human history of early hominids in Africa. The climate was so warm and damp that all the structures and clothing rotted quickly. If they carved statues out of wood, that wood was long gone. And to find evidence of what psilocybin mushrooms meant to them seemed impossible. Çatalhöyük might be almost as far back into prehistory as humans could reach in the search for the interweaving of hallucinogens and spiritual thoughts.

The earliest form of what is now called religion was probably a memory of ancestors. Early people might confront a new experience, but remember that a grandfather or grandmother had mentioned dealing with that very problem, and might mentally ask them for help. Humans carried on conversations in their minds all the time, as people all know well. If they relaxed with hallucinogens, they would actually "see" the ancestor who remained with them here, under their floors. Many, many of the houses had the skulls of ancestors that had been removed from graves and decorated with plaster. Why do that? To respect them and ask their blessing and advice?

Blue said, "Mellaart thought there were shrines, but we now see that he was just looking at some fairly large rooms in people's homes. There were other things going on there that you wouldn't do in a shrine. Cooking, knapping obsidian—"

Tabitha said, "So these weren't shrines, because people lived their daily lives in them?"

"Oh, they were probably shrines all right. But not public shrines. Pretty much every house had them. They were private personal religious objects, if you could call it religious. There was lore, but not organization."

Perce said, "Of course this was a goddess religion, Blue. You've got statues of women with infants at their breasts and women giving birth. Seated women. Dancing women. Jeez Louise! If there were statues of a man in a helmet carrying a flaming sword, people would have no problem saying they worshiped a god."

Blue said, "That's true. But there are pictures and statues of men hunting."

There was some irony here, Blue thought. Ana Cruz, in Peru, was researching a male-dominated society. Perce, here in Turkey, was researching a peaceful, agrarian, probably matriarchal society.

"Blue, you were too tentative in *Goddess*. This was a goddess culture, pure and simple."

The part of the mound covered by the tent was maybe an acre or less, a small fraction of the more than thirty acres which was the city at its height. But inside the tent, the excavation seemed huge. In three places the staff was at work, marking off certain parts of the walls for detailed attention. The final conservatorship of anything removed was done off-site in the dig house.

"They're chipping plaster off the wall here," Perce said, taking us to the nearest house. The exposed walls surrounded a three-room dwelling. Interior walls framed the rooms. There was one larger room maybe fifteen feet long and twelve wide, and two smaller rooms. Even after the passage of seven thousand years, the clay storage vessels in one of the smaller rooms were visible.

"You can see the painting under the plaster."

They did see. Three local women, wearing the *hijab*, the veil, scarf, and long coatlike dress, sat on the ground, scratching carefully at the plaster. Partly visible was a running bull with long horns.

"We have a kitchen midden here," Perce said pointing.

This was a square room outside the house that didn't seem to be part of the house next door. Presumably it would be filled with stuff archaeologists love—kitchen waste, broken pottery with traces of food, dried residues of beverages, maybe even smoking materials. There was nothing an archaeologist liked as much as a good garbage dump. Blue said, "I'd like to get some samples of what they were throwing away."

Bengt said, "And some samples from the storage jars inside?"

"Absolutely," Perce said. "Now come this way, carefully."

They walked carefully and approached a second house.

Perce and his team had excavated down about fifteen feet, and they entered the excavation down a ladder, then a second ladder. As they descended, Perce gestured.

"Here, you see, they were using pottery. Notice the soot line here. There may have been a fire. Five thousand years ago. Now here"—he stepped down two steps—"we're a thousand years earlier. Roughly fifty generations have lived and died between here and here. See, they are just beginning to use pottery."

The rest of them, who had preceded him down the ladder, watched as he descended.

"Here"—he pointed a couple of feet lower at the remains of two woven reed bowls—"they have not yet learned to make pottery."

Brad's eyes were huge as he watched.

"We have a lot of burials. I assume you want human samples?"

"Yes," Bengt and Blue said together. Bengt added, "Especially bone and liver."

"There's more disease in cities than in a nomadic life. More closeness, more pathogens inhaled, more feces. More pollution in the water. Higher infant mortality."

Blue's little party looked subdued.

"There were a lot of deaths in childbirth, although that was true in nomadic cultures, too. But for some reason, the incidence seems higher here. We have one we're just uncovering. A young pregnant woman. I would guess there are thousands and thousands buried here at Çatalhöyük, in a city of this size. You can see the skeleton of the unborn child, still in her abdominal area. She was buried with some jewelry. The preservation is excellent."

She lay in the dried clay, in a folded position, with red ochre around her skull. Some of her dark hair still clung to her head. Lapis beads, a beautiful blue, made an arc near her jawbone.

She lay as she had lain for seven thousand years.

And Blue's imagination moved back in time.

The girl was fifteen or sixteen at most. She was quite thin, except for the distended belly, so huge that the skin looked shiny. Her black hair was long and soaked with sweat. There were three women surrounding her; one elderly, with gray hair.

The girl shrieked. One of the women massaged the huge belly, as the girl continued to shriek. "No more! No more!" she screamed. She sobbed and gasped and then quieted, shivering.

She was half reclining in a sort of wooden chair with arms and a U-shaped seat. A birth chair. The room was lit only by a door in the ceiling through which stabbed a thin beam of sunlight.

The old woman dipped water from a bowl into a cup and placed it at the girl's lips. She sucked a few drops, then turned away. Her legs were trembling, a symptom of the chill she must be feeling. In childbirth, the peripheral circulation shuts partway down to prepare for the upcoming blood loss.

She rolled her head from side to side as the next birth pang struck, and Blue could see that the hair at the back of her head was matted from thrashing in labor. She began to moan, and then screamed, a bubbling, gasping scream that shredded the air. The two younger women moved to each side of her and grasped her knees, pulling her legs as far apart as they could. The older woman said something about curling around the baby, and the girl pulled her upper body forward. But the pain was too great for her to hold the position. She lurched back, throwing her head from side to side and emitting a shrill keening. After half a minute more the pain stopped. She sank back, her neck slick with sweat.

The two women who held her legs relaxed briefly. Blue could see blood dripping from her vagina. The old woman bent near to her ear and spoke to her.

Then the girl's eyes widened in terror as another birth pang built. The two women pulled her knees apart again, and the girl screamed and, as Blue watched, a gush of water flooded from her body, down her buttocks and over the chair. The old woman nodded and said, "Yes, yes."

With the amniotic fluid gone, the pressure of the baby on the girl's tissues increased. She whimpered now, little gasps of agony, then took a breath and shrieked.

The old woman had said "Yes, yes," but she was worried, and so were the other two. As the pressure of the contracting womb increased, the old woman reached into the girl's vagina and frowned. The girl said, "Don't!"

After a full minute, the pain ebbed. The old woman thrust her right hand farther into the girl's vagina and pushed on one side of the distended belly with the other.

She was trying to turn the baby. It was breech. Blue could even see the bulge of the baby's head, too high on the girl's left side. She screamed "No! Nonononono!" as the old woman pushed. She kicked and flailed with her arms.

Then the old woman stepped back half a step. She exchanged a glance with one of the younger women.

She had not been able to move the baby.

Another pain struck the girl. She began to scream "Get it out! Get it out! Oh, mother, help me!"

The old woman thrust her hand inside the girl again, pushing the baby's rump up toward the right, hoping to bring the head down. For a moment, Blue thought it moved. She pushed, the girl screamed for help, beating at the old woman with her fists. The baby seemed to turn a little and then it fell back to the breech position.

When the old woman drew her hand out, it was slick with blood.

The girl made whimpering sounds like a mewing cat as the pain died away again.

One of the younger women bathed the girl's face. The girl looked at her with huge, terrified eyes. The woman touched her face and smiled. The other woman bit her lips together and looked at the floor.

Another pain struck.

Another.

And another, for hours. The old woman came to her with a brownish liquid made from dried poppy sap in a horn cup. The girl-child quieted a bit from it between pains, but whatever it was, it didn't lessen the shrieks when the pains came on.

The lozenge of light from the ceiling that fell on the floor moved slowly across the packed plaster, a sundial marking agony.

Without a hemorrhage to bring death quickly, it could take days to die of labor like this. Blue saw the sun set and the girl screamed and screamed. She saw it dark outside. Inside the house, there was only the light from the oven and the hearth, now grimly fed by one of the younger women. Blue saw the oily light on the girl's agonized, sweating face, her lips pulled back from her teeth in pain.

After a while, she began to scratch at her face in agony and the two women had to pin down her hands.

Blue saw the light of dawn come faintly through the opening in the roof.

She screamed and screamed until her voice was hoarse and then she was too weak to scream and just whimpered with the agony each time a pain crested. A few times she begged "Get it out, oh, get it out," but she said it hopelessly, not even to the three women in the room any longer but to the air, the sky above, whatever she saw that wouldn't help her. "Oh, mother, oh, mother." Still her body tried to get rid of the now-dead, now poisonous thing in her womb. If it stayed there to putrefy, it could take days for her to die of septicemia, and the pain from that would be continuous.

There was more blood as the light became bright from the sky, but still she didn't die. She lasted until twilight of that day, when a long, thin clot like a slice of red liver slid from her body. She convulsed and then a river of blood came out. Her skin paled. She cried a little, and then mercifully she died.

The women stretched out the corpse, which was twisted from fighting against pain and death. They washed it and then laid it back down.

"Blue?" Perce said.

Blue said, "Thousands and thousands."

Tabitha said, "Professor Eriksen? Are you okay?"

"Fine. I was just spacing out, I guess."

47

By noon the troop had walked four miles of Anatolian plain, with Brad carrying Adam on his shoulders a large part of the way. Perce insisted on carrying him, too, after hearing that Blue had broken ribs and couldn't do it. Adam was totally in his element. The local women came over and made much of him. Perce's students cooed at him.

Adam could take really quite a lot of admiration.

Adam also loved the wide fields. He ran as fast as he could, away from them, frequently falling and getting up again. They pretended that catching him was terribly difficult, shouting "Catch him!" and "Where's Adam?" as they tumbled and ran this way and that. Finally Blue grabbed him and they rolled on the ground giggling, Blue barely able to protect her ribs. She realized that the wide open horizons of the Anatolian plain delighted him. She had taken him many times to parks in Evanston, but they were always closely bounded by buildings. Maybe he didn't realize that the world could be this open and endless. Even the dig houses and tents were dwarfed by the broad extent of fields and sky.

Finally, they set Adam up in the corner of Perce's office in the dig house as they got out their sandwiches. Blue took a jar of pureed carrots from her canvas hold-all. Adam was going through a pureed carrot phase and she had two dozen jars at their hotel, despite her certainty that in about a week he would give her one of those looks that said, "Are you trying to poison me?" as he extruded pureed carrots from between his teeth—he had only six teeth, with major gaps, and when he extruded he looked like a pasta machine.

"And now watch," said Perce.

The dig house was plain, functional, and full of papers and books and specimens. There were seven tiny bedrooms for seven students to live—five students were currently in residence—and two larger bedrooms, one for Perce and one for a colleague currently in Bulgaria. The office-cum-dining-room where they now sat was furnished with folding chairs and card tables. There was a nice small Turkish rug on the loose-plank floor. On the rug was a cooler full of bottled water. Perce picked up the cooler and moved it and swept back the rug. The rug proved to cover a two foot by three foot sheet of plywood over a second very large Styrofoam cooler sunk into a depression in the ground, and when Perce swept the cover off, inside were at least thirty bottles of Turkey-brewed beer: Türk Tuborg and Efes Pilsen.

"Voila, beer!" said Perce.

"BEER! WALL! BEER!" shouted Adam at the top of his lungs. Then, apparently having expanded his education someplace, sang "Nimey-nime balls beer *wall*!"

Perce nearly fell over laughing.

"Gor blimey, as we Brits are popularly believed to say. Blue, you trained him right."

"Actually, it was Brad," Blue said.

Brad was blushing.

"There's a story here," Perce said.

"As a matter of fact, there is," Blue said. "It's all about when Brad was a genuine, solid gold hero." Brad's ears turned red.

So she had to tell Perce the whole story.

Telling it pulled its fangs a bit for Blue. It was still so terrifying she quailed inside, but at least she could talk about it.

She had one beer, cool from being sunk in the ground, and she needed it. Andy and Brad had two. Bengt, Drake, and Perce each had three. Tabitha drank part of one, put it down, and said, "Beer makes me feel funny."

Drake, edging closer to her, said, "Beer is supposed to make you feel funny."

"Ah, children," Perce said. "The same all over. Night and day they waste in pleasures."

"Indolent wretches," Bengt said.

Perce said, " 'We never asked them to work behind the ox, or to bring firewood.' "

Bengt, chuckling, said, " 'Your kin provide ten gur of barley each and you none.' "

Blue said, " 'Why can't you be more like your older brother?' " The three of them fell about laughing, as the Brits say.

Brad said, "What's going on?"

"Well, Bradley," Perce said, "does this remind you of anything?"

"Um, sure. My grandfather telling us to straighten up."

"Yes! Yes!" Perce shouted in delight. "And it was written four thousand years ago on a Sumerian clay tablet. Pushed into wet clay with a cuneiform tool."

Bengt said, " 'You didn't go to school. Where did you go son?' The son answers, 'Nowhere.' "

Giggling, Blue said, "It's the four-thousand-year-old version of 'Whatever.' "

Bengt shouted, " 'I never, never made you carry reeds to the canebrake.' "

" 'Why can't you be more like your *younger* brother?' " Blue said.

Laughing uproariously, Perce said, " 'Why do you idle about? *Go to school!*' "

Bengt shouted, " 'Why can't you study? Become a scribe, like your father?' "

After a few moments, they all simmered down. Sighing, Perce said, "Does human nature *never* change?"

After lunch, Tabitha very kindly offered to stay in Perce's office with Adam, who had fallen asleep with his head almost in his pureed carrots. This was his way of telling his mother he'd like to take a nap. Blue knew

Tabitha was babysitting so that Brad could go out with the team. Blue said thanks, but she planned to find a chance to thank her more specifically later. Tabitha was maturing almost before Blue's eyes, not at all the haughty young woman she had been a few weeks before.

Perce fixed up two extra sheets of plastic roofing over his window, making the room a little darker. He had apparently never thought to install curtains.

Perce was going to give them what he called "the medicine walk."

Andy had been very quiet. In fact, he'd said very little since they landed in Turkey. He'd gone along with everything. He'd helped carry equipment. But he wasn't really all there. Blue sidled over to him and asked, "How're you doing?"

"Oh, fine," he said, but he wasn't. *Now,* Blue thought, *I'm their teacher, not their mother, but unless he begins to show some energy, sooner or later I'm going to have to get him some counseling. Maybe I should have discouraged him from coming in the first place.*

Meanwhile, Perce gestured widely at the world.

"You have to think of psychoactive substances as falling into three categories. The stimulants, like coffee and coca and the theobromine in chocolate."

"Chocolate has stimulants?" Brad said.

"Absolutely. Very similar stuff to caffeine," Bengt said.

"But when I was little my mother used to give me hot chocolate before bed."

Drake Rakowski snorted "Awwww!" at this.

"Well, she *did.*"

Perce said, "I'm sure that was very consoling. But nevertheless, hot chocolate is basically a stimulant." He paced far enough ahead to turn and pause a couple of seconds looking back at the others.

"To continue. Okay, we've got the stimulants. Now the depressants, like alcohol and opium and so on."

"Alcohol is a depressant?" Drake said. "But people get silly on it, and run around and dance, and like that."

Bengt said, "Yes, alcohol is a depressant. You get enough of it and you'll fall asleep, or into a coma. Or die."

Drake couldn't believe this. "But people do wild things—"

Bengt said, "Alcohol is a depressant that has an anxiolytic effect. It dissolves anxiety. Reduces fear, in other words. In World War I they used to give soldiers a tipple of rum before they went over the top of the trenches to charge the enemy lines."

"Which is why," Perce said, "it works well at cocktail parties and bar scenes. You lose your social anxiety."

Bengt said, "You're not as scared of making a fool of yourself."

They paced on a bit farther.

Perce said, "Then there are the hallucinogens, which is what Blue is interested in. Stimulants or depressants don't give you hallucinations unless you get a big dose of them. True hallucinogens, like peyote or LSD, do."

Blue was well aware that many archaeologists averted their gaze from the presence of psychoactive drugs in the cultures they studied. There were whole tomes written about sites with literally not one word about the hallucinogens the people indisputably used. The archaeologists in these cases, she thought, were too afraid that they might be called some sort of hippie cultist. Blue thought they were being dishonest.

Perce was not one of these timid souls. His specialty was tracing the effects of diet on the health of ancient people. Bones and mummified tissue told him stories. And that included hallucinogens.

"When James Mellaart first came to Çatalhöyük, he found the whole mound covered with Syrian rue."

"Syrian rue contains harmine and harmaline, like the ayahuasca the Moche in Peru used," Bengt said. "They're both hallucinogenic. Very interesting stuff. It's said to cause visions that include animals. Like leopards."

"Which of course are painted on walls all over Çatalhöyük."

"Syrian rue was called 'ruin plant' by explorers because it grew on the ruins of vanished cities."

"You mean here?"

"Not just here. It's all over the Middle East and Asia. And it's been spread basically all over the world."

"Why don't we know this?" Brad said. Everybody laughed.

"Another hallucinogen we know was available here is hemp."

"I've heard of that!" Brad said.

"Bet you have."

Blue said, "They used hemp to make cordage. I'd like to find some evidence that they smoked it, but my guess is for hallucinations they ate the seeds."

Drake said, "What about opium poppies? Doesn't a lot of opium today come from this part of the world?"

"Well, sure, generally," Perce said. "But so far we haven't been able to find any poppy seeds right here, so we can't prove these people grew poppies."

"The climate may have been wrong?"

"Or the type of soil. A lot of the ground around here is marl."

"Which doesn't mean they couldn't have traded their products for opium."

"Right. This was a major trade route. If they couldn't grow poppies, you'd think they'd have traded their goods for the sap or some kind of extract. It was one of the best painkillers. Still is, for that matter."

"This is Syrian rue," Perce said, pulling up a stringy weed.

"No kidding," said Brad. He pulled up a piece and stared at it. It was tough and dry.

"And they had hallucinogenic mushrooms. Hallucinogenic mushrooms follow cattle. They grow on the droppings."

"And they had amanita muscaria. It's a mushroom that grows in pine woods on the ground."

Blue and Bengt exchanged glances. Amanitas were good sources of the hallucinogen muscimol.

"And they brewed beer," Brad said.

"Ah, yes. Beer." Perce sighed. "Compared to most of these plants, alcohol is a sledgehammer to the brain."

"But you love it," Drake said.

"I surely do. But if I'd developed a taste for peyote at the early age when I developed my taste for beer instead, I'd be a better person today." He smiled hugely to show that he was kidding. Sort of.

He flapped his arms. "Time to get to work."

"Can I help?" Brad asked

As they headed back to the dig house, Bengt said, "I'm sorry Tabitha has missed this discussion."

Perce said, "I'd be happy to go over it again with her." He thought a couple of seconds and added, "Maybe I could take her to dinner in Cumra."

"I can tell her all about it," Drake said.

At the site, Blue glanced once more at the place where the pregnant woman and her unborn child lay. The house that enclosed them was large, with three rooms, two smaller storage rooms, and the one big room fifteen feet square, where she had lain under the plaster for seven thousand years.

Blue imagined the family opening the top of that northwest platform for her, chipping away the existing white plaster and exposing the bones of older relatives, deceased years before.

By the time they had dug out the earth under the plaster and piled the soil neatly to one side near the timber post, it must have been late in the day. They would have to wait until light tomorrow to go to the source of marl and plaster.

Blue saw in her mind the two younger women taking the refuse of urine-soiled straw, bloody straw, blood clots, and feces and placing them in reed baskets. They climbed the ladder to the roof, crossed the roof and the corner of a nearby roof, to the midden. Into the midden they dumped all the trash.

With their grandmother, they flexed the body so that it lay in a roughly fetal position, then gently draped a necklace of beads around the young woman's neck. They placed a boar's-tusk necklace near her chest then wrapped the body in reed matting.

They and an old man packed the earth that had come from under the platform back around and over the body, tamping it down to wait until tomorrow for the final plaster sealing.

By now it was dark outside. A trapezoid of moonlight entered the door in the roof, but the interior of the home was lit mainly by the fire in the hearth. Shadows played across the walls, shadows of the head of a wild bull set into the east wall, a real head with horns, plastered over, and the horns and muzzle painted red with ochre. It looked as if the big animal had forced his head through the wall and stopped there, looking into the room. On the north wall, barely visible in the firelight, were wall paintings of vultures, headless bodies, and modeled protruding breasts.

The tusks of three boars and the head of a ram protruded from the wall near the paintings of vultures. Their shadows moved.

Sorrowfully, the grandmother sat down on a reed mat, facing toward the hearth. There was water in a reed basket and into the basket she dropped hot ceramic balls that she plucked from the fire with two flattened wooden sticks. The water hissed and steamed. Into the hot water she dropped several dried mushrooms, brown and curled like ears.

The two younger women, the old man, a young man, and a boy who was almost a man all sat quietly. Outdoors were the sounds of men coming into the city with meat, with grain in baskets. The ceiling creaked as people walked overhead on their way to their own homes. A breeze sucked the smoke out the door.

The mushroom tea was cool enough now to drink. The old woman drank some and passed the basket to the old man. As she did, she noticed that the basket was beginning to leak in one spot and she tried to decide whether it would be better to mend it with pitch inside or to make a new one. By the time the tea returned to her, she had decided to use the old basket for grain and make a new one for water.

She drank again and passed the basket on again.

At the far side of the room was a human skull, plastered over many times. She believed it was of the father of her father's father.

Now in her eyes the firelight took on the color of the sky, with a halo around it of the rainbow. The rainbow contracted and expanded. The woman felt that it encompassed all her family, and she could see that though they were separate, they were all one. The bulls that leaned into the room through the walls were alive and with them as well, as they were one with the fields and the mound.

She felt warm. It seemed to her that the pains in her legs, which had been worse lately, were part of some sort of blessing, like honey or sunshine.

When her granddaughter rose from her burial place in the corner and came to stand at the fire, the grandmother welcomed her. The girl swayed. She had grown younger. Not so much that the grandmother couldn't recognize her, though. She looked very much as she had before she became big with the child.

The grandmother could see the fire, right through her granddaughter's knees. The fire was purple now. It pulsed.

Her granddaughter smiled. The grandmother realized that she and her granddaughter were the same. And so was her daughter, who sat near her son, closer to the fire.

The fire was made of sparkles now, like the sun shining on the lake. And the sparkles were the colors of spring leaves.

The grandmother held up her hands, palms outward, toward her granddaughter. The granddaughter did the same, a mirror image, and came forward, and they blended into one.

The old woman was happy.

48

Marcus rolled over in bed, taking his hand off Diana's hip.

"Diana?"

"Mmm?"

"Look. Watch this."

Diana rolled toward Marcus, but he was clicking the TV remote. The screen came to life.

"That isn't what I thought you wanted me to watch."

Marcus laughed, giving her a kiss on the ear, hoping she would laugh, too, and after a hesitation she did. "Don't be mad at me. Just tell me what you think of this."

"Please. Not Hacker again."

"Just for three seconds. Oh, well, two minutes. But look at this."

"Yes. Yes, okay."

The O'Hare security video showed Hacker, in his Las Vegas shirt, bouncing happily down the ramp. Marcus let her see twenty seconds of that, and as Hacker passed out of the frame, Marcus fast-forwarded through

316

some New York video to Hacker, slumped and defeated, looking ten years older and fifteen pounds heavier. No Las Vegas shirt. He looked fat and unhappy. He looked exactly like a factory worker who had lost his job.

"Okay. Which is his real mood?"

"Marcus, you know Hacker is a wannabe method actor. You can't tell what he's really thinking."

"Well, just look and guess. Help me out here."

"You shouldn't have taken these tapes out of the office."

"I didn't. These are copies."

"You shouldn't have made copies."

"But come on. Which looks like the real Hacker? Happy or grumpy?"

"Or Doc or Sneezy or Dopey—"

"You know, I've kind of changed my mind. He looks like he's acting in both. Underneath, I think he looks angry."

When Diana had sunk into a sound enough sleep that he didn't need to worry about waking her, Marcus got out of bed. Diana might not think he could find Hacker, but if he did, she would see his persistence had been worth it.

His office techie stuff was one corner of his small living room. He sat down and e-mailed Horace Pollard. In less than two minutes Horace phoned him. Marcus grabbed the phone almost before it finished the first ring, trying not to wake Diana.

Marcus said, "How did you know I was awake?"

"You just e-mailed me. It's got the time on it."

"Well, why are you up at this hour?"

"Case ran late."

From the bedroom, Diana called, "Marcus? Is that the office?"

"No, hon. Go back to sleep."

"Busy?" Pollard said.

"Well, I'm talking to you. I'd call that busy. Listen, that murder case—"

"Well, what else would you be calling for at this hour? What do you want to know?"

"Were you satisfied it was a simple break-in?"

"No."

"Just like that? No?"

"Nothing stolen, so not a pro job. There was some anger involved. He stomped a bunch of knickknacks. But nothing disgusting strewn around, so not teenagers. The baby wasn't killed, so it wasn't somebody trying to terminate the Eriksen genetic line. Like for inheritance or whatever. And they did know the baby was there. Did I tell you the killer went upstairs where the baby was sleeping?"

"After the murder?"

"Yes. After, because he left a smear of the vic's blood on the wall. He may have been scared off by some sirens in the area. There was a grass fire."

"No, I didn't know that he went upstairs. That's very interesting. Almost as if he was looking for somebody else."

"Like the wife."

"Like the wife." Marcus thought a few seconds. "Is she okay? What's happened to her since?"

"Haven't got any idea. I sure haven't heard that she's been killed. You realize, of course, that my job doesn't end with one single case in June. I have a few others on my plate."

"Can you find out?"

"How she is? I guess so. Let's see what people here know. I'll get back to you tomorrow. Can't do anything useful at this hour." In the background came the voice of Pollard's wife.

"Honey? Is that the office?"

"Two minds," said Marcus, "with but a single thought."

Marcus was still cautious about the phones at work. He had arranged that when he went out to lunch the next day he would call Pollard at area headquarters. "Any time after noon," Pollard had said. Marcus used his cell phone this time. You couldn't get totally paranoid, he thought.

Of all the people killed in Chicago on May twenty-eighth and twenty-ninth, Dr. Edward Eriksen was the only one who really wasn't

ordinarily supposed to be where he had been. Whether this was important, Marcus couldn't guess, but he was looking for anomalies.

When he reached Pollard, he heard a tone of regret in the man's
voice.

"Eriksen's got her house on the market."

"To sell?"

"Well, yeah. That's what you do if you put it on the market. She's got
a possible buyer lined up, too."

"Did you talk to her?"

"She's not living there. She's out of the country the neighbors say."

"Did they say where?"

"They don't know. It's some sort of school thing. You knew she was
a professor?"

"Then you could find—"

"Find out from the school. Okay, I'll get on to Northwestern."

"And you'll—"

"Call you right back. Yup. I know."

He called back after twenty minutes of convincing Northwestern
functionaries that he really was the cops and he really ought to be told.

"She's in Turkey. An archaeological field trip. Someplace called
Shatall Hooyook."

49

Arsène Dou deplaned quickly, aiming to get ahead of Hacker. There was no likelihood the man would recognize him. Arsène had been younger when they crossed paths, and they had not exchanged a word or even looked at each other then, except for the brief glance Arsène gave Hacker before foolishly dismissing him as a suspect.

There were no services at the Konya airport. No food court, no lounges, not even a snack shop. The Turkish Air Force Military Base was adjacent; in fact, it looked to Arsène as if the military and commercial planes used the same runways. There were two C-130s at the far end.

Where were the Turkish police Arsène had asked his junior to request? There were no police marching to arrest Hacker. Or to meet Arsène, either, for that matter. Were the Turkish police as uncaring as that, or had his idiot assistant, Henri Nez, simply screwed up? Told them the wrong town? Maybe he called the wrong country. Somebody could be looking for him and Hacker in Denmark!

Arsène looked longingly around the spare airport. He was hungry.

He would settle for just a small food stand, maybe a stuffed pita. With onions and hummus. In his brief daydream, Hacker would pause long enough for Arsène to order and pay for the pita. Then—yes—he could cover the fact that he was watching Hacker by eating the pita. Maybe with an Orangina.

But it was not to be, of course. Hacker was not pausing; he was going out the door. Was Arsène to go forever without food?

Maybe he could locate a policeman.

But he didn't have time. He was surprised to see Hacker walk purposefully toward the military base entrance. A fence surrounded the base, with a gate at some distance, but Hacker went toward a warehouse at one side, then around the corner and disappeared from Arsène's view.

Arsène hurried after him.

50

There was Internet access in Blue's hotel, so making contact with home was easy. She e-mailed Paula a couple of times, just to say Adam was doing well and to ask how Tiglath Pilaser was. TP apparently had discovered a taste for small sardines packed in olive oil. Blue told Paula they'd be back in a week. This trip would take ten days all told, including travel time. Blue was still struggling with the question of what to do about living in Chicago. The idea of Adam in the middle of the Kennedy Expressway had so spooked her that she cringed at the thought of the city. Still, that was irrational. She couldn't allow herself to get foolish like that, especially when she didn't admire that sort of behavior in other people.

Plus, her job was there. Maybe she could find a position at some other department of archaeology in some other university, but the job market was tight these days.

Or she could move to a house nowhere near a superhighway.

Oh, come on! He wasn't going to crawl out onto a highway again.

Her contact with the Realtor was encouraging. The last two e-mails told of three different couples who had looked at the house, and one was coming back this weekend for a third look.

Bengt was receiving e-mails at the hotel, too, from his assistant back in the U.S., and he reported to Blue happily. "We're getting what we hoped for from the Peru samples, Blue. Ayahuasca, hallucinogenic levels of nicotine, and some mushrooms that I still have to figure out how to classify, but are clearly the psilocybin type."

"Good."

"And a message from Professor Oudendyk. He's seriously interested in going ahead with your program."

Blue received an e-mail that was disconcerting.

MAIN IDENTITY

From: Ana Cruz <ana@forthwith.net>
To: Blue Eriksen <b-eriksen@northwestern.edu>
Sent: Friday June 19
Subject: Scree slide

Hi, Blue—

I don't know whether this will be the good news or the bad news. Several days after you left, Clodaldo found footprints near the top of the scree slope. This is of course at our still-somewhat-secret find. None of us had been in that area before or after the slide. This most likely means that guaqueros had found the site. Perhaps they followed us, or had backtracked on the student hiker. They could have started the slide hoping to scare us away.

In replying, please do not identify the place. Jorge and Clodaldo and another are on guard.

Ana

Blue was stunned by this. Not an accident? She replied immediately.

MAIN IDENTITY

From: Blue Eriksen <b-eriksen@northwestern.edu>
To: Ana Cruz <ana@forthwith.net>
Sent: Friday June 19
Subject: Scree slide?

So it wasn't an accident? You're right—none of us had gone up there before the slide. I supposed the pile was just unstable, but if it was, how easy for somebody to pull away a log or even roll a large rock down onto it from the top.

I am in Anatolia right now, and for about the next eight days.

Please let me know if you discover anything about who may have done this.

Blue

MAIN IDENTITY

From: Ana Cruz <ana@forthwith.net>
To: Blue Eriksen <b-eriksen@northwestern.edu>
Sent: Friday June 19
Subject: Scree slide

I doubt we can be sure they caused the slide intentionally. It is possible that their presence, in walking about, simply destabilized the pile of rock.

I had wondered whether to send you this information while you were on an expedition. However, I believed that you held yourself to blame for Professor Martello's death. You can see now that it was surely not your fault.

Ana

MAIN IDENTITY

From: Blue Eriksen <b-eriksen@northwestern.edu>
To: Ana Cruz <ana@forthwith.net>

Subject: Scree slide?
Sent: Friday June 19

Well, thank you for letting me know. Do the footprints give anything away about the person? Big? Small? Type of footwear—locally made or not?

Take care of the site. It will be a major find. Have you begun to map it?

Blue

MAIN IDENTITY

From: Ana Cruz <ana@forthwith.net>
To: Blue Eriksen <b-eriksen@northwestern.edu>
Sent: Friday June 19
Subject: Site

The prints were apparently of a mass-produced hiking boot, not a native shoe. Of course, they are available everywhere. We do not know the brand. You must realize that the footprints were made in a mix of sand and gravel that does not permit a detailed cast.

We are protecting the site well. We are keeping the location as secret as possible consistent with the fact that an investigation had to be made into Professor Martello's death. Clodaldo and Jorge and the new man, Javier, are armed. The best news is that the University has issued a grant for investigating the site. There is rumor of additional moneys from the Peruvian government. I have been to the site several times now, and truly believe that it will prove to be the greatest Moche find of the century.

Ana

Sometimes Blue looked on the bright side when being more pessimistic would be wise. Except for a deep terror of expressways since Adam's crawl onto the interstate in Chicago, she was not an easily creeped-out sort of person. But the murder of Edward had been clawing at her thoughts uncomfortably since it happened. It probably was what the cops thought it was, a burglary gone wrong. Except they hadn't really. Detective Pollack—no, Pollard—Pollard had offered that explanation as plausible, not as if he were convinced.

Burglary? Blue's house wasn't the richest-looking in the neighborhood. In fact, it was probably the least impressive. And it also wasn't predictably empty during the day. Blue was home a lot, taking care of Adam, and when she wasn't there, Paula was. Blue was not known to have valuables lying around, mainly because she didn't own any valuables.

Still, anything can happen once, Blue thought. That's why we have the word random.

Twice was too much. The news from Ana that the scree slide was not a simple accident changed everything. Paranoid as it sounded, somebody might be after her.

There were a lot of possibilities, if she looked at it right. Over the years, she had failed a few students. It wasn't like the old days, when grades really meant something, but there had been students so lazy—or so *absent*—that she could not pass them in good conscience. She was sure some of the ones she had failed really hated her. She had also on very rare occasions refused to write a recommendation for a student who needed one for an application to grad school or for an employment application.

That kind of thing was true of almost all teachers. But the most likely people to hate Blue were the people who were outraged by her book, *Goddess*. She still received several pieces of hate mail every week—and the book had come out three years ago. There were zealots who believed that if Blue said some ancient people worshiped a goddess rather than a male god, that meant she was denying their religion. This was absolutely irrational, she thought. There were a lot of other religions in the world for them to get angry at, and why these people were so outraged at a simple archaeological description, she could not understand. Why not be furious at people who worshiped snakes? Or the sun?

Their hatred was increased by the fact that the book had been very popular, of course. And maybe they were enraged by the air of respectability that being published by a major university gave it. Also, the photos and chemical analyses and citations from scholars. Maybe her scholarly caution made it paradoxically more threatening to them. Maybe its very tone of respectability made it all the more poisonous to people like that. And there were, going by the vocal evidence, many thousands of them.

But would they kill Edward for it? Even if by accident?

Let me put that the other way around, Blue said to herself. Can I be sure that *no one* in those thousands of haters is insane enough to try to kill me?

No.

Then what can I do?

Blue supposed she could e-mail or phone that Detective Pollard about the rock slide. He hadn't seemed convinced that a random burglar killed Edward.

But what was he going to do? He'd found what evidence he could. He wasn't going to jump on a plane and rush to Peru to take casts of foot-prints. Footprints Ana said scarcely existed anyhow.

Even Ana, who was there, couldn't do anything to help investigate in Peru, as far as Blue could imagine.

Blue didn't know any private investigators. And if she did, she couldn't tell them where to start. Well—start with the hate mail, she sup-posed. Thank goodness she was enough of an academic to have kept it all. But only some of it had been signed and had a return address. A lot of the people brave enough to tell her she was a spawn of Satan were not brave enough to put their names on their letters. But an investigator could begin with the ones who did. And there were tapes of TV and radio interviews Blue had done with vitriolic opponents. Articles and op-ed pieces and fly-ers from some of the outraged churches would be easy enough to find. Even anonymous e-mails might be traced. Altogether, there would surely be enough to give an investigator someplace to start.

Searching through the thousands of people who hated her would take ages, wouldn't it? And much more money than she had.

But she *could not* ignore a threat if it was real. Not with Adam in the line of fire.

What investigator? If only she knew somebody good.

Then she had an idea. *I wish I knew where ideas come from. I would send for them in large batches.*

Joseph Stryker. Blue didn't think he was a licensed investigator in any usual private-eye sense. He was more of an art theft investigator. He traced things. Maybe he could trace this thing. Back in Chicago, when Blue had her Greek dinner with Stryker after Jasper's funeral, she had urged him to tell her more about himself. He avoided it for a while, asking her what archaeological era or what ancient people she was most interested in.

Finally, though, she got him onto the subject of Joseph Stryker.

He finds things. Blue wondered whether his need to find things and Jasper's to find out things, both forms of a search for truth, had to do with their dismay at their father's utter dishonesty. Truth had meant nothing to Arthur Hammer.

What appealed to Blue about Joseph was he seemed like a person who could think outside the box.

He had every reason to want to find the killer, if there was one—the death of his own brother. He had more reason than anyone Blue could hire would ever have.

In addition, he was clearly comfortable with working in many parts of the world. It was frightening to think that the—the what?—the person who was hunting Blue?—might have been skillful enough to go to Peru, follow the team as they climbed that first valley, probably cross over the crest into the next valley, having overheard them plan the second climb, and then have the wit to quickly take advantage of a natural danger. Maybe he carried a gun and would have finished Blue off with it if that landscape hadn't provided the scree slope.

This argued that he was very smart.

Blue didn't think she was just imagining the threat. If there was a killer, the facts also suggested that by now he would be really, really angry, having missed twice.

She booted up her laptop and e-mailed Joseph Stryker.

51

The phone rang in Marcus's apartment.

"Hello?"

"Is this my son the doctor?"

"What? Dad, you don't have a son who's a doctor."

"If I did, would he call me? Or possibly this is the son I never hear from?"

"Dad! We talked two days ago."

"Oh, *now I know!* It's my son whom I only hear from when he needs something."

"Damn it! Let's make an appointment right now to take you to Fruit of the Sea on Saturday night."

"Make it the Harp and I'll go."

"And I want you to meet a girl."

Dead silence. Twenty seconds passed. Finally, "Ahum. Aha. Well, in that case, either restaurant will work okay, I guess."

Thinking *gotcha!* Marcus said, "I assume you have something for me."

"Indeed I have. Your Mr. Hacker has been sighted in Nice."

"Nice, France?"

"That's where I keep Nice. And he's on his way to Turkey."

"Turkey? Is that near Istanbul?"

"Istanbul is *in* Turkey. Where were you educated—"

"Gotcha!"

"He's been sighted by an agent of the French Direction Centrale de la Police Judiciare, who appears to be following him. This man, Dou, phoned his office. Hacker's plane isn't going to Istanbul, though. He's gone to Konya."

"All right. You've got me with that one. I'll look it up."

"Saturday night. Or else."

Marcus had the phone off before he thought: Turkey! Isn't that where Blue Eriksen went?

52

"Look, I don't want to scare you," Joseph Stryker said to Blue.

"Don't treat me like a child, either, Joseph. I appreciate your kindness in coming here. But I e-mailed you because I hoped you could tell me something, not keep something from me."

They were on the outdoor terrace of Blue's double room in Konya. Adam was falling asleep, Blue hoped, in the bedroom just inside, and Joseph, Bengt, Perce, and Blue were sitting in bentwood chairs on the tiny balcony. Joseph had asked straight out whether she was okay with them being here for the discussion, and she said of course. They had been in danger, too, and maybe because of her.

On the other hand, she was glad that Tabitha, Drake, Brad, and Andy had gone to a dinner at a well-known outdoor grill in some famous courtyard that Drake wanted to photograph, and were planning to go to a movie afterward. It was good for Andy to get some fun, and Blue didn't want to involve them in any heavy discussion until she knew what Joseph was talking about.

She said, "So you don't think you've come all this way for nothing."

"No. I don't."

Bengt said, "There's clearly *something* wrong, Blue. You've told Joseph. Now tell us about it."

She did. Everything, starting from Adam's crawl onto the highway, which made Bengt wince, through the police finding Edward's body, Horace Pollard's doubts that it was simple burglary, the scree slope disaster, through Ana's e-mails.

Bengt said, "I knew there was something funny about that rock slide. You three hadn't walked onto the scree. It came down on you."

"Vibrations from all of us talking—"

"Blue, please!" Bengt said, impatiently, "That's ridiculous. Thunderstorms crash over that mountain. Lightning. Jetliners fly over it. A few people talking quietly? Please!"

"Joseph, do you really think some religious nut is out to kill me?"

"No."

"Well, then!"

"But somebody is."

Blue felt chilled. Sitting on that balcony, looking out over Konya, with the *muezzin* beginning the sundown call to prayer from the Iplikçi Mosque, where calls had echoed for nine hundred years, conspiracies and mysteries did not seem so improbable.

Joseph said, "The people who were angry at your book, *Goddess,* have been angry for—how long? When was it published?"

"Three years ago."

"The reason I'm pretty successful at what I do is that I know what looks mysterious is usually simple. When you have a mystery, go to the closest answer first. Occam's razor. Exactly what are you doing now? I Googled you. You're a public figure. Your latest project is on psilocybin as a treatment for drug addiction. You talked about it on television. That could get you in trouble."

"So you think some religious zealot is after me?"

"That would be my second guess."

"Then what?"

"My first guess would be people who make money from drugs."

"Why would they care about me?"

Joseph said, "You think you may have a cure for drug addiction."

"Or a way to prevent it."

"Good God, Blue! If there's the slightest possibility you're right, you're threatening the biggest monopoly on earth."

"What monopoly?"

"Drugs are a trillion-dollar, worldwide business. Would you really expect a business that large, that sprawling, and that complex to be run by hundreds of thousands of little mom and pop operations?"

"Well, there's the mafia."

"Peanuts by comparison. Yes, of course, Mob guys moved into drugs when alcohol was decriminalized. And there were Asian cartels. And Latin American cartels. But they all got gobbled up."

"Gobbled up? Why?"

"Think of OPEC. You don't have people with half a dozen oil wells producing, refining, and selling their own oil a few barrels at a time like boutique wineries."

"No."

"Nobody says, 'Ah, a modest light sweet Kuwaiti with just a bold hint of crude.' "

Bengt chuckled. Joseph went on. "Drugs are very much like oil. They're produced all over the world. There is refining involved. Transporting the product is difficult. And they have the one thing oil doesn't have—the prices are already artificially inflated because they're illegal."

"Although," Bengt said, "OPEC holds back supplies to raise prices."

"Bingo. It is similar. And brings me to this: Think what would happen to the people who profit from drugs if that artificial inflation were removed."

Perce said, "They'd all be out of a job."

Bengt said, "But is there really any such organization?"

"Yes. And they will terminate interlopers who try to take a market area away from them. And people who want to take the market away from them the other way. They've terminated legislators who favored decriminalization."

Blue said, "But I'm just—jeez!—I'm Dorothy the Small and Meek."

"Right. You're small potatoes to them. Except you made one big mistake."

"What?"

"You're not a nobody. You got famous for your first book. So they know your new project is going to get a lot of media attention."

"Who are they?"

"Businessmen. Big, big businessmen. Bigger than Halliburton, and we know how public spirited Halliburton is. Bigger than Enron ever was. A thousand times bigger. I don't know what they call themselves, if that's what you mean. Law enforcement groups nicknamed their consortium DOPEC. The OPEC comparison was pretty obvious."

Blue said, "You mean people know they exist?"

"They're very well hidden. You don't see them except by their actions."

Perce said, "It would explain something I've wondered about."

Blue said, "What?"

"Drugs are sold by small, warring gangs. This is true in London, anyway."

"Okay."

"And these gangs are supposedly in murderous competition with each other. Each has its own turf. Invade the next gang's turf and they'll kill you."

Blue said, "But then they're not really organized—"

"Hear me out. What happens with prices, oddly enough, gives the lie to some of that. If the price of, say, heroin, rises in one part of London, it rises in another part," Perce said.

"That's true in New York, too," Joseph said.

"So—you'd think the second group would keep prices relatively low to get more business."

"Yes. Simple economics," Bengt said.

"Yes. But instead of prices being set from the bottom, by small entrepreneurial gangs, it looks as if they're set from the top down. By an organization that controls supply and sets prices to optimize everybody's profits."

The call to prayer echoed from the buildings. The air began to cool. Blue shivered.

After a minute or so, Perce said, "Joseph, how do you know this?"

"And *do* you know it?" Bengt added.

"It's an open secret. What's not known is how far it extends. Put another way, it's not known exactly who's in their pocket. Which of the guys on what you might call our side are actually on theirs."

"There have always been cops paid off by drug dealers."

"Cops are little guys. Who is being paid off by the gigantic drug dealers?"

"Big guys."

The muezzin had ended his call. There would be another at full dark. The sky was purple in the east and a pale fragile blue to the west. Thin mist, water vapor or dust, softened the skyline. Blue wondered at all the conspiracies this part of the world had seen. Templars and Janissaries, their lives pledged to their order, and ruthless churchmen of a hundred sects. Hittites with their great trading empire, and sultans with absolute power over their subjects.

Bengt said, "I can see that the amount of money involved would be irresistible. The OPEC analogy is a good one. Even so, before anybody came out on top, there would have been major wars. There must have been thousands of people who wanted control."

Joseph said, "You bet."

"And casualties. Dead bodies."

"There's a lot of ocean on the planet."

Perce said, "What would happen to OPEC if the price of oil were reduced ninety percent?"

"And what would they do to prevent that?"

Bengt said, "So, Joseph, they wouldn't have minded killing your brother in the scree slide, either. They'd see it as collateral damage."

"I suppose."

"Since he died, they might believe that Blue's been scared off her research."

"They might have, but—"

Blue said, "If they've read the Dutch newspapers, they know I haven't been."

53

Congressman Jacko Holton called his son Marcus at his office in the Agency at 9:00 A.M. Marcus had been about to phone him to cancel their dinner date. Marcus was going to his boss, Reed, to demand permission to leave for Turkey.

"I have some news, Marcus," the congressman said, without preamble. Jacko had what Marcus thought of as his "newsboy" voice on. Marcus could picture his old man swinging from side to side in his swivel chair, too much energy to sit still.

Marcus was about to say he didn't like using this phone, but his dad was calling from the congressional office building. Wasn't there some sort of regulation forbidding listening in on members of Congress? Plus, Marcus was in a hurry.

"What, Dad?"

"It's not exactly good news."

"Don't keep me waiting."

"The police in Konya found the French agent, Arsène Dou."

"'Found' doesn't sound good."

"No. It isn't. He was found dead near an air force base there. From what they tell me, I guess the civilian airlines and the air force use the same taxiways."

"Was there any sign of Hacker?"

"I would tell you if there had been, Marcus." There was no joking in Jacko's voice now. He realized what this meant to his son. He didn't even mention dinner.

"Thanks, Dad." Marcus kept his voice steady until he shut off the phone. Then he jumped to his feet and ran down the hall.

"I need to take my vacation days this week, sir. Right now," Marcus said to Reed, his immediate superior.

"Need to? Why?"

"I—does it matter?"

"Haseltine has told me about your obsession with that assassin. You're going after him, aren't you?"

Marcus liked Reed. He didn't want to lie to him. "Hacker is a killer."

"You don't have any right to arrest him in a foreign country."

"I know that, sir."

"Then what do you plan to do?"

"He may be in Turkey." Marcus liked and trusted Reed, but he didn't want to tell him everything. "I'm not even taking my sidearm."

"They'd let you send it through boxed on the plane—"

"But I can't carry a concealed weapon in Turkey."

"Or practically anywhere else on the planet."

"I just want to locate him. Then I'll bring in the Turkish police."

Reed looked down at his desk. "Marcus. I want you to be careful. Don't break any international agreements. Don't trash your career. You're good for us."

"Thank you, sir."

"I mean it. Play it on the up and up."

"Does that mean I can take my week?"

"Go and God bless."

Marcus, for years, had kept a suitcase always packed. Thinking how smart he had been to do that, he called his ticket broker from his cell phone as he headed to the parking lot to get his car.

"No, I don't care about price. I don't care what the seating is. I want whatever flight gets me there soonest."

"Make that two seats, big spender," said a voice behind him.

"Diana!"

54

The fifth day in Turkey, they took the entire day off from the dig and stayed in Konya to shop. Adam's birthday was tomorrow, and, general favorite that he was, there was a whole lot of giggling and smiling behind hands as they left the hotel. Brad was going off with Tabitha, an event that made Drake huffy. But he and Dr. Jungstedt started out together, until Jungstedt realized that this left Andy with no one to stroll the city with. They had all been taking Andy under their wings a bit.

Andy said, "I might just stay here."

"No, hey," Joseph said. "Help Blue and me out. We may need you to carry something. I'm hoping to buy Adam a mountain goat."

This got a weak half smile from Andy.

Blue suspected that Joseph was hanging around her in case an attacker was watching her. Certainly, he kept scanning the faces of the people around them. There was a large number of Turkish military men on the streets, hardly surprising as the Turks had the second largest army in NATO, and the Konya police were visible as well, which gave Blue some sense of security, but she kept a closer eye on the other shoppers than she ordinarily would have.

Blue had e-mailed the department secretary, asking her to submit three articles, one she had written in the spring and two she had updated recently on her work so far. Since patient trials had started with psilocybin, she included a review of the literature, an extensive description of her deductions from the end-of-life therapy, and a careful summary of the first patient results. Two would go to professional journals, one to a popular science press. It seemed to her now that the more work there was "out there," the less to be gained by killing her.

When she told Joseph, he said, "That's kind of bold."

"Unfortunately, it'll be months before they hit the presses."

Adam, Joseph, Andy, and Blue wandered off down the street toward the market, said to have existed on this spot for a thousand years. Blue had rented a stroller for Adam, who was walking pretty well now, but not very far. Also, if left to walk, he picked up all kinds of stuff off the street and immediately put it in his mouth.

The bazaar was a hodgepodge of Turkish fruits and vegetables, including beautiful strawberries, lettuce, and early squash, plus baked goods, candy, cloth, clothing, household items, miniature Turkish rugs, lace, and also a disappointing but probably predictable array of Turkish and imported plastic stuff. Toys, hairbrushes, plastic tourist ware of all sorts, including dolls and snow globes with famous mosques in them, rubbed shoulders with exquisite metal work and bright fabrics, pottery, and fine china.

And rugs. Rugs, rugs, rugs! Blue wanted every one of them. She stopped and stared at a multihued array of rugs, stunning as a dozen stained-glass windows.

Andy touched a small one, showing the first glimmer of enthusiasm he'd displayed in days.

The weather was summerlike now in late June. Many of the women wore traditional headscarves. Blue saw worry beads wrapped around the hands of many people. This was a very conservative Muslim place. Despite occasional rallies for secular rights, the entire area, in fact all of Turkey, was religious and strict, and Konya was one of the most conservative cities in Turkey. Blue had been careful to tell her group to dress conservatively. She asked Tabitha not to wear shorts, and to keep to high T-shirt-style necklines.

Konya was a mixture of people. There were Greeks from the south, Jews, Armenians, and Kurds. There were very conservative Muslims, most but not all of them the older generation. Then there were the twenty-somethings, especially college students, who were mostly nontraditional, wearing "modern" clothing, jeans and polo shirts and sweatshirts.

Most of the produce sellers came direct from small local farms. They passed a woman selling garlic. The woman had set out a table and sat directly on the table cross-legged, surrounded by bunches of garlic. The stems remained on the garlic, and pretty blue ribbons were tied around the stems, making garlic bouquets.

"Why do they do that?" Andy asked.

"They expect you to hang them up in your kitchen and use the garlic as you want it. Pick off however many cloves you need at a time."

Andy said, "If I bought a small rug for my mother, could the shop-keeper ship it home? Her birthday's in September."

"Get the hotel to ship it," Joseph said. Andy wandered away toward a display of rugs in jewel colors, but he didn't look particularly enthusiastic. The rugs should have cheered anyone up. Blue thought Andy would be best off going home, too. She didn't want to suggest it, for fear he'd think he was being rejected. No matter how carefully you phrased things, people heard what they wanted to hear or what they were afraid they were hear-ing. Maybe he'd be more involved and less sad if he went out to spend the last couple of days they were going to be here in Perce's dig house. He could help out with the conservators.

A few minutes later, as they inspected some ceramics, including a green-glazed frog Blue decided not to buy, Andy approached them, carrying a rolled rug over his shoulder.

"Meet you at the hotel," he said.

"So—what shall I get Adam for his birthday?" Joseph said.

"Well, nothing heavy. We'd have to ship it home. You shouldn't feel you need to give him anything."

Joseph took over pushing the stroller and zoomed in swerves right, then left, then right, making hooting noises, like a train. Adam chortled with glee. The people on the streets smiled at them. Some waved at Adam. What nice people they were.

"I see a possibility," Joseph said, giving Blue the stroller. They had just passed a booth with clothing for children, little coats and robes strung on clotheslines. Some of the garments would have fit dolls. Joseph scanned the people nearby again. Apparently seeing no one ominous, he said, "Don't go too far. I'll catch up with you in two minutes."

He ducked into the booth.

Blue had walked just a few paces, when Adam suddenly stood straight up in the stroller. "Dere!" he said, which meant "there."

She had already heard the jingling of bells, but hadn't paid much attention. A tiny, rug-draped booth half a block ahead displayed bells, most of them hanging from a wire running between two poles across the top of the booth. When the breeze pushed a paddle, the bells rang. As they drew up in front, she could see that there were bells of many sizes, and of many materials—silver, steel, brass, copper, ceramic, and even wood. By now Adam was shrieking with delight, and the booth's owner, beaming with equal delight, rang bells for him.

There was a tiny silver bell with a high-pitched, clear sound. A big cowbell that gronk-gronked like a frog. Hanging across the front of the booth on a lower wire were graduated bells that looked like they were made of steel. The owner tapped them one at a time with a tiny silver hammer, producing a haunting melody. Adam bounced up and down.

The man picked up a brass bell about four inches wide, shaped like an eight-fingered claw with a handle on top. The clapper inside did not hang from a hook as most did, but bounced around inside the claws, producing clear alto notes as it struck them. Adam reached out both his hands.

He said, "Ooooeeeeh!"

The man placed the bell in Adam's cupped hands. Blue thought he couldn't break the bell, so she let him take it. He held it by the handle, swung it, and produced beautiful sounds, just as if he knew what he was doing. He laughed and did it again.

The man knew he'd made a sale. Blue gave in happily.

Turkey had converted to the New Turkish Lira since Blue was here five years earlier. Lira now came in five-lira, ten-lira notes, and so on, easier than the old style. There were a hundred yeni kurus in one lira. A lira was worth about sixty-three cents American. The man wanted two lira, a dollar and a quarter, which he probably didn't expect to get, but Blue was so happy with Adam's delight—he was now hugging the bell under his chin—that she paid without haggling. Well, there you go, careless American throwing money around. But the shopkeeper didn't suggest any such thing. He was watching Adam, too. Just then a woman who might have been his wife slipped into the back of the booth. The man pointed at Adam, now crooning "Beeeeer. Waaaaall," to his bell. The woman broke into a smile of immense sweetness.

Adam cuddled the bell to his chest.

Blue turned the stroller to go back to the store where Joseph was shopping.

Out of nowhere, she felt creepy.

Adam leaned back, his body and legs rigid. "Unnnnh-unnh!" he said. His reaction when he was scared.

"What?"

"Unnnh!"

Blue looked. Adam pointed at the fruit stand across the walkway, but the rugs that shaded the fruit from the sun made it hard to see beyond it.

At that instant, Joseph came out of the clothing store, smiling, carrying a wrapped package.

His smile faded. His gaze went to the fruit stand they were looking at. At a run, he ducked behind it. But a moment later he appeared around the other side of it, his head swiveling back and forth. Then he returned, shrugging.

He said, "Maybe we should go back to the hotel."

55

"Listen up, all," Blue said.

Drake stopped trying to stroke Tabitha's hand. She folded her arms and looked at me. Everybody else was already on alert.

"We're going to have Adam's birthday party this evening as planned," she said, at which point Tabitha, Bengt, and Joseph cheered. "But we're not going to do it out at the dig."

"Why not?" Bengt asked.

"I want Joseph to explain. He believes Jasper's accident may not have been an accident. It may have been connected with the murder of my husband."

Joseph did a good job. He laid it all out, explaining DOPEC in even more detail than he had to Blue.

When he finished, Drake said, "That's gotta be the biggest load of crap I ever heard."

"Drake!" Tabitha said.

Joseph was remarkably calm at Drake's remark. Bengt said, "I'm not so sure it is. Crap, I mean. Once Joseph told us last night, it made sense. There's too much money in drugs for it not to attract organization."

"Still, it's hard to believe," Tabitha said.

Blue said, "Well, whether it's true or not, I want to act as if there is somebody out to attack me and doesn't care who gets in the way."

"Good," said Bengt.

Blue said, "Instead of having a picnic out on the exposed plain near Çatalhöyük, I want to hold the party this evening in the hotel's courtyard. It's enclosed by a wall, and there are employees all around."

"This is stupid," said Drake, looking directly at Joseph. Maybe he saw him as another rival for Tabitha's affections. If so, he wasn't going about this in a way that made Tabitha happy. She glared at him, but his ego was in control and he couldn't stop himself.

"This is conspiracy-theory stuff. You're paranoid." He said this to Joseph, but it was Bengt who answered.

"Better paranoid than dead."

56

Tabitha had bought Adam a tiny, solid stainless steel hammer, not some baby plastic kind, and a little steel trowel, and she apparently had ordered made to her specifications a sifting screen about eight inches across, small enough for him to hold. She then gave him a bag of sand, saying to Blue, "It's clean. I sieved it and steamed it. And you know how he loves sand." Blue wondered what she meant until she sat right down on the floor with Adam in the dining room, spread out a large towel, and showed him how to sift the sand, as he had seen Perce and the rest of them do at the dig. He poured some sand into the sieve. It went through the mesh and left behind—*a dinosaur animal cracker!*

Adam shrieked, straightened his whole body, and flopped over backward in glee.

Perce, who was out at the dig, had sent a small drinking cup of brass, which with some imagination could be mistaken for a tiny beer mug, but wasn't, really.

Andy gave him an embroidered Turkish vest. Blue had told him, and for that matter all the others, not to get Adam anything expensive. Especially she had told the students, as students never had enough money. And she was touched that they had put little money into it, but much thought.

Joseph gave Adam a hat much like a jester's hat or elf hat, with brass bells on the points that actually rang. Adam found that if he shook his head back and forth he made music.

Brad gave him a small wooden cart, which looked like the large ones they had seen carrying produce.

The waiter placed a huge tray of appetizers on the long table. There were tiny tomatoes cut to resemble roses, a dish of fava beans and garlic, and dolmas, which were pretty much the same as dolmades, stuffed grape leaves.

They were going to have roast lamb, a favorite of the Turks, who, being Muslim, don't eat pork.

The large hotel courtyard contained at least thirty tables, with diners at several, even though the birthday group was eating earlier than most tourists or Turks would. The restaurant would fill up by nine or ten.

Around the courtyard were high walls, which gave Blue a feeling of security. A wide bank of six French doors opened into the lobby of the hotel and stood open now. But it seemed unlikely that an attacker would come in through the busy lobby, which was filled day and night with visitors, newspaper vendors, flower-sellers, little boys selling a sort of sweet syrup that they poured over shaved ice, and of course hotel employees carrying suitcases, fresh laundry, and so on.

On the other side of the courtyard, big arches opened into the kitchens. There were two kitchens: One, with ovens and spit-roasters visible, was given over primarily to meat. The other seemed to be breads, sauces, vegetables, and desserts.

They had picked Adam up off the floor, bundling the tools into the towel, and sat him in a booster seat. They were parceling out the gifts, giving Adam one at a time and not waiting for after dinner, so that he'd stay patient through dinner. Adam was sweet and good-natured, but he was a one-year-old, and he was capable of a major crying meltdown if he was bored.

"You'll call me paranoid—" Joseph began.

Drake said, "Yeah."

"I'd like to go out and just walk around the hotel once."

"To catch the lurking madman?" Drake asked. He chuckled. Nobody else did.

The hotel occupied the whole city block. Of the four streets that bordered it, the two on the south and east were major, busy thoroughfares. The one on the west was quiet but well-used, and the one on the north was not much more than a big alleyway. The only doors were in the front into the lobby and in this back alley. The food for the kitchens was delivered at the back, and the alley probably had more people who were aware of who should be there than the front did.

Blue said, "I think that's a good idea. But be careful." Earlier in his life, Joseph had been a Marine, and while she was uneasy about him going out, he probably knew what he was doing.

But as Joseph got up, three people came in from the lobby side. One was the desk clerk, saying, "Sir! Sir, the guests are at their dinner—"

The other two were a man and woman, American from the look of their clothes.

Joseph immediately moved to place himself between the arrivals and Blue, and Bengt jumped up and stepped toward them to intercept them.

57

"So it's not our imagination," Blue said fifteen minutes later.

Their identification lay on the table: Diana McCullough and Marcus Holton. Not just their Agency IDs, but their passports and their driver's licenses. Joseph had not relaxed his vigilance until they had all but emptied their pockets. And according to Marcus, he was right to do so.

Blue and Brad had pulled another table over to make seating for all ten of them.

When Marcus explained what had brought him to Konya—the trail of death Hacker had left behind him—Brad's eyes grew as big as pitas, but he sat next to Adam's high chair and kept an eye on the little guy.

Adam was experimenting with how finely a piece of boiled potato could be mashed. The results: pretty darn fine. It looked like library paste.

Joseph said, "We've been keeping an eye out, even before we heard this."

Blue said, "And this Hacker killed Edward?" She found it so hard to wrap her mind around that she realized she had only half believed Joseph's idea.

"And he could have killed the baby, too—" he hesitated as Blue winced.

"Go on."

"We think he was interrupted when he heard sirens. There was a grass fire around the other side of the block."

"So a grass fire saved Adam's life?"

"I can't be sure. But when he heard the sirens, he might have thought the neighbors saw him go in your place and called 911."

Firming up her back, Blue said, "Go on."

"A French agent, Arsène Dou, spotted Hacker leaving Nice on his way to Konya yesterday and followed him," Marcus said. "Dou was found near the Konya airport today, dead."

"Why didn't Dou get backup?" Bengt asked, reasonably.

"He had very little time to follow him, but he called his office from the air."

"And?"

"And his assistant thought he said 'Calais' not 'Konya.' "

They were all silent for a few seconds. Blue expected Drake to say what they were all thinking—that these are the agencies that are supposed to protect us. Fortunately, he kept quiet.

"I'll go out and take a walk around," Diana said.

Bengt said, "I can do it."

Diana got a bit steely-eyed. "I've been a federal agent for nearly fifteen years now. I can walk around a building perfectly well."

"Certainly," Bengt said.

"And I *certainly* don't want to risk the lives of civilians." She strode away.

"Feisty," Drake said, with a grin.

"The one thing we don't know," Marcus said, "is who Hacker's working for."

"As a matter of fact," Joseph said, "that is exactly what we were talking about before you got here."

He described DOPEC. Surprisingly, Marcus nodded when Joseph made the analogy to OPEC. Joseph said, "It would explain a lot. The amount of money is unimaginable."

"You're right. It would explain a lot of things," Marcus said slowly.

Drake said, "The meeting of Paranoiacs Anonymous is now in session."

Diana came back. "Looks okay out there to me."

Adam bent forward over his tray and licked the potato paste. A dime-sized circle of it painted his nose.

The roast lamb came in on a huge platter, carried dramatically from the kitchen by two young men in white coats, followed by a chef brandishing a carving knife and two-pronged fork.

The chef carved thin slices from the bone, the meat just slightly pink in the very center. The scent of rosemary and mint leaves was wonderful.

The desk clerk entered from the lobby with a small white box and approached their table. In his French-accented English, he said, "The gentleman said to give this to you, madam."

"Not to Adam? It's his birthday," Blue asked. But she pulled up the lid. The whole table heard her intake of breath and saw the little green glass frog spill onto the table.

Joseph said, "Blue! What's wrong?"

Marcus said, "What's that?"

"Why, it's very pretty," Tabitha said. "Why are you so upset—"

"He took it. When he came to my house. He's here." Blue's voice shook.

"The killer?" Joseph reached for the frog. Marcus scanned the room.

At that instant, Adam reared up in his seat and screamed. "Baaaad!" He was facing the vegetable-and-bread kitchen.

It is not true that you see a crisis as a stroboscopic mix of sights. It's pictures, but out of sequence.

Adam is pointing at a man in a baker's apron, carrying several long loaves of bread.

Adam's warning gives us a couple of seconds to react. Brad grabs Adam and dives under the table. One of the bread loaves explodes. Andy gulps and stands up. Joseph dives at the bread man. Marcus rushes at the bread man. A diner at a table behind us screams. Diana shouts, "Oh, God!" I push two tables over between where Adam and Brad are crouched and the gunman, who I now realize is a gunman, not a man with exploding bread. Drake, on hands and knees, crawls rapidly to the lobby doors and disappears.

Tabitha is running at the bread man's back.

Diana crashes into Marcus, but I think that was later. Or earlier. Andy bleeds onto the floor. Joseph lurches back. The gunman enters the room, but I know that was a few seconds earlier. Marcus falls over something that makes a clanging noise. Bengt falls. The gunman vanishes. Bread flies all over. Shots hit the table over Brad and Adam and me. No, that was two seconds earlier.

I huddle over Brad and Adam. I feel every part of Adam and nothing seems to be bleeding. Then he screams, piercingly. He's hopping mad. That's wonderful. Screaming. Wonderful!

Everything was wonderful for only an instant.

When Blue clawed her way up from behind the double table barricade she had made, she saw disaster.

Brad was bruised from Blue pulling the table down over him. His forehead was bleeding, but he wasn't injured badly. Diana stood near Marcus, her arms wrapped around herself. Marcus held her waist, but he was bleeding from somewhere on his shoulder or upper arm. Joseph sat on the floor, rocking back and forth. Andy lay curled in a fetal position, twitching and surrounded by a pool of blood. The other diner at the back who had screamed also lay in a pool of blood. Hotel employees were all over the place, several of them just wringing their hands, but a man in a chef's hat strode to Marcus and wrapped a towel firmly around his arm. A young man who worked here as a gofer crouched near Joseph, asking him something and holding a towel to his leg.

Coffee bubbled. A man barked orders in Turkish. Smoke drifted across the ceiling.

Blue didn't see Tabitha! What?—Oh, there she was. She was helping an older woman, who had been at a table eating dinner. She held the woman's hands and gently backed her into a chair.

Every muscle in Blue's body twitched. *Aren't there any doctors?* But the man from the registration desk shouted something very loudly. Blue could see his lips move, but couldn't understand the words and couldn't figure out whether that was because she was in some sort of mental shock or because he was speaking Turkish. When she heard a word that sounded like "infirmiers" she hoped he had switched into French and was saying that the paramedics were coming.

Blue knelt near Andy. An elderly man from the older woman's table knelt near him, too. Andy curled around an abdominal wound, breathing in shallow, bubbling gulps. Blue looked at the man and gestured "shall we turn him over on his back?" The man shook his head.

Staring down at herself from some eye outside her body, Blue behaved very sensibly. She looked back at Brad and saw him amusing Adam, who had calmed down as soon as—Blue hated to even think the phrase—as soon as the shooting stopped. Brad had Adam facing him, away from the carnage, and was making clown faces.

The air smelled of spilled food, hot gunmetal, blood, feces, coffee, and urine. Only one person still screamed.

Andy bubbled and trembled. A paramedic arrived. He took out a stethoscope and reached toward Andy's shoulder to turn him over. The man who had been crouching next to Andy spoke to the medic in a language Blue didn't understand. The medic nodded his head and stopped, holding his stethoscope. The older man must be a doctor.

Then Andy died.

The police found the driver of a baker's van unconscious from a head wound that had smashed the side of his face. He was under his vehicle, out of the sight of passersby. His apron and hat, and of course some bread, were all missing.

Joseph had a severe leg wound. Marcus was wounded on the upper arm, but not badly, in the sense that neither important nerves nor large arteries nor large veins were severed. Fourteen stitches closed it up. Bengt had taken a bullet in the side of his face, smashing his cheekbone and seriously injuring his left eye. Drake Rakowski was gone. Blue heard later that he took the first taxi he could find to the airport and flew home.

Tabitha and Diana were reasonably okay except for small lacerations from glass and broken pottery.

Felix Hacker had gotten clean away.

58

They touched down at O'Hare at 9:50 P.M. local time. Adam had fallen asleep in Blue's arms. Blue thought she would never sleep again.

"I have a car waiting," Marcus said. "We'll get you to the Hilton and safe, first of all."

"What about Tabitha and Joseph and Brad?"

"I made reservations for them, too."

"I can go home," Brad said.

Tabitha said, "I could go to my apartment, but there's nobody else there. Maybe I'd feel safer in the hotel."

"I wish you'd both stay there tonight at least," Joseph said. "Tomorrow we can work out how to keep you safe after this."

"He won't try again, will he?" Blue asked. "It's gone too far. There's too much publicity."

"Well, we've left him behind for now," Marcus said. "But he knows where you all live."

"I mean, everybody would know it was him now."

"I wish I thought that would stop him."

Diana, who had been quiet up to now, said, "He's a professional. He's got to drop it, because now the risk isn't worth the benefit."

"I think," Marcus said, "that he's gone nuts."

Blue was grateful to Marcus. They would never have been allowed to leave Turkey this soon if it hadn't been for Marcus and the Agency's influence. As it was, it had taken three days. Andy's body was being held another week for the Turkish authorities to finish their investigation. Blue had talked twice with his grieving parents and she would have to visit them tomorrow or the next day, which she dreaded. His father would be going to Turkey for the body, but not until it was released for burial.

Bengt's family was mostly in London. Blue had talked with them on the phone. They said eye surgery was scheduled, but the prognosis wasn't good. He might lose the sight in that eye.

She had talked with Brad's parents, too, and Brad had talked with them, of course. They decided to pick him up at the hotel later tonight. *They don't want to leave him near me too long.*

When the plane touched the earth, she burst into tears. Poor Bengt. Poor Andy. It was sad beyond anything.

Adam must have sensed that his mother was upset, because he woke and started to cry.

Then Tabitha started to cry, and Brad started to cry, and even Joseph, who didn't know any of them well, pressed his lips together, his eyes swimming with unshed tears. Marcus and Diana held hands. Both looked grim. The other passengers around them, some of whom were jumping to their feet to be first off the plane, stared at the seven of them.

59

At Marcus's request, the Agency had sent a car that could carry all of them, and sent sidearms for Diana and Marcus to replace the weapons they had not been allowed to take on the flight to Turkey.

"A baby seat!" Blue said. "Who thought of this?"

"Yeah, well." Marcus was embarrassed. "I have nephews and nieces, so——"

There was an Agency driver Marcus introduced as Harold.

Harold said, "Let's get you tucked up in the Hilton before Hacker knows where you've gone." He added, "Like the old Irish saying 'May you be in heaven half an hour before the devil knows you're dead.'" Nobody chuckled. "Well, maybe not the most felicitous choice of sayings."

"It's okay," Blue said. He was trying to be nice, after all. And he had been extremely helpful. But nobody else spoke and the car became deathly quiet.

Adam was in the child safety seat right next to Blue, and she played with him, nuzzling his fist and making popping sounds on his cheek, which he loved. It was the only sound in the car, except for Tabitha sniffling. Then even that stopped.

Blue gave Adam a teething biscuit. He made a ghastly mess when he gnawed on one, but she needed him happy. They had swung onto Interstate 90 toward Chicago, and in another ten miles they would pass over the spot where Adam had crawled into the highway.

Blue kept telling herself that it was silly to let a specific place bother her. The event was in the past. But she was tense, anyway. She wondered whether she'd cringe every time she used that highway.

They drove on in silence.

There was her old neighborhood. This was the place. People had died on this highway, and because of Adam. *Not his fault. Not my fault. Certainly not poor, dead Edward's fault. Maybe it was my fault. Like the woman with the protestors had yelled at me, I should have been home.*

And then they were past it, heading in to downtown Chicago.

There was the John Hancock Building ahead.

As they approached the Division Street exit, they saw red taillights come on ahead. Harold braked just in time and Blue saw him glance uneasily into the rearview mirror, wondering whether the car behind them could stop. It did. They inched forward. Harold picked up his radio. "What's the problem on the Kennedy near Chicago Ave?"

"Rollover accident. Take a side street if you can. They say it's packed solid after Ohio Street."

"Damn," he said. "I should've got off at Division."

It was just five blocks to the Ohio Street exit, but it took them twenty minutes. The exit brought them into town just east of the Chicago River.

Harold said, "I'm going to take Lower Wacker if that's okay."

"Fine," Blue said, and Marcus said, "Okay."

Diana said, "I'm texting the hotel." She punched at her handheld.

Lower Wacker was a street under a street. When you drove around The Chicago Loop, what you were seeing was the top layer. Another whole layer of streets and alleys lay underneath. Lower Wacker was the biggest of the underground streets.

When Chicago was a young frontier town, the swampy areas were mostly left as they were, filled with water and mud and garbage, and as the town grew, filled with the poor, living in tents and shacks. After the Great Chicago Fire, things were different.

There was big money in Chicago—lumber money, meatpacking

money, money from making harvesters and combines, money from the burgeoning railhead. Big money went into improving the city. The downtown streets were raised above the swamp or flood level. Whole areas of The Loop were built on iron stilts, the pavements were raised, and gradually the sidewalks were filled in and the vacant land stuffed with buildings until you could walk from one end of downtown to another and not realize it was underlain by swamp.

The only remnant of all this was a series of secondary streets below the level where the sun shone. Some, like Lower Wacker, which ran under Wacker Drive along the Chicago River, were regularly used and were favorites of taxi drivers and city cognoscenti for getting places in a hurry.

Others were used primarily by trucks and delivery vans, picking up and delivering to the subbasement levels of glitzy hotels and posh restaurants. Still other narrower tunnels down here carried heat conduits, sewer mains, or parts of the underground transportation system. It was all held up by cast iron pillars and groins.

It was like you were inside the rib cage of the city.

They were headed south on Lower Wacker, right under The Loop, when Harold, the driver, said, "Oh, jeez."

About a second later they were hit from behind. Blue swung around and saw a Hummer that looked as big as a house revving up for a second strike at them. Harold gunned the engine, but so did the Hummer and it was faster. It turned slightly to the left, to hit the left rear of their car, sending them into a spin. They bounced off the pylons on their right with a sharp crash and all Blue could think of for a second was Princess Di.

Blue reached for Adam's car seat as they came to a crushing stop. Marcus and Joseph shouted "Out! Out! Out!" Shots pinged off the left side door. One went through the windshield.

The driver of the Hummer leaped out and onto the concrete divider.

Harold was motionless behind the wheel, his head leaning toward the gear shift.

The left rear door wouldn't open when Brad tried it, but Blue thought maybe that was just as well. The assailant was shooting from that side. Marcus had fired once at him, which backed him away behind the Hummer. Then Marcus jumped out the right front door and shot again from over the hood of the car.

Meanwhile, Joseph, Tabitha, Diana, and Blue, with Brad carrying Adam under his arm like a football, dove out the right rear door. "Get away!" Marcus yelled.

Joseph yelled, "Run!"

They scattered. Joseph and Tabitha were on the left side where the shooter could see them. Joseph pushed Tabitha into a low dirty space behind a grate. He squeezed in after her. Blue heard his shirt rip.

There was a cross tunnel to Blue's right, still out of sight of the shooter, she hoped. Brad pelted toward it, carrying Adam. Blue sprinted after them.

60

"It's Hacker!" Marcus shouted at Diana. She already had her sidearm out.

Marcus ran a few steps forward and fired at him. Diana, behind him, fired and her bullet struck Marcus in the right side of his back, passing through and exiting under his arm, the surprise and shock causing him to slide to the ground ahead of the car.

Hacker leaped down from the concrete divider, cut around the front of the Hummer, then in front of the car and ran into the tunnel after Blue, Adam, and the others.

"Go after him, Diana!" Marcus said.

"I don't think so."

"What? You have to! He'll kill Blue and the baby!"

"No."

Marcus stared at her, not taking in what she meant. "It's safe enough. He won't see you following him. He's entirely focused on Eriksen."

She shook her head. After a few seconds, Marcus asked quietly, "How did he find us so fast?"

"I told him. Text-messaged him."

"What?"

"Otherwise, he'd still be on the Kennedy, wouldn't he?"

"What?"

"What? What? Is that all you can say? You're so stupid." She held her gun pointed at him. His own weapon was in his lap, pointed at the ground as blood ran down from his chest onto his forearm. The gun trembled in his hand.

"Diana, stop playing games. We have to help Blue!"

She stood facing him. "Where do you think your job would be if she got her way?"

"I don't know. Gone, I suppose."

"So would mine." She held her automatic pointed at his gut. Marcus sat splay-legged on the floor of the tunnel, leaning against the wall. His gun was slippery in his bloody hand, but slowly he pointed it in her general direction.

"You can't shoot me," he said. "They'd identify your gun. Ballistics would show it came from the gun the Agency issued you."

"You are so naïve. Don't you get it? The Agency gave us these weapons."

"No. I don't get it."

"The Agency! The Agency will show an entirely different weapon issued to me. This is one I picked up after some nameless, gloved attacker dropped it."

Marcus blinked.

Diana said, "After the nameless, gloved attacker shot you. Twice."

"Twice." Marcus stared at her. Several seconds passed. "Who else is involved? Haseltine, of course. Who else? Everybody? The Agency is a great, huge, criminal boondoggle."

"It's a moneymaker. Fights drugs. Gets millions from the government. Everybody loves us. Better than building pyramids. Keeps the economy chugging along."

"Is the President involved, too?"

"Who knows? Probably. He sure doesn't think all the money they're throwing at the Agency does anybody any good, does he?"

Marcus's brain was speeding, while his body felt slower and colder. "Haseltine took me to see the President so the President could jump all over Haseltine and make himself look golden?"

"Probably." She gestured at his face with her weapon. "Maybe it was a little playlet. Aw, Marcus, you look like you just discovered there's no tooth fairy."

Marcus rocked back and forth, his left hand holding his armpit and his right holding the shaking gun.

Diana said, "And you know something else? I never was the fat kid in grade school. I was built more like a greyhound."

"With the morals of a liver fluke."

"Now you get it."

He was shivering hard now. Blood loss and fear. Sinking into shock. "So you're really going to kill me?"

"Like I say, now you get it."

"Unless I shoot you first."

"You won't, Marcus. You're too much of a wimp." Her aim stabilized and her finger tightened on the trigger.

He shot her.

61

Blue, Brad, and Adam were about two city blocks into the tunnel, not knowing where they were going, but knowing they had to run, when they heard somebody behind them. Hoping it was Marcus or Diana, Blue turned to look.

It was Hacker.

He fired a shot, which pinged off the concrete wall, making sharp echoes rebound from somewhere ahead.

Blue screamed, "Run!"

But they had been running. Blue had taken Adam back from Brad a few seconds earlier, but now he snatched him from her arms, a smart move because even carrying Adam, he could run faster than she could.

The tunnel branched. Blue said, "That way!" not having any particular reason, except that it was dimmer, and she thought Hacker would be less able to hit them if he couldn't see clearly to aim.

Without Adam to carry, Blue could just about keep up with Brad. "Don't wait for me," she yelled. "Just get Adam out of here!"

. . .

They ran down the tunnel, slipping on mud that had drained in from the roadway above. Blue still kept up with Brad, but her broken ribs felt like the ends were grinding against each other. They ran at least another two underground blocks, and now she had no idea where they were. She thought they must have gone west from Lower Wacker—maybe. Somewhere up above them, the Eisenhower, the Kennedy, the Dan Ryan, all major interstates came together five blocks from Wacker.

Hacker was gaining on them. A shot splattered against the wall ahead.

"Over here!" Brad called. He had spied a metal stair going up. Blue thought it was a bad idea to climb it, because it would slow them down and Hacker could stand at the bottom and fire at them. But Brad was up it in a second. When she followed, she realized he had guessed right; there was a turn halfway up and the wire mesh that ran along the railing kept Hacker from being able to shoot at them easily when they made the turn.

Just at the turn, Brad handed Adam to Blue and said, "Hurry."

Hacker rounded the turn at that instant and Brad grabbed both side rails and kicked out at him. Hacker screamed, fired a shot that hit the concrete someplace overhead.

Brad kicked him in the head and he dropped the gun. Blue heard it clang into metal somewhere down the stairs. Brad had disarmed him!

Stop and help Brad or try to save Adam?

Blue kept going up. As she reached the surface, she looked back to see Hacker grab Brad's knees and fling him backward down the steep stairs. Brad screamed, "Shit!"

Hacker was right behind her. She ran out into the light.

Blue and Adam were on a concrete island in the middle of the expressway. The Kennedy or the Eisenhower. Or the Ryan, and who cared which? They were isolated on a long slab of concrete with only low guard rails separating them from lanes of traffic on both sides. Cars and trucks flew past, trailing slipstreams of dust.

Blue froze. It was her nightmare come to life. She had to run across the lines of cars—

But in that instant of indecision, Hacker crashed into her from behind. As she reeled, he grabbed Adam.

Adam shrieked. "Baaaad! Baaaad!"

Hacker brandished Adam over his head. He stepped into traffic, over the guardrail, jumping to the white dashed line, so that cars were roaring past on both sides of him.

Why didn't somebody in the cars do something?

Blue yelled, "Hey! People! Hey, call 911!"

What's the matter with them? Doesn't everybody have a cell phone in the car? But she realized it couldn't have been more than five seconds they'd been out here.

Blue had already run after Hacker, who was taunting her. "Come and get him." He wanted Blue to get close so he could shove her into an oncoming car. That was fine with her, as long as she got Adam out of danger.

"Bastard!" she screamed. "Bastard, bastard! Bastardbastardbastard-bastard!"

A truck the size of New Hampshire bore down on Blue, its front grille a dinosaur mouth. She dodged. A red sports car clipped her hip, spinning her. It hurt but she didn't go down. The driver honked. *Idiot! Does he think I'm out here just to get in his way?*

Hacker held Adam at arm's length, as if to toss him into traffic. An SUV honked at him. *Isn't anybody smart enough to stop? Take a chance, maybe, of being hit, but be a hero? Somebody do something smart! Stop your car! Block the road! Hey, be a hero!*

Hacker pirouetted as an orange Wolley taxi narrowly missed him, then he reared back, holding Adam in his right hand, as if to throw him like a football.

Blue leaped for Adam, and as she reached for him, she pushed him instead of pulling him away from Hacker. She put her foot behind Hacker's ankle and pushed at the same time. Falling backward, he let go of Adam to save himself.

He fell directly into the path of a cement truck.

Blue heard his head crush. She heard his skull pop. *I heard it pop! I heard it and I'm glad! I am so glad!* Blue cheered and cheered and cheered.

62

Marcus went back to the Agency to clear out his desk. Nobody attacked him. Only Reed and Malkovitch spoke to him at all. Reed said he was sorry that Diana had died trying to apprehend Hacker. So that was the cover story, Marcus thought. As far as Marcus could tell, Reed was sincere. But he no longer trusted his ability to assess people.

Malkovitch came in as Marcus was dumping the contents of his miscellany drawer into a box.

"I guess you see the problem," Malkovitch said, his angry Santa Claus face glistening.

"You're not one of them?"

"Why do you think I never got anywhere in the goddamn organization?"

"Then why don't they get rid of you?"

"What would be the point? I'm an old deteriorated malcontent."

"Well, all right. Then why don't you leave?"

"Again, what would be the point? I need the work and nobody's ever going to beat them. There's too much money in it."

Marcus turned away in disgust.

Malkovitch said, "It's not everybody, you know."

"I don't know anything anymore."

"It's a sort of cadre. They're in power now. They might not always be."

"It'll take too long for me." When Marcus looked around, Malkovitch had gone.

He had just packed the second R-Kive box, the two boxes adding up to everything he owned in the office, when Reed came in.

"Which are you?" Marcus asked. He'd always liked Reed.

"I'm not your enemy." Reed mouthed without sound. The lip movements—and gestures—made his meaning clear enough.

Marcus mouthed, "Some day, I'll have them dead to rights."

"Well, I hope to meet you again in the future," Marcus said aloud. They shook hands.

Marcus wrote up everything he knew or suspected, in precise detail. It took him a week. He didn't e-mail the result, but sent paper copies to half a dozen reporters he knew in the print media and four in TV. Two of the print media, the smallest, least important, most muck-raking, printed a version of what he had written.

Except for a few dyed-in-the-wool conspiracy theorists, nobody anywhere of any importance paid the least attention.

63

Brad withdrew his college enrollment and is going to spend a year at a local community college. He wants to get his grades up, his ACTs up, and he also wants to take physics and trigonometry, which he never had any use for before. His goal is to get into the University of Chicago as an undergrad, or if that doesn't happen, do his undergrad work at another school and perform so spectacularly that he can get into the University of Chicago graduate archaeology program, which is said to be the best in the country.

Ana Cruz received permission from the INC to organize and lead the dig at the mountain site. Once she knew it was definite, she invited Tabitha to be part of the team. Tabitha goes around with a constant smile on her face, which she tries to conceal because she realizes people have died. Her happiness bursts out all the time, though. Blue would advise her to let the smile happen—after all, life goes on and she's young. But Blue realizes Tabitha doesn't need her advice. She's fully fledged now.

When Tabitha goes back to Peru, she will have a lot to send Blue. Ana reports that they have been permitted to remove specimens from the grave they are calling the Guardian's, the grave that was partially washed away. The feeling was that it was already so exposed to the elements that covering it with a tent would help but not help enough. Early tests on the Guardian's medicine kit show hallucinogenic tobacco, coca, and ayahuasca.

Blue has not talked with Drake, but he sent in his photos of Anatolia. They were exquisite.

Joseph is spending time in Chicago lecturing on art theft at the Art Institute. Blue has a new home, downtown, and he comes over for dinner once in a while. Paula comes in to be Adam's nanny, and Tiglath Pilaser likes the new place, especially the south-facing windowsill.

Adam is showing all the other one- and two-year-olds at the park sandbox how to dig for dinosaurs with the tool set Tabitha gave him. He hasn't found any bones yet. Doesn't bother him. It's the digging and the dirt he likes.

Brad went to the park yesterday with Adam and Blue. Adam was thoroughly delighted. He kept flopping over backward, ramming the back of his head into the sand. Blue recently figured out he did this mostly for her reaction, so she now gives it every time.

"Oh no! Shampoo night!"

Adam crawled over three of Brad's textbooks. Brad didn't object.

Brad said, "I've been thinking about the people at Çatalhöyük."

"What about them?"

"Thousands of people lived there for thousands of years and nobody lives there anymore. What happened?"

"We think the climate changed. It got drier, and maybe the food plants died out and then the animals left."

"But that would happen slowly." Blue nodded. He said, "I was thinking about the last people. I mean, as people moved away, there would be a few families left. Fewer and fewer. And maybe sand blew in around the old houses. And weeds grew over them. Like that ruin plant. And then maybe the last man was there all alone looking over the place where thousands of people had lived. And then he just walked away."

"Probably so."

"And the whole city slowly got covered with sand and weeds. And finally it just looked like a hill, so people came to picnic on it. And nobody even remembered it had been a city once. Full of people."

"Yes."

"But they were real," he said. "They really lived."

"Yes."

64

Mr. Pavia sat in the wing chair near the fire, in the common room at Leeuwarden. Mr. Ratigan entered, flipping a few sheets of blue paper back and forth. Mr. Pavia recognized this as agitation on Ratigan's part.

"Have you a worry?" he asked.

"He's failed again. And this time Hacker has gotten himself killed."

"I knew that, Mr. Ratigan."

"And in a high profile way! Exactly what you wanted to avoid."

"I knew that, too."

"Well, hell!" Ratigan threw himself heavily into a chair. "What about Mexico?"

"Ah, much progress. It looks like the other six cartels are willing to be run by Obrador."

"Really? I wouldn't have believed it possible."

"Well, the Federales rolled the six leaders up at the meeting, with the DEA lending support."

Ratigan sucked in a deep breath. Then, quietly, he said, "And why did they miss Obrador?"

"After the place for the parley was set, I sent word of the location to the Federales and the DEA. Then I suggested to Obrador that he might get the date wrong by a day."

"Exactly what you said you wouldn't do!"

"No, you said it."

"We don't work with *police*!"

"Unless it helps us. Think of it this way, Mr. Ratigan. Clausewitz said 'War is the continuation of politics by other means.' But we can say 'politics is the continuation of war by other means.' We can be careful and politic rather than wage obvious war."

"Mr. Pavia, this is in contravention of everything we have always stood for. I've noticed you sliding for some time now. I am afraid it's time for you to retire. Mr. Wong has said so, too."

"I knew that."

Madame Versluis entered, after a soft tap on the door. She carried a tray.

"Good afternoon, Madame Versluis," Pavia said. Ratigan nodded at her.

"Good afternoon. Morton wishes you to try these chocolates with your coffee. As you know, chocolate is now being handled and marketed much like wine. The area where the beans are grown and the year of the vintage is a selling point these days. Today he is offering Dagoba Organic Chocolate. The beans are handpicked. He would like to make a final selection before the August general meeting."

Ratigan reached a hand to the chocolates. "Thank you."

Pavia said, "Let's table the question of my retirement for a time and consider Blue Eriksen. If she had a fatal accident now, it would attract much too much publicity."

"If I may make a suggestion," Madame Versluis said.

"Indeed, Madame Versluis."

"Discrediting her would be quite an easy matter."

"What did you have in mind?"

"You might put it about that she holds drug parties with students on digs."

Pavia said, "Good thought. But she—and the students for that matter—will deny it."

"Well, of course. They *would*."

"So people would think."

"We could even leak it to the Reverend Hommiller. He'd love it," said Madame Versluis.

"And Lauriette Blessing. She'd use it on her radio show."

"A fine suggestion, Madame Versluis," Pavia said. "Maybe we should have done this in the first place."

Mr. Ratigan said, "This chocolate is too bitter."

"It's bittersweet," said Madame Versluis.

"There's no goddamn *sweet* in it—"

Mr. Ratigan could not catch his breath. He turned pale, then purplish, and then fell to the floor. "Aaagk," he said.

Mr. Pavia and Madame Versluis watched. When he stopped breathing, Mr. Pavia said, "Thank you, Madame Versluis."

"You're welcome, sir."

"He never really understood the importance of subtlety."

Endnote

40,000,000 YEARS AGO primitive apes appeared.

13,000,000 YEARS AGO orangutans diverged from the chimp-human family tree.

6,000,000 TO 5,000,000 YEARS AGO chimps and humans diverged.

> Ninety-eight percent of human and chimpanzee genetic material is identical. Chimps are closer to humans than to other apes. Therefore the present belief is that they had a common ancestor 5 to 6 million years ago.

> Since both chimps and humans are self-aware, the common ancestor may have been self-aware. Orangutans, which diverged 13 million years ago, are also self-aware, so self-awareness may go back that far. Except that the gorilla isn't, or isn't much. And the gorillas diverged 7.5 million years ago. So some other factor may be at work.

9,000,000 TO 5,000,000 YEARS AGO protohominid evolution to upright posture occurred.

3,000,000 YEARS AGO there were at least three protohominids in East Africa: *Homo africanus, Homo boisei,* and *Homo robustus.* Also *Homo habilis,* the first true hominid. *Homo sapiens* probably arose about 250,000 years ago in Africa and moved out across the planet.

2,600,000 YEARS AGO hominids made chipped stone tools and buried their dead. They spent two and a half million years as hunter-gatherers.

900,000 YEARS AGO, *Homo erectus* were using boats and rafts.

500,000 YEARS AGO, hominids developed the anatomy that permits speech and the area in the cerebral cortex to manage the ability. Some think language appeared 2 million years ago. Some say only 40,000 years.

400,000 YEARS AGO, hominids used wooden spears. The oldest known fossils of *Homo sapiens* are 250,000 years old.

150,000 YEARS AGO anatomically modern humans, *Homo sapiens sapiens,* appeared.

> 63,000 years ago:
> According to paleontology professor Juan Luis Arsuaga, Neanderthal people, predecessors of modern humans, engaged in dental hygiene. Two molars were found in Spain with grooves indicative of habitual cleaning with pointed sticks.

60,000 YEARS AGO there were humans in Australia.

50,000 YEARS AGO, humans invented the bow and arrow.

26,000 YEARS AGO humans were just as intelligent as we are (or are not) now.

18,000 YEARS AGO the last Ice Age began, and it ended 10,000 years ago.

15,000 YEARS AGO or earlier there were humans in the Americas.

15,000 YEARS AGO, in Europe during the Upper Paleolithic, fetal-position burials became common, as if expecting rebirth.

14,000 YEARS AGO sedentary village life appeared in multiple centers.

12,000 YEARS AGO humans domesticated cereal grains, including wheat.

10,000 YEARS AGO the walls went up around Jericho.

9,000 YEARS AGO the people of what is now Jiahu in China had been brewing beer for an unknown but probably long period of time.

9,000 YEARS AGO humans in Mesopotamia learned how to make pottery.

8,000 YEARS AGO the first construction began at Stonehenge.

> Elaborate hallucinogen kits (medicine pouches) have been found with mummies in Peru and Chile dating back at least 5,000 years. The kits contained seeds of hallucinogenic snuff called *wirca* or *huillca* from the *Piptadenia colubrina*.

6,000 YEARS AGO the Sumerians invented cuneiform writing.

> About 4,000 years ago in Sumer, the word "freedom" was used for the first known time in written history in an account of a tax reduction program.

Acknowledgments

Thanks to:

Linda Klepinger, Professor Emerita, Department of Anthropology, University of Illinois at Urbana-Champaign.

David Heinzmann, journalist and novelist (*A Word to the Wise*, Five Star, Dec. 2009) for information about the drug traffic and drug wars in Chicago.

Janice Kim for her personal description of Chinese food.

Ricki Nordmeyer for finding the greatest site explaining how many cars go over any piece of road in Illinois.

Professor Andrew Koppelman, Northwestern University School of Law, for calling my attention to the Good Friday experiment.

Thanks to Judy Greber, who writes as Gillian Roberts, for her insights into Turkey and her photo.

Thanks also to Dr. Charles Zugerman for his recollections of Turkey and his photos.

The most important person is the one who keeps us from making horrible mistakes. Sarah Wisseman, Ph.D., Illinois State Archaeological Survey, University of Illinois at Champaign, and novelist (*The House of the Sphinx*, Hilliard and Harris, 2009) deserves all my gratitude.

And to my writing group and severest critics, as always, thanks—Jeanne Dams, author of a new Dorothy Martin mystery (Severn House) and Mark Zubro, *Fool proof*, Tor/Forge 2009.

Especially to Robert Gleason, executive editor at Tor/Forge, and Deborah Schneider, agent and splendid critical reader. They made suggestions that produced a far stronger, more focused book.

And to Ashley Cardiff, who shepherded the manuscript to the final book.